PRAISE FOR

# GRIMSPACE

"A terrific first novel full of page-turning action, delightful characters, and a wry twist of humor. Romance may be in the air. Bullets, ugly beasties, and really nasty bad guys definitely are."

—Mike Shepherd,
national bestselling author of the Kris Longknife series

"An irresistible blend of action and attitude. Sirantha Jax doesn't just leap off the page—she storms out, kicking, cursing, and mouthing off. No wonder her pilot falls in love with her; readers will, too."

—Sharon Shinn,
national bestselling author of *Reader and Raelynx*

"A tightly written, edge-of-your-seat read."

—Linnea Sinclair, RITA Award–winning author
of *The Down Home Zombie Blues* and *Shades of Dark*

"An unflinching tale of survival, redemption, and serious ass kicking. Jax's brutal eloquence will twist your heart when you least expect it."

—Jeri Smith-Ready,
award-winning author of *Voice of Crow*

"*Grimspace* is an exciting, evocative, and suspenseful science-fiction romance, reminding me of *Firefly* and *Serenity*. Characters and a world you'll think about long after the book is done. Fascinating!"

—Robin D. Owens,
RITA Award–winning author of *Heart Dance*

*Ace books by Ann Aguirre*

GRIMSPACE
WANDERLUST

# WANDERLUST

ANN AGUIRRE

**THE BERKLEY PUBLISHING GROUP**
**Published by the Penguin Group**
**Penguin Group (USA) Inc.**
**375 Hudson Street, New York, New York 10014, USA**
Penguin Group (Canada), 90 Eglinton Avenue East, Suite 700, Toronto, Ontario M4P 2Y3, Canada
(a division of Pearson Penguin Canada Inc.)
Penguin Books Ltd., 80 Strand, London WC2R 0RL, England
Penguin Group Ireland, 25 St. Stephen's Green, Dublin 2, Ireland (a division of Penguin Books Ltd.)
Penguin Group (Australia), 250 Camberwell Road, Camberwell, Victoria 3124, Australia
(a division of Pearson Australia Group Pty. Ltd.)
Penguin Books India Pvt. Ltd., 11 Community Centre, Panchsheel Park, New Delhi—110 017, India
Penguin Group (NZ), 67 Apollo Drive, Rosedale, North Shore 0632, New Zealand
(a division of Pearson New Zealand Ltd.)
Penguin Books (South Africa) (Pty.) Ltd., 24 Sturdee Avenue, Rosebank, Johannesburg 2196,
South Africa

Penguin Books Ltd., Registered Offices: 80 Strand, London WC2R 0RL, England



WANDERLUST

An Ace Book / published by arrangement with the author

PRINTING HISTORY
Ace mass-market edition / September 2008


Cover art by Scott M. Fischer.
Cover design by Lesley Worrell.
Interior text design by Kristin del Rosario.


For information, address: The Berkley Publishing Group,
a division of Penguin Group (USA) Inc.,
375 Hudson Street, New York, New York 10014.

ISBN: 978-0-441-01627-3

ACE
Ace Books are published by The Berkley Publishing Group,
a division of Penguin Group (USA) Inc.,
375 Hudson Street, New York, New York 10014.
ACE and the "A" design are trademarks belonging to Penguin Group (USA) Inc.

PRINTED IN THE UNITED STATES OF AMERICA

10 9 8 7 6 5 4 3 2 1

*For Andres.*
*Who doesn't miss a beat when I IM with questions like*
*"Should they steal a ship or be rescued by space pirates?"*
*I couldn't ask for more in a partner.*
*I hope you're half as proud of me as I am of you.*
*(The dog thinks you're awesome, too.)*

# ACKNOWLEDGMENTS

I'm indebted to Laura Bradford, my agent. She is a person of great wit, verve, and discernment. I feel so lucky to have met, worked, book shopped, and eaten omelets with her. Her great spirit humbles me.

This book wouldn't exist without Anne Sowards. Her expertise makes her a pleasure to work with, and her insights never fail to improve my books. I'd also like to thank the talented staff at Ace for their hard work.

Finally, thanks to my friends, who respond to my ramblings as if I make sense. Much love to Lauren Dane, Carrie Lofty, and Angie Fox, who put up with me daily.

# CHAPTER 1

***The hearings have been going on for days.***

I don't know why I thought it was over, just because we got the truth out. There are always people who refuse to believe it, or want to analyze what they've seen seventy-four times before they even try to accept that reality has changed. I've been answering the same questions under oath for them for the last week, so I'm at the end of my patience when I'm summoned, yet again.

The room-bot tells me, "Your presence is required in conference room 7-J, Sirantha Jax."

Well, of course it is. My eyes burn as I step out into the pristine white corridor. I feel oddly fragile, as if my bones have grown too big for my skin. I haven't been sleeping well in what used to be Farwan's staff dormitory, and they won't let me see March. They're keeping us sequestered to make sure we don't synchronize our stories, I guess. The Conglomerate-appointed Taskforce has a great interest in getting at the truth, which is understandable, given that we've known only what the Corp chose to disseminate for decades now.

The Conglomerate spent countless centuries as an impotent coalition of planetary representatives, holding sessions and debating issues that never changed anything. Now all the representatives are gathered on New Terra, jockeying for power and trying to fill the void left by Farwan's fall. At this point, the Conglomerate can't be blamed for its zeal. They don't want someone else to seize control while things whirl in a chaotic spin.

Doesn't mean I enjoy these constant, courteous interrogations. I find it difficult not to flash back to all the "counseling" sessions I suffered after Kai died. Kai was my pilot first, then my friend—and then he was . . . everything. I'd never known it was possible to love as he did—with complete devotion yet devoid of promises. The crash of the *Sargasso*, engineered by Farwan Corporation, reshaped my world, and for a while I wasn't sure I'd survive the shift.

That's behind me now. The world has changed because of Kai's death. People won't forget him, and that assuages the loss. The other day, I saw on the news, they're building a monument in Center Park, a small reproduction of the *Sargasso* with a brass plaque graven with the names of the dead.

The Conglomerate mines its representatives from corporations and special-interest groups. Only a few come from genuine free elections, devoid of corruption, kickbacks, and nepotism, and I can't honestly say whether I've done a good thing by destroying Farwan. If nothing else, they were stable, and now we have a great chasm at the center, around which everything trembles.

But I couldn't let them get away with murdering Kai.

People nod at me as I pass through the hallway and into the lift, heading for the seventh floor. I'm a public figure now. I always was to some degree, I suppose. The news vids often flashed images of me, returning from a successful jump, and the gutter press loved to publicize my barroom brawls.

Bracing myself, I step through the open doorway into conference room 7-J. To my surprise, I don't find the usual panel of judges and planetary representatives gazing at me with poorly concealed disapproval. Maybe they finally believe I'm telling the truth, but they don't like me for it. Thanks to me, the status quo has been destroyed, and now we have multiple parties rushing to fill the vacuum, some of which are worse than Farwan. Sometimes the truth doesn't set you free; it just presents a different set of problems.

Instead I find Dina, March, and the Chancellor of New Terra. March smiles at me with such warmth that my heart contracts. They've cleared him of charges since nobody died during the standoff, plus the resultant broadcast knocked him clean off center stage.

When he thought I was dead, he stormed Corp headquarters and took the whole building hostage. March didn't think it would bring me back. He just wanted to watch the man who gave the order die.

The woman, Dina, looks good, as if she's been getting some sun, and her blond hair shines with new highlights. When she feels my scrutiny, she discreetly flips me the bird. I barely restrain a smile.

*You all right?* He comes into me quietly.

Right after I met March, I thought I was going crazy—and perhaps I was, but not because I sensed him inside my head when he shouldn't be. Since he's Psi, he can skim surface thoughts as if he were dipping a net into the water. With most people, that's all he can do without causing irreparable harm. Our theta waves are compatible, which means he can share a *lot* more with me.

I answer with my eyes and a slight smile. Just being in the same room with him makes things better. Easier.

The Chancellor gazes between us as if sensing subtext. He's a sharp one. Suni Tarn is a big man, rawboned, with disheveled salt-and-pepper hair, but he wears real silk. A study in contrasts, then. His smile seems sincere as he invites, "Take a seat, Ms. Jax."

Warily, I do so. "What's this about?"

I expected to find another panel wanting to hear the

same story yet again. For some reason, this assembly makes me nervous. March offers a look of quiet reassurance, and some of the tension fades. If it was bad, he'd warn me, surely.

"The Conglomerate has served as figurehead long enough, and we're determined to restructure so that regulatory functions return to our control. No longer will the private sector control tariffs and jump-travel training. After reviewing your testimony, we'd like to repay you for your loyalty to the Conglomerate. It can't have been easy, staying one jump ahead of Farwan when they were so determined to suppress the truth."

After replaying his words in my head, they still ring with governmental doublespeak. "I'm not actually sure what that means."

"They intend to make you an ambassador," Dina says with a smirk.

*Mary, I've missed her.*

"True." Tarn nods, folding his hands before him. "There are a few formerly class-P worlds that have reached the correct level of technology to be considered for addition to the Conglomerate. There are also a number of xenophobic planets from which we need to recruit representatives. If they are allowed to secede, they will presume they are exempt from travel regulations and tariffs as well. And that's how wars start."

We share a grim silence, remembering the casualties from the Axis Wars. In the aftermath, Farwan stepped into the breach, offering impartial mediation. They took control by centimeters, and nobody noticed the bloodless coup until the Corp had stripped the Conglomerate of all decision-making autonomy. Oh, the tier worlds still elected representatives every ten turns or so, and they went around talking about "issues," but Farwan held the real power. Until now.

"I'm flattered," I say carefully, because this mission sounds like a great way to get killed. Maybe that's why they want to send *me*. I'm no stranger to the notion of people wanting to space me to tie up loose ends. "But my first obligation is to finish what I've started. I have people on Lachion counting on me to help them get what they need to found a jump-training academy."

March studies me with an inscrutable expression, but I receive a sense that he's proud of me. This opportunity would keep me in the limelight, almost like being a nav-star again, but I don't want that life anymore. I want to make love to him in my shabby glastique flat on Gehenna, see how Doc's doing, and then go find out how we can help on Lachion.

"They have everything they could possibly need," Tarn tells me. "When we seized Farwan's assets, that included their research, and we disbursed the information to all interested parties. Your friends aren't the only ones engaged in genetically engineering a race better suited to the nav chair. We're living in an exciting time, full of innovation and change, but we'll have to wait and see what happens, just like everyone else. However, that leaves you at loose ends, I believe."

I can see how Tarn got elected. He has a charming, toothy smile and a persuasive manner. Maybe it's a reflex left over from dealing with the Corp, but I don't trust him. He has a point, however.

If they have all the data they need, which I'll verify with Keri, then the rest is lab work for Doc to do on his own. I remember those poor women on Hon-Durren's Kingdom, and part of me shies away. In my time I've seen some horrific things, but few things have lingered like that ward of helpless breeders, catatonic females condemned to be used as wombs.

I don't like the idea of genetic engineering, but thankfully, it's not my responsibility. The Conglomerate will appoint arbiters and navigator activists when the time comes, I have no doubt. Still, there won't be a class for me to train for a while yet, and I'm not the only teacher anymore. Everyone who used to work at the Farwan Academy is now looking for a job, too.

"If they don't need my help on Lachion, I'd rather go back to jumping for its own sake," I answer finally. "Logging new beacons. That was what I loved."

Tarn arches a brow with an indulgent air, almost as if he's talking to a child. "And who's going to pay you to do that, Sirantha? That isn't a Conglomerate priority at this time, I'm afraid, and your ship will have expenses: fuel, food, miscellaneous supplies. Not to mention a living wage for the crew."

Shit. I've never needed to think about a paycheck before. I'm not even sure how much I have in my personal accounts. Living on Farwan stations where they comped everything, I didn't have to worry about such details.

If they have no use for me on Lachion right now, then I'd just be living off Keri's largesse, and they're already going through tough times because of me. Then it sinks in. I actually *need* a job, and I'm probably not in a position to turn down an offer at the moment.

I'll need to check my financials as soon as possible, assuming my assets haven't been frozen because they came from Farwan. Surely that's not possible. I won't feel easy about it until I find out, though.

"Why me?" That's a last-ditch effort to refute the inevitable.

"We want you and your crew to start with Ithiss-Tor. You're in a unique position, as . . ." Tarn checks his notes on the datapad. "Velith Il-Nok, a bounty hunter of some repute, is willing to travel with you to his homeworld and help you traverse the obstacles that tripped up other ambassadors.

"Needless to say, this mission does present its share of dangers. Given the current state of the shipping lanes, you will be fortunate to get there in one piece." He pauses to let the gravity of his statement sink in.

Oh, how I wish he were kidding. But Tarn doesn't seem to have much of a sense of humor. And he's right. Pirates, raiders, smugglers . . . they all know there's no strong Corp militia coming to kick their asses anymore; the time has never been better for them to ply their trade and push the lawless frontier a little closer to civilization.

It's going to be a fucking mess out there. And it's largely my fault. I sigh and scrub my hand over my face as Tarn continues, "So I'll allow you twenty-four hours to discuss the opportunity with your crew. You'll find the Conglomerate most generous, however, if you should choose to join our employ."

"Does this mean we're finished with the hearings? We're free to do as we please?" I wouldn't quite call what they did to us house arrest, but it was close. As I mentioned, we weren't permitted to fraternize with each other at all.

Tarn nods. "We have all the testimony we need from you. Now, if you'll excuse me, I'm expected in 12-H for a bounce-relay chat with Ielos." With that, the Chancellor heads for the door.

I sigh. Sure, we'll discuss it, but I know the smell of an offer I can't refuse.

# CHAPTER 2

***"So what do you two think?"***

If I go, they're going with me. That much is a given.

Dina grimaces and pushes to her feet. She's a stocky woman who could kick my ass with one hand tied behind her back, but luckily, she doesn't want to anymore. I don't think.

"I think it's a sucker's job." Then she grins. "And we're just the suckers to do it. How bad could it be?"

I stare at her. "Why do you have to say shit like that? Seriously. Why?"

"Because it makes you nervous?"

"Big deal," I mutter. "Everything makes me nervous. It's a wonder I haven't developed a tic."

"You have," March puts in, ever helpful. "Your left eye sort of—"

"Thanks, baby. You're a gem."

He smirks, the expression that used to make me want to slap him. Now it makes me want to tie him up and do things to him until he says he's sorry.

"We should check with the Chancellor's assistant. I'm sure they have an itinerary for us," he adds.

I shrug. "We have twenty-four hours. After all this, they owe us some rec time."

For once Dina agrees with me. "Do they ever. This place is a dump." She dismisses the sterile conference room with four blank bisque walls with a contemptuous gesture. "Isn't there anything to do here?"

Thinking back to my training days, I try to remember. "Not by Gehenna or even Venice Minor standards. But there are a few good bars in Wickville over on the west side. At least there used to be. Place called Quincy's had a trio that played folkazz, good stuff. But remember, I've been gone a long time—"

I find myself talking to her back. If I know her at all, she'll catch a lift over to where she's likely to find a party and leave the details up to us. Our ship's mechanic lives for a good time and makes no bones about it.

Oddly, I respect her for that. Dina doesn't dwell on everything she's lost. The woman surpasses me in that regard, but she doesn't brood over it. Doesn't use it like a weapon to make other people feel sorry for her.

Without a word, March pulls me into his arms. I hope nobody else needs the conference room because it doesn't feel like he's letting go anytime soon. He rests his cheek against the top of my stubbly head. Just after we landed on New Terra—before the bounty hunter snatched me—my crewmates decided I'd be less recognizable without my hair. I still can't believe they shaved my head for nothing.

March tightens his arms around me, and I luxuriate in his heat. This separation has been harder on him than on me because first he thought I was dead, and then before he could make the mental adjustment, they quarantined us to prepare for our testimonies.

A shudder runs through him. "Sometimes I'm afraid I'll wake up and you won't be here."

Part of me—the part that's still raw over losing Kai—

wants to back away from such unabashed need. I'm afraid I can't handle it, that I'll hurt him again like I did on Gehenna. Part of me needs him every bit as much, though. I'm afraid of that, too. I wasn't always such a contrary bundle of fears. That's new.

I like the person I am now, though. Jax the nav-star didn't care for anyone but Kai, certainly didn't care about the state of the universe or acting in the interest of the greater good. I'm not sure I'm cut out to be a hero like March, but I want to try. Not for the fame and glory but because I want to leave something behind that matters more than the number of jumps I made. I want things to be better because of me. He lifts his head, and his gaze meets mine.

"I'm not going anywhere," I say aloud, though it isn't a surety I can truly offer. Life is precarious, and it turns in a flash. As if he knows this, his lips drift over mine, delicately possessive. His kiss sparks a chemical reaction, endorphins careening wildly.

Lifting his head, March exhales slowly. "You want to—"

A throat clears behind us. "We have a meeting scheduled," someone says in the polite tone that conceals amusement.

We break apart like kids caught necking on the front doorstep. I smile over that as we hurry out of 7-J. Once we get some distance down the hall, I pause and gaze up at him. He's no prettier than when I first laid eyes on him. March still looks mean as a black-tailed rattler, but as always, I focus on his dark, gold-flecked eyes fringed in those ridiculously luxurious lashes.

It's just as well he has such a hard-hewn face. With those eyes, he'd just be too pretty if he were anywhere close to handsome. Besides, I look like a war refugee these days, scrawny, scarred, and bald as an egg, so I can't have some beautiful man outshining me.

"Do I want to . . . ?" I arch a brow at him, as if I don't know perfectly well what he's going to suggest.

He grins. "Go to Wickville and listen to some folkazz."

Okay, he got me. He's the mind reader, not me, which is

just as well. I'd be dangerous if I could do what March does. Hell, I'm dangerous anyway.

I shake my head. "Not really. Not in the mood."

We start walking again, meandering along the corridor to the lift. "You want to bounce a message to Lachion? Double-check what Tarn told us?"

I nod. "We should try to find an independent relay computer, too. I don't trust station terminals."

March doesn't argue as we step into the tube. A whooshing sound sends us to our floor, and as we get out, he asks, "You sure this isn't more paranoia, Jax?"

He has a point. My instincts are a mess. I'm prone to flipping out for no reason after the Psychs finished tinkering with my brain.

"I don't know. But people who want something from you never tell the whole truth, so I need to check his story. See what Keri says. I don't want to have traded one corrupt master for another."

"Absolute power corrupts absolutely."

I stop outside my quarters. "Are you saying all this was for nothing? The Conglomerate will eventually be as thoroughly raddled with dirty politics, kickbacks, suppression of information, and borderline tyranny as the Corp?"

He hesitates as if weighing his words. "It's change. Who knows exactly what's in store? Right now everything's in a state of upheaval. Historians will draw the conclusions, not me."

"Heh. With my luck, I'll be known as the one who ended an era of peace and prosperity, huh?"

"Maybe, but you'll be dead, and you won't care. Now go bundle up, and I'll do the same. Meet you back here?"

I remember we're in Ankaraj, which means snow, and the wind tears through you like a steel hook. "Nah, just wait for me downstairs."

One of these days, I'm going to get ready faster than he does. But not today. By the time I find an overcoat and layer my clothing to withstand the winter chill, I find him lounging in the foyer.

He takes in the navy s-wool coat with hood and muffler paired with clunky brown boots. To think I used to be considered one of the best-dressed women in the tier worlds—in fact, I made the list twice. I sigh a little. On the plus side, I gained ten kilos in clothing, and the way I look now, that's a good thing.

"Cute," he pronounces.

I wish he'd shot me. "Bastard."

First order of business is to find a non-Corp, non-Conglomerate terminal where we can bounce a message to Keri. That will cost money, so we'll need to hit a bank first. Maybe March can cover it, but I need to be independent. The idea of being dependent on anyone, for anything, makes me feel odd and queasy.

That means checking on the status of my personal accounts, which Simon, the estranged husband who tried to have me killed, better not have fucked with. I also need to have a new pay-card issued. Mary only knows the turmoil of the currency situation. Maybe Corp credits have been devalued entirely. Shit, I hope not.

Drawing my hood up around my ears, I head for the door. Stop short.

The woman drawing back a gorgeous, filmy thermal scarf looks eerily familiar. She shakes a few flakes of snow from her ink-dark hair, managing to look graceful and elegant while she does so. Her perfectly painted mouth rounds into an "O" when she registers me.

"Sirantha?" she chokes out.

"Mother?"

For March's sake, I make the introduction. "This is Ramona Jax, my mother. Mother, this is March."

Let them make of each other what they will.

# CHAPTER 3

***Half an hour later, we're sitting in a café near what*** used to be Farwan headquarters, though it's now the Conglomerate Command Center on New Terra. Few patrons are sitting in the restaurant this time of day, too late for breakfast and too early for lunch. The place is done in tones of amber and gold, heavy, fringed shades giving the room a diffuse, smoky glow, frosted by the ice on the outside of the windows.

It's eerie. My mother doesn't look a day older than when I left. Either she didn't worry about me, or she spent my father's money on antiaging treatments. My credits, assuming I still have some, are on both.

"The shock killed him," she's saying. "Everywhere he went, someone asked, 'Isn't that your daughter?' when they flashed that horrid picture of you. He just couldn't take it anymore. I always knew there was something wrong with it, though."

"You did?" I've barely recovered from her first tactless announcement, and a stabbing pain between my shoulder blades prompts March to regard me with concern.

*Can't believe nobody told me.*

"You loved working for the Corp. Mary knows you defied everything we wanted for you to do it, so I knew you wouldn't have run off without a good reason."

Heh. She calls everything I went through after the *Sargasso* "running off." This fundamental disconnect would be why I left New Terra in the first place. I can't believe my dad is gone, though it explains her glamorous interpretation of widow's weeds.

"No, she wouldn't," March puts in.

I can see Ramona assessing him, trying to figure us out. With a faint half smile, he makes it easy for her by curling his arm around me. I lean in, watching her warily. She wants something, or she wouldn't be here. But what does she think I can do for her? That's the question.

The small talk continues, and she sidles around the subject of the crash and my dead lover, unpleasantness we shouldn't dwell on, according to her. Ramona does mention that she knows a lovely cosmetic surgeon who could help me with those "unsightly marks" via laser therapy. I set my jaw.

"No thanks," I say quietly. "I want to keep them."

We've been together less than an hour, and already exasperation shows in her tone. "Well, for Mary's sake, why, Sirantha?"

"You like to pretend bad things never happen. I prefer to remember, so I won't make the same mistakes again." I flick a glance at March. "Besides, guys dig them."

He grins. "I do. They make you look dangerous."

This place is automated. Most places have a human programmer who supervises the equipment, but otherwise, the café is nearly empty, just us and a couple of others across the room. I shift long enough to tap out an order for hot choclaste on the wall panel. The kitchen-mate at our table handles basic requests. Anything complex or exotic would be forwarded to the gourmet unit in the kitchen, and an autoserver would bring it to us. March doesn't like them, but I think they're cute, little beverage carts on wheels, equipped with a primitive AI chip.

My mother pauses to regroup, studying March with what would be a narrow-eyed stare, except that might cause wrinkles. Still, the impression remains via the intensity of her regard. He doesn't flinch. At last she looks away, and I have the sense he's won something without knowing what it is.

"I understand they plan to appoint you as ambassador for New Terra," Ramona begins.

Talk about a subject change. We're finally getting down to the meat of why she came looking for me, though. It *wasn't* to hug me and bask in her gratitude that I'm all right. My mother doesn't possess a scintilla of pure maternal sentiment.

I raise a brow. "How could you possibly know that?"

"Oh, I hear things." She waves a hand in an airy, elegant gesture that would look ridiculous from anyone else.

"Do you?" My dry tone is lost on her.

"Indeed. Do you plan to accept the appointment?" She seems nervous, almost frightened, in fact. Her red-lacquered nails tap out a subliminal statement on the glastique table.

"I thought I'd become a junk dealer." Yes, I'm baiting her deliberately. "Maybe do salvage runs, or possibly just settle down on New Terra and go to work in recycling. Have some brats. Would you like that?" I ask March.

*You're so evil,* he tells me silently.

Then he chokes out, eyes watering, "Whatever you want."

Shit, I wish I'd recorded that. I can think of any number of situations where playback would come in handy.

"No! Oh, Sirantha, you mustn't even joke." She reaches for my hand, where it's curled around my cup. "You simply must take the post."

*Here we go.*

My choclaste has cooled enough to drink, so I take a sip to cover my annoyance. This means pulling away from her, of course, which was the whole point. I intend to accept Tarn's offer, but my inclination toward a course of action always plummets in direct correlation to someone's demand. Call me contrary.

"Must I? Why?"

"We need someone like you on Ithiss-Tor," she replies. "Just go and be yourself, and everything will be fine." Her posture reflects anxiety and duress.

Since Ramona has been trying to annihilate my personality since I was eight years old, I tense. Something really isn't right. March confirms my impression with a nod. Now he's frowning as well.

"Who's 'we'?"

Her eyes dart around the nearly deserted coffeehouse, as if she suspects an eavesdropper. This isn't like her, at least, not the woman I remember. She's a society darling, a flighty little butterfly, and I was supposed to be one, too.

"People I owe money," she whispers, and her dark eyes well up with tears.

I'm staggered by that. "What? Who? What happened?"

It takes her a moment to collect herself. "We owned stock in Farwan. When . . . everything happened, we were ruined. I didn't know; your father didn't tell me. I went on, as I always had, spending . . . it wasn't until your father . . . died that . . ."

I can piece together the rest. My father killed himself over their reversal in fortune. Who could possibly expect *him* to get a job? People came to his gallery because he had money, not because he had impeccable taste. Once the cache was gone, the gallery would've gone straight down, too.

And my mother kept spending money she didn't have. What I don't understand is why her creditors want me on Ithiss-Tor.

"What does this have to do with me?" Maybe that sounds cruel.

Perhaps some women would be overcome by sentiment and obligation, despite the long estrangement, but they didn't lift a finger to help me when I was in trouble. I can count on one hand the people who did, and Ramona doesn't make the A-list.

"We cannot allow a successful diplomatic mission to Ithiss-Tor."

I start at the deep, mechanical voice emitting from a jeweled brooch on my mother's jacket. No wonder she's been watching her words. They're monitoring us.

Do I answer it? My mother's face pales until her skin looks like clotted milk. Her hands tremble, so she squeezes them into fists and rubs them against her thighs.

March makes the decision for me. "Why not?"

There's a hint of feedback as the pin replies, "Sliders, Bugs, whatever you choose to call them, represent a threat to our way of life. We cannot take the risk that they will respond favorably to Conglomerate overtures and make plans to infiltrate our society on a widespread basis."

I really don't get it. If that's their stance, however xenophobic, doesn't it make more sense to ask me *not* to go? Ramona says nothing, seeming paralyzed with fear. Oh, the irony—she probably spent money they didn't have on that piece of jewelry, which her new masters then turned into an electronic leash.

"How does Jax play into that?" I'm content to let March ask the questions. He'll cover anything I want to know; there's a real benefit to this whole symbiotic bond, apart from mind-blowing sex.

Absently, he strokes my upper arm. It's strange to be having a conversation with someone I can neither see nor picture in my mind's eye. The voice coming from my mother's left bosom sounds distorted and altogether lacks any human quality. Who could have bought up her marks?

"Ms. Jax has a history of strewing destruction and disorder wherever she goes. We are content that if she goes to Ithiss-Tor, the natives will want nothing more to do with the Conglomerate. We cannot take the risk that Chancellor Tarn will select a candidate greater skilled in oration, tact, and diplomacy."

"If you don't go," my mother whispers, "they'll kill me."

# CHAPTER 4

***"I wouldn't have put it so dramatically," the pin says.*** "But that is, in effect, correct. On the other hand, if you take this assignment, we will see clear to forgive your mother's debts. I should imagine even you have this much filial affection."

I don't even know what to say to that. They're so convinced I'll fuck this up, they aren't even asking me to *try* to make a mess of it. It's enough that I go? I don't think I've ever been insulted so casually in my whole life.

"However," the voice continues, "if by some unlikely chance, your diplomatic mission proceeds well, then I'm afraid we shall be forced to collect our pound of flesh."

Ah, there we go—the stick by which they try to force me to do their bidding. My mother whimpers. Above my left eye, I swear I feel twitching; maybe March wasn't kidding about the tic.

"I'd already decided to take the job," I say coolly. "More than that, I will not promise."

The thing responds, "That will suffice . . . for now. We

will reevaluate your mother's situation once we see how your task proceeds."

Her brooch crackles as it stops transmitting. Ramona looks older somehow, as if her maquillage has cracked, revealing worn skin beneath. "You've bought me a little time," she manages at last. "For that I thank you."

"Don't thank me." I feel savage. I'd like to slap her for being so silly. "Who the hell did you borrow money from?"

At first she tries to bluff. "I'm not sure, so many documents, and it's all so complicated—"

But she doesn't know about my ace in the hole. I didn't ask him to do it, never would, but sometimes need-to-know outweighs right-to-privacy. I'm glad March has to weigh those concerns instead of me. If he left the judgments in my hands, I'm afraid I would use him like an inquisitor.

*The Syndicate?* Even in thought, I hear his incredulity. I know—I can't believe she's that stupid either. They've taken organized crime to a whole new level.

No wonder my father took a safe, painless death. At least I hope he did. I should ask if he used a state-sanctioned Eutha-booth. That requires a Psych profile and an affidavit attesting someone is in his right mind when he decides to end it all. This precaution removes all possibility that a bereaved family will sue the state because the situation could have been ameliorated with medication or dream therapy.

Somctimes death presents the ultimate solution, though. I've never been one to look at it like that, as I want to make sure I suck every last drop out of this life before seeing what comes next. I used to believe it was nothing, just a void, but now I'm not so sure. I've seen miracles happen. Lived to tell of them. At this point, I'm willing to concede I just can't know.

Ramona stares across the table at us, growing visibly unsettled. If I'd known how well silence worked at keeping people off balance, I'd have curbed my tongue years ago. Okay, probably not. But maybe I'd have tried harder.

"The Syndicate?" I say aloud.

Her eyes widen, showing threads of red in the white. I see every fleck of mascara she's used to thicken her lashes, and the dark liner beneath looks spidery somehow. Her prettiness is an illusion now, cunning layers of paint to hide the truth.

"How did you—" She stops, likely realizing her words comprise an admission.

"That's not important." I take another sip of choclaste.

I'll never give March's secret away. Too many people would want to destroy him if they knew. He's never been through Corp training; he doesn't have the safeguards in place that prevent him from raping another mind just because he can. Maybe that should terrify me because of our bond, but I know he'd never hurt me on purpose. He's had ample opportunity since we've been together—and as for the rest of the universe, it can look out for itself.

"You're different," she observes. "And I'm done for. They think you'll go out there and make a mess of it. But you won't, will you?"

I won't lie. It hurts a little to make the admission. "Not on purpose. I won't set out to create an interstellar incident, not even for you."

Ramona smiles, a soft tremulous twist of her mouth. "Then I suppose we're finished. I should follow after your father if I have any sense."

"Did he . . . ?"

To my surprise, she picks up the cue. Neither one of us specializes in subtlety or subtext. I suppose you adapt or die. "Yes. Dr. Harmon certified him. It was quick."

"Good." I swallow back the lump in my throat. "Look, I have some business to take care of before our departure. I'll wish you luck, however you sort things out."

March pays our tab with a swipe of his card. Mary, why do I feel this ridiculous weight as I walk away from her? She looks so alone, sitting in the coffeehouse with her stupid big hair and her black dress with the jewelry that monitors her movements.

At the door, I collect my layer of outer garments and wrap up again. We step out into the white swirl of an Ankaraj winter. He takes my hand, and I feel his warmth through two centimeters of s-wool.

"So that's it?" he says. "You're not giving her another thought?"

"Would you?"

He considers for a moment. "I can't say. My mother died when I was five. My father remarried, and my stepmother never cared for me, but she had Svetlana . . ." The wind carries his words away, or perhaps he simply doesn't want to talk about her. "Anyway, I don't know. It just seems strange."

"What does?" When I spy a gap in traffic, I make a break for it. We're getting our own Skimmer, dammit. I'll try to talk the guy at the garage into loaning us one. I need to find a bank.

"I just didn't think you ever gave up on people you love, that's all."

Ouch. Low blow. We duck into the tunnel that leads down to the vehicle-maintenance bays. The Corp owned a fleet and a half, and the Conglomerate is still taking inventory. They won't notice if one vanishes for an hour or so. The ramp winds down and around for quite a ways, but at least we're out of the wind.

"I haven't seen her in sixteen years. And I didn't *like* her when I lived with my folks. Sometimes I find it hard to believe Ramona is my biological mother."

Lucky break, I know the guy working this level. Squid washed out of the academy because he suffers from heterochromia iridium, which he hid by wearing one tinted contact. Unfortunately, two different eye colors meant he didn't possess the J-gene, and he lost some IQ points inside the simulator before they got him out. These days he's only fit to patrol the vehicle-maintenance lot.

The thermal vents mean I can pull off my hood. Should have known something was wrong when my mother didn't say anything about my hair, or lack of it, as soon as I bared myself at the café. I wave to Squid, who glances behind him to see who else I might be signaling.

Damn, what's his real name? Ira. Huh, Squid might actually be better, though the name was meant as a jab at his IQ.

"Hey, Ira! How's it going? How've you been?"

"Uhm. Okay." He pauses with an expression of what I take to be perpetual confusion. "Do I know you?"

I smile at him. "It's been a long time. We were at the academy together. You think you can hook me up with a Skimmer?"

His moon-pale brow wrinkles up in a scowl. "I'm not supposed to let anyone take them. They've been . . ." Ira struggles over the word, and I wince in sympathy, though he doesn't notice. "Confiscated!"

"I'm sure that doesn't apply to the newly appointed ambassador of New Terra," March says smoothly. "If you don't believe me, confirm with Chancellor Tarn. Of course, he might be annoyed with you for making the ambassador wait, as well as interrupting his conference with the Ielosian representatives."

Damn, the man is good; poor Ira looks bewildered. I imagine I don't look like an ambassador, but then again, how many would he have seen, spending his life roaming around vehicle maintenance? If this works, this gig might have perks I hadn't even imagined. Assuming I don't die horribly on the way to Ithiss-Tor.

"I didn't know you were an ambassador," Ira says finally. "You should really have a badge or something. I can let you borrow a B-class Skimmer, but you have to bring it back before my shift ends at five. Please?" he adds, as if remembering he needs to be polite to me.

"Absolutely," March assures him. "We have no plans to leave the city."

That sends a cold chill down my back. Famous last words, best-laid plans, and all that. March takes the codes that will start the engine, and I follow him toward the black-and-red-striped one in the far corner. Ira trails behind us, obviously conflicted. I gather he likes following the rules, and we've made him break them.

"Who're you anyway?" he asks March.

Who flashes his saturnine smile. "I'm the guy who kills anyone that messes with the ambassador."

Wow, I like the sound of that. Ira doesn't venture any more questions before the engine purrs to life. Then we're up, up, and away.

# CHAPTER 5

***There's nothing like riding a Skimmer, even when it's*** this cold.

The speed, the control, the hint of danger as we swoop around the city. Ankaraj isn't a pretty settlement, glittering metal bones jutting from the snow with more determination than grace. I've never been sure why the Corp chose to center its headquarters here. Even though New Terra can't compete with other worlds in terms of natural beauty—and functions as nothing so much as a farm colony—it certainly possesses sites more scenic than this.

I hold on tight to March while the wind whips against my face. For these moments, I am perfectly, gloriously free. I don't need to think about the future, my obligations, or what's in store for us on Ithiss-Tor. March knows I can't stand feeling trapped. Shit, being planet-bound is bad enough. He intuits what those days trapped inside the cave, then later confined to quarters because of the Conglomerate inquiry, meant to me.

If not for Velith Il-Nok, the bounty hunter slotted to accompany me to Ithiss-Tor, I would have died in a Corp asylum, after taking the blame for any number of their crimes. He and I spent several nerve-wracking days riding out a storm in a cave off the Teresengi Basin, after he killed his own crew on my behalf. They were monsters, no doubt, but he'd hired them in good faith. To someone like Vel, his word is his bond. But I can't think about what I owe him, or guilt will set in. I'm not used to owing people debts so big, I have no coin to pay.

By the time we park outside a Transplanetary Bank, my fingers feel vaguely numb. I can't even remember the account numbers to get past the first security check, so we're forced to push the call button. An irritated blond man flashes onto the vid screen above the double doors.

"This location doesn't handle transplanetary wires or open new accounts," he tells me brusquely. "For that, you need to visit our wonderful new branch in the city center, just two blocks from the AquaDome."

Before he can turn off the feed, I answer, "I have an account here already, I just can't remember the code."

He sighs as if I'm mentally defective. "I'll send someone."

At least fifteen minutes pass before a stocky brunette appears to unlock the doors manually. Her expression radiates disapproval for customers who forget their account codes. If I'd entered them, the door would have verified them as viable with in-house security and their AI would have unlocked the doors for fifteen seconds. It's not a foolproof system, but it cuts down on passersby asking to use the lavatory, at least.

"How can I help you today?"

"By looking up my account information," I say, as she leads us toward her workstation.

"I need to scan your thumb and index finger. You can provide additional information if you like, but it is unlikely to be required."

"Not a problem." I let her zap me with her wand.

Transplanetary Bank doesn't believe in embellishing the workplace: beige walls, beige carpet, and one fake plant. Her desk is even beige, built of heavy synthetic wood. A prominent nameplate reads SILVIA KUYEIDI, which means she's descended from the original settlers. I wonder whether her distant ancestors, who revered raven and wolf totems, would approve of her career in banking.

Then again, so what? My distant ancestors specialized in spending money and putting on airs. They wouldn't be impressed with me either.

While she taps away, I unwind some of my layers, my least favorite part of a cold climate. They don't offer chairs for clients unless you're important enough to be ushered into a private suite. I guess we don't qualify.

When March grins, I don't need to be a mind reader to know he's considering a reprise of the whole ambassador bit. That's going to take some getting used to. I fidget, trying to ignore the unusual aches and pains I've acquired along the way.

Ms. Kuyeidi bites her lip. Uh-oh. I know that look.

"I'm sorry, I have bad news, Ms. Jax. When you were . . ." She makes a moue that I interpret as discomfort. ". . . declared dead, your husband filed a next of kin claim, and we consolidated your accounts. And when the Conglomerate froze all Corp assets, that included the personal accounts of Corp executives, such as your husband, who are now awaiting trial."

"Which means . . . ?" I don't really need her to say it. I'm broke.

"Your accounts have been closed." Ms. Kuyeidi refuses to meet my eyes, which tells me she's aware how shitty this is. "I can provide you with the amount that your husband received at the time of your . . . er, death," she adds. "Perhaps the Conglomerate can see about retrieving the wrongfully allotted funds. Such inquiries take time, I'm afraid."

"Of course they do," I mutter.

"I'm sorry I couldn't be of more assistance, Ambassador." She speaks the last word with a conspiratorial air. I must have looked perplexed because she adds, "I saw the announcement on the news just before you arrived. I didn't recognize you right away, though. Your hair . . ."

Great. My mother doesn't comment on it, but the bank lady does. I muster a smile. "Yes, I look quite different now."

Silvia sees us to the door. After thanking her, I stomp out into the cold and immediately regret the impulse. I shiver from head to toe as I rewrap myself. Feeling me tremble, March powers up the thermal vents, which help a little.

"So what now?" he asks, as we climb back on the Skimmer.

These little beauties can toggle between hover and ground mode with the flick of a switch. Speeding over the ice is the closest thing on earth to flying, and it carries a unique thrill. Any other time, I'd beg him to break some records on the tundra—final remnant of the Jax I used to be—but right now I need to get this sorted out.

"Back to headquarters, I guess."

"You think Tarn can help you?" he calls over the roaring wind.

I shrug, knowing he'll catch the movement as well as the accompanying thoughts. Tarn will offer to "look into the matter," but my hope of recovering that 100K hinges on how things go on Ithiss-Tor. That's politics for you, a filthy polyglot of one hand washing the other until everything's unclean.

Suddenly glum, I rest my chin against March's back. If I succeed, they'll kill my mother. If I fail, I'll be jobless, penniless, and the laughingstock of the tier worlds, assuming the Bugs don't execute me for some breach of etiquette.

And that doesn't begin to factor in the danger we'll be in, trying to get to Ithiss-Tor. I didn't realize how much the clockwork Corp patrols factored into keeping the star lanes safe. I hope pirates and raiders will be too busy jacking cargo vessels to mess with a small cutter like ours.

A surge of heat beneath me catches my attention, but it's the high-pitched whine coming from the Skimmer that alarms me. I hear March mutter, "Shit," as he lets go of the controls and rolls hard left. Since I'm holding on to him, I fall as he does.

We hit the ground and tumble, careening into packed snow and stacked garbage cans. My hip feels like it has ground glass embedded in it. The Skimmer continues in its flight, but it slows without a hand on the throttle. Midair, it shudders and then blows into shards, raining fire and ash down on us.

I cover my head as the larger pieces plummet to earth. The icy air smells of burning metal. *Ah, shit. Ira's gonna be pissed. Hope he doesn't get in trouble, poor bastard has enough problems.* Then again, if being an ambassador *means* anything, I should have the power to promote him out of it.

"You all right?" If I had a credit for every time March has asked me that question, I wouldn't be mourning my missing money.

"I'll live." I can't restrain a whimper as he pulls me to my feet. "What are the chances this was a routine malfunction?"

Mouth compressed to a white line, he shakes his head. "Slim to none."

I test my left hip, the one that took the impact, by taking a step, and fire streaks up my thigh. To cover this, I try to sum up our situation, ticking off the points on my gloved fingertips. "So one faction—the Conglomerate—wants me to succeed on Ithiss-Tor because they want to strengthen their position as the galactic governing body. Another faction—the Syndicate—wants me to fail because periods rife with chaos are good for the smuggler's bottom line. And an unknown faction doesn't want me to get there at all."

March nods his agreement. "This was meant as a preventive measure. I'm not sure if they thought they'd end you like this or just put the fear of Mary in you."

I snort. "That'd take more than a bunged-up Skimmer, at this point."

"They don't know you like I do." With careful fingertips, he traces a feathery touch over my brows, and I feel that lovely little spark. Now's not the time, though. "Can you walk?"

I rake a quick look around the alley. "Do I have a choice? This looks like Wickville, where auto-cab stands are few and far between."

His face looks sharp and harsh within the shadowed frame of his black hood, but his eyes soften his whole mien. March swings me up into his arms. "You always have a choice, as long as I'm around. If you'd rather, we'll hop a ship to Maha City, claim some land according to the New Homestead Act, and plant rutabagas or something. Is that what you want, Jax?"

For a moment, just a moment, I consider it. Imagine being planet-bound, no more grimspace, no more wildfire, no more notoriety. Just a quiet life easing into a quiet death. I could almost, almost manage it, with March by my side.

Then I shake my head, smiling. "I don't think I'm what Chancellor Jackson had in mind when he set out to attract honest, hardworking citizens to New Terra. Besides . . . I didn't become a jumper to die old and gray."

Something flashes in his dark eyes, something stark and raw. His answering smile looks like it hurts in ways I can't conceive. "I was afraid you'd say that."

# CHAPTER 6

***As he carries me through the Wickville warren, I re-*** flect on what it means for March to love me.

The man's known nothing but loss his whole life. With me he can expect more of the same. I'm a jumper to the core, complete with all the reckless, thrill-seeking urges. Though I've changed since I first met him, and I'd like to believe for the better, I'm never going to be a safe bet.

I'm not a woman you bring home to Mother, pick out china patterns with, or Mary forefend, breed. I've seen a chunk of the universe, true, but there's still so much more to see. I doubt I'll ever cure this wanderlust, and I'm content with dedicating my life to failing to sate it.

Then again, maybe if I checked with him, he'd say he would rather have two weeks with me than twenty *safe* years with someone else. After all, that's what I'd say if he asked me. Kai taught me nothing comes with a guarantee.

The sky darkens overhead, heavy with impending snow, and on the far horizon, the setting sun smears the white plain with a diffuse glow. Each breath stings the inside of my nostrils, puffs out like smoke. It's becoming clear we are unequivocally lost, and we're starting to draw attention. With March carrying me, we look vulnerable. That brings out the predatory instincts in people.

Buildings low-slung and close together separate Wickville from Ankaraj proper. There, everything shines with chrome and glastique, and even the gutters stay clean. Here, you can find whores, chem, contraband, and wicked music.

During my academy days, I spent as much time as I could out here, away from rules and regulations. I even had a boyfriend, an insanely gifted sax player named Sebastian, who called me a stroppy little bitch. We fought and fucked and fought some more. In retrospect, it's a wonder I made it to graduation day.

The crunch of footsteps demands my attention, somehow ominous and stealthy. "Put me down. It's better if I walk."

Maybe I was getting heavy anyway because he complies without protest. More likely, he figures he may soon need both hands to fight. March offers a nod as a group of hooded thugs step into our path.

The leader says, "Maybe you didn't know, but this is a toll road. You need to pay us fifty credits each in order to use it."

First, it's not much of a road. I'd call it an alley, myself. I can't help it; I'll die a smart-ass, maybe right here in this alley. "Is that fifty credits from each of us or fifty credits to each of you? Or—"

"Shut up, woman." March doesn't even glance at me. This better be manly posturing to impress the gangers, or he's sleeping alone for at least a week. Even that threatening thought doesn't rouse a reaction from him, though. "How about I beat the shit out of you, and we call it even?"

Whoa, there are seven of them. He's sure feeling his oats after plunging ten meters off a doomed Skimmer. I don't think I'm going to be much help in a fight, and I don't have a weapon.

To my astonishment, the head man breaks down into a

belly laugh. "March, you rat bastard, how you been? We haven't seen you dirtside in at least five spins. I almost shat when I saw you on the vid."

While they exchange backslapping hugs all around, I relax muscles I hadn't realized I'd tensed. Dammit, they all had me going. And now my hip really hurts because I slid into a fighting crouch out of reflex.

*Men.*

"I'm all right, Surge. Except we find ourselves a bit disadvantaged in your territory. Our ride went down a ways back, and I have no idea where we are."

"Let's get you out of the cold, catch up a bit, and then see what we can do about a lift home. Where *is* home these days?"

Maybe it's the waning light, but March looks grim and weary. "Nowhere, now. I lost the *Folly*."

His pal shakes his head. "Rough luck, mate. Let me stand you one."

They lead us into a pub via the back door, ignoring the red-faced woman who shouts at them. When Surge peels off his winter wraps, I decide he got his name because his wild, springy hair looks like he conducts large amounts of electricity as a hobby. I limp through into the common room, which is grimy, dimly lit, and full of mismatched furniture.

*Ah, home.* I might've been here with Sebastian, fifteen years ago.

Once we settle at a sticky table, I find out they aren't gangers at all but guys March knew in the old days. From what I can gather, they fought together on Nicu Tertius. Mercenaries go wherever they get paid best, and the Nicuan Empire is always in turmoil, so much that half the time they can't even participate in galactic politics.

By the time the server puts a mug of hot tea in my hand, I don't care whether the cup is clean. I sip and listen while they catch up. Apparently Surge and his boys are working salvage at the moment; they got tired of fighting other people's wars. Someone named Buzzkill died in the last insurrection, and that's when they called it a day.

"Is there a bounce-relay anywhere in this dump?" March asks.

His friend points to the far wall. The thing is positively ancient, dates back before the Axis Wars. It doesn't even have a card reader; you key in your digits by hand.

"Let me send a message to Keri. That was one of our goals today, wasn't it?"

I nod. "Make sure she got the data, as Tarn claims."

"And don't flash your cred too wide around here," Surge cautions.

March's gesture says Surge and I are both nervous old women. Well, he's got that half-right. A few minutes later, he returns, looking satisfied. "She should have it in ten to twelve hours, so we'll hear back by early morning."

That'll have to do. Tarn will want my decision then, but I'm not making it unless I'm sure they don't need me on Lachion.

"So what's the story with Tarn?" March takes a seat and picks at a plate of fried . . . something. You'd think I would be used to the way he follows my thoughts by now, but it always seems a little bit eerie. Just like the first time.

Surge shrugs. I can't remember the names of all his guys, which is fine, because they're drinking at other tables now. One of them watches me out of narrowed icy blue eyes. He's a pretty one, if a little grimy around the edges, and I'm not sure what has him so interested. Maybe he's never seen a bald chick before.

"He was a nobody before last week," Surge says. "Now he's pushing to make New Terra the Conglomerate capital, and the fact that Farwan fell apart here is lending him some momentum, but as far as I can tell, he has no more power than any other representative."

Our waitress sets a carafe down at my elbow. I sniff it. The fumes decree that it's extremely alcoholic, so I tip some into my weak tea. There's probably a still in the basement. In Wickville they make the homebrew out of whatever they have to hand. Hopefully, it will take the edge off the pain. Medicinal usage aside, if I drink enough of this brown lightning, I won't care about my hip anymore.

Some things never change. In poor districts, people do the jobs that bots perform in more affluent sectors. Here, the owners can't afford maintenance, replacement parts, or chip upgrades. Humans are infinitely more expendable. If a woman wears out, you can find twenty more just like her looking for work.

The one working our table looks pretty close to busted. As if she feels my stare, she meets my eyes, but she doesn't have enough spark left in her to mind. Her gaze slides away from mine as she trudges on back to the kitchen to schlep the next tray.

March drums his fingers, looking thoughtful. "He's ambitious then."

"And I'm his cat's-paw." The guys glance at me in surprise, as if they've forgotten about me. We can't have that, can we? "What else is new?"

"You certainly have a history of finding trouble," Surge says.

Annoyance sparks through me. This prick doesn't know the first thing about me, other than what he's read or seen on the vids. And okay, maybe things tend to unravel at the seams wherever I go, but is that *my* fault?

"Lay off her," March says. He's smiling, and his tone remains deceptively gentle. "You don't want to make her mad."

I liked how he began, but now I'm not sure where he's going with this. If he expects me to put on a show—*You know, honey, do bitchy Jax for my buddies, come on!*—well, that's just not happening. I'm too tired.

Surge regards me with bloodshot eyes, a forest bristling from his jaw. "Oh yeah? Why's that?"

"Because if you upset her, you'll have to deal with me. And I don't think you want that."

We're in no position to pick a fight with the people who

are helping us. Then again, I suspect I don't get the whole guy thing, because Surge cracks up again. Fucking men, right?

"Shit, she's got you trained right and tight, lad. When you donning the collar?"

With a sigh, I down the rest of my spiked tea and feel the warmth washing over me. It's been a while since I drank anything this strong.

"Jax doesn't believe in that," March answers.

"I did once. It didn't work out." I scowl, thinking of Simon. "I don't suppose you know people who could get to him? He's being held in a secure facility." It's a throwaway remark, one I don't expect to bear fruit. I should have known better. These are former mercs, after all.

"There's always a way," Surge tells me with a wicked smile. "But it'll cost. Depends on where, of course, but we probably know someone doing time same as your ex. How bad do you want the man done?"

# CHAPTER 7

***I'd love to see Simon dead.***

When his superiors asked for a scapegoat, he tried to sacrifice me. He knew they planned to murder everyone on the *Sargasso*, and he decided to rid himself of me as well. There were probably insurance payments to collect, my death benefits. Mary knows he cleaned out my personal accounts before my alleged body was cold.

He deserves to suffer in ways I can't articulate for what he's done. Seventy-five souls trusted us to get them safely to Matins IV. Eighty-two died in the crash.

Even now, I still have dreams. I wake up screaming, and I can't stand the smell of cooking meat. March watches me thinking it over, and I'm sure he's tapped into my bloodthirsty thoughts. Then it occurs to me. Doesn't matter how bad I'd like to get this dirty job done. I can't afford it.

I'll have to content myself with imagining bad things happening to the bastard. If he's been sent to Whitefish, I won't have to wait long, though. Someone will shank him for being an officious little prick.

"I'll think about it," I say, because there's no way I'm

telling Surge about my temporary financial embarrassment.

The merc looks disappointed. "Right, then. Another round?"

"One for the road," March answers. His expression becomes speculative. "What would you suggest for someone in deep to the Syndicate?"

"A Eutha-booth." Luckily, the other man has his eye on March while he laughs, so he doesn't catch my wince. There are home truths, and home truths, if you know what I mean. "Oh shit, you're serious? Dunno, lad, that's some steep ground. They were fighting a smugglers' war on two fronts between Hon's raiders and the gray men, but the world looks a whole lot rosier for them now, thanks to your girl here. Maybe she could ask them nicely to call off the debt."

Well, that's not helpful. Mr. Jewel Brooch didn't seem inclined to believe he owed me any favors when we talked at the coffeehouse. Was that just a few hours ago? Long day.

"We'll sort it out." March pushes away from the table. "Can you call us an auto-cab? Where's the closest stand?"

"At the corner," Surge says. "And already done. Should be there by the time you make your way down. It was good seeing you, mate. I hope you and the ambassador here get things sorted."

Every time someone says that, I fight the urge to look over my shoulder. It's like being the butt of a joke everybody gets but me. I sure as shit don't feel like any such thing. Maybe it takes a while to sink in.

From the next table I hear Surge's guys speculating that I'm bald because I had a terrible case of nits. I run a hand over my stubbly head and struggle to my feet. Yeah, it's definitely time to go.

"There's some wreckage four blocks up and over from where we met you. You should get a good price for the big pieces if you get right over there." With a wave, March heads for the front door with me trailing behind him like a gimp puppy.

I guess diva-Jax still dwells somewhere inside my scrawny breast because that doesn't set well. Then he holds the door for me and offers his heart-melting smile. As we step outside, I forget my minor complaints because nightfall in the north is fucking brutal.

Our hike down to the auto-cab stand feels like kilometers. There's a reason people drink so much, living here. I'd nearly forgotten that part. A group of homeless men huddle near a trash barrel where they've lit a fire. Such things are illegal, but who's going to protest?

The Corp wrote this place off decades ago, and gangers run it now. Starving artists produce the most amazing music, though. Sweet strains wend through the smoky dark toward me, notes of throbbing warmth that seem to hang in the crystal-cold air like tropical fruit. People in Wickville live with singular abandon; it's not hard to behave as if every day might be your last if it truly might be. Until now, I hadn't realized how much I'd incorporated that idea into my personal philosophy, if I could be said to have such a thing.

"I didn't realize how much time you spent here," March says softly.

I make no response as we climb into the blessedly heated cab. He doesn't know as much about me as he supposes. I wonder what he'd say if he knew I almost threw everything away—my future with the Corp, my promise as a jumper—for a saxophone player.

First he swipes his card and then taps out our destination on the panel. With a soft swoosh, we're on our way.

Numbness sets in. Not from the cold, though I can't seem to warm up all the way. Too much has happened. I can't parse it all.

*My mother, my father, my past . . .*

Everything feels like it's on a collision course. No matter what choice I make, somebody loses. In the old days I wouldn't have cared. Fuck the lot of them; what did they ever do for me? I'd have gotten drunk, flashed my tits, and danced on a table. I'd have thought of nothing but my next jump. For Mary's sake, these days, I even regret the trouble the exploding Skimmer will cause poor Squid.

*When the hell did I develop a conscience?*

"When you came for me." March answers the unspoken question with an expression I can't interpret.

There's something to be said for a man who tunes into your moods like this. He wraps an arm around me and leans his head against mine. Sometimes I sense in him a deep-seated fear. It's like he wants to hold me so tight I can't get free, but conversely, he's afraid of frightening me away with such visceral need.

He's right to fear that. I love him, but he terrifies me in some ways.

"It's a pain in the ass."

"Get used to it," he says dryly. "Once you start caring, it's hard to stop."

"Great."

We ride the rest of the way in silence. I feel a little queasy from the homebrew, or maybe it was the microorganisms in my tea. By the time we climb out in front of headquarters, I'm grateful for the shock of frosty air. Wickville seems farther away than the kilometers we traveled.

"I'll walk you to your door." In his eyes, I glimpse an endearingly roguish twinkle that warns me he doesn't intend to leave me there with a chaste kiss.

I'm not in the mood for love, but I'll deal with that when the time comes. We're questioned once by the automated security system. Luckily March remembers the pass codes. To my mind, modern life just offers too many numbers that we're supposed to keep track of.

Up on the eighth floor, I key my room open and stare. "What the fuck . . ."

The place has been ransacked, well, as much as an impersonal, nearly empty room can be. I don't *have* anything. Anyone who doesn't realize that is dumb as a rock. Correction, March gave me back my PA, 245, which he found at the hostel where Velith took me.

She is literally all I own, and I keep her with me at all times now. Discovering that I'm dead broke makes her all the more valuable. Since she has perfect recall, she'll make an ideal assistant for an ambassador who needs to get everything just right from customs to mealtime etiquette. Just last night, she asked me to get her a droid frame, so she can better serve in that capacity.

So she's my most important asset. I'm like the tinker and his horseshoe nail from the stories. Numbly I step inside and start tidying up.

"Shouldn't we call security? They might be able to find out who did this."

I shrug. "If you like. I don't feel up to dealing with it tonight, though."

He takes a closer look at me. "You don't look good, Jax."

"Thanks. You're fantastic for my ego." I manage a wan smile. "It's been a long day, and dropping out of the sky didn't help. I'll be fine after I get some rest."

"Hope so." Maybe it's because I know him, but he's not doing a good job of hiding his concern.

I understand why. This isn't like me. I'm not the pale, listless type, and I can count on one hand the number of times I've been sick in my life.

"You want to stay?" Even as I ask, I press the button to enlarge my bunk from a single to a double.

We've been assigned to executive quarters, so I have a san-shower in the suite, a vid station, and a customizable sleep unit. The only thing we don't have is a wardrober, but the Corp was run by a bunch of skinflints. March has his own room on ten, but I don't imagine he'll be returning to it. He smiles at me and hangs his things next to my winter gear. It doesn't take long to set the room to rights, given how little I have in here. Nothing seems to be missing.

"I was hoping you'd ask," he says. "Shower?"

"Yes, let's."

Maybe things will look better in the morning.

# CHAPTER 8

***I'm having the strangest dream.***

Dina sits on my chest while trying to convince someone I'm part of an expensive rug she wants to sell. Vaguely I know this isn't right. I'm not made of loose threads and badly woven s-wool. Am I? When I wake up, I find myself snuggled against March's big body while Dina peers into my face. As always, I'm surprised that she smells of flowers.

"I got us a ship," she says.

"A what?" The neurons in my brain aren't firing at capacity yet.

"A ship," she repeats, slower this time. Like I'm a head case. Since I need a chemical boost to jump-start my wits, she probably has a point.

March is awake now, and thankfully, he heaves over so I can crawl out of bed. Damn, I ache. Guess I'm not as young as I used to be . . . so I can't fall out of the sky with equanimity. I wish Doc was here. He'd give me a shot of something and say, *You're fine, Jax. Get out of my med bay.*

"How'd you manage that?" he asks.

Maybe she doesn't think I notice the way she averts her eyes, but I do. In utter exhaustion I fell into bed in my skivvies last night. This morning, she's caught me in a tank top and shorts, revealing my scars in all their glory. They're never going to fade entirely. I don't even want them to, so it's just as well March can handle them. I'll never go to a cosmetic surgeon and ask him to burn away the marks.

"Won it," she answers. This means she hustled someone, the poor bastard. "In a magnificent hand of Pick Five. I spent the night going over it. I'm dog tired now, but she'll run. And she's ours. You can rename her when I handle ownership transfer. We'll just have to pay license and filing fees."

"What's it called now?" I ask over my shoulder.

Since we showered last night, I don't feel dirty pulling on a fresh jumpsuit, straight from bed. When you don't have any hair to manage, it's amazing how fast you can be ready. I just need to wash my face, clean my teeth, and I'll be set.

Dina grins. *"Bernard's Luck."*

As I laugh at the irony, March wears a thoughtful frown as he gets dressed. "I've *heard* that somewhere before. Ah well, it'll come to me. Let's not rename it; I'd rather not meddle with a man's luck."

She raises a brow at me, and I shrug. He can be unaccountably superstitious for an otherwise reasonable man. Then again, with eyes like his, it wouldn't matter if he threw the bones before every flight.

Our station beeps, signaling we have a message. Through static and white solar lines, Keri says, "We've received ten gigs' worth of genetic data, and it's advanced Doc's research by years. He arrived a week ago, and we're—"

End message in a snowy gray blur. I suspect something must be the matter with the satellites near Lachion, or we wouldn't consistently have this problem with messages. Or maybe she was about to say something we weren't supposed to hear. Unfortunately, I have no ability to judge anymore.

If the Psychs can be trusted—which they can't—I suffer from borderline paranoid dysfunction. I suspect *everyone* of treachery and subversive plots against me. But like the old adage goes: *Just because you're paranoid doesn't mean they aren't out to get you.* Why, then, do they want to send a half-cracked nut like me off to Ithiss-Tor? That question begs for an answer, but I don't have all the pieces of the puzzle just yet.

In under half an hour we present ourselves in conference room 7-J again. My hip still hurts, and I have my doubts about this whole endeavor, but when Tarn enters the room, I manage a smile. His expression alters subtly when he takes in my outfit.

"If you intend to take this position, Ms. Jax, you'll need to dress the part. We cannot have you representing New Terra looking like a garage mechanic."

This is my favorite blue jumpsuit, dammit.

I glare at him. "And if you think I'm donning ceremonial robes, you're out of your mind."

"You *are* interested then, I take it?"

March and Dina regard me in silence. I think about all the factors, and in the end, it comes down to one thing. It's a job that gets me off this rock, at least for a little while. I'll be jumping again, all expenses paid. Plus, I've never been one to back away from a challenge.

"Yes, I'm interested. I'll dress up more when we arrive."

Tarn smiles. Oh, I really don't trust that look. "Excellent." He depresses a button under the table, and the door to the conference room slides open.

I don't recognize the man who joins us then: medium height, brown hair, average features. In fact, if I didn't know better, I'd say his face is some amalgamation of a thousand others I've seen, so relentlessly average that I've forgotten what he looks like as soon as my gaze shifts away.

I test this three or four times, bemused by it, so I'm

distracted when Tarn says, "I believe you already know Velith. He'll be accompanying you as your cultural liaison. I'm sure I don't need to stress the importance of internalizing Ithtorian customs to prevent giving insult and destroying our nascent accords. And above all, please take care with your jumps, Sirantha. There may be raiders lurking in highly traveled hot spots."

"Vel!" Though I know what lurks beneath the human skin, I can't resist. I leap from my chair and startle him with a hug. I never had the chance to thank him. There's no question; I wouldn't be here if not for him.

He fields me with awkward perplexity. "If I am to begin your lessons at present, Sirantha, this would be construed as an aggressive act on Ithiss-Tor."

Well, since I'm not normally a touchy-feely person, I think we'll be okay. I nod, though, and make a mental note. *No hugging of random Bugs.*

"This is March, my pilot, and Dina, ship's mechanic."

They exchange polite words while Tarn observes us. What's he looking for? Something isn't right here, but I can't put my finger on it.

I'm all but certain Vel isn't in on it, whatever the Chancellor is plotting. What was the point of saving me if he only meant to take me to his homeworld and get me killed? Logically, it just doesn't track, and Vel is all about things making sense.

"When do we leave?" Dina asks. "I have some preparations to make."

Tarn raises a brow at her. Oh, she's gonna go all "her highness" on his ass. "Your vessel is already adequately supplied."

"I wouldn't touch that 'vessel' with a ten-foot pole," she says, eyes narrowed. If her chin juts out, he'd better run. "We have our own ship, and I trust you'll approve all necessary expenditures to equip it as the ambassador's team sees fit."

Before the veins in Tarn's forehead explode, March puts in, "We prefer not to trust our fate to those inexperienced with long jump-flights." Chalk one up for diplomacy. "However well-intentioned they may be. I hope you understand."

I can't believe this ambassador stuff works, even on the Chancellor. He's the one who *appointed* me. But I suppose once you claim someone has power, you can't decry it without making yourself look like a jackass.

Clearing his throat, Tarn makes an attempt to regain some lost ground. "I'll approve the same budget for your provisions as were spent on the Conglomerate ship. You may allot it as you choose."

"Can we get under way tomorrow, Dina?" March gets to his feet, signaling the meeting has adjourned. Tarn isn't going to like that either. As for me, I'm still standing with Vel, near the door.

"Depends. If their commissar can requisition everything we need, it'll be a snap. I'm having *Bernard's Luck* transferred to the Conglomerate docking bays today."

He nods. "That's your top priority then."

"I haven't briefed you fully," Tarn protests, as we head for the door.

I shrug. "Send the files to the ship. I'll read it en route."

If he expected me to be easily controlled, he didn't pay enough attention to recent history. I don't owe Chancellor Tarn a damn thing. He wants me to go to Ithiss-Tor and try to persuade the Bugs that it's in their best interests to join galactic politics. And that means I work for the Conglomerate, a glorified bureaucrat.

Whether it's best for Ithiss-Tor to join the party, I'm not sure. If they refuse, I'm positive the Conglomerate intends to make an example of them somehow, perhaps to frighten other non-tier worlds into towing the line. Tarn lost sight of one thing, however.

I'm nobody's pawn, not anymore. And if he tries to orchestrate my moves on some celestial chessboard, he'll be sorry.

# CHAPTER 9

***Dina has to be kidding.***

If the *Folly*—the ship we crashed a couple weeks ago—looked better on the inside than I expected, well, my luck has turned. This vessel looks like something out of old vids; it's positively ancient. The outside promises a dirty, cramped interior, and I'm not disappointed when I clamber through the hatch.

It's only a six-seater. I pass through a narrow corridor to the central hub. At least the safety equipment looks to be functional. From the hub, halls lead left and right. If this ship conforms to standard layouts, there will be three small bunk areas on either side. Straight ahead we have the cockpit. Since this junk bucket is so small, I rather doubt it possesses any extra amenities.

*Bernard's Luck* doesn't even boast a boarding ramp. Instead it has a pressure door on the side and a retractable ladder. I wouldn't put it past the former owner of this ship to have lost it on *purpose*. Okay, probably not—he could've gotten something for it from the scrap yards.

Dina interprets my expression correctly. "I know she's a

little rough around the edges, but the *Folly* wasn't a diamond when we got her. I'll polish her up as we go."

"A little?" I shake my head. "As a jumper, I always knew my odds of going out on board a ship were pretty high, but do you have to stack the deck like this?"

"It's not that bad," March says, then nearly loses his head to a dangling ceiling panel. Though I'm not a mechanic, I feel pretty sure that ought to be soldered to the wall. He exercises remarkable restraint as he adds to Dina, "You might want to fix that before we get under way."

She hurries off to get her toolkit. As I head to check out the cockpit, Velith boards. I hear him say, "Is this wise? Perhaps we ought to reconsider and accept the loan of a Conglomerate ship."

Though I hate the idea of being dependent on charity as much as the next person, I have to say, I'm with Vel on this one. Sadly, I'm not surprised when both Dina and March call, "No!"

"It is quite . . . compact, is it not?" Vel glances around.

He has a point since five steps takes me around the hub. Another five steps carries me to the pressure hatch. I take a quick look around, and damned if crew quarters aren't so cramped that passing gas in there might result in methane poisoning. There's no med bay on board, just a maintenance closet, so it's just as well Doc won't be traveling with us this time.

Halfway to the cockpit, the metal panels appear singed, as if there's been a fire. Mary help us. "Dina!" I call. "Did you check electrical?"

"Do *you* want to fix this thing? Of course I did. It's sound. I already told you that. That's purely a cosmetic flaw."

"What's the obsession with this piece of junk anyway?" I mutter.

"If we decide to leave Ithiss-Tor unexpectedly, we can't be accused of theft by the Conglomerate," March answers from behind me.

After considering everything that could go wrong, I have to say, "I see the value in that."

"I thought you might. Let's take a look at the cockpit."

Right. We continue to the front, where I intend to inspect the nav chair. That's life or death for me. If it doesn't look right, I'm not going up in this, no matter what. I can live with being accused of theft. In fact, that might make a nice change from mass murder and general, wanton acts of terrorism.

I'm pleasantly surprised to find a relatively clean environment. The newest pieces on the ship have been installed up here, no signs of systems failure, no loose wiring. The nav chair is an older model, but it looks like it's in good shape. After checking the port, I don't doubt this ship will run.

"How's it look in your end?"

March shrugs. "Old interface, but I can manage. We'll be all right, Jax."

"We're stopping on Lachion first, right?" He said something about it last night, but honestly I was half-asleep. "Is that Conglomerate approved?"

"I don't give a shit." He grins at me and runs a hand over my stubbly head. "We know our message went out clean, but I'm not so sure about Keri's. I just want to make sure everything's all right. I owe her that much."

I am absolutely *not* jealous over his concern. It's paternal, that's all. So what if Keri is young, lovely, talented, and terribly important? For a moment, I remember how much I resented her at our first meeting.

"I don't know about paternal," March says, tormenting me with a thoughtful pause. "Fraternal. I'm not *that* old."

Before I can hit him in the head as he so richly deserves, the sound of raised voices echoes toward us. The acoustics in here are such that I can't make out what the fuss is about, so I head back toward the hub. March's friend Surge towers over Dina, looking ready to clobber her.

"You cheated!" Surge roars. "If you think I'm letting you take my ship—"

"My ship," she corrects. "I have all the documentation,

and you better get your smelly ass off of it before we take you up and boost you out the garbage chute."

I register March's amusement as he comes up behind me. Funny, he hasn't made a sound, but I can *feel* his smile. Wonder if this sensitivity results from jacking in with a Psi pilot.

"I see you've met Dina. I *knew* I'd heard that ship name somewhere. She rolled you in a game of Pick Five, huh? You must've been pretty drunk."

"Maybe a little," Surge admits. "I didn't even realize what I wagered till this mornin'. Talk about a rude awakening. Now my crew's stranded here."

Dina snorts. "Serves them right for signing on with a scruffy, shamefaced mash-brain like you."

"You can't leave us here," Surge protests. "Let us ship out with you. You could use an extra pilot and jumper to spell you, right? And my guys won't eat much." His tone turns wheedling. "Come on, mate, it'll be like old times."

There are seven of them and four of us. Even with March and me in the cockpit, that leaves a shortage of safety seats in the hub, and I doubt anyone is going to volunteer to have his brain scrambled. Staying on New Terra isn't that bad.

By his expression, March is thinking along the same lines. "Look, I'm sorry you gambled away your ship, Bernard." He *does* sound sympathetic. "But she won't carry twelve. I can take three of you: pilot, jumper, plus one more. The rest of your crew stays dirtside. We're on a diplomatic mission, but we're stopping on Lachion first, so I can take you that far."

"We might be able to find work with one of the clans," Surge says with a sigh. "Right, then. Done. I'll call my boy, Jael, and our jumper, Koratati. It's rather urgent for her to get off world. She's nonhuman, doesn't have a valid visa. I expect you've heard about the new Conglomerate immigration laws?"

I haven't, actually, but Velith has. "Yes, it shall likely prove difficult to move about once they enforce them."

March shakes his head. "That's one way to enforce the status quo."

"They really want to get a lock on things, don't they?" With a sigh, Dina fastens a tool belt around her waist. "I'm just afraid it's going to backfire, like it did on Tarnus."

"Periods of political upheaval are often accompanied by widespread disorder and lawlessness," Vel observes.

"It used to be confined to the Outskirts," I say. "And Corp patrols kept the tier worlds safe. You think the Conglomerate's organized enough to prevent piracy and smuggling from becoming widespread?"

We all exchange a dubious glance.

"If nothing else, they can make life difficult for folks on the tier worlds," Surge answers at last. "As for the wider reaches, I doubt it. It's gonna be every man for himself out there for a while yet. I'd put money on the Syndicate running things before the Conglomerate gets itself sorted."

Sadly, nobody disputes his assessment.

"Pick your bunks, people. Surge, I want your other two on board in under an hour. We're taking off in seventy, hell or high water." Now that's the March I know and love.

I throw my meager possessions into a miniscule room at random and then return to the cockpit. March is already running diagnostics, a pretty array of lights glimmering on the instrument panel. I even know what some of them mean now, and I prove it by saying, "Isn't that reading a little low for life support?"

He grins like he's proud of me. "Yeah, give it some time to power up all the way. This ship won't be doing any lightning-fast getaways in its current state. Give Dina some time with it on Lachion, though. She'll upgrade, add all the pretty bells and whistles you admired on the *Folly*."

I check the port one last time. "So what do you think?"

"Surge isn't telling us something," March says. "But I couldn't get a read on what. I'll be watching him, don't worry."

I raise a brow. "I thought he was a friend of yours."

"More accurate to say, we belonged to the same company at one time. He's doing his best to appear affable, but I think there's more to it."

"You think he lost the ship to Dina on purpose, so he'd have a reason to attach himself to us?" There goes my paranoia again.

"I don't discount it." March wears a thundercloud scowl, long fingers dancing over the instrument panel. "Never forget, he's a merc at heart, and he doesn't own an ounce of sentiment. He goes for the biggest payday, every time."

"If you think he's out to get us, why is he on board this ship?" I ask. Seems like a basic error in judgment.

"I prefer to keep my enemies close enough that I can go for their throats." By his grim expression, he's remembering something he'd rather not discuss.

# CHAPTER 10

***It feels good to be in the chair again.***

We've finished diagnostics and everyone's on board. Jael is a handsome, cocky bastard. I don't know what he's good for on a ship, but he makes fine eye candy. And he's just the type I used to love: slim, blond, and too pretty for his own good. The way I look now, though, he spends his time flirting with Dina. He's more likely to get blood from a stone than make headway with *her*.

That stings my feminine vanity a little. I used to be able to command a man's attention by walking into a room. I had an indefinable *something*.

Now I'm damaged goods, but it's enough that March loves me. I don't care if some stupid space cowboy can't appreciate what's beneath the surface.

Koratati is . . . big. She arrived swathed in a gray cloak, and I didn't get a good look at her before we came up front. We know she's nonhuman, so she might be one of the jumbo races. Surge did right to get her off planet, as hiding her wouldn't prove an easy task in Wickville. Hopefully, she can wedge her ass into the safety harness when we need to make the jump.

March contacts docking control on the relay, which crackles in a tinny, old-fashioned way. After a few minutes, they respond, "You have clearance, *Bernard's Luck*. Have a good flight."

Over the rush of the thrusters, I hear the hangar doors groan their way open. On some planets, the shipyards are out in the open, but it's too cold for that in this part of New Terra. The subzero temps would damage the instruments if we didn't keep the ships inside a climate-controlled hangar.

As always, I admire March's skill on the controls, the smooth way we swoop out into the sky. I know from experience, that isn't as easy as it looks. As we gain altitude, I feel it in my eardrums before the pressure inside the ship stabilizes.

The little *Luck* shudders as we push past the atmosphere and into stark, silent reaches where I feel most at home. There's nothing like seeing stars through the sensor screen and knowing only a few centimeters of metal separate you from vacuum. Just thinking about it sends a thrill through me.

March shakes his head at me, I hope with affection. "You're crazy, Jax."

"I know."

That's not the first time he's said so. I could counter that he's mad for loving me, but that might make him question it. And I don't want that, even though I'm afraid of hurting him, afraid of losing him.

Afraid of damn near *everything*.

But I refuse to let it paralyze me. I won't be the woman who cowers behind four walls, never taking chances. I want to die like I've lived. I always wanted to be larger than life, but lately it feels like I'm shrinking—literally, like old women do.

March cuts me a sharp look—he hates when I think about dying. He says it's macabre. Well, the subsequent thought should make him smile because I'm not ready to go anytime soon, not until I've seen more, *done* more. After this is all over, we'll spend a glorious week on the beaches of New Venice, maybe luge down the glaciers on Ielos. There's too much left to do for me to want the ride to end so soon.

"Glad to hear it," he says softly. "I'd miss you."

*Understatement.* I have no words for the holocaust I saw inside him when he thought he'd lost me. He went to a place beyond loss, beyond madness. I don't deserve him. But I put aside those thoughts because they make me ache.

He seems a little tense. The last time March and I left the cockpit, the *Folly* wound up targeted by New Terra's Satellite Defense Installations, and we were lucky to reach the surface in one piece. I don't blame him for wanting to make sure we make it to the first jump intact.

Moreover, we can't trust everyone we have on board, so if we leave the cockpit, there's a chance that Koratati and Surge will hijack us and deliver us someplace we don't want to be. I can't imagine who else might be gunning for me—or maybe it's March they want this time—his past is far from an open book at this point. Regardless, it seems better to be safe, which means keeping our asses in these seats.

Dina and Velith will keep an eye on Surge, Jael, and Koratati for us. And if they start something, my money's on Vel. See, I watched him take on a clutch of Morgut and walk—okay, limp—off to tell the tale.

My fingers go to my newest scar, a slash across my right wrist. Though it's healing well enough, it still itches a little.

March slants me a smile. "So . . . you wanna play Pick Five?"

I roll my eyes. "Not really. You'd just read my cards and know what you needed to discard."

He lays a hand over his heart. "I'm cut, seriously. You're implying I'd cheat?"

"Wouldn't you?"

His expression becomes wolfish. "Absolutely. I always get what I want."

"Should that worry me?"

"Everything worries you."

I can't argue that. He must find me the most ridiculous bundle of contradictions. I suspect everyone of perfidious motives yet I long to hurl myself into dangerous situations to forget my fears. Forget aversion therapy, that's the way I live.

Apart from the noises of the ship, it's so quiet up here. This is what freedom feels like. In some ways that's an oxymoron—I'm only free when I'm confined to a ship as opposed to having a whole planet to move around on. But there you have it; it's how I've felt since the first time I went up. My parents took me on a pleasure cruise when I was thirteen, and I was never the same thereafter.

That line of thought leads me directly back to my mother. I can't believe she expects me to save her ass, after they disowned me. They probably celebrated when they heard Farwan "brought me to justice."

"That's not true," March says, unaccountably gentle. "She was happy to see you. More worried about herself, but genuinely glad you're all right."

I sigh. "Ugh. Don't we have enough to worry about without you analyzing my feelings about my mother?"

"We have time to kill before we make the jump." He grins.

"I'd rather play Charm, New Venice rules."

"I expect you would. But think how shocked people would be to find us sexing each other up in the cockpit, just like the porn cliché."

A smile tugs at the corner of my mouth, but I won't give him the satisfaction. "You saying you can't see me naked without being overcome with lust?"

"Try me."

I suspect he's full of shit, but damned if he's not good for my ego, which has taken a beating lately. Most days I don't even feel womanly, let alone sexy.

"I think we better not," I answer finally. "I don't want to scare anybody."

Mainly I'm glad he's not bugging me about my mother

anymore. That's where it's a little unequal. He knows exactly what he can say without tearing open old wounds. I don't have any such clarity where he's concerned.

Of course I'm curious about the shit he's done, the battles he's fought, and the hell he went through before he wound up on Lachion with Mair, Keri's grandmother. But I don't want to hurt him—I don't want to ask about stuff he's trying to forget. The old Jax would've ranked her curiosity above any possible harm and called it candor. I've since learned there's a balance between candor and cruelty.

"You can ask me anything you want to know," he says without looking up from the instruments. His playful mood has faded, though, as if in anticipation of what I may say.

Okay, then. This is an olive branch, so I take it. Maybe he wants to open up, but he doesn't know where to start. "How many, March?"

He answers without looking at me. "Body count, you mean?"

I nod, knowing he'll catch the movement in his peripheral vision.

"Thousands," he says, after a long pause. "On Nicu Tertius alone. I did the job they hired me for, no matter how bad it got."

"That was war. That's . . . different. And it's not what I wanted to know."

"You want to know how many men I've personally ended?" he asks then.

*Do I?*

"Yeah."

"Between ten and fifteen." He sounds dispassionate. "Depends on whether the ones whose minds I broke are still lingering."

"But you had good reason, right?"

Before he can reply, Dina's voice comes over the comm. "I think we have trouble."

"When don't we?" March mutters. "What's wrong now?"

"Their jumper seems to be having a fit, and we don't have a doc on board."

# CHAPTER 11

***I put aside my misgivings about the man March used to*** be. People can change; I'm living proof of that. "You want me to take a look?"

March manages a smile. "Unless *you* want to drive."

I'm just never going to hear the end of that. When we made our escape from Hon-Durren's Kingdom, I banged the hell out of the *Folly*. Shaking my head, I push out of the nav chair and make my way back to the hub. Koratati flails uncontrollably, but she's still wrapped up in that heavy cloak, so I can't tell what's going on.

Surge looks frantic, Jael appears unconcerned, and Vel . . . he's observing the scene, putting the pieces together before he makes a judgment. Dina has made herself scarce. I guess she figured she discharged her duty when she notified March.

"Has she been sick? You idiots, we don't have facilities on this ship. She'd have been better off dirtside, new immigration laws or not." I bend toward her, and Koratati lashes out.

"Don't touch me!"

Her fist feels like a hammer as it connects with my cheek. I reel back, steady myself on the wall. That's gonna leave a mark.

Under her voluminous robe, something . . . moves. Okay, this really isn't right. I wish Doc was here.

"She's not ill," Velith says while I rub my cheek. "She's in labor."

"I had to get her off world." Surge paces around the hub, watching Koratati with a worry that tells me she's not just his jumper. "She's not due for days yet, though—"

"Imbecile." Even *I* know that stress can jump-start this breeding business, and I'm not exactly an expert. "You know we can't jump, right? Did you even consider what the pressure and/or environmental shifts could do to an unborn child?"

"I . . . no." Surge shakes his head. "I just didn't want my kid to suffer or be treated like a second-class citizen because of those new immigration laws. At least if he's born up here, they don't apply."

"She!" Koratati pushes her way out of the cloak. She has a jutting jaw, a fine dusting of gold fur, and powerful haunches. Mary help us, she's Rodeisian. Wait, *his* kid? I didn't even know they could crossbreed with humans. They're a large, humanoid race from a small planet in the Outskirts.

"You knew you needed to get off the planet in a hurry, and you gambled away your ship?" That makes no sense.

The woman's scream of pain derails my train of thought. We need medicine, a doctor, somewhere she can lie down—

Shit, why am *I* in charge?

"When they broke the news about the reforms, I didn't have the credits to provision the ship," Surge explains. "Or even refuel it. Then I ran across you and March. Did some digging to see how it could help me, and when we saw your mechanic drinking in the Den . . ."

"You saw your chance and took it. Then you pushed

your way on board, talked March into taking you up, and the rest is history."

Koratati screams again, and March's voice comes over the comm. "What the hell is going on back there?"

"It appears we're having a baby."

"We're *what*?"

I realize how that sounds, but unfortunately, I don't have time to tease him with it. "Surge brought his wife on board, and she's about to deliver any minute."

"I'm not his wife," Koratati grits out.

I don't know enough about Rodeisian customs to understand why she's so adamant on this point. Whatever, it doesn't matter. More to the point, what the hell am I supposed to do?

"Let's get you to one of the bunks where you can lie down." I try to help her up, but she shoves me away.

I stagger back, and Mary, either her adrenaline is running amok or she's the strongest woman I've ever met. Dina isn't going to like that. I've never sparred with a Rodeisian partner, but then again, most of my combat experience comes from being liquored up and starting something in a station bar.

"That will only make it harder," she grunts. "I need to stay upright so gravity will help me."

Great, we need one of those old-fashioned birthing chairs. I glance around the hub and don't see anything better suited than the seat she's already sitting in. She can't have a baby *here*; this ship is old, filthy, and—

"Vel, help me out here!"

The bounty hunter turned cultural liaison lifts a brow at me, appearing completely at ease. "What do you expect me to do?"

"I . . ." Have no idea.

Thankfully March appears in the corridor leading from the cockpit. He'll take over, right? The man takes in my frantic expression and scrubs a palm across his face. "You were serious." Turning to Surge, he adds, "You smuggled a pregnant woman on board my ship? We're tied to hauling straight space now, and I don't know what kind of provisions Dina laid in. We expected a clean jump to Lachion!"

As if responding to a summons, she appears with an armful of odds and ends. "We have enough organic to run the kitchen-mate for a week, if we eat light, enough paste to keep us going for another two weeks."

March mutters, "Fuck. All right, let me check the charts to see what our options are, given fuel and supply levels." He narrows his eyes on me. "You. That wasn't funny, not even a little bit."

"Do I *look* pregnant?"

"You look like a refugee," Dina says while laying out the things she's collected.

To my vast relief, she handles the situation, spreading a blanket that I hope she's sterilized somehow beneath Koratati's feet. I don't even mind the slam, which stings more because it's true.

"Give her your hand," Dina instructs.

After all the abuse I've taken, I'm not precisely eager, but I don't want to wind up orchestrating this comedy of errors. So Koratati squeezes down, and I'm pretty sure I hear my bones popping. That can't be a good sign.

From somewhere behind me, Jael says, "If we don't need to be strapped in, then I'm off to quarters. I'd rather not watch."

"You prefer the baby-making, do you?" I'm amazed Koratati can find the wind to be flippant, but she manages to make an obscene gesture at Jael as he retreats. "Go on then, get out of here, you gormless coward!"

"If you insist." Surge pretends he thinks she's talking to him, heads for the hallway, and calls to Jael, "Slow up, lad, maybe we can get a game together."

This looks insanely painful. If I'd ever been inclined to romanticize motherhood, this would've dispelled those illusions straightaway. Koratati's belly roils with her labor, and she sits forward, knees splayed wide. The golden fur running down her neck is wet with sweat. She smells funky, too. By the way Kora bares her teeth, it's just as well Surge took to his heels.

A gush of fluid spatters the blanket Dina laid down. The mechanic whispers soft words of encouragement with a surety and comfort that astonishes me. She correctly interprets my surprise and shrugs.

"Back on Tarnus, I was present at my mother's bedside for every birth. I had three sisters. It was tradition."

Her family is dead now. I wonder what she'd do in my place, given what my mother has asked of me, what Dina would've done to save them, if she'd had any power in the matter. Koratati growls low in her throat, signaling that she should be the center of attention, as she crushes my fingers in hers.

"You're doing great," Dina murmurs. "I'm timing you, and it's time to push."

That's Vel's cue. Despite our racial differences, he's still quintessentially male, and this is a woman thing. I sigh.

*I wish I had a penis.*

March's amusement ripples through me. *Yeah, that's going on the list of things I never want to hear again.* I grin, knowing I'm not going to explain the context.

"I think I will go see what they're playing," Vel says, and hurries off.

I'd like to say the birth affected me profoundly, that it was beautiful and miraculous. Maybe even report the experience changed me forever. But that would come across as pure bullshit to anyone who knows me.

So I'll tell the truth: The ordeal struck me as painful, bloody, smelly, messy, and a whole lot of trouble. I can't believe women go through it on purpose. Kora looks positively beatific when we lay her daughter in her arms, though, a wrinkly, squalling little thing with tufts of gold hair. So I suppose she must think it's worth it.

As for me, I resolve never to pass along my genes. The guys return when the coast is clear, first Surge and Jael, then March and Vel. They admire the child dutifully and then break open a bottle of homebrew Surge brought on board. He knew he'd have something to celebrate.

The mood on board shifts from tense to festive, but I know it won't last. I can tell by March's expression he has crucial information, and we may not like it. Then again, when do we ever?

Like a good captain, he lets them celebrate for a while, though. Doesn't want to bring the mood down too soon. Dina coaxes some music out of the ancient comm system, and Jael shows off a surprisingly deep singing voice. Kora basks in Surge's proud fatherness. I don't think I've ever shared a moment like this with anyone.

Finally, March has to speak because time marches on, as that's what time does. I'm shocked to find we've been up hauling straight space for over twelve hours. "I have bad news and worse news. Which do you want first?"

Shit. I hate this game.

# CHAPTER 12

***As the hub devolves into many voices talking at once,*** Vel takes a seat near me, where I've collapsed. "Is it always like this?"

I think about that. "Pretty much. Except sometimes there's shooting and things blow up."

"Give it time," Dina mutters.

"Let's have the worst news first," I suggest a little louder. "Maybe the bad news won't seem so bad."

March motions for all of us to shut up. "I've looked at the routes, and we have two choices. We can go back to New Terra—" Jael immediately protests, and March tries to continue over the noise. "Or we can make for an emergency station two weeks out. If we can't jump, there's just nowhere else in this sector."

"What's so bad about the emergency station?" I'm sure I'm not the only one wondering that.

I stopped at a few in my Corp days. They're a little grim, true, with their bare-bones floor plans, and they offer only basic amenities, but I don't remember them as terrible places. We should be able to drop Surge and Koratati off there. They'll be able to work for their keep until another ride comes by.

It might be a while since most ships jump at the nearest beacon, six hours out of New Terra, but the kid needs to be old enough to don protective headgear anyway. Looks like she'll spend her first few turns on an emergency station. That's not the end of the world.

"According to reports I pulled, Emry Station is full of Farwan loyalists. They don't care what the Corp did; they just want to preserve the status quo."

I raise both brows. "You mean they don't accept that it's over? There's no Corp *left*. Doesn't that technically make them rebels?"

"Whatever you call them, they won't receive us politely. They're demanding the Conglomerate acknowledge them as an autonomous outpost, or they'll refuse to aid distressed ships in this sector."

That could be catastrophic. In time this area will turn into a graveyard, ghost ships floating, full of people who died from someone else's inaction. Add that to the already astronomical risk of being hit by raiders, well—we can't let them get away with that.

This will put us off schedule, but we don't have a choice. In reflex, I curl my right hand into a fist, and the left tries to follow suit, but instead pain shoots all the way to my elbow. For a moment I see stars, and I'm nowhere near the sensor screen.

"I'm not going back to New Terra," Jael says flatly. "I'll kill you all before I let you turn this ship around."

Before March can respond to that, Vel glides to within a few meters of the man issuing such wild threats and examines him with a detached air. "You would try," he concludes. His ever-so-average appearance lends him menace that borders on spooky.

If I were Jael, I'd step back. See, this young merc is just too pretty to be as dangerous as he thinks he is. You don't keep a face like that if you spend your life fighting. He'd have a broken nose or something by now if he actually mixed it up. Instead I find it curious that he reacts so strongly to the possibility of going back. What's he running from? And is it going to hunt us down?

March poses that very question aloud as I frame it mentally. It's almost like he's Psi or something. *Oh, right.*

Jael doesn't want to answer. It would be my luck to discover Pretty Boy was my mother's business partner, now running from the Syndicate. Possibly her former lover as well, as I doubt she's kept herself to an immaculate widowhood.

Mary. I'll never see my dad again. Ridiculous it should hit me so hard, right now. Maybe it's because of the baby. Once upon a time, before they took me on a ship, I used to be his little girl. He had high hopes for me. Sometimes I wonder what I'd have been like if I hadn't discovered joy and freedom up here.

As much mind as she pays us, we might not even be here as far as Koratati is concerned. Her whole world rests in the crook of her arm. When she starts feeding the kid, I have to look away, and I intercept a meaningful exchange between Jael and Surge. It's almost like a lightning-fast argument, conducted silently, a glance, a couple of head shakes, and then:

"He's Bred," Surge explains, apparently against Jael's wishes. "If he stays dirtside, he'll be subject to discrimination, according to the new laws."

"It's almost like they're trying to force a caste system," Dina says thoughtfully.

Vel nods his agreement. "In a backward manner, it makes sense. While they are trying to engender a wider alliance with other races, hence the diplomatic missions, they also want to cement human privilege on the homeworld."

The tone of the new immigration and citizenship laws is downright xenophobic. Page seven, last paragraph restricts nonhumans from holding office and owning land. "It's going to be ugly for a while. We're better off up here."

"Not with a baby aboard," March says. "We can't plod

along forever in straight space, and we can't jump with her unprotected. I won't take the risk."

I study Jael. No wonder he's so pretty, and no wonder he doesn't want to go back. Normals hate his kind. Bred humans tend to be faster, smarter, healthier, and generally superior to their counterparts. With the reforms kicking in, it'll be worse.

"Our best bet is to head for the emergency station," I say. "And hope we can talk some sense into those idiots. Maybe they don't realize how isolated they are."

They're Farwan loyalists, not a military group. At best, they'll be former corporate wage slaves and disgruntled technicians. We should be able to cow them.

"It's settled then. We haul onward." March reaches for me and tows me toward the quarters I picked out earlier.

I don't protest because I could use a break. Aching from head to toe, I follow him into the room he apparently intends to share with me. When the door shuts behind us, he draws me into his arms.

"I'm worried about you," he whispers.

Ordinarily I'd discount that as pointless, but I haven't felt right for a while. Most likely I should've had a checkup before we left, but I intended to have Doc check me out when we hit Lachion . . . I should've known things never turn out the way we plan.

Wrapping my arms about his waist, I lean into him and close my eyes. "There's something wrong," I admit, low.

I haven't wanted to admit it, but I'm not healing like I should. I'm tired all the time, and sleep doesn't seem to help. I'm no good at being sick, but I think I might be.

So gentle it makes my heart constrict, he presses me close for a moment, and then he steps back to look at my hand where Kora squeezed it. "I think she snapped your fingers."

"Me, too." I wasn't kidding when I said I couldn't move them. Pain shimmers through my fingertips in odd, erratic pulses when he turns my hand to examine it. Then his fingers trace over the dark bruise forming on my cheekbone.

That, too, feels swollen, damage out of proportion to the blow.

"You look breakable." His gaze lingers as if seeing me for the first time. "And that scares the shit out of me."

"Hey," I murmur. "Don't worry. We'll figure it out. We always do."

He doesn't argue with me, but in his face I see pure, unadulterated fear. That's why March separated me from the others. He didn't want them to see it. Nobody else pays attention to me like he does, so the others probably won't notice that I'm ill.

Wouldn't you know it? I even go out different than the other jumpers. I've spent my life courting death in various ways, living for the thrill, the rush, the risk. I jack in, knowing it might steal my mind away, knowing March may not be able to save me this time, and I keep doing it.

Grimspace beckons; I can't resist the call.

I don't even want to. I don't smoke, rarely drink, and I gave up chem years ago. *This* is my vice.

Even now, I'm faintly irritated that I can't just jump, take us where I want to go. Fuck straight space travel. But it's more than that. It's an itch under my skin, and I can't scratch it, no matter what I do. The longing won't go away until the colors come roaring through me, and my mind blossoms to ten times its size. At this point, I must admit it might be killing me, albeit differently than most jumpers go out.

Question is, what am I going to do about it?

# CHAPTER 13

***Hell is two weeks on a ship with an infant.***

If you don't believe me, try it. By the end of week one, I'm ready to space both Koratati and her squalling bundle of pee. Dina says there's nothing wrong with the little rotter; that's just what babies do.

To make things easier for the new mother, we've instigated a rotating care schedule. This wasn't my idea, by the way. I eventually caved to majority rule, but I did so with poor grace and a lot of mumbling.

I manage to keep my sanity on this straight haul by hiding out. There are six crew rooms. March and I snag the largest one, probably intended for the captain. Surge and Kora share another, while Dina, Jael, and Vel each claim their own. The galley's on the other side of the ship. That leaves one room vacant, just before the maintenance closet with the hatch leading down to the holds.

I fill this space with spare chairs from storage and other odds and ends to make it more of a sitting room. The bunk can recess completely into the wall, making my job easier.

Mostly I'm waiting to hear from Doc, but the satellites are old and tetchy out here. I'll be lucky to get anything before we make Emry Station.

I tend to hunker down in there when the kid is crying because there's more metal between us. Sometimes it helps, but you'd be surprised how that racket carries. When all the doors stand open, it's an acoustic nightmare.

Sometimes my esteemed crewmates join me, like I need company. I'm quite occupied with feeling sorry for myself, thanks. I had a great-aunt whose main hobby included reading about strange diseases and then trying to match her symptoms to whatever exotic ailment took her fancy. Based on my depressive behavior this week, I suspect I may have more in common with my great-aunt Tallia than I would've previously guessed.

Today Jael joins me. He's just come in and doesn't seem inclined to let me brood. With a faint sigh, I put 245 aside. People never understand why I talk to my PA, an ongoing experiment of sorts. Her AI chip seems incredibly sophisticated, and the more we interact, the more she learns, adapting her communication style to mirror my own. This fascinates me.

"Are you busy?" Without an audience, he sheds most of his bravado, and in an oddly tentative movement, he occupies a chair opposite where I sit.

"I guess not. What's up?"

"People always treat me different," he says. "After they find out. You haven't. So I'm wondering why."

I figure he's talking about his origins in the Ideal Genome Project. "This is pretty basic, but . . . it's because I don't care."

The Corp implemented the program shortly before I was born. They offered designer babies for a premium price, and a few wealthy families took advantage of it. They used the profit margin to fund a side research project, seeking to perfect the human condition. Forget antiaging treatments; they wanted to develop bodies that don't age, don't suffer from illness, and require reduced amounts of rest.

Few of their Bred experiments survived to adulthood, and the Corp officially shut the program down after religious outcry that outweighed any theoretical value. Who can say what went on behind closed doors? Or what became of lab babies like the one sitting across from me? He's the first I've ever met.

Jael looks puzzled. "You don't care as in . . . you're disinterested? Or you don't care as in . . . it doesn't matter to you?"

"Both?" Yeah, it's definitely both.

Why does that intrigue him? He sits forward in his chair, hands clasped across his knees. "I don't get you."

Great. He's interested because I'm *not*? Men.

"You don't have to get me. In fact I'd rather you didn't since you're disembarking next week, and I'll never see your face again."

"Nope." He shakes his head. "I already spoke to March, and he said I can stay. You don't have a gunner, and I know this ship's weapons better than anyone else."

Now why didn't March tell me that?

"What do you think will happen on Emry?" I steer the conversation away from personal topics. At this point I'm not interested in playing mother confessor, nor in soothing the scrapes on his soul. Plus I think it's possible we may need weapons to cow the fools playing at resistance out here.

As long as nobody questions it, they can call themselves autonomous. And the Conglomerate is notorious for taking forever to determine a course of action. I'm amazed we got clearance to head for Ithiss-Tor so fast; we probably have Tarn to thank for that.

Jael gives the question due consideration. "Hard to say. Best to play it by ear once we get on station and see how they're running things. I don't think they've officially declared that they won't honor a ship's request for aid as yet. They're waiting to hear from the Conglomerate."

"It'll get messy," I predict. "The Conglomerate will say, 'Fine, if you're autonomous, you're also self-supporting, so you can pay for your own supplies, pay for station repairs on your own,' and so on."

"I wonder if they've thought of that."

I shrug. "Probably not. They're Corp wage slaves. This is the first burst of independent thought they've enjoyed in a while. One can't blame them for being rusty. But if that threat doesn't work, then Tarn might send armed enforcers to clean the place out."

"The Corp would've just blown the place up and built a new one," he says.

"Like they did DuPont Station?"

"I heard about that. They were looking for *you*, weren't they?"

"Yeah. Big scary terrorist, that's me."

He snorts. "You don't look so tough."

Well, he's right. At the moment I feel like the baby could snap me like a twig. It's not a good idea to reveal your weaknesses, however.

"Appearances can be deceiving."

The man flinches like I hit a raw nerve. "I know that's right."

"Aw, don't tell me people think you're pretty but dumb. That must really sting." This conversation is finally getting interesting. "Do they suggest you should be in vids or wearing clothes professionally?"

"Bitch."

Dina sweeps into the room in time to hear the invective. "Making new friends, are you, Jax?"

I flash her a grin. "You know, with a winning personality like I've got—"

"We'll have ten different factions trying to kill us again within a week or two," she interjects.

"Ten? That seems a little on the high side, even for me."

"I figure we've already got the Syndicate. The Ithtorians, who don't really want to receive us in the first place and so aren't going to be happy with this delay. The folks on Lachion are going to be wondering where we are, too . . . so that's three already."

"You think Keri would hunt me down? I thought she kinda liked me by the time we left last time."

"No, she enjoyed beating the shit out of you."

Wearing an expression of tentative amusement, Jael listens to us banter. It seems like he wants to join in but isn't quite sure whether he's allowed. I don't tell him that picking on me is practically an official pastime around here.

But she's brought me a mug of hot choclaste. My brow arches even as I accept the offering. I can't help peering into the cup with suspicion.

"Did you pee in it?"

"Of course not." Dina waits until I've taken a sip before adding, "The baby did."

I manage not to give her the satisfaction of spluttering. "Mmm. I thought it had a special something."

"You're nasty, you know that?" She shakes her head.

"Did March send you?" The question comes out loaded.

When her gaze meets mine, I see that she's figured it out. I thought staying out of sight would be enough until I figured this thing out. Shit. I don't think I'll be able to handle it if Dina starts being nice to me. Treats me like an invalid.

"What did I miss?" Jael glances between us, sensing subtext. He really is smarter than he looks. That just might keep him alive with this crew.

"Nothing," I answer before Dina can. "Okay, you did me a favor. Now what do you want in return?"

She pins on a smile that troubles me. Mary curse it, she's worried about me. "It's your turn to watch the brat."

"Oh, it most certainly is not. I just—" I trail off because it's been days. I hoped if I stayed out of sight, people would forget.

This "team" child-care thing sucks. I've never been near an infant so young before. The kids I cared for on Gehenna were all toddling, at least, which gets you a whole different set of problems.

I down the choclaste in one gulp. “Fine. But any longer than two hours, and I’m not responsible for what may happen. Wars have been started over less.”

“Don’t worry, it’s Jael’s turn after yours. I’m sure he won’t forget.”

“As if I’d let him,” I mutter, heading for the door.

# CHAPTER 14

**"Bernard's Luck** ***to Emry Station. Requesting permis-*** sion to dock." March has been sending that same message on a timed loop ever since our sensors first picked up the station.

So far no response—and that worries me. Comm silence seldom results from a beneficial cause. Things may be worse than we've been led to suppose. Emry Station never qualified as a hub of activity, and no telling what's going on there now. The last we heard, it was full of Farwan loyalists, but a lot can change in a few weeks.

The whole universe has changed, after all.

"What do you think?"

"We have to stop, no matter what. We can't go on as we are."

I certainly agree with that. This crappy little cutter doesn't have the storage for long hauls. We need to fuel up, refill our water tanks, and get some more supplies on board: nutri-paste at the very least. Mary only knows who's going to pay for it. The one good thing about the Corp, I never had to worry about that.

We've already received two angry messages from Chancellor Tarn, wanting to know where the hell we are. I haven't decided what to tell him. I intend to blame nonreceipt of his messages on sunspots, rogue comets, and anything else I can think of along the way. Hopefully, he's a politician to the bone, and he'll make up a convincing story that doesn't leave the Ithtorians wanting to kill us on sight for insulting them.

"But we can't just dump Surge, Kora, and—what did they name the kid again? If it's dangerous."

"You know perfectly well they named her Sirina."

"I do?" I don't remember registering that, actually.

He nods, checking our distance from Emry. At our current cruising speed, we'll be there in under an hour. "It's a combination of Sirantha and Dina . . . since you two helped Kora through her labor, Rodeisian tradition. Makes you like a . . . godmother or something."

"It does not." I can't hide how appalled I am. "You're making that up."

"Don't believe me?" He grins. "Just ask Kora."

"What obligations does that involve? Am I supposed to remember her birthday? Send gifts?"

"In the oldest Terran sense you're responsible for her moral fiber. Set a good example, keep her on the straight and narrow, all that."

"Now that you *must* be making up."

His grin delights me. "It's true. You can verify it with 245 if you like."

"You're enjoying this far too much." I make a mental note to do just that, not that I don't trust him, but . . . well, you know.

"For Rodeisians, I suspect it involves something else entirely. You and Dina might be responsible for supervising Sirina's vision quest or something like that. Ask 245 about that as well."

For a moment, I try to imagine Dina and me coordinating *anything* as a team, let alone an outing that involves out-of-body experiences and mild hallucinogens. Thankfully that's years away yet. I sprawl back in the nav chair and turn my face upward, appealing to a grungy gunmetal ceiling. "Why me?"

"Because you fight so hard against attachments?" Though delivered casually, I register the intent quality of the question.

I force myself to answer lightly. "Yeah, that must be it. What's the plan?"

March raises a brow. "When do we ever have a plan?"

"We always have a plan. We just don't stick to it."

"So what's the point of making it? Why not just wing it?"

I glare. "Are you in the *mood* to argue with me?"

"Actually I'm in the mood to fuck, but our timing's off."

"Isn't it always? Dance lessons might help."

The smile kindles in his dark eyes before it reaches his mouth. With a wonder that actually steals my breath, I watch its genesis like a mini-sunrise lighting his whole face. I don't know how I got by without him, or why I fought so hard against this. The first impression scares the shit out of me, but it's breathtaking, too, like when you push off a cliff and feel the wind against your face. At that point, you're not thinking of anything but free fall.

Landing comes later. That's what hurts. Then again, what doesn't?

I can close my eyes and construct this man's face, feature by feature. Could I ever do that with Kai? I can't remember anymore. I know he had blond hair and green eyes, but he's faded, like someone I knew a long time ago. And I'm not sure if that's okay, or if it just makes me fickle.

He answers my thought without looking at me. "It makes you human."

That sounds like an equivocation to me, but then, I know he doesn't like finding me thinking about the love I lost. That's tough shit, I'm afraid. I can't forget about Kai. I never will. He was different than March in every conceivable way, so it puzzles me how I could love two such dissimilar men.

I have this dream sometimes where I'm in a white room, no furniture, but there are two exits. Kai stands before one door and March stands before the other. I'm caught in the middle, and I have to choose. I know this is a bullshit crazy-ass thing because I'll never have to pick.

Kai is gone. I'll never see him or touch him again. I'm happy with March. I love him, I do. But the dream still wakes me up in a cold sweat.

How do you measure love? Quantify it? It's not something you can put on a scale or pour into a beaker to examine its volume and viscosity.

Crazy Jax, worried about choosing between the living and the dead. Some days, though, I feel like I'm closer to the latter than the former, and it's not improving. If anything, I'm getting worse. The bruise Kora inflicted on me two weeks ago should be healed. Instead it's just starting to turn blue-green.

My hair should be growing back. I should have a short, nappy crop of curls on my head by now, but it still looks much as it did after we shaved it. When I look in the mirror, it's like I can see ghosts swimming in the glass. They can't touch me yet, but my head echoes with their whispers.

"Please don't think that way." March finally cuts me a look, away from the instrument panels and readings he doesn't need to monitor.

I remember that from the old days, before I knew how he felt about me. He used the controls as a way to distance himself from me. And the fact that he's doing it now tells me he thinks we do, indeed, have something to fear.

"Have you ever heard of a jumper wasting away like this?" There, I finally said it out loud. Now it's no longer the pink orangutan that everyone pretends not to see.

"No, but that doesn't matter. After we wrap things up here on Emry, we're heading straight for Lachion, so Doc can take a look at you. Don't worry, Jax. We'll fix it."

I don't argue with him, but I have a feeling it won't be that simple. At this point we don't even know what "it" is. There are any number of medical facilities we could jump to from here, no need to target Lachion, except I trust Doc, and I won't have somebody I don't know poking around in my head. Or my intestines for that matter. Those days are done.

Further complicating matters, we really shouldn't jump to Ithiss-Tor until we're certain I'm not infectious. Most likely any illness I've contracted wouldn't translate to their systems, but I prefer to be sure. I'm not killing off a whole race as an unwitting plague carrier.

Unless that's what someone intends. What if I've been infected on purpose? What if—

"Jax." With a word, he reins in my paranoia.

One thing's certain, though. I'll choose a trip to a Psych and a Eutha-booth over some long, lingering illness that has no cure. Either March is distracted, or he prefers to ignore that. Just as well, I don't want to fight. Too tired.

Still no answer from Emry. We've reached real visual range now, no more distant images picked up by the sensors. I lean in, studying the energy readings, though I don't know enough about it to draw conclusions.

"How's it look?"

"Like something's wrong."

"Wrong like they all caught some exotic disease and died, and the station is now infected with deadly parasites that kill you with bloody hemorrhaging out the eyeballs? Or wrong like they don't want to encourage visitors?"

March regards me for a moment and then shakes his head. "Ever an optimist, aren't you? Your imagination scares me sometimes, Jax."

"You know, the Psychs always said that about me, too."

Truthfully, I'm getting a bad vibe from Emry Station. Not like what waited for us on DuPont, nothing as harmless as Hon and his raiders. It's too quiet here, too still.

Something's down there. And it's not in the mood to talk.

# CHAPTER 15

***Whatever has gone wrong inside, the automated sys-*** tem still works.

As we glide toward the bay doors, the sensors detect us, and Emry opens up. I try to squelch the mental image of the docking mechanism as a gigantic maw waiting to devour us. Comm silence has become eerie.

By now someone should have come on, asking about the nature of our emergency. Instead the station AI coordinates our arrival in mechanized silence. Through the view screen, I watch as the inner doors seal. They won't reopen until the outer doors close, and this area regains sufficient pressure and oxygen levels to support human life. Typically that takes about two minutes.

Emry is an ugly station, designed with function in mind: two circular decks that rotate slowly in counterpoint to create artificial gravity. I wait until the docking procedure completes and then swing out of the nav chair. March follows me down through the hub, all the way to the hatch.

"Who's going with us?"

"Kora and Dina need to stay with the ship," he says at once.

That must be because he wants one of our people making sure Surge and Jael don't fuel up and repo this thing, leaving us stranded. March grins and offers an infinitesimal nod. I guess he doesn't trust Vel completely yet, for all the guy saved my ass a few weeks ago. I can't blame March; he takes a while to warm up to people.

"I'll go," Vel says quietly.

I'm not entirely sure that's a good idea. We might need him on the ship to help Dina, if our passengers get any bold ideas. That is, until Jael adds, "Me, too."

I relax a little. Dina can handle herself against Surge. Kora should be too busy looking after Sirina to start anything. Plus if Dina is really her baby's godmother, there should be some Rodeisian rule against attacking her.

"Let's gear up then."

What gear? I've been a galactic vagabond since the *Sargasso*, owning little more than a change of clothes. I'm not sure what he means, unless the *Luck* has a hidden cache. Over the last two weeks I've been over this junk-bucket starboard to stern and didn't find anything. Then again, maybe I just didn't know where to look.

March heads for the maintenance closet. I watch as he keys open a smuggler's cupboard, where they've hidden a supply of shocksticks and a disruptor. He takes the latter and shoves it through his belt. With a shudder I remember how the thing mangled his arm, how I used it on other human beings. I'll never be able to use one again: Sometimes in my sleep I still hear their screams. Before DuPont Station, I'd never killed anyone.

I don't know how much use I'll be in a fight, but I take a baton nonetheless. Jael follows suit, but Vel just shakes his head and turns toward the exit.

Since I've seen him fight bare-handed, I know he doesn't need a weapon. He'll have to slip his human skin, though. Jael will probably piss himself if that happens.

"Leave the light on for us," I call to Dina.

She grins. "Try not to get yourself killed, dumb-ass."

"It's a tough job, but someone's got to do it."

March pauses and then says to Surge, "See if you can get the fueling system to engage, but do *not* leave the docking bay."

I'm not sure if the guy's dumb enough to venture out alone. I tend to say no—he was smart enough to get off planet when he didn't have enough creds to provision his ship. I think they'll be okay. Plus he's got a wife and kid to think about, so Surge won't do anything stupid. He's not the one we need to worry about cowboying all over the place. I glance at Jael and sigh.

March is the first one out. He skins down the ladder with a grace I can't help but admire. Or maybe it's his ass. Anyway, I go next, hitting the ground with an extra bounce that tells me we're in light G. The station's crew probably take supplements to prevent suffering long-term physiological damage.

Vel lands lightly beside me, and Jael doesn't bother with the ladder, just leaps. Despite my best intentions, his recklessness appeals to me on a visceral level. In another time, before the *Sargasso*, I suspect I would've found him irresistible.

March cuts me a look, but thankfully he doesn't say anything, at least not about that. I'm glad he has some common sense. From the look of the docking bay, we might be the last humans left in this sector. Sputtering lights hint at some unknown electrical problem, and my sense of foreboding doubles.

"You think it's safe to go on?" I hesitate, looking at the far doors, which lead into the station proper.

"Probably not." March flashes me a smile. "You still in?"

"Yeah." It goes unspoken that I was ready to die at his side weeks ago. That hasn't changed.

"We work in pairs then. Vel, you're with Jax. Jael, you come with me."

Falling in with Vel, I can't help but raise my brows. I didn't expect we'd split up. "You sure this is a good idea?"

"We're sticking together, Jax. I'm not stupid. But you never know what might happen inside, so it's best if you have someone designated to watch your back."

That makes sense. "Okay, I'm guarding Vel."

More like the other way around, but the bounty hunter is kind enough not to say it aloud. The automated system has opened the doors into the station for us, but I can't see beyond a turn in the dark corridor. A wisp of something brushes my face, like a spiderweb, but when I turn I can't see anything. Maybe it's nerves.

Nobody speaks as we push onward. All my aches and pains fade to a low hum. The instincts that have kept me alive for thirty-three years kick to the fore, leaving me clearheaded and alert. I feel Vel at my back, like he's my mantid guardian. Shit, he might be for all I know.

In my right hand, I feel sweat forming around the shock-stick. The air doesn't smell right as we move deeper, following the external corridors toward the inner reaches of the station. The security doors are all stuck wide open.

Yeah, something's definitely wrong.

As we come into the commissary, I see the place has been ransacked. Crates and barrels torn open, but the supplies have been left behind. What the hell were they looking for? Chem? Contraband? Anyone with half a brain knows you aren't going to find that on an emergency station. Smugglers avoid these places like the plague.

Here, you can fuel up and buy paste, maybe some organic for the kitchen-mate if they've stocked up recently. You can also find basic medical assistance. And that's all a station like this offers.

Sweet. Something smells sweet and raw. Almost like a butcher shop gone bad.

Overhead, the lights flicker and go out.

Wordlessly, Vel produces a torch-tube from his pack. Ever prepared, he is. When he bends it, the chemicals mix and emit an eerie yellow-green glow. The silence is starting to get to me. I can hear the hum of distant machinery, but no human movements, no voices echoing.

Just silence. Darkness.

Vel raises his light just as I step into a puddle of something dark and sticky. Blood. Oh Mary, it's like being trapped on the *Sargasso*, but without the overlying stench of burnt meat.

I feel March curl his hand around my shoulder, reassuring me. "Did anyone else bring light?"

Like a stupid newb, I have to shake my head. Apart from the shockstick I didn't bring a damn thing. Sweat rolls down my spine, pools in the small of my back. My jumpsuit sticks to me, and I'm sure I stink of fear.

*You'll be fine. I'm not going to let anything happen to you.* His presence fills my head, pushes back the panic. Maybe they're empty promises, but March has never let me down.

Jael has been oddly silent, so he startles me when he finally speaks. "I've been through something like this before," he says, as if he doesn't want his voice to carry.

I still don't hear anything. It's as if we're being hunted, unseen predators creeping closer while we wheel blindly in the dark. At this moment I'd sell my soul for a pair of night-vision goggles.

"What happened?" March asks. "Where?"

The guy just shakes his head. "I don't want to upset anyone." I glare, not that he can see me. It doesn't take a genius to figure out he means me. Before I can tell him off, he continues, "If I'm wrong, then there's no need for me to talk about it." His voice grows taut. "And if I'm right, then Mary help us all."

# CHAPTER 16

***From behind, I hear the sound of the inner docking*** doors clanging closed. Now we're effectively separated from the others until we find a way to get them opened. Divide and conquer. It's the oldest trick in the book, but we couldn't have taken a new mother and her child with us to explore the station.

Our fate hangs on Dina's preventing Surge and Kora from stranding us here. I have a lot of faith in our mechanic, but we may have stuck her with an impossible task. They have a pilot and a jumper on board, but I hope they won't want to risk scrambling their daughter's brains.

Transport companies won't have an infant on board on interstellar voyages—too much liability involved. As far as I know, they deny children under the age of two, and even transporting children older than that requires a special ship outfitted with miniature jump gear.

With a sigh, I glance around the commissary, seeking anything we can use. I spot a box of uncracked torch-tubes. Though decidedly unglamorous, I'm glad I'm wearing this baggy jumpsuit because it has six pockets. I stuff them full, a total of ten.

Vel's stick won't last forever. When the chemicals burn out, we'll be left flailing in the dark. So here's a little insurance against that eventuality. We can ration them. I don't know what I'll do when the lights go out.

*Can't think about that.*

A little more rummaging unearths eight packets of paste. I hope we won't be here long enough to need them, but I snag the food nonetheless. Nothing else catches my eye as immediately useful. There are spare parts and fuel cells for weapons we don't possess. They wouldn't carry charge packs for the disruptor March carries, given that it counts as contraband.

Going forward seems like our only option, even if it's into the trackless dark. I shudder a little. It was dark when the *Sargasso* went down, and I spent twelve hours pinned. My scars flare with phantom pain.

Wish I'd stayed on the ship, even if it meant changing Sirina.

"It seems obvious that something happened to the original station crew," March says. "We have to figure out what, or it might take us, too."

I feel Vel at my shoulder, oddly reassuring. "If we can get to a terminal, I can patch into their security cams and see what went on before our arrival. Knowing our enemy will help us formulate the best course of action."

"Sounds like a plan." March leads the way.

Shadows play hell with my peripheral vision as we move out of the commissary. We'll worry about supplies once we have a way to get them off station. I try to focus on that—we *will* get out of this.

"Watch for webs." Jael sounds cold and collected, not the pretty, useless ornament I initially took him for. I suspect he's seen something, noticed something, that slipped right past me.

*Webs.* As I process that, Vel adds, "And cocoons."

Does everyone know what's on this station except me? In the distance, I register a skittering sound, oddly familiar. Where have I heard that before?

I've almost got it when Vel tackles me, and we hit the floor hard. I lose my grip on the shockstick, not that I'm in any shape to fight. It clatters along the floor, throwing tiny sparks of light. Ahead, March and Jael scatter to opposite sides of the hallway. A sweet stench hits me on a breeze that shouldn't be, which means—

Movement.

Something white and filmy rebounds down the hall, passing between the four of us. A trap? It looks like a web, just as Jael said.

"They may have set venom mines as well," Vel murmurs near my ear. "If it spatters on your skin, the rest of you will be immobilized."

Not him, though. His physiology renders him poisonous to them. Now I know what we're facing—the Morgut. That's human slang, because they're more gut than anything else. The last time I saw some of these fuckers, they tried to eat me.

Then again, I *was* asking for it.

I start to suggest turning back and then I remember they've sealed us in with them. Nothing like playing with your food a bit before you eat it.

"Noted," March says from a few feet up. "You mentioned you've been through something like this before," he adds to Jael. "So tell us what you know."

Call it paranoia, a quality I possess in spades, but I don't think we should stand here talking. Maybe stumbling blindly ahead isn't the best idea either, but they may be monitoring these hallways. Homing in on their prey. Us. So the longer we hang around, the easier they catch us.

I've never been hunted before, and I don't much care for the sensation.

Surprisingly, Vel echoes my thoughts. "Not here. It is vital we get to a terminal. I need to know what happened here."

"I'll tell you," Jael says, as we round a corner with maximum caution. "We interrupted their dinner, and now they plan on having us for dessert."

"Tell us while we move then." March doesn't sound like he's in the mood to negotiate on this point.

Jael seems to recognize this, but his voice holds a raw, unwilling note. "I signed on with Surge, maybe four years back. You'd already quit the game," he says to March. "The rest of us were still willing to bleed for Nicuan. They had the money, and they never tire of the fight. Nobody wins, everybody dies."

We creep along by millimeters, staying in the shallow circle of light. Maybe we'd be better off to douse it, but I can't face the dark. I'll lose my mind. The ventilation system kicks in, sending a hiss of air past our faces. I'm already on the floor, jumpy as a chem-head after two days without a fix.

Jael gives me a hand up, tugs me to my feet with a Bred strength belied by his slender build. He continues tonelessly. "Someday, after we're all gone, archaeologists will find cities of bone on that world. Our commanders were useless, soft, pampered imperial types, who came up with strategies from the comfort of their manor houses. Body count didn't matter to them. They offered hazard pay and death benefits to the soldiers' families."

"What happened?" Despite our situation, I almost succeed in forgetting about the living night all around us, haunted by mechanical noises and suspicious thumps in the ducts overhead. Almost.

"My CO sent us off world to investigate trouble at a satellite weapons factory, built outside of terrestrial tariffs. They kept a skeleton crew on-site to monitor the automated production system, make necessary repairs. And then one day, the place went quiet."

"Like Emry," Vel observes.

"Just so. This is how the Morgut prefer to operate. Pick a small, unimportant outpost and devour everything inside. If they're left undisturbed, they'll sometimes nest. Breed, before moving on to their next hunt."

"But you got away from them." I cling to that as a beacon of hope while the dark swims around us, eddies and ebbs in fluid waves that keep me jerking in all directions. I don't know when I've ever been this scared.

"Yeah," Jael says. "And lightning doesn't strike twice in the same place."

He's a regular bundle of cheer. I didn't need to be reminded that I've stretched my luck until it's transparent.

*Stay cool, Jax. This is no worse than a bad jump.*

The hell it isn't. At least grimspace can only steal my mind, not suck all the juices out of me, devour my flesh, and pick its fangs with my bones. My fingers tighten on the shockstick, not that I think it'll do me any good.

From what I remember they're insanely fast. On the *Silverfish*, after Vel captured me, I tried to feed myself to them instead of going back to the Corp. Yeah, I was desperate. A monstrous marriage of arachnid and humanoid, the Morgut have fanged mouths, jointed limbs, and hairy bodies that bulge in obscene, unnatural ways.

I try not to think about that as I stay close on Vel's heels. I'm guarding our rear flank, and I can't help but remember the scary vids where the person in back gets yanked away to some hideous fate, and nobody notices for like ten minutes.

"I'll always come for you, Jax." Distracted by the need to watch our every movement, March answers me aloud.

The other two don't seem to wonder what that's about, though. Vel shines his light before we move a single meter while March pans with his disruptor. Anything that moves in the dark is going to get its innards rearranged. I'm not sure what to make of Jael. He's too calm and unshaken.

We're coming up on a two-way split in the corridor. Without a layout or a peek at station plans, we have no way of knowing which way we should turn. Down one of those halls might lie a nest or something worse.

"Right." Jael points without elaborating as to why we should go that way.

After Vel shines the light both ways, I don't have an

opinion, but I do know my skin is crawling all to hell. It feels like I'm passing through wisps of webs, not enough to entrap me, but they do stick to my face. I refuse to let myself start slapping at my skin, a complete breakdown of impulse versus intellect. I won't be the one to go nuts and flee, shrieking in the dark.

The hum of machinery grows louder as we make the turn Jael suggested. Maybe we can find a terminal here, so Vel can patch in and see how many we're looking at. I'd rather know the odds, straight out. I saw the bounty hunter handle a full clutch of Morgut on board the *Silverfish*, so maybe our chances are good. Maybe.

I continue the silent pep talk as we continue, step by step. The coppery stink increases, the closer we come. By the time we hit maintenance, I have to cover my nose and mouth with my shirt.

*Mary, no.*

I don't want to look, but it's a compulsion as Vel lifts his light. I register impressions as flashes that burn themselves into my retinas. I'll see this room again, frame by frame, in my nightmares, as if rendered on some old-fashioned film.

They've been here. Chunks of flesh litter the floor. I imagine the hunger, the frenzy that drove them to this. I imagine the spilled blood as an intoxicant, reacting on their alien body chemistry.

To them, we are, quite simply, delicious.

# CHAPTER 17

***The blood has dried, leaving dark, tacky patches on*** the metal floor.

If left untended, it will rust. Don't ask me why I've focused on that, but I want to scrub all this away, as if that would mean it didn't happen. Lives weren't lost here.

I should know better than anyone how impossible that is. Cleaning up a mess doesn't negate it. And some things can't be swept under the proverbial rug.

The Conglomerate will have no choice but to deal with the Morgut now. In its day, the Corp dealt with them in terms of property damage. They didn't care about loss of life, only the bottom line. But these monsters are growing bolder now. They've acquired a taste for human flesh, and they don't believe the human authorities have the power to stop them.

And maybe they're right.

Vel sweeps his light in a slow circle. This room holds half-repaired bots and cleaning droids, spare parts, and bins full of wires. Against the far wall, there's a terminal meant for diagnostics, but maybe it connects to the rest of the station.

We can hope. By the low hiss of the unit, we still have power, even if the lights aren't working. Vel sets up at the terminal while March and Jael take up guard positions in front of the door. Since we're doing two things at once now, not moving as a unit, another light might come in handy. Plus I want them to be able to see anything that tries to get at us.

I hand a tube to March, who snaps it immediately. Now we have two anemic pools of yellow-green light. Because Vel is supposed to be watching my back—and vice versa—I head over to his side. He keys with unbelievable speed, but before I can try to assimilate what he's doing, he's inside their system.

I've never seen anyone crack code like he does. Most hackers rely on gadgets, portable AIs that run all the possible combinations. With Vel, it almost seems intuitive, like he can hear machines on a level that we can't.

Another few clicks, and a grainy image comes up on the screen. Routine bot surveillance, these units perform basic cleaning, maintenance, and repairs as well. We see what the little machine sees, a corridor that could be anywhere on the station.

"Anything yet?" March asks without glancing our way.

"Yeah, we're watching a bot—" I break off because even the low-quality images can't conceal what's sliding past.

I recognize the jerky, multijointed movements. Here's visual confirmation, and a chill rolls over me. When this recording ends in static, Vel switches to another. And another, until we've seen every last droid destroyed.

There's no record of the people who died here, screaming unheard. No bloody images the talking heads can use on the vids to rouse people to a vocal outcry. And the truth is, nobody dirtside gives a shit what happens to the folks up here. Maybe they even privately think we deserve such things for taking the risk.

We may find their names later on the outpost manifest or on duty rosters. If we survive. And it will be up to us to remember.

"It's a full clutch," he says at last. "At least ten."

"There may be more if they've had time to nest," Jael adds. "They breed fast. And they'll be utterly savage if they're protecting young."

"They are always savage." After checking to be sure he can't get primary systems online from here, Vel powers down the terminal. "But I concur, that would make it worse."

"Would they lay eggs on a station without a renewable food source?" That's such a disgusting question.

March shrugs. "We're here, aren't we? Maybe they counted on a ship arriving now and then."

"Pointless speculation," Vel says.

Jael adds, "We need to find and exterminate them. The time for talking is over."

I actually agree with Jael. Now that we have a rough idea how many we're facing, the hunted need to become the hunters. Vel had an advantage against them on the *Silverfish*; they couldn't lair up there, or spin webs and traps. In close quarters, he has the edge since they use their fangs on prey—and if they bite him, they'll die.

But here on Emry, they've had time to get comfortable. They have the upper hand. We'll need to be tough, smart, and careful to make it out alive.

The instant I conceive that thought, the door slams shut. March and Jael spin as one, weapons drawn and ready. But there's nothing to fight. How do you combat what you can't see?

A hiss from the ventilation system gives the first warning.

"They're going to gas us," Jael says grimly. "Fragging cowards."

Vel lifts his face, breathes in. "It's nontoxic, designed to make you dizzy and noncombative."

"But it's not bothering *you*," Jael says, his words already slurred.

He's finally figuring out that Vel isn't as average as he looks. What I wouldn't give for a rebreather. My stomach lurches, and my head starts to spin. The room seems smoky, and I can't make my eyes focus.

I see two Vels standing before me, and his voice seems to come from very far away. "Don't go to sleep, Sirantha. Do you understand me? Stay awake."

But I'm so tired. If I could just lie down for a minute, I could figure everything out. I'm positive of it. I've lost track of March and Jael.

My knees feel like they're melting. Vel jerks me upright and gives me a shake that rattles my teeth in my head. When that doesn't help a whole lot, he slaps me full across the face. That stings enough that I try to fight back.

And that's when the things drop down from the ceiling.

My head spins too much to count them. When Vel knocks me flat, I have the sense to stay down, though the blow feels like it may have cracked a few ribs. Ironically, the pain clears my head to some degree.

I try to breathe through my shirt, and that helps a little, too. On my belly, I crawl along the floor, taking refuge behind a crate of machine parts. The fighting seems blurred and distant, too far away for where I'm hiding.

My vision can't be relied upon. I hear March swearing steadily as he fires. He's taken cover somewhere nearby. I hear the wet, splattering sound of the disruptor rearranging meat. The Morgut don't scream when they die; they keen.

*Jael* screams. My whole body tenses in response to the anguish of the sound. Backlit by a fallen torch-tube, I see the Morgut hold his body aloft, skewered on one of the creature's forelegs.

Vel almost seems to fly as he crosses the room, severing the limb with a sonicblade I didn't even know he had. But he's got a pack of them following hard on his heels, so he can't do more for Jael, who hits the ground in an agonizing arc. The wounded thing shudders; blood spatters, hot drops raining down on my face.

The bounty hunter wheels on the ones sinking their teeth into him from behind. His weapon hums as he carves a gory map into their flesh. And the one that's missing a leg turns on March, who's waiting for the disruptor to power up again. The weapon cycles up, the lights on its grip indicating when it will be ready.

I give myself another good slap, fighting the effects of the gas. I can't say whether it's will or something else, but I manage to clear my head a little more. My own cry strangles in my throat. I taste the copper of Jael's blood, the flavor of terror and despair. Vel goes down beneath a wave of them. They'll die in agony, but if they hurt him bad enough, he'll perish, too. Grim comfort.

The disruptor won't do March any good this time; he's used it too much, and it's taking forever to charge. The Morgut advances, trembling with lust. Its fangs drip with the salivary fluid that paralyzes us. One scrape, and he will be done. The Morgut hesitates, and then, with a careless swipe, it knocks the useless weapon from March's hands.

It clatters to the floor a few meters from me, skidding into Vel's sonicblade. I can't cower here. I have to *do* something. I'm not the only jumper for once, so my life isn't more valuable than anyone else's.

Knowing any movement could draw their lethal hunger, knowing I might feel a spear through my intestines at any second, I crawl along the floor toward the sonicblade. I could *die*.

Well, I'm willing.

I pinch the soft skin of my inner wrist. I need pain, need it to focus and stay in the here and now. I can't give in to the fuzziness building inside my head.

The swarm atop Velith finally processes that they aren't sucking down sweet, delicious blood. Some fall into convulsions, a putrid froth boiling from their fanged maws. Some stagger away, weak and dying. Only two look as though they could fight. That's three too many, and they're all stalking March.

At this point, they don't register anyone else as a threat. We're beaten. Food.

He backs toward the terminal, trying to lead them away from me.

*Oh, no you don't. We have too much to do yet. You're not dying for me.*

"Who better?" he says aloud.

*No.*

As it lunges to dismember him, I hurl the knife.

# CHAPTER 18

***The blade whistles as it spins end over end and buries*** itself in the Morgut's faceted eye. Lucky shot. Though its brain has shut down, it will take a while for the body to figure that out. Its high-pitched death shriek distracts the other two long enough for March to dive toward Vel's body. At first I think he's lost his mind because he rolls across him, smearing himself with the bounty hunter's blood.

He muffles a pained sound. I imagine it stings like hell, but now I get it. Suddenly, he's tainted meat. They can't just sink their teeth in and feast. He'll need to be hosed off first.

*Damned inconvenient, isn't it, you greedy bastards?*

The other two chitter and clack, clawed forelegs waving with genuine menace. Maybe they're discussing the best course of action or marveling at the ingenuity of their prey. Maybe they're considering unconditional surrender because we might all be Ithtorians beneath the skin.

Hey, I can dream.

But even if they want to parlay, we have no way to talk

to them, and I'm sure they don't speak universal. Why would they bother? Humans certainly never troubled to learn bovine back when we were still eating cows.

Vel might have translated—but he's out. He needs medical attention, and Jael *must* be dead. I can help best by keeping out of trouble. They might have qualms about going after March with their fangs, but I have no such protection.

So I stay low and scuttle along the floor, slippery with blood, bowels, and insect innards for which I have no name. The smell nearly compels me to add my dinner to the mess as I try to make my way toward the fallen Morgut with the knife in his head. If I can get that to March without being seen, he may have a chance. He stands in a battle-ready crouch, waiting for their strike, most likely in unison. They'll use their claws, not fangs, but if they coordinate it well, he's doomed.

The room is queerly lit by fallen torch-tubes, a flickering yellow-green glow that gives the maintenance shop a surreal, hellish air. Smoky gas lingers, ebbs, and eddies, adding to the infernal atmosphere. I pass into pockets that make me light-headed. I'm tempted to rest my eyes until it passes. Sleep will make it better—

*Can't. Vel told me to stay awake.*

I shake off the confusion with sheer will. *Please don't let them notice me.* My own movements look oddly staccato as I slide behind boxes and barrels, and then crawl on my belly through the muck toward the twitching monster. The blade makes a sucking motion as I yank it out, and then the faint hum kicks in. Good, still functional.

I slap it across the floor so it bounces against his boot. Low G gives it extra lift when he kicks it upward and catches it by the handle as if we've orchestrated the maneuver hundreds of times before. The Morgut lunge for him as one, but he's got a shot now.

"Fuck it," March says, as he wheels into the fight. "I'll play the doomed hero another day. Don't worry, Jax."

My chest feels tight. Even now, he reassures me.

Maybe I've given him the edge he needs, but I can't watch. I need to stay away from the action, or I may offer these monsters a hostage. Worse, they might stab me through the throat on the backswing.

I take refuge behind a crate of machine parts, come around the other side, and find Jael's body. Blood still bubbles sluggishly out of his gut wound around the limb that skewered him. His face looks impossibly young, pure and clean, despite the filth that surrounds us.

When his eyes snap open, I recoil. In the distance I hear March swearing steadily. That's good, means he's still alive, for now. Holding his own.

Before Jael speaks, I'm sure I know what he's going to ask of me—a mercy killing. End his pain. But I don't have a weapon. Lost my shockstick, the disruptor won't charge, and March has the blade. How can I let this poor bastard suffer?

"Pull it out." His voice comes out thick and wet. I can hear fluid in his throat, probably from his internal injuries. "Do it fast, damn you."

"You'll bleed to death." Stupid to protest, he's dying anyway.

"Don't make me hurt you."

I choke out a laugh at that. He can't even lift his head, and he's threatening me? Trembling from head to toe, I do as he asks. Wrap my hands around the severed leg and tug hard. With some part of my mind, I register that it sounds a lot like the knife coming out of the Morgut's skull. It takes all my willpower not to hurl.

"Seal the wound with your palm." Even as he barks the order, Jael lifts weak hands, trying to do it himself.

I don't know how the hell he thinks this will help, but I can't refuse a dying man his last request. Even if it means feeling his guts beneath my hand—

Except the wound isn't as wide as it ought to be, and unless the gas has completely fried my brain, it's getting smaller. I touch him gingerly, exploring his lower abdomen, and I find only wet skin. Bloody, but whole.

"Okay, what the hell—"

"Not now," he says, lurching to his feet. "Your boy needs help over there."

With that, he dives into the fray, armed with the foreleg the Morgut stabbed him with. The fury from remembered agony must lend him strength because Jael shoves it straight through the creature's neck. My first shocked thought—*He wasn't kidding on the ship when he said he'd kill us all.*

I have to see, have to know. So I scramble to my feet and slip-slide over to March, who's on his knees, sonicblade still in hand. Entrails spill along the floor, twisting bits of flesh that seem so inexpressibly alien that I shudder just looking at them. He's bleeding from about a hundred cuts, but he seems to be in one piece.

A sob escapes me. I touch him briefly on the shoulder, a gesture that says everything as I pass by.

Vel played bait for the rest of us, and I already owe him so much. I want to know him better, perhaps more than he'll ever allow. And it might be too late.

I kneel in his blood, feeling it sizzle against the fabric of my jumpsuit. I can't tell how wounded he is through the tattered human suit he's wearing.

"How bad?" March asks, coming up behind me.

"Don't know. I need the knife. Let's cut him free."

March hands me the sonicblade, and I go to work, feeling like a serial killer skinning her victim. Amid all the other smells I detect the faint scent of decomposition. He needed to slough this skin soon anyway.

"Shit, you're butchering him!" Jael lunges like he's going to steal the weapon, but March steps in between us.

"Easy, she knows what she's doing." Well, that may be an overstatement. I'll do my best, though. I always do. "How's your gut?" March adds.

Since I'm slicing off Vel's faux skin as if peeling fruit, I don't see his shrug, but I hear it in Jael's voice. "I'm all right."

I delve in my jumpsuit pocket and find a fresh torch-tube,

crack it so I can better judge the damage. I count a dozen bites on his thorax alone, but they don't look deep. I need to keep cutting in order to finish assessing his condition. Not that I know what to do about it.

Why don't we have Doc with us? Fuck him for being safe on Lachion, puttering around his lab when we need him so bad. I don't know enough about medicine to save Vel if he's in critical condition. And Mary curse it, we don't have much more than a first-aid kit on the ship. There's a basic med center here on station, though, if we can get to it. The medical AI may know what to do for him; it should possess exobiological treatments.

As I shift Vel to pull the rapidly rotting flesh away, I count five more bites. His mandible works slowly, and it takes his vocalizer a few seconds to translate it to a pained sound within our hearing range. I could almost cry in relief. In fact, I feel tears stinging at my eyes, but I won't let them fall.

"That would've killed most guys," March observes.

"I'm not most guys." Jael kneels beside me, watching the procedure with horrified fascination. Vel's features flash into sight. "Right then, what the fuck—"

"If I don't get to ask," I cut in, "then you don't either. This isn't the time for talk anyway. You two should really figure out a way to get that door open, just in case there are more of them. We're in no shape to fight."

For once, I get the last word, and they both snap to work.

# CHAPTER 19

***While I work on Vel, they jury-rig wires between the*** terminal and the door. His blood stings my skin, and I spare a moment to hope it won't kill me, if slower than it does the Morgut. Even if it might, I wouldn't stop.

"If this works," March says, "it's going to take out half this room."

Doesn't it figure? Our security guy is laid out while the two mercs, who tend to solve problems with a hammer, take charge of getting us out of here. Vel could probably hit two buttons and get the door to open.

I resist the urge to stare at Jael, knowing he probably expects it. Everything we know about the Bred comes from rumors from the gutter press, sensational gossip seasoned liberally with speculation. Like an Ithtorian bounty hunter, who ever expects to meet one?

His wounds appear to be coagulating nicely, but then, I don't know what to expect, given his physiology. I lack all but basic emergency training. Then again, I can't blow a security door either.

"Keep your head down, Jax." To my surprise, this terse order comes from Jael.

"March, line up some crates in front of Vel, if you can. Give us some cover."

He nods to indicate that's a good idea. "Don't set it off until we're settled," he tells Jael.

How morbid—the slimy floor provides a ready lubricant, so our makeshift barricade slides easily into place. March crouches beside me.

"Ready," he calls.

Instinctively, I bow my body over Vel. Any debris that rains down will catch me in the back. Jael hits the switch to short out the terminal, and the current crackles along the wires, shorting out the electrical lock that holds the door in place. It blows wide with a boom, slamming backward into the corridor.

The sound shocks Vel awake. I sense the moment he rejoins us, side-set eyes glittering up at me. His mandible moves, and his vocalizer kicks in a few seconds later. "Are you taking advantage of me, Sirantha?"

"Was that a joke?" Sheepishly I ease off him.

"And we're out of here," Jael says. "Is he conscious?"

"I am." Vel answers for himself. "Can you help me up?"

Since I was just about to ask if he could walk, I certainly can. Between March and me, we haul him to his feet. As Vel drops a foreleg around my shoulder, not out of affection but from a need for support, I flash back to our hike out on the Teresengi Basin.

Vel seems to follow the thought because he sounds almost wry. "This is becoming a rather unfortunate tradition."

"I'm sorry," I murmur, once March and Jael move off to scout ahead. "You sure got the short straw when they partnered you with me."

"I'm alive," he says. "There are those who would've left me for dead, dismissing my injuries as too grievous to make me worth the risk of hampered travel."

Damned twice over, I don't know what to say. He received those wounds trying to protect me, and once before, in another life it seems, I considered leaving March after a fight went bad. A wave of nausea washes over me, not because I'm covered in gore, or embracing an Ithtorian, but because I hate that Jax.

Does changing for the better absolve you of all the wicked shit you did before?

*No.* March fills my head like a warm glow. *Instead you receive the twin delights of guilt and regret.*

So he knows then. I've always wondered.

*It's what you do that counts, not what you* consider *doing.*

He always knows exactly what to say. I swear to Mary, I could be dying, and he'd ease my final jump into the dark.

*I thought we agreed you aren't going to think like that?* But he sounds resigned, as if he knows I'll never stop thinking about two things: grimspace and my own death. Loving a navigator pretty much guarantees the dual obsession.

So far the hallway looks clear. March and Jael round the corner and disappear from sight. Of necessity, Vel and I move slower, but March will warn me if there's trouble. I'm surprised nobody has asked how I know certain things before now.

"If we can find the control room, I can purge the vents," Vel says.

"And that's a good thing?"

"It might save our lives."

Well, I'm all for that. "Clue me in?"

"They prefer a secure enclosure for their nests, and on a station like this, only the ventilation shafts make sense. The Morgut cocoon a corpse along with their eggs, and their larvae eat their way out. The young develop rapidly and could pose a significant threat before help arrives."

He's right. We can't just drop off Kora, Surge, and baby here, as intended. Anyone with a glimmer of conscience would wait for the cleanup crew to arrive to secure the station, and I'm no exception.

"So what happens in this purge?"

"A burst of superheated air surges through the ducts and is vented into space. It works on a system of locks, so the station doesn't decompress. They use it to clean debris out that bots can't manage . . ." Vel hesitates. "And on more populous stations, it . . . discourages nomads from taking up residence there."

"Or they wind up cooked and then spaced for vagrancy? Harsh."

"The universe often is. Had you not noticed?" Yes, there it is again, the hint of humor. Since he's so formal all the time, it's difficult to discern, subtle and droll.

"I catch on slow, but I'm starting to get it."

We come around the corner to find the hallway empty. Where the hell did the other two get to? I notice that their blood-smeared tracks simply end, which means they must've gone . . . up. Surely March would've touched base if trouble hit, though. *If he could.* If he's dead or unconscious—

*No. Not thinking that way.*

Though my head is full of images, mainly the Morgut webbing them and hauling them up, I can only deal with one problem at a time. The bounty hunter leans on me harder, and we've only walked fifty meters. He needs the med center. In my considered opinion, purging the station can wait until I have him stabilized.

Plus, a purge might fry March and Jael, wherever the hell they are. Weak and dizzy from blood loss, Vel's not thinking as fast as usual, or he would've noticed by now. Maybe I can keep him from worrying about it.

Time is ticking. My skin stings, my hip aches, and I can't use my left hand. Why does shit always come down to me? But maybe I'm getting ahead of myself. Maybe March and Jael are fine.

"I know," I say aloud. "Let me ask 245 for a sample layout of an emergency station. It won't be exact, but it might give us an idea where to turn."

My PA wouldn't have helped earlier, because even *pre-*

*cise* blueprints don't include dangerous Morgut nests, more's the pity. In any case, I didn't think of her until now. I pull the unit from my pocket, input my codes, and ask for the information I need.

She actually seems a bit miffed that I don't have time to chat. Maybe I've talked to her *too* much during our ongoing experiment. Maybe she's learned a uniquely human trait: loneliness.

"Yes," she says, after a few seconds searching. "As part of my helpful information database, I have plans for emergency stations. They are designed to aid interstellar travelers in distress. Are you currently in distress, Sirantha Jax?"

"Yes, I most certainly am. Can you tell me where medical would be, assuming they didn't deviate from the standard design?"

"Please wait." Her new voice rings completely feminine. A few weeks back, while we were confined to quarters, I decided if I talk to her as if she's my best girlfriend, then she should sound the part.

Then she flashes the location on-screen. On the plus side, it should be located on this level. On the minus side, it's on the other side from where we are. That means we have two hallways to cover . . . without getting caught by whatever took March and Jael. I hate thinking like that, but it's the only thing that makes sense.

I have to cordon off the terror and pain. Vel's my responsibility right now. March made him my partner in case we got separated, and I'm not going to let Vel bleed to death while I go tearing around after the other two.

At this point, I tell myself, it's better if the remaining Morgut snag March and Jael instead of us. I know that sounds callous, but they're former mercs. They have a better shot at surviving than we do right now.

"Let us move," Vel says. "I do not know how much longer I can stay vertical."

*One crisis at a time, Jax.*

# CHAPTER 20

***The distance seems a lot longer than it actually is.***

I remember Vel mentioning there might be traps laid, so we proceed with care. I try to stay to the edges of the hallway. My shoulders ache from the strain of holding him upright. He's not helping much anymore, moving on sheer determination.

If he goes down, I don't have the strength to get him on his feet again, so we have to keep shuffling toward Med Bay. Or where it ought to be. My PA sulks in my right front pocket; I don't think she quite grasps the urgency of the situation.

The silence troubles me. I send a few experimental thoughts toward March, but I get nothing back. It's more than his lack of response, though. The station itself seems oddly still. Could be my paranoia, I suppose. Maybe nothing's left but us.

When we turn the corner into the last hallway, a web snaps down toward us, but we're not quite in range. We stagger back a few paces while I try to control my heart rate. Lucky they placed the trigger off a few centimeters or we'd be finding out firsthand what became of March and Jael. I suspect they let themselves be taken . . . because it's more comforting than the other options.

Why would they do that? I can't even speculate, unless it sprang from some heroic urge to take on the rest of the Morgut without endangering Vel and me.

I spare a moment of gratitude that the med center is where 245 predicted. As I suspected, it's unmanned. Vel collapses on a cot while I commandeer a workstation.

"Power on." I hope these aren't coded to require certain voice patterns. Then again, that wouldn't make sense, given the budget for these outposts.

Pure relief surges through me when the screen lights up. "Access emergency medical database. Seeking treatment for an Ithtorian suffering from multiple bite wounds and blood loss."

"Accessing." This AI sounds cool and collected, which is reassuring in a medical system. "Recommend sonic cleansing and immediate application of liquid skin, type four. Contains antibacterial agents and macrobiotic, further intervention is not required unless patient exhibits signs of infection. Augment treatment with a transfusion of synthetic intravenous fluid, program med-bot to use type 1345AB."

*Liquid skin. Med-bot.* Vel's gone under again, which is probably best. Thankfully the station provides some guidance as to where I can find things. My hands tremble as I carry out the instructions.

They keep the med-bot in a cupboard, charging until he's needed again. He powers up at my voice command, and I'm able to program him with treatment instructions that way as well. In efficient, mechanical motions, he handles the infusion, which should help Vel stay conscious.

As for me, I suck down a packet of paste. Won't do any good if I pass out. I'm fucking exhausted, and I ache all over. For good or ill, we're holed up here until we both feel better. I hope to Mary that March and Jael are all right, but I can't save them. I just can't. When they disappeared, I chose to stick with Vel.

That's a fucking agonizing decision.

I *love* March.

I feel like I'm abandoning him, but presently he's not my lover; he can't be, or I'll go nuts. As my captain, he gave me an order: *Guard Vel's back.* I've never been much for authority, but I trust his judgment. So I force my worry down, compartmentalize it. I'm an old pro at that.

I'd kill to get cleaned up. That's when I notice the san-shower, probably kept in here so the doc can wash up after dealing with messy injuries.

I hesitate only a few seconds. "Do you have a quarantine protocol?"

"Affirmative."

"Activate it and secure the doors. Require my voice imprint to override."

"State the name of the attending physician and the nature of the infectious illness for station records, please."

*Shit.* I wrack my brain, hoping it won't check my name against a credentialed list of physicians. Then I solve the problem. I hope.

"Saul Solaith, logging a case of advanced Jenner's retrovirus."

The machine pauses, which suggests I was right about the database. "Acknowledged, Dr. Solaith. Activating quarantine. Outside access to medical facility will require your authorization."

Heh. Technology often manages to be both brilliant and wonderfully stupid. It apparently doesn't care that I'm the wrong gender, or maybe it doesn't register pitch and match it against official records. They run on a shoestring budget in places like Emry, and they wouldn't have the latest innovations, luckily for me.

I take a look around Med Bay, most specifically at the ceiling. It lacks the access panels to the ducts that we encountered in the maintenance room. In here the vents are tiny, not big enough for anything to drop down. I decide it would take a cutting torch to get to us.

Vel appears to be stable, and the med-bot stands ready,

monitoring his vitals. That frees me up to rummage. There's no point in washing, if I have to put this filthy jumpsuit back on. To my delight I uncover a spare pair of scrubs. If I'm impersonating Doc, I might as well go all the way, right?

Before I hit the shower, I fiddle with the terminal a little. The comm channel doesn't respond, however, and I can't reach the ship. Not that I expected to.

It seems insanely mundane to strip down and step into the stall, but why is it better for me to sit around covered in blood? If I go running around the station, looking for March and Jael, I may only succeed in getting myself killed. Plus I leave Vel vulnerable. We're safe here, and we need to stay that way.

I refuse to do something stupid. At least that's what I tell myself as I wash up. I'm just being smart. Aren't I? I can't sort good sense from cowardice at this point. Guilt weighs me down too much.

One thing's for sure. I'm beating the shit out of March for putting me through this. When he finds us.

After stepping out of the san-shower, I dress quickly in the castoff clothing. Coming around the partition, I see that Vel has struggled to an upright position. I interpret the clicking of his claws as agitation. The movement slows when he registers my presence. I don't say anything because I'd freak if he disappeared on me, too.

"You have become a medical professional? How long was I out?"

"Not more than an hour." I check the med-bot to confirm.

"Any word from the others?" Trust him to strike at the heart of the matter.

"We might be the last people left in the universe for all I know," I answer quietly. "Nothing on the comm channel; it appears to have been disabled. And I haven't heard a peep from March or Jael since you passed out."

"You did a nice job patching me up," he says, ignoring the rest for the moment.

I shrug. "Anyone could've done it. I just followed instructions."

"Anyone did not." His rounded eyes glitter as he regards me. I'm used to his natural face now, just wish I could read him better. "You are a constant surprise to me."

Not sure what he means, if he thought I'd dump his unconscious body, first chance I got. No fucking way—while the Morgut can't eat him, they can sure as shit kill him. I could spout some shit about responsibility, but it's more than that. I need to acknowledge it.

"We're friends," I say softly. "You'd do the same for me."

He ignores that as if he doesn't know what to say. "You look done in, and you must be worried about the others. I will stand watch for a couple hours, Sirantha. Get some rest. When you wake up, we will decide our next step."

I hope he doesn't suggest a purge again. I can't permit that without knowing the fate of the other two. Yet at the same time, I don't like the thought of what might be growing within Emry's bowels.

"It seems like we need to head for the systems-control room. See if we can get the bay doors open. We need to warn the others. They can bounce a message to New Terra, explaining the situation and requesting a cleanup crew."

"Later," he says with gentle insistence.

"There's paste in my jumpsuit." I lie down at last, feeling the tension in my joints pop in celebration.

"I would rather die."

Though we're a bit more comfortable now, this occasion reminds me of the cave, where we relied on each other once before. Life or death, no second chances.

I *love* March, but Vel is something else entirely. He's one person I'd trust at my back, no questions asked. Funny how that worked out, considering the Corp hired him to hunt me. I relax, and the minute my eyes close, I'm gone.

Darkness wins.

# CHAPTER 21

***I don't know how long I've been out, but a thump jerks*** me out of a fitful sleep.

My heart thuds as I take stock of my surroundings: cots, cupboards, various bits of equipment. *Right. Med Bay, Emry Station.* I find Vel at the workstation, zipping through files that mean nothing to me.

"Did you hear that?"

"Yes," he answers. "I am trying to get external cameras online, but it is not working. I have no idea who—or what—is out there. And I cannot seem to open the door." He pauses with certain ironic inflection. "Dr. Solaith."

"Yeah, well." I roll off the narrow bed, feeling somewhat better.

*Jax? Open the door, baby. It's me. I'm all right.*

A rush of relief nearly deposits me on the floor. I didn't realize how scared I was until this moment. This silence might have lasted forever. Even as I go to the terminal to deactivate the quarantine, my knees still feel weak.

"Saul Solaith," I tell the computer. "Requesting override. Access to medical facility now permitted."

Vel cocks his head at me. "Are you sure?"

I don't answer. Instead I turn toward the door and key it open to find March there with a small body in his arms. Jael stands a few paces behind, and they both look as though they've been to hell and back. I have no idea how he knew I'd be here, but I'm so happy to see him—

"You dick!" Not the first words I thought to speak, but it's what comes out. "I can't believe you worried me like that. Thoughtless asshole."

March shakes his head. "I'll explain later. Right now, I need to help her."

That's when I notice the child's chest rising and falling. They managed to save someone? *A miracle.* March heads straight for the med-bot. After he programs it, the droid goes to work on the girl. The tiny little thing can't be more than four years old. At present, she's dirty, her hair matted with webs. I can't tell anything else. Maybe Surge and Kora will foster her.

"March found her." Jael sounds as if he's been strangled. He drops down heavily on the cot I just vacated. "Weirdest fragging thing I ever saw. We went through the vents for hours. He'd stop and listen, and then go on again, like he was homing in on her somehow."

*Yes.* That's exactly what he was doing. And why he couldn't touch base with me. If he stopped focusing on her thoughts, even for an instant, he might've lost her. He couldn't take that risk, particularly not to reassure me. Sure, I was scared shitless, but I was safe, unlike this poor girl. Once again, March proves he's a bona fide hero. My anger melts away.

"They cocooned her, but the eggs hadn't hatched yet," March says then. "She's terrified, dehydrated, and malnourished. Can't imagine what it was like for her."

Vel studies me for a moment. Once he has some time to reflect, he's going to put the pieces together about March's ability. I just don't know what he'll do about it.

"I've been studying the station grid," the bounty hunter says. "And I'm going to the sys-control room. I'll open the interior docking door and purge the vents. Then I'll head back to the ship. We'll bounce a message out."

"Are you sure you're strong enough? Do you need me to go with you?" Just a few hours ago, he passed out on me. But maybe the synth-blood he received provided more of a boost than I realized.

"I can handle this," Vel assures me. With that, he slips out.

Jael has closed his eyes. He seems inert until his lips curve into a faint smile. "This is the first crew that ever made *me* feel normal. Thanks."

That doesn't seem to require a response, so I cross to March's side. He watches the little girl with pained tenderness. I get the feeling he doesn't really see her at this moment. He's picturing all the people he failed to save. I fucking hate that expression, so grim and bleak. It hurts me just looking at him.

"Is she going to be all right?"

He shrugs. "She has a shot now. That's more than she had before."

"Good work out there today." That seems to register where nothing else has.

"Thanks. You, too. You did exactly as I hoped you would. You got Vel medical attention and kept safe."

"You scared the shit out of me," I admit, low.

March turns to me then and pulls me into his arms. I drop my head onto his chest, even though he's covered in dried blood. "I know. I took my turn, trust me. You must've been asleep when I started trying to find you again, Jax. It was like . . ." He pauses, and I know he's thinking of when Vel took me. When he thought I was dead. "I'm sorry I put you through that, but I couldn't—"

"I know," I say softly. "I just thought, well, I was *afraid*—"

"You didn't let me down."

"Do you two ever finish your own sentences?" Jael asks.

Shit, I forgot he is here. If he didn't look so beat-up, I'd hit him. "Rarely."

I expect him to make some wisecrack, but he merely says, perhaps a touch wistfully, "Must be nice."

"It has its moments. I'm going to clean up, Jax. Keep an eye on things for me." He means the girl.

I nod. "Of course."

Within a few moments, I hear the san-shower kick in. Until he went quiet, I didn't realize how much I'd come to count on his presence, wandering in and out of my head. Maybe that sounds crazy, but for a jumper, it's almost commonplace. I'm used to sharing mind-space.

*Time to take a look at our patient.* The med-bot hasn't noted any problems with her vitals. I suspect she received some of the sedative saliva before going in the cocoon. I hope it doesn't have any lasting detrimental effects on the nervous system or cognitive functions.

Dammit. At this point, I'm considering a crash course in medicine. I search through the database for information. I don't find anything about the residual effects of the saliva, though, probably because the Morgut tend to digest the evidence.

"Why do you have a Bug with you?"

In a way, I'm glad Jael chooses to ask about Vel. I'd lie for March, just not sure how *well*. "He's the bounty hunter the Corp hired to track me down when they were trying to pin the *Sargasso* crash on me. Fortunately, Vel respects the truth more than a payday. Plus they pissed him off when they tried to fry him."

"I guess that would do it," he agrees without opening his eyes. "It was rough up there. They snapped us up in a web, pulled us into the ducts, but March still had the blade in hand, so we cut our way out."

"There were more?" I'm not sure if I really want to know.

"We killed six up top," he says.

"You're a lot tougher than you look." Duh. I pulled something out of his gut and *felt* him heal. That may be the stupidest thing I've ever said.

His mouth curves into a half smile. "So are you." Jael

cracks his eyes open to study me. For the first time I notice they're a pale, icy blue, like frozen rivers in the Teresengi Basin. "I figured you'd freak when we vanished, but March said no." He hesitates. "I've run with some tough bitches in my day, fought under a couple who were scarier than any men I've met, but they were mercs. I've never known a civ-chick to handle herself like you did. You were cool, Jax, dead cool."

Is that a compliment? "I'm not at the top of my game right now."

His eyes drift closed. "You should let the bot take a look."

As I consider that, the workstation beeps, indicating an incoming transmission. To my surprise, when I accept the message, I find Vel's face on-screen. "I got the comm channel back online, and I've sent a message to Chancellor Tarn, explaining the delay to our mission. He's promised to get a cleanup crew out here as soon as possible." Vel pauses. "His exact words were: 'What the devil are you doing at Emry Station! You're weeks off course!' He doesn't seem overly impressed with our heroism, Sirantha."

I snort. "He wouldn't." The man's a politician. They don't give a shit about the welfare of individuals, only electoral points and obscure polls. A thought occurs to me. "Hey, if he cans me, would you serve with another ambassador, Vel?"

The bounty hunter considers. "No. From our past dealings, I know you are honest, and I could not bring such assurance to my kinsmen about another candidate."

"I guess that makes me uniquely qualified, doesn't it?" Talk about job security.

"It would seem so. Everything all right there?"

I nod. "We may as well choose quarters and get comfortable. It looks like we're going to be here awhile. Did you get in touch with Dina?"

"Affirmative. The purge is complete as well. Emry should be secure now."

March steps around the partition, looking damp and

battered, but inexpressibly dear. "Much better. How's our girl?"

"Still sleeping. How do you feel about station life?"

He cocks a brow at me. "It tends to be slow and boring. Why?"

"Because we're in charge until the cleanup crew arrives."

Jael and March swear in unison.

# CHAPTER 22

***Thus commence the longest days of my life.***

There's nothing like running an emergency station to make you feel like you're alone in the universe. At first I live in fear that another Morgut ship will dock, and then I'm afraid New Terra will never send the promised crew.

By day eight, I'm genuinely worried we'll be stuck here with dwindling supplies and a couple of kids. Staying much longer will drive me nuts. If I wanted this kind of life, I would've stayed where there's a whole world to move around in. I need new sights and sounds, constant change, in order to keep from feeling twitchy, and the fact that I haven't jumped in weeks only exacerbates my station fever.

To make matters worse, March insists on having the med-bot run some tests on me. I suppose it makes sense, but nobody on board can interpret the results, which leaves a diagnosis up to the emergency medical AI. Maybe it's primitive of me, but I would feel better if Doc were here. I don't think technology can figure out what's wrong with me.

Until it does.

"Acute degenerative bone disease of unknown origin," the AI says. "Recommend immediate and aggressive treatment via daily injections of vitamin D3, calcium, and phosphorus. If underlying cause cannot be determined, however, this regimen may provide only limited long-term therapeutic value."

*Bone disease?* Jumpers don't die of such an old woman's illness. And I'm not that *old*. That can't be right.

But a few days ago, the med-bot set the broken bones in my left hand. I'm wearing a small brace now to keep them in place while they heal—and that could take a while. No wonder Kora snapped my fingers like dry twigs.

March tries to smile, but I can tell he's troubled. Well, that makes two of us. "Take your medicine. I'm sure you'll feel better in no time."

Maybe I don't always eat right, but there's no logical reason why I would come up calcium deficient. While undeniably disgusting, nutri-paste provides all necessary nutrients to maintain good health. And I suck down the stuff more than I'd like to admit, so it's not like I'm living off cheap homebrew and sweets.

"You can't possibly trust that thing," I protest. "It's probably a hundred years old. It'll poison me."

"It's a sound program, Jax. And that *thing* saved Tiera and Vel."

Tiera is the little girl. She has terrible nightmares, but she took to Kora straightaway. I hope she won't remember much of this ordeal as she gets older.

We found the duty roster. Twelve souls died here, including her parents. Tiera doesn't seem to understand the idea that they're gone for good. She's too young to learn something so painful—that sometimes people don't come back.

Like always, I think of Kai. Part of me will always ache for him. A divided heart offers a strange sensation. I love March enough to die for him, but I still miss Kai. Is that wrong? Do other people feel like this? Sometimes he feels agonizingly close, as if he's watching me, as if I could touch him. I never would have believed it possible before. Medical science disproved it. But I've seen miracles in my day.

By his taut expression, March knows what I'm thinking, but he doesn't say anything. It's impossible to lie to him, and I wouldn't want to, even if I could. He has to take me as I am, broken bits and all.

"I do," he says. "But you're not going to get better by ignoring the problem, and I won't lose you." His voice comes out raw.

Dammit, he's right. Maybe the workstation itself is a bit antiquated, but the database updates frequently via bounce uplinks. Besides, I do feel like absolute shit. Maybe this will help.

I sigh. "Fine. I refuse to be stupid on principle."

"Yes," he says, dark eyes twinkling. "You always have impeccable reasons for acting like an imbecile."

Why do I put up with his shit? I grin reluctantly. "Damn right."

With poor grace, I let the droid do its thing. I refuse to linger in Med Bay, though. The bot might decide to turn me into a man.

"Mary forefend," March says, following me out.

I have no idea where the others are. With two levels, it's easy to lose track, but I feel reasonably safe. Vel has done four purges, just to be certain, so if there was anything left in the vents, he fried and then spaced it.

This isn't the first station the Morgut have ravaged, and unless the Conglomerate pulls its head out of its collective ass, it won't be the last. They don't fear us. They see us as food, and you don't respect something that lets you eat it.

I stride along the corridor toward the lift. The dull gray-green walls offer little in the way of cheer, but nobody expects to find that here. This is a last resort, a place nobody comes by choice. Not even the crew that mans it.

"Where we going?" he asks, as we step into the tube.

"Up." I smile, knowing he hates when I'm cryptic.

A smile begins in his eyes and works its way down his mouth. "Private quarters are located on the second level."

"So they are."

But when we step off, I don't turn toward them. I'm sure he's disappointed when I stop outside the training room. We haven't had sex in quite some while, and now I hesitate. I don't want him to see me like this, so thin and sickly. I couldn't bear it if desire transmuted to pity somewhere amid the kissing.

"That would never happen," he assures me.

"You say that now."

The door slides open to admit me, offering us free use of limited equipment. A serious health enthusiast would be appalled, but I just want to burn off some nervous energy. I feel trapped, as if even my skin's too small. I need to run until I can't think about how much I want to jump.

I miss the colors and the astonishing splendor of the universe rushing through my open mind like wildfire. My chest hurts. If I didn't know better, I'd call it a cardio problem, but I've been through withdrawal before. It's bad this time, and it'll get worse. I've seen jumpers who opt out devolve into screaming fits before they burn it out of their system, before the memories fade enough to be bearable. The ones who recover make fine teachers.

I'm sure March would rather I fuck him senseless to help me through this, but I just can't. Not now.

"I'm going to use the treadmill a bit. You're welcome to join me if you like."

"Is that a metaphor?" he asks. "Just when I think I'm about to get somewhere, you invite me to run in place."

I misunderstand deliberately. "It's good for you."

"Is it?" March raises a brow. "I expect certain ascetic brotherhoods would agree with you."

"What are we talking about again?" I begin my stretches, careful not to look him in the eye.

"You know perfectly well."

Well, of course I do. He's my pilot, isn't he? I just don't want to deal with it. Avoidance isn't my style, though. Never has been. I need to bring it out in the open.

"What do you want me to say?" Sufficiently limber, I

climb on the machine. It registers my height and weight, and then sets my initial pace accordingly.

"I want to know what the hell's going on," he bites out. "I thought we were—"

"Together?" I supply.

"Yes, that. And we make decisions as one, don't we? When did we decide on celibacy, exactly? I'm dying to touch you."

I don't look at him as I run, arms curled high against my sides. "It wasn't a decision. It just happened. First they separated us, and then—"

*I got sick.*

No. I just can't say that aloud. But he's strong and fit, whereas I'm fragile. I can't wade in beside him with a shockstick and a kiss-my-ass smile anymore. I don't have the stamina or the speed. I can't be an equal partner to him now. Maybe I never can be again.

The old Jax wouldn't have cowered with Vel in the med center. She'd have found a way to do both, somehow. She'd have saved Vel and managed to find March, too. I can rationalize it, but I've changed. I'm not up to my old weight.

*Weak.*

Before I can alter the status quo, I need to hear what Doc has to say. It's not fair to tie March to someone who may have a shorter life expectancy than your typical jumper—and that's saying a lot. That truth hurts so much that I'll never be able to speak the words. Not to him.

But he knows.

Deliberately, March steps off his machine and heads for the door. Even though I'm not Psi, I feel the pain rolling off him in raw, angry waves. Without turning, he says, "I had no idea you were such a fucking coward, Jax. You think you love me enough to die for me. Big fucking deal; you don't love me enough to *live* for me. You've quit on us before we ever began."

# CHAPTER 23

***It's just like that first time, all over again.***

I've finally got what I wanted so bad. Here I sit in the nav chair, ready to jack in, next to a pilot who wants nothing to do with me. I already tried to apologize, but he's having none of it.

That scrapes the wrong way since I want to keep us from making a terrible mistake. If I pull back, then hearing the worst will be easier on us both. And if we get good news, then we'll be dying to get back in bed, anticipation and all that.

March thinks I'm full of shit—that I'm inventing reasons to push him away. That's not true. I just don't want him to suffer like I did when I lost Kai. I have to know there's hope before I let this thing between us go any further. So maybe it's better this way, better if he hates me. He's so afraid of losing me that he can't see I'm scared out of my mind, too. I'm trying to be strong.

How can you miss someone who's right beside you?

I put all that aside as we run a systems check and prepare to depart. I'm a professional. Doesn't matter how I feel, or that my stomach flips like a dying fish at the thought of being part of him again. The desire to jump twines painfully with the desire to jump *March.*

This ship vibrates a lot more than the *Folly*. It's smaller, for one thing. Not sure if we possess any weapons at all. If we don't, Dina'll want to collaborate with Jael on it. I haven't had a chance to ask if she made any upgrades while we waited.

All told, we spent fourteen days on Emry Station, but the cavalry has arrived. Surge and family will remain on station, but Jael's coming with us. I'm not sure we need a gunner on a diplomatic mission, but given my track record, it's not a terrible idea.

"We'll stop on Lachion first," March says. "Doc needs to see you, and I need to take care of personal business there, too."

"Tarn isn't going to like it."

"He'll like it less if you drop dead."

Yeah, he's back to the old March where I'm concerned. It hurts to look at him, so I jack in, though we haven't left the station. The cockpit disappears.

We're waiting for clearance. I've already checked the star charts to translate the distance I need to navigate.

They've disabled the automated docking system until they decide what to do about the Morgut threat. I heard them kicking around the idea of having Conglomerate ships outfitted with a special device that signals the system it's safe. Such technology can be cracked, though. The other solution is requiring the docking bays be manned twenty-four/seven. Either option requires a bigger budget.

March gets on the comm, hailing the guys in the office. "We're good to go."

"Roger that. Thanks for everything, *Bernard's Luck*. We'd have lost a lot more lives out here if you hadn't happened by."

I feel the lift as we maneuver out. Though I can't see, I picture March's hands on the controls. He's sure and graceful as he flies. I hear him telling the crew to strap in, so we'll be making the jump soon.

"You ready?"

*No.*

But I nod, bracing myself for the moment when the universe unfurls. And then March jacks in beside me. Partitioned, of course. He doesn't want to share anything with me right now. Well, I can do it, too; I've learned a lot from him. I won't give him a damn thing either.

The ship shudders as the phase drive powers up. Dina reports all clear just before we make the jump, and then the world flashes out.

*Fucking beautiful.*

My mind expands to infinite space. Grimspace feels like flying, the only place I'm completely free. I sense the beacons, alluring as innumerable heartbeats thudding in time. Somehow there's harmony in the chaos.

For a moment, just a moment, I think I might understand *everything*, but then it shifts to something else and floats away. I can't hold on to anything here, not even my own soul. The sense that everything's connected on some level I can't grasp haunts me. But I'm not here to suss out the secrets of the universe today.

I just need to find the beacon nearest Lachion. I've made this run more than once, so the path comes easy. Funny how March and I can do this so coolly, sharing nothing, where we used to be one mind.

Well. Funny, like a needle in the eye.

He knows what grimspace looks like, its mad, consuming beauty. Few people do if they aren't jumpers themselves. They've never managed to develop a camera that can reproduce what it sees, the impossible patterns and oscillations found here.

I sense the adjustments he makes, guiding the ship in response to my cues. The pulse roars in my ears. *We're here.*

And then I go blind again while the ship trembles its way back into straight space. No wonder mudsiders think spacers are crazy. Anytime we make a long haul, we could be lost forever. Over the years, they've reduced the odds considerably, but freighters still vanish now and then. A gamble at good odds is still a gamble.

Taking care with my bad hand, I unplug. My head hurts, more than it used to when I left. It sucks a little more of my soul each time. There will come a day when I'll simply be empty. Even if March manages to drag me back again, the next time I cruise too close to burnout—assuming he'd bother now—I'm not sure there would be anything left.

And I don't care. Beneath the tired aches, serenity flows through me like a river dammed too long. This is a jumper's lot. I don't know how the instructors do it. Since they want me to teach on Lachion, though, I guess I need to figure it out.

His voice startles me. I thought we wouldn't be speaking for a while. "We'll be there in a couple of hours. You did well."

"Thanks." Courtesy feels awkward.

I want to tell him to go fuck himself if he can't understand what I'm going through. It's not all about him. March has abandonment issues, and it's not my job to soothe them. Just now I can't muster up the energy.

"Your fire's gone out," March says. "You used to feel like a live wire, Jax."

"All the more reason for me to step back," I tell him with a fraction of my old bite. "If that was what you loved about me, and I've lost it, then what's left?"

"You really don't get it, do you?"

"No."

March rakes a hand through his dark hair. Over the past weeks, his has actually gotten longer where mine has stopped growing entirely. He looks rough and a little menacing with the stubble on his jaw.

"You're killing me here. You're asking me to leave you the fuck alone just when you need me most. How can I do that?"

"I'll make it easy for you." I push from the nav chair and duck out of the cockpit. Nothing ever hurt like walking away from him.

I can't accept that I'm crazy for asking for time, though. Why can't he understand that I need some chance to be strong again? I don't want to lose myself in leaning on him. If I can't stand on my own two feet when I need to, then I might as well be dead.

Suddenly my dad's plan—the Eutha-booth—doesn't look half-bad.

Instead of stopping to chat with the others, I pass straight through the hub and head for my quarters. I have two hours to kill. Maybe I'll dump my problems on 245 and see what she suggests.

To my vast annoyance, the AI tells me I have company, almost as soon as I flop down on my bunk. As the door slides open, I growl, "I thought I told you to leave me alone."

Dina steps back, feigning surprise. "Did you? I didn't hear for all the bitchy stomping around you've been doing for the last few weeks. You need to get laid."

I lie back with a sigh. "No, I don't. I need to find out from Doc just how bad off I am."

"You're completely fucked," she says at once, but it's more of a reflex. "I brought biscuits and choclaste. I thought we could talk about hot guys."

That makes me raise up on an elbow. "You don't do hot guys."

"But *you* do. We can talk hot chicks if it makes you feel better," she offers. "Kora wasn't my type, but I liked the doc they sent along from New Terra."

"I bet you did." Despite my misery, I eat a cookie. "Wonder who she pissed off to get that assignment."

"She punched someone for feeling her up." Dina grins.

I raise a brow. "And you discovered this while feeling her up?"

Dina shakes her head as she commandeers the chair beside my workstation. "Afterward."

"Of course. Why are you being so nice to me?"

She shrugs. "Someone has to be. You look like a fucking death's-head."

Nobody else on the ship knows. Since she's a smart woman, she noticed something's wrong. But she doesn't know what. It might do me good to confide in a human being for a change, one who isn't interested in screwing me.

So I do.

# CHAPTER 24

***Talking with Dina eats up the hours.***

"Fuck it," she says, downing the last biscuit. "We all die. If Doc can't sort you out, then go do whatever the hell you like. Don't waste the time you have left."

"Always thought I'd go out jumping, you know? I think I was meant to, earlier. March called me back." That spills out before I can stop it.

She dips her chin, studies her booted feet for a moment. "He loves you, Mary knows why. I don't know what you mean to do about it. Not my business, really—"

"But you're presuming to advise me about het-sex relationships, even though you don't know the first thing about them?" I lick my finger and collect some of the crumbs from the cookie plate.

"It's the same principle, you stupid twat. You don't deserve my advice."

"Probably not, but you can't resist. That way, when I ignore it, you can call me an ignorant bitch later, after I've fucked things up beyond all recognition."

"At least you're honest," she says with a grin. "And reasonably self-aware."

"It's a gift. Go on then."

"Be gentle with him." Dina sits forward, arms crossed on her knees. "I've known him a long time, and I don't want to see him hurt again."

*That makes two of us.* The silence builds, charged with things I don't feel able to articulate. Finally, I answer, "Noted."

It's not nearly enough.

My first clue that we've arrived comes from the bump that signals planetfall. They've built a hangar inside the Gunnar-Dahlgren compound, so the merger must be going well. I can't wait to see Doc, even Lex and Keri for that matter.

It's not quite a homecoming. I won't feel like that until I return to the glastique garret that didn't have a shower. Inexplicable, the places our hearts tie us to. I miss Adele. She was like the mother I always wanted, not the one I've got.

"We should get the hell off this ship," Dina says then.

With a stretch, she pushes to her feet, leaving the dirty dishes for me to worry about. I grin a little over that. I'd worry if she ever turned up *too* nice. I might find her laying out my funeral clothes the moment my back was turned.

"Yep. The other guys must be wondering at this layover since we're already behind schedule."

She pauses at the door. "Let them wonder."

I have no quarrel with that notion. They don't need to know about my illness or March's sense of obligation to the clan. Right now I can understand Dina's attraction to other women. I'm rather fed up with Y-chromosome bastards myself. I roll off the bed, and my reflected movement prompts me to look in the glass beside my bunk. What I see startles me.

"Need to change first. I look like an inmate . . . or a san worker."

"Clothes won't help." She's back to mocking me, which

I appreciate, because it means she thinks I'm strong enough to take it. I think I'd go back to bed if she became solicitous. "You need a new head . . . or at least a new face. Maybe Doc's friend on Gehenna can hook you up."

"Ordo?"

"Yeah, that's the one. Still, do your best, won't you? Spackle on some paint, maybe use the wardrober to manufacture a wig. They're all queued up to see the ambassador from New Terra."

"They are not." I rummage through my bag, sighing over my meager possessions. Impossible to believe—I used to be something of a clotheshorse. Back in the day, I loved dolling up in short skirts and long boots, tiny tops that showed more of me than they hid. Now I'm hard-pressed to find something that doesn't make me look as though I repair Skimmers for a living.

"Tarn panicked. He was afraid the Ithtorians would take offense to our meandering progress, so he's 'leaked' the fact that New Terra's ambassador is wending her way toward them on a goodwill tour."

"No."

"Yes."

We could go on like this all day, I expect, so I choose not to be juvenile. I know; it stings a bit. "Do I have an itinerary?"

"You'd have to inquire of Chancellor Tarn."

"I'd rather make it up as I go along." I shake my head over the absurdity of the situation. Tarn should have replaced me weeks ago, but he won't. Because of Vel, I am indispensable. "Get out, or you're going to see me naked."

"I'm going!" she protests, heading out. Her final words drift back to me as the door slides shut. "You're such a stroppy bitch."

Since March just accused me of having lost my spirit, I certainly like the sound of that. Not surprisingly, it takes me a little while to make myself presentable, given the raw material. Finally, I unearth a simple black vest and a pair of skinny black and gray thin-striped slacks.

I hesitate because the shirt reveals my scars, and then I decide I want it that way. They mean something. That's why I kept them.

In the end I take Dina's suggestion with regard to cosmetics. I paint some color into my complexion and cover up the circles beneath my eyes. I refuse to wear false hair, though. Maybe I'll start a trend for women who fancy wearing theirs a centimeter long but always lacked the nerve before now. When I emerge from quarters, I find Jael waiting for me.

"I'm to be your protection," he says without preamble. "Isn't that a laugh?"

"From what?"

"Assassination attempts like the one you didn't report on New Terra. You tried to pass that off as a crash."

It takes me a moment to parse what he means. *The Skimmer explosion, right.* I just wanted off world, didn't want to wait around for another inquiry. "Did they find the cause? It wasn't a mechanical fault?"

"Yes, and no. Scavengers found the parts, but they were confiscated when they tried to fence them. The authorities found the remnants of a primitive incendiary device, assembled from common household items."

"So someone definitely tried to murder me." I feel oddly numb about that.

"As a direct result of several lengthy communiqués that bordered on interrogation by the Chancellor, I'm now responsible for preventing them from succeeding. I'll warn you, Jax. Tarn is paying me well, and I intend to take my job seriously."

"You've been keeping him off my back?"

I admit it; I've been shirking my responsibilities. As a nav-star for Farwan, I had just one. Take my pilot and make my scheduled jumps. That's all. My life used to include a fair amount of holiday time, and nobody trying to disperse my molecules.

*Different world, different life.*

Jael smiles for the first time, charming when he stops

radiating belligerence to compensate for his pretty face. "Done my best."

"If I had any creds, I'd pay you for that myself. Unfortunately, I'm broke as a joke just now."

His smile becomes a grin. "You don't need creds. The Conglomerate is picking up your tab, aren't they? You should charge a bunch of stuff before you lose this gig."

"You talk like that's inevitable." What am I saying? I laugh reluctantly because I see his point. I have a solid record for diplomacy in regard to class-P planets. I know how to impress superstitious natives.

The Ithtorians? Not so much. I hope Vel can save my ass yet again.

Jael spreads his hands in a defensive gesture. "I'm just saying, buy some new clothes, maybe some sparklies."

Tarn's reaction to my draping myself in diamonds at his expense would be priceless. Despite myself, I rather like this merc's sense of humor. In some ways he reminds me of Kai: cheerful, cocky, and irreverent.

"Anyway." I try to refocus the conversation. "I enjoyed some peace while we waited on Emry, though. I appreciate that."

"All part of the job," Jael tells me easily. "You look better, less like you're about to turn toes up."

"You're a smooth talker, aren't you?" I don't mean for the words to come out flirtatious. Mary knows, I have enough problems in that regard, and it's not like he's interested. He's just saying I look less like the walking dead, which is a long haul from a true compliment.

March clears his throat. From his taut expression, he thinks he's interrupted something. Mary, I'd like to smack him in the head, but at this point, he'd probably take it as foreplay.

"Let's get this over with," he mutters.

He brushes past the two of us without another word, and Jael cocks a brow at me. "Trouble in paradise?"

"You don't get to know about my personal life," I snap at him. "Just go clear the way or whatever bodyguards do."

"Darling," he drawls. "Soon I'll know everything about you, including how many times you breathe per minute, and if your heartbeat sounds a smidgen off."

"Will you know when I . . ." I lean in to whisper the rest.

"That depends. Am I in your room at the time?"

"No!" Nothing I say fazes him, so I stalk past to the main hatch.

Great, I need another man poking about in my business. Like I need to settle down and study rutabagas.

# CHAPTER 25

***Lachion hasn't changed a bit.***

Then again, why would it? It hasn't been as long as it seems since I was here. The horizon stretches pale and endless beyond the compound walls, bounded by dry plains. This place offers extremes—heat or cold—depending on the season.

After discovering the scary things that live in the caves, the clans stayed because Lachion meant freedom from the Corp. Nobody has ever given a shit about what happens on this planet. Despite the new world order, I don't see that changing anytime soon.

To my astonishment, this looks like a formal delegation, not the casual welcoming party I expected. Far cry from the last time I touched down here. And is that the gutter press, lined up behind Keri and Lex?

Shit, it *is*. I recognize the guy with the poorly implanted ocular cam. In the old days, he stalked me through spaceport bars, hoping to get a shot of my tits for the midnight bounce. *Nice.*

Keri's smile looks decidedly artificial. "We're delighted

that you chose Lachion to kick off your interplanetary goodwill tour."

A smile tugs hard at the corners of my mouth, and it's all I can do not to burst out laughing. "Of course. I'd love to see a greater level of governmental participation from the clans."

Since freethinkers and outlaws abide here, that will go over like the monkey-pilot experiments from the turn of the century. The clans don't want to legislate, vote, or pay extra tariffs. For Mary's sake, they settle grievances in the arena.

"We'll discuss that during your visit," she responds through gritted teeth.

I suspect Keri's going to kick my ass again, which is sad because she's just over half my age. The girl is tougher than she looks. As I move forward, a barrage of questions greets me.

"Ambassador, can you tell us anything about your plans?"

"How do you feel about the proposed integration of Ithiss-Tor into the Conglomerate?"

"Why is your itinerary shrouded in secrecy? Our sources say you may be targeted for retaliatory action from Farwan loyalists or other extremist groups. Is there any truth to those claims?"

"Can you comment on the recent rumors that you detoured en route to thwart a Morgut attack on Emry Station?"

I ignore them all, trying to move forward while the guy with the bulging eye cam watches me like I'm about to yank up my shirt right here. In addition to the fact that those days are behind me, it's also too damn cold. Why don't I ever have a coat when I need one?

March stands somewhere to the right, just behind me, but he won't be coming to my aid. Yep, just like the last time. I've lost track of Dina, but she's somewhere behind me, and Vel doesn't like cameras, as they possess a small chance of ferreting out inconsistencies in his appearance that would ID him as nonhuman.

Jael pushes his way up beside me. "The ambassador isn't answering questions at this time. Clear the way." He looks almost friendly as he says it, but there's a high shine in his pale eyes that says he wouldn't mind cracking some heads in time for the midnight bounce.

As if they sense it as well, the reporters get out of the way. Keri leads my entourage along the drive, her own people straggling behind. Five of them wear purple armbands; I'm not exactly sure what that means.

When we've left earshot, she mutters, "You always bring trouble, don't you?"

"Everyone needs a hobby." I used to say that to March in regard to thinking about my own death. Does that mean I've made emotional progress?

"Perhaps you'd consider horticulture."

Outbuildings line the path to the main house, an old-fashioned stone structure. The wire-and-steel security fence crackles, reminding me why it's there: to keep the monsters out. Remembering that endless night where so many people died, I stifle my smart-ass reply.

A while back, March liberated me from my cell, after the crash of the *Sargasso*. He saved me from a lifetime of torment and delivered me to Lachion, where I was intended to help Clan Dahlgren start a renegade jump-training academy. Unfortunately, their rivals, Clan Gunnar, wanted to get their hands on me as well. Anyone who controlled a supply of jumpers would possess an edge—and on more than just a planetary scale. So they came at us on the ground, forced us to stop.

Tired of being jerked around, I started a melee between the clans right out in the open, not knowing that blood would draw the Teras, awful winged monsters that sweep across the plains like a plague, eating everything in sight. And because of an evolutionary boon, you can't see them coming—just hear the sound of their wings.

Despite my best intentions, I can still hear the Gunnar warriors screaming as they were swept away on that hungry tide, an unseen army of claws and talons rushing around me in the dark. I shiver. *No more thinking of that. Not now.* It's safe here behind the electrical perimeter, and nobody is bleeding.

I make myself smile at Keri. "I swear I didn't intend for this to turn into such a—Doc!" I spot him about thirty meters out and take off at a dead run.

Part of me had worried I'd never see him again. What if Vel had lied about leaving him in a trunk when he took his place? That's how the bounty hunter managed to snag me; he pretended to be Doc. So there's some truth to the Syndicate's worry that Sliders—a human slang term for Ithtorians, or Bugs, as they're also called—present a threat to our way of life.

But Vel didn't lie. There Doc stands, solid and sturdy, still wearing his salt-and-pepper goatee, and his hair shorn close to his skull. Come to that, we have the same haircut now.

He breaks into a broad smile and meets me halfway. His hug practically pulverizes my ribs, but I don't care. My eyes sting. Doc was the first one to treat me like I wasn't dangerous or criminally insane, responsible for the lost lives on the *Sargasso*. I'll never forget him for that.

"I missed you," I say shakily. This probably isn't ambassadorial behavior, but I don't give a shit. "You're really all right?"

"I'm fine, Jax. Good to see you, too. Er, you can let go now." Yep, it's definitely Doc. I expect him to comment on my fragile appearance, but he has more tact than that. I've been surrounded by the likes of March, Dina, and Jael too long.

My bodyguard says, "They'll have you on the news, speculating about an illicit affair with him, by morning. Possible impropriety by the New Terran ambassador?" he intones, just like one of the talking heads.

"Please. Nobody cares." But I step back nonetheless.

Doc scans all our faces and seems to focus on Vel. "You. I believe you mistook me for luggage on our last meeting."

Since Vel looks like everyone and no one, it's a logical

leap, and Doc excels in that area. I can't imagine what he makes of the situation we currently find ourselves in. Hopefully, he'll be able to help me. I can't think too long about the possibilities otherwise.

"Sorry about that." I must say, Vel doesn't *look* sorry. "Farwan supplied me with erroneous information."

For a long, tense moment, I think cool, calm pacifist Doc might sock the bounty hunter in the nose. Then he says, "I suppose everyone makes mistakes. Let's go inside, shall we?"

The gutter press follows at a discreet distance, filming the whole time. I'd suggest feeding them to the Teras, but that might strike a sore spot with Keri. I've already hurt the poor girl enough.

March throws brooding looks over his shoulder now and then. I bet he'd like to pound them on principle. Mary, I don't know what to do about that. I know I'm hurting him. And I want him; I miss him. But I can't let myself *need* him, not because I'm physically incapacitated. And if he doesn't understand that, then he doesn't know me at all.

Just from this short walk, my fingertips have gone numb, the icy wind ripping right through me. When I picked out the vest, I forgot it was still winter here. Time is fluid, so the moments where everything feels perfect pass in a wink, and those where you're on your knees in despair drag on like the death of a thousand cuts.

As if he notices my discomfort, Jael presses up against my right side in a manner that's destined to provoke March in the worst way. The merc can be such an asshole—he's just doing it for the entertainment value. I pretend I don't notice either of them.

*Fucking men.*

We pass into the warmth of the house and shut ourselves away from prying eyes. I hope. I muster a smile, even though I'm already tired as hell. Yeah, just from that short hike. *Couldn't have been more than half a kilometer.*

Keri's home is lovely as ever, with all the elegance that surprised me the first time I visited. The place possesses the old-world charm of handcrafted moldings, shimmering marble tiles, and carpets so thick I'm afraid to walk on them. They've redone the foyer since I was here last, though: red and black now, a little more foreboding than the chilly silver and white elegance her grandmother had favored.

The tiles form a pattern I can't identify, though I've seen it somewhere before. I stare down, absently rubbing my hands up and down my biceps. Up the stairs, she offers capacious guest suites, and hallways lead in either direction. An enormous silver-gilt mirror with acid-etched leaves dominates the far wall, offering distorted hints of the people standing in the foyer. I can't help but shiver, as if we've been granted a glimpse into the afterlife, nothing but vague shapes and shadows.

"Looks beautiful," March says. "It's completely you, Keri."

"Thank you." Her cheeks pink with delicate color as she turns toward him.

Just like that, she forgets me. I'd also forgotten the huge, unrequited crush she had on March the last time we stopped here. The little darling—she's all of nineteen, fights like a chi master, and had started to learn advanced feats before her grandmother passed away. On top of all that, at her age, she acts as joint chieftain to her clan. Keri has smooth skin, a sylph's shape, a spill of night-dark hair, and eyes that gleam like pale jade. And by March's smiles, he's noticing for the first time how lovely his mentor's granddaughter has grown to be.

I fucking hate the bitch.

# CHAPTER 26

***"Where's Lex?" That's one question sure to snap Keri*** out of the March-induced daze she currently enjoys. Lex is the big lug she's supposed to marry as part of the clan merger. To say she hates him would be an understatement.

She spears me with an icy stare and bares her teeth in what would be considered a hostile act on some worlds. "War council. You came at a bad time, Jax."

*What else is new?*

"What's going on?" March asks.

I recognize his solicitous tone and barely manage to keep from rolling my eyes. He thinks Keri is delicate and needs his protection. I'm sure he feels some obligation as well, given that Keri's grandmother took him in when his gift had ravaged him and taught him to be human again. And Keri is all that his mentor left behind. I guess he doesn't know that Keri whipped my ass without breaking a sweat.

Beside me, Jael sizes up Keri's men, as if he suspects any situation I'm involved in could turn ugly on a moment's notice. I didn't realize he knew me that well.

"It's bad. I'll tell you about it on the way. I'm sure Lex will want to see you." With a definite proprietary air, she takes hold of his arm. "Saul," she adds over her shoulder to Doc. "Can you get everyone else settled for me? Thanks."

Her honor guard, or whatever the hell they are, spins as a unit and follows her down the left hallway. None of them said a single word from the time we met her outside the ship, until now. *Fucking creepy.*

"They move like military," Jael murmurs. "Well trained, too. I wonder what's happening on this backwater world."

I shrug. "Hard to say. They're always fighting over something here. I think it cuts down on boredom."

Doc favors me with a piercing look. "Don't be flip, Jax. When two clans join, it's time to strike. It's well-known here, both clans are weak, or they wouldn't need a merger. Waiting until things are stable doesn't make good tactical sense."

"What's the point, though?" Jael asks. "From what I saw, the whole planet is pretty bare. What the hell is there worth fighting over?"

"Gunnar-Dahlgren controls the magnesium mines on planet," Doc answers briefly. "I probably don't need to outline all the goods that encompasses."

In my case, he does. But Jael nods, ticking them off his fingertips. "Flash grenades, imaging technology, pyrotechnics for festivals, certain metal alloys, which translates to machinery that needs to be strong and lightweight—"

"It's used in some medicines as well," Doc says with a nod. "And if we can't defend the mines, they'll wipe us out."

*Us?* I didn't realize Doc was from Lachion. Based on his friendship with Ordo Carvati on Gehenna, I would've guessed he came from the Outskirts somewhere.

I sigh. "I didn't understand what I'd done the last time I was here."

Not really, anyway. I didn't have anything like the big picture, even when we left. Keri has been fighting her own uphill battle ever since we left. And by the look of things, it's not getting any easier.

"When do you ever know what you're doing, Jax?" Dina grins at me.

Ignoring that, Doc tries to herd us toward the stairs. "You can pick out the rooms you like best. Perhaps you'd like the one you occupied last time, Jax?"

Yeah, I like the Blue Room, very serene, and it has handmade rugs so soft I sink into them. "Sure, that sounds fine."

At this point, I notice that Vel has disappeared. I wonder if he has camo that I don't know about because he has a habit of doing that: there one minute and gone the next. He can take care of himself, though.

"I don't care. Assign me whatever." Dina sighs. "If I can find parts and mod kits, I'm heading back to the ship. I have work to do."

Jael surprises me—and evidently Dina as well, judging by her expression—by asking, "Need help?"

She narrows her eyes on him for a long moment before shrugging. "The ship needs a lot of upgrades. So if you know how to handle your tools, I won't say no to an extra hand."

The merc risks his life by draping an arm about her shoulders. "Darling, I'm *expert* with my hands."

She shocks me when she doesn't immediately drive her elbow into his stomach. I can't believe he still flirts with her, even knowing he has no shot. Maybe he suffers from a chronic disorder. I expected he'd stick to me like glue after the lecture he just gave me, but I'm glad to get rid of him. As they go back out into the cold, I hear her reply, "Your own opinion doesn't count, dumb-ass."

That just leaves Doc and me. To avoid the questions in his very kind eyes, I head up the stairs. I should have known that wouldn't matter.

"What's wrong, Jax?"

I pause on the fourth step, but don't turn. "I was hoping *you* could tell me. That's part of why we're here. Tarn cooked up this other nonsense."

"I deduced as much," he tells me.

Without looking at him, I confide the droid's diagnosis. I expect him to laugh or tell me it's ridiculous. Instead I receive silence that lasts until I wheel and gaze down at him. He looks troubled.

"I wish I could say I'm surprised, but I found a number of anomalies in your test results that puzzled me. If my hypothesis holds true, then this would explain everything. Let's get you to the lab then." Doc tilts his head toward the right corridor, opposite from the way March went with Keri.

*Hypothesis?* This is my *life*, not a science project. I like Doc, but sometimes I think he doesn't realize that I'm more than an "interesting specimen." He's the only one I trust to help me, though, so I have to accept his bedside manner.

I come down again and fall into step with him. As I recall, the house is laid out in wings. We move off toward his research facility, but before we've gone ten paces, the lights flicker, as if somewhere, someone has drawn an absurd amount of power.

Doc breaks into a run. "Hurry, Jax. We don't have much time."

"Before what?"

He doesn't pause to answer. I trot behind him nonetheless because Doc isn't one to manufacture crises. We've just reached the door to his lab, which is oddly—and ominously—made of reinforced metal, when I hear screaming.

"Doc?"

"Get inside. Now."

I do, and he seals the door. "You want to tell me what's going on here?"

"Teras," he says briefly.

Just the word alone sends a cold shock through me: hideous subterranean creatures you can't see coming. Just hear the rush of their wings through endless night. And once the dying starts . . .

With some effort, I shake myself out of it. I rub my

hands together, trying to warm them. We survived them once, and we're safe inside this time. It should be fine.

"What about them?"

"I haven't deduced how, but Clan McCullough has figured out a way to train . . ." He pauses, listening to the distant sounds of combat, cries of rage and pain. "Well, if not train, then *use* the Teras. They seem to strike on command now. It's not safe to leave the compound. They hit us at all hours, no rhyme or reason to it."

"Doesn't the shock field help?" I remember the way they fried the monsters. The smell the next morning nearly did me in.

"We can't keep it up all the time," he says tiredly. "Not enough juice. We run on solar panels and wind turbines, mostly the latter during the winter. Gunnar-Dahlgren is officially at war, Jax. Clan McCullough wants everything we have, and with the Teras on their side, they think they've figured out a way to get it." He sighs. "I'm not sure they're wrong."

No wonder Keri said I came at a bad time.

"I guess jump research isn't at your top priority at the moment."

He manages a wan smile. "No, they've got me trying to sort out why the Teras are attacking like this instead of their usual feeding patterns. We're weakening by the day, and I don't think the McCulloughs have lost a single man."

How do you fight when you can't see your enemies? It would take bioengineered poisons or type-three battle droids to clean this planet out. I have no idea how the loss of the Teras would impact the planetary ecosystems either.

"Do you have the resources to build battle droids with heat imaging?" Lame, I know. I remember the way the Teras dismantled the Rover. Could they find their way into the main house as easily? Are there weak spots?

Doc shakes his head. "That's not the way things were done here. The McCullough has changed everything. He doesn't risk his own men or his own life for a hostile takeover. Instead he's killing us by centimeters."

Again, I find myself cowering while others take the risks on my behalf. That stings like nothing ever has. No. I won't do this. Not again.

March is out there. Jael. Dina. March. I have to help them.

I stride over to the door, tap on the panel. "If it's that bad, I should go see what I can do."

"You can't get out," Doc tells me. "The doors are sealed until the attack ends. And I'm not going to release you when you're clearly ill."

Bastard. Is he trying to make me feel useless? My hands curl into fists, but who am I going to hit? Doc? He won't fight back. Nothing like impotent anger to make you feel ineffectual.

"Fine," I bite out. "If I'd known, I wouldn't have come in here with you, though. I can't believe you tricked me into hiding out."

Again. I hate this. I've got to find some way out of here, or I'll never be able to live with myself. I can't devolve back into the selfish bitch who doesn't care whose ass is on the line so long as it isn't her own. I won't let fear become my mistress.

"I know," he says gently. "That's why I didn't tell you. Try to ignore the noise. It'll be over soon. They never stay long; not sure why that is either. If I can put the pieces together, we might have a chance, even weakened as we are. At any rate, let's get started on your tests."

"Then cure me. Or kill me. Because I can't live like this."

# CHAPTER 27

***Soon as Doc looks away, I lunge toward the emergency*** override panel. Unfortunately, I'm not as fast or agile as I used to be, and he wheels round to catch my wrist. He radiates frustration, but before he can yell at me, a boom sounds.

The whole house shakes.

I hit the floor, expecting the roof to come down on me. "I didn't know Lachion was prone to quakes."

"It's not," Doc says grimly. "They're bombarding us."

I'm not even sure what that means. For a moment, I envision Clan McCullough dropping giant rocks on us. "They're what?"

On his hands and knees beneath the exam table with me, he looks as though he's considering one of his university-style explanations. Then he shakes his head. "This is a hostile takeover, Jax. Welcome to stage two."

Shit. We *did* come at a bad time.

Between Teras who attack on command and the McCullough war machines, things don't look good. Oh, Mary, I might never see March again. Dread threatens to close off my throat. It can't end here, before I can make him understand.

"I guess we were lucky to land before they struck."

He stays low, duckwalking toward the back of the lab. "I suspect your arrival prompted them to step up the attack. They can't take the chance the ship carried reinforcements, or that the Conglomerate means to interfere with local politics. You're not just Jax anymore, Ambassador. Not that you were ever 'just' anything."

He can't be serious. I did this by showing up? I *am* the fucking butterfly, causing ripples everywhere I go.

"It's a tiny little cutter," I protest, crawling after him. Wherever he's going, I'm headed there, too. We weave around a tall metal cylinder that quivers like it wants to crush my spine. "What the hell could we possibly haul? And it's not like we could've carried many mercs in it."

"A fair number of Threshers would fit into the cargo hold," he answers over his shoulder.

The McCulloughs hit us again, and this time, the walls tremble. Dust spills from the ceiling, powdering my head. Not far away, something collapses. Mary curse it, I hope Doc has a plan.

"I would've brought Threshers," I say, "if I'd known you were at war."

Made by Veratech, Threshers represent the gold standard in killing machines for terrestrial combat. I couldn't have afforded them, but he doesn't need to know that. Let my financial embarrassment die with me.

"Keri tried to tell you. Didn't her message go through?"

I remember the way it hissed and cut out. "Not all of it. Not the crucial bit. We thought there might've been a problem with the bounce-relay. It's never stable here."

The freedom of a backwater planet also comes with a certain amount of technological disadvantage. There's no grid in place, no warning system for natural disasters, and no help forthcoming if people get in trouble. To the folks who live here, that's a plus.

Advance teams told Farwan that Lachion offered nothing

special in the way of natural resources, no money to be made via exploitation, so they packed up and left the place to the settlers. That's why the Corp called this place a frontier world and paid them no mind. So for the last fifty turns, the Clans have policed themselves and made it up as they went along.

Another hit sends me sprawling. As he rights me in a casual motion, I note the pack slung across his shoulder. Doc pushes a heavy piece of equipment over to the side with the sheer physical strength that never ceases to amaze me. Head down, he looks like a short, squat ox.

"Plan B," he says.

That happens to be a small escape hatch built into the floor. The house will come down around our ears if we don't get a move on. Even so, I hesitate to skin down the ladder after him, gazing into a vertical shaft that measures less than a meter. He descends carefully to accommodate his shoulders.

Soon he disappears from sight. A cold sweat breaks out over me, but I don't make the leap onto the skinny little ladder until another boom threatens to collapse the ceiling on me.

"Close it!" Doc shouts, an echo inflating his voice.

I yank on the short chain to seal us off from the surface world. The light vanishes. My hands feel slippery on the rungs, and I can taste the dark, thick as rancid meat grease.

Down one step. *I can do this.*

The shaft shudders. Overhead, huge chunks of rubble slam against the trapdoor. If I hadn't moved, I'd be crushed up there, along with all of Doc's expensive equipment.

We're buried alive.

Pure terror paralyzes me. They're going to find my bones on this ladder, twenty turns from now. Trembling, I remember the *Sargasso*, how I felt while buried in the wreckage.

Why isn't March here? He promised, damn him. He said I'll always come for you. That probably doesn't hold true anymore, though. If it ever did.

What a dickhead. Why couldn't he understand I just needed some time? Anger, even the manufactured variety, lends me some strength, but it's not quite enough. I can't make myself move.

"Jax?" I can't see him, but I hear sympathy and understanding in his voice. "One step at a time. Closing your eyes might help. Forget about the dark."

How embarrassing. He knows. Sirantha Jax, afraid of the dark. Nonetheless, I take his advice and squeeze my eyelids shut. Feel my way down.

Somewhere along the way, I miss a rung, but I don't fall far. Solid as a brick wall, Doc's placed to catch me. I think he could hold a baby elephant. He holds me for a moment, effortlessly, while we listen to the sky falling above us.

I'm sure it's just my imagination, but I swear I can hear the rustle of wings. "Is this a good idea? I mean, don't the Teras live underground?"

"Clan Dahlgren dug the bunkers," he assures me. "And secured them. They don't connect to the natural caverns where the Teras make their home."

"If you say so."

I remember what he said about magnesium mines. You couldn't pay me enough to work down there. Or maybe it's all automated, like some of the moon mining facilities, just a skeleton crew to oversee and repair the droids.

Doc sets me on my own feet and cracks a torch tube. I've never been so glad to see chemicals mixing. Soon the ambient light bathes our faces in a sickly yellow-green glow.

"I'm afraid your tests will have to wait."

*Really? I thought you'd produce a pocket lab and cure me this minute.* Somehow I manage not to snap at him. He's the only thing standing between me and madness down here.

"Yeah, I gathered that. Where do these tunnels lead?"

"To the main bunker. It's a honeycomb, and unless you know the way, you could wander for days and never find the way in."

"I guess that's the idea." I fall behind him, keeping one hand on his shoulder. I don't care if he thinks I'm touchy-feely, overly familiar, or just scared shitless. The latter is true, and he's seen me melt down before.

"Exactly. This is our final fallback. They can reduce the compound to rubble, but they'll never find us." He sounds so calm at the prospect of living for an undisclosed period of time below ground.

The very idea makes me sweat. I can smell my fear, sour and sickly. My fingers trail along the sides of the tunnel as we move, puffs of powder drifting into the wan light. I fall quiet, listening to our footsteps scrape over the dry stone. Time slows, becomes impossible to measure.

Just Doc and me, surrounded by an island of night. I want to hide my face against his broad back. Instead I walk on, trying to think of this as a test. If I come out of it unscathed, I'll be stronger.

*At least there are no Morgut down here.*

I don't know how long we've been walking, but my throat aches. So I tug on his pack. "Do you have any water?"

"Of course. I should've offered. Let's rest a moment."

There isn't room for us to relax, but I sink down onto the tunnel floor and take a long drink from the lukewarm water in his flask. He probably has paste, too, but I can't face the thought of it, not yet. I'm simply not hungry enough.

If I was paying Jael, I would so fire him for leaving me with a pacifist to protect me. I hope he's all right. Dina and Vel, too. I can't think about March. My stomach wants to tie itself in knots over him, and I have to stay calm. It'd be far too easy to lose myself in the dark.

I squeeze my eyes shut to combat the panic boiling up in my throat. Steel bands tighten around my rib cage, making it hard to breathe. I swear the walls are getting closer together.

"Easy, Jax." Doc tugs me to my feet. "We need to keep moving."

So we do. More trudging. I'm just about to ask for a packet of that disgusting paste when the torch-tube flickers. Hope to Mary he has a replacement. I can't walk in the dark. As it is, I'm barely hanging on. The solid rock above me registers as a tangible, menacing presence. Our tomb.

We come up against a dead end. Shit. Doc doesn't know this honeycomb as well as he thought he did. We're lost.

I can't take this. I need the open sky. Need to see the stars and feel the wind on my face. I need to jump. This isn't where I'm supposed to die.

"What now?" I ask finally. "We can't stay holed up forever."

"Guerilla war," he tells me. "The monsters can't serve the McCulloughs in here, nor will their killing machines. So they'll come looking eventually. They can't claim clan assets as long as either chieftain lives. When they make that mistake, we'll kill them, one by one. Keri's trained her men for tunnel fighting."

"Won't they just starve you out?"

In answer, he depresses a hidden button in the wall and the door to another world swings open.

# CHAPTER 28

***There's an entire city hidden here.***

Well, on second glance, it's more of a scavenged, retrofitted, grungy underground settlement. The survivors have pitched tents and set up chemical heaters. Here and there, I see salvaged ship parts doing double duty as furniture. A couple of dirty-faced kids bounce on a broken nav chair.

They pause as we pass by, whispering. Then one of them calls, "Doc! The Dahlgren's looking for you."

He nods. "I'll find her. Thanks."

I'll never get used to the way her clan refers to Keri. My breath comes easier as I register a ceiling so high I can't even see it. I'll never take the open sky for granted again, though. Ambient noise gives the space a low roar, part people, part machinery, and the air smells faintly of spices, like someone is cooking.

The kids giggle and whisper a little more, and then: "So is Rose!"

"She's alive?" he breathes. "She made it! Where?"

They point. To my surprise, Doc alters course, practically running. March better be down here somewhere, or I'll never forgive him. Or myself.

I'm not Psi, so this is probably pointless, but I build his face in my mind's eye, feature by feature, and focus on him. All my fear, yearning, and need, I bundle up and send outward, hoping he'll sense it.

Silence answers me.

Shoulders slumped, I follow Doc through the throng. Everyone looks tired, worn. In the far corner, they've set up an infirmary, rows of bodies on blankets. Blood. The tang of antiseptic. It's all so astonishingly primitive that I can't believe people choose to live like this. But folks do crazy things in the name of freedom.

Naturally, Doc heads straight over. Two Dahlgrens are trying to patch up the wounded, administer treatments and medicine. A weary-looking woman with a sweet face, capped by red-and-silver-streaked hair, greets him with a kiss. Not a polite one either. She melts against him in a way that makes me look away, a private moment flaunted. I guess I know now what keeps him on Lachion.

"This is Rose," Doc says, drawing my eyes back.

I manage a smile. "Nice to meet you."

"Likewise." Her tone is cool, and I sense she wants to be rid of me.

Doc adds, "She could use my help here, but I'm sure you want to find the rest of the crew as soon as possible."

Nodding, I leave my fear unspoken. "Thanks for seeing me through the tunnel."

I part from him there and thread my way through the camp, searching through the smoky, intermittent light. In here it feels like perpetual twilight, faces emerging out of the shadows to peer at me, startled and curious. All strangers, all clansmen.

I find Vel first. He sits apart from everyone else, of course, watching them eat. I hurry toward him, remembering not to hug just before I grab him. That leaves me standing there, not knowing what to do with my hands.

He gets to his feet in a motion that doesn't entirely ring true as human, now that I know what to look for. To my surprise, he does the hugging, awkward and tentative, like a dance step he isn't sure he's mastered. And he doesn't have it quite right either. His hands cup the back of my head, smoothing my shorn hair as if I'm a baby bird with ruffled feathers.

It's oddly comforting. Even though I know what he is under the skin, it doesn't matter. In fact, I register awe at his versatility; the ability to assimilate new customs seems enviable.

"Our situation is less than ideal," he says, when I finally step back.

I have to smile. Typical Velith statement. He probably thought it a "trifle inconvenient" when we were holed up in a cave on the Teresengi Basin.

"You can say that again."

He cocks his head at me. "Why?"

Right, he tends to be literal. "Never mind. Have you seen the others?"

"No. I made one sweep before settling here. Are you hungry?"

I am, actually. "Is it real food?"

"S-meat with potatoes and peppers," he answers. "You'll want to eat something. They're closing up in a few minutes."

That decides the matter. I take a bowl and get in line behind the other stragglers. Short and gristly, the woman scraping food from the grill looks a little like Keri's grandmother, the clan matriarch who sacrificed herself for us. She narrows her eyes on me.

"In case you don't know how this works," she snaps at me, "that bowl is yours now, Ambassador." Her tone gains an ugly stress. "Keep up with it, and keep it clean, or you don't eat. You're just like everyone else down here."

For Mary's sake. I'm steaming by the time I rejoin Vel in the far corner. They act like I've put on airs and demanded all kinds of special treatment when in fact we'd barely landed before all hell broke loose.

As I sit, I realize I have no utensils, so I take a quick look around to see what everyone else is doing. They use their fingers to scoop the food into their mouths, which seems basic enough. It's messy, but practical.

"What was it like out there, Vel?" I have to know. My imagination will create a thousand terrible scenarios to torment me otherwise. "I was in the lab with Doc."

He steeples his hands in a familiar gesture that tells me he's thinking the question over. "Bad," he says finally. "Those creatures swarm, as if from a hive mind. When the bombardment started, I thought the buildings would break wide open and the beasts would devour us. I am more than a little amazed to be alive." His stark, quiet tone makes it worse somehow.

A shudder runs through me. I don't ask anything more, not while I'm eating. I'm not sure I can hear more, not until I know whether we all made it. When I finish, I watch the others scrape their bowls clean with dry granules, but I don't have any. I hate being unprepared. Vel tips some into my bowl wordlessly, and I smile my thanks.

Gotta love his bounty-hunter travel pack. I should get one.

I feel a little better now, slightly stronger. "I'm going to look for the rest of the crew. They must be around here somewhere."

The alternative is unthinkable.

He regards me for a moment with an inscrutable expression. "Have you applied for a place to sleep?"

"What? No. Do I need to talk to someone about that?"

Leaning around me, he points to another line fifty meters away. "Lex is handling that."

I can't miss him. Lex is a mountain of a man with big, rough features; he also happens to be Keri's co-chieftain. If she ever gets over hating him, they'll wed to seal the deal. She doesn't seem likely to do that anytime soon with March on scene.

"Have you already arranged for . . . accommodation?" A kind euphemism for the shantytown we have going down here.

Vel pats his pack. "I have everything I need."

Well, of course he does. "You want to come with me?"

"It seems pointless to waste energy moving about when that might make it more difficult for the others to find me."

That makes sense, but I don't know if I can sit and wait. Patience isn't one of my well-developed virtues. "Vel . . . is there room with you? If I ask Lex, I'll end up sharing space with the clansmen."

If what Doc said is true, the McCulloughs went full throttle because they were afraid I was intervening on the side of Gunnar-Dahlgren, bringing supplies or reinforcements. I don't want to guilt him, though, so I leave the crucial part unspoken: *And they aren't too happy with me right now.* Since it was just a personal visit, serving a dual purpose, and I didn't bring anything but trouble, it's safe to say Gunnar-Dahlgren wishes me to perdition.

But I needed to make sure Tarn told me the truth, and I wasn't abandoning my obligations to Keri. I had to make sure I wasn't forsaking people who helped me out of a jam. And on a personal level, I needed Doc to check me out. I just don't trust anyone else. If I'd known stopping would prove so disastrous, you can bet I would've gone another way.

But hindsight is twenty-twenty.

The silence grows awkward. I toy with the idea of reminding him he's supposed to watch my back, and he owes me for sticking by him on Emry, but I don't say another word. I figure he knows those things already.

No clue what thoughts run behind his eyes, but the silence starts to make me uncomfortable. Maybe he's not used to such . . . intimacy? I can't imagine that he is, given his race and what he does for a living. I'll say it's that, and nothing personal. Mary knows, enough people hate me as it is.

"You can stay with me," he says finally. "Are you still going to look around?"

"Yeah."

"If I see"—he pauses—"anyone, I'll tell them where to find you."

His hesitation tells me he's worried about March. That makes two of us.

I'm none too eager for my own company, considering that everyone blames me for the increased furor of the McCullough attack. It feels like the Hate Jax backlash that followed the crash of the *Sargasso*—only this time, it really is my fault. Nothing I did on purpose, but bad mojo follows me just the same.

With a wave, I set off into the crowd. I have people to find, or I'll die trying.

# CHAPTER 29

***The place is bigger than it looks.***

Concealed rooms branch off from the main bunker, offering an illusion of privacy. From the looks I receive, I'm not welcome either. So I slide back out like a shadow, weaving between the tents.

I want to scream. My stomach has tied itself into knots, worrying about the man—

Who steps out of a large tent, right behind Keri. He's blood-spattered, wounded, and filthy, but more or less whole. As March turns, the whole world slows, receding into the background.

I see his lips move, mouthing my name, even as he pushes past the people between us. Not walking. Running. I'm afraid to smile, but I meet him halfway. He wraps me so tight in his arms that it hurts, but I don't complain. Not when I can feel his heart beating against mine. He spins me in his arms as if I weigh nothing.

"Jax," he whispers.

With shaking fingers, I touch the pale bandage at his temple. It looks like he'll have another scar for the collection. In turn he brushes rough fingertips across my cheek. I'm surprised to see them come away wet.

I have no words.

For now it doesn't matter how complicated things have become between us. It only matters that he's here.

His breath hitches. All around us, people enjoy their own tearful reunions, paying us no mind. The same can't be said for Keri, whose angry gaze bores into my back. She has another reason to hate me, among so many others.

"They're waiting for us in tactical," she tells him, gesturing at one of those semiprivate alcoves.

I can't imagine what strategy will get Gunnar-Dahlgren out of this mess, but the clans never give up. I admire that.

To my surprise he doesn't let go. "Do this one without me."

He gives her no opportunity to argue. I intended to look for Jael and Dina as well, but he swings me into his arms and carries me toward one of the larger tents. If I wasn't so damn happy to see him, I'd probably struggle. As it is, I lay my head on his shoulder and close my eyes for a moment. He smells of smoke and unseen battles.

March ducks a little to get inside, sets me on my own two feet, and then seals the flap after us. It's dim within, a plain canvas shelter that underlines the gravity of our situation. I've been in a lot of messes in my day—at this point it's sort of my specialty—but I do believe this one frosts them all.

"You made it." He sounds hoarse.

I imagine him shouting orders until his voice gave out, helping organize the retreat. March knows about killing. I have only a passing acquaintance with that side of him.

"I have Doc to thank for that. I never would've made it through those tunnels without him. I wanted to run out and look for you." With a long sigh, I drop onto the sleep mat he's unrolled.

He smiles. In the faint light, his face looks even rougher than usual, all harsh planes and angles. His eyes glitter like uncut amber, pure cognac gold. "Of course you did. I'm so fucking tired, Jax."

"So sleep." Okay, so that's not how I imagined this would go, but I don't want to fight with him anymore.

"I haven't been alone with you in weeks," he says. "Do you really think I'm going to doze off? I can actually see your heart beating . . ." As he collapses beside me, he touches the base of my throat. "Sometimes I forget—"

"What?" I tilt my head back, registering a pleasurable shock.

*How fragile you are.* When he fills my mind in a hot rush, I realize how lonely I've been. How much I've missed him. I don't even take umbrage at being called fragile. Right now I am, physically, and there's no value in denying the obvious.

But that reminds me. "Why didn't you . . . make contact? Let me know you were alive?"

He pulls me back into his arms as if he's loath to lose hold of me even for a minute. "Sometimes I forget you don't know everything about me. If you think back, I've never touched you across long distances."

Shit. He's right. Most of our contact occurs when we're on ship together or in the same room. Here I thought—well, never mind. Relief surges through me. March wasn't punishing me with the silence, which is good, because I don't know if I could've forgiven him that.

"Do you still love me?" When the question comes gusting out, my face burns like I've been splashed with acid.

March leans his head against mine. "What do you think?"

"You're the psychic. It's mean to toy with me."

He eases down until our noses touch, lips mere millimeters away from a kiss. "I don't always agree with your decisions, and you drive me out of my mind sometimes. Like you pushing me away when I want so bad to be there for you. I'm *still* trying to understand that. But yeah, I love you."

"Don't you understand?" I ask tiredly. "I'm trying *not* to hurt you."

"The last few weeks, you've been breaking my heart." Such a stark tone, unadorned truth.

I have no defense against that. Mary help me, I want him so bad.

And he knows.

I see it just before his mouth takes mine in a kiss that I feel like I've waited for my whole life. Heat. Need. He cups my face in his hands.

At this moment I don't care about the people outside these fragile walls. The world shrinks to him and me. My fingertips brush the curve of his ear, and he shivers in reaction. I know all his hot spots now.

He laughs softly, trailing his lips down my throat. I suck in a shaky breath. Yeah, he knows mine, too.

"This is only a temporary truce," I whisper into his jaw.

He gives me a slow simmering smile. "I can live with that."

March pulls my vest over my head, skimming my skin with his palms. For just a moment I feel scrawny and self-conscious, but it's nothing he hasn't seen before, scars and all. Plus he has more than his share, and I relearn them all as I tug his shirt over his head.

Even in the dim light, I can tell he's a mass of bruises. I don't even know how he can stand for me to touch him. I hesitate, my good hand hovering over his chest.

"You're sure? I won't hurt you?"

A soft laugh escapes him, as if he can't believe I've asked. I know he's twice my size, but he's wounded, dammit. And I've been known to bite.

"We're both a little bit broken," he says quietly. "But we'll take care not to cut each other on the sharp edges."

I smile. "We'll manage."

Quiet lightning surges between us, a longing that cannot be channeled or contained. He touches me with exquisite gentleness, lips trailing heat wherever he claims me with his hands. I arch against him, melting.

His penis feels so hard, it almost hurts where it jabs me. I undo his pants with unsteady hands. In this moment I need nothing more than March.

Primitive.

*Mine.*

"Yes," he gasps, though I don't know if it's because of my thoughts or my fingers curling around him. I love how I short-circuit his higher brain functions. "You, on top. I want to watch you."

"Lazy bastard," I manage to tease as I climb on.

His eyes drift shut as I sink down, sheathing him. He fills me, pure heat. I start slow and easy, but I can't control myself for long, not that he'll let me. March cradles my hips in his hands, moving me on him. Showing me how he wants it.

"Take me, Jax." I can't resist his whispered plea.

*Faster.*

*More.*

I don't know whether that's him or me, but we both crave it. Our breathing changes tempo, staccato urgency. Once we find a hungry rhythm, his hands roam my body as if he owns me. Or wants to.

When his fingers drift down my belly, stroking lower still, I bear down and let the orgasm come. Liquid lust wracks me in hard, frantic waves.

March offers a wicked smile, holding me upright. "Don't pass out, baby. I'm just getting started. Lost time and all that."

I manage to snort, though I feel shaky as hell. "You wish. I'm still woman enough to wear you out."

"Take your best shot."

His eyes shine as he settles back, preparing to make me work for it. I roll my hips on him as aftershocks spark through me. But he's not ready for what I do next.

Lean down, nip his throat. Grind. I suck, tugging his skin with my teeth. That's going to leave a mark.

He shudders, breath rushing in noisy gusts.

I whisper, "Every time I've touched myself in the last four months, I thought of you. Every. Time."

And then he's all mine, groaning, shaking, and breathless beneath me.

# CHAPTER 30

***When I come to, he's dressed and about to slip out*** on me.

That's probably fitting, given the way I ran out on March the first time we had sex. The universe has a way of rewarding people with what they deserve. I'm not sure what this says about me.

No, I do, actually. It says things I don't enjoy hearing.

I push up onto my elbow. "You weren't going to wake me?"

"I didn't want to bother you." That sounds like an excuse.

"I need you more than sleep." The words feel barbed coming out of my mouth. There, I said it, damn him.

"You don't need me," he says with quiet finality. "You want me. You might even love me. But you don't need me. I wish you did."

Is this because I wouldn't lean on him? Didn't want to become physically dependent?

He goes on, "They need me in planning sessions. Though we've retreated, we can't just hunker down here.

We need to talk strategy and coordinate the war effort. The McCulloughs won't settle for anything less than a full hostile takeover, so we have to exterminate them." He sounds so cold.

A chill courses through me. March tries so hard to suppress this side of his personality, the darkness where he lost his soul once before. In the shadows his face looks almost inhuman, taut and graven. I've never seen him wear an expression quite like this, as if he's switched his feelings off.

"Don't let me keep you." I want to get dressed, but I won't crawl out from under the blanket. His eyes sear like lasers.

He hesitates, as if there's something more he wants to say. And then: "I'm glad you're safe, Jax."

I just nod. Not exactly an impassioned declaration, but this isn't the moment for them either. As soon as he leaves, I scramble for my clothes, still scattered where we threw them earlier. I'm not sure how long I've been out.

Noise levels outside indicate some of the clan has retired for a few hours at least. I dress quickly and push my way out of the tent. They've left guards posted, which makes sense, in case Doc is wrong, and the McCulloughs *do* find us. The diminished crowds mean I can make my way around easier.

In the hours I slept, they've done more work on the encampment. Makeshift barricades now sit before the two exits to the tunnels, along with motion detectors. Well, at least nobody's sneaking up our backsides.

I don't know what I'm supposed to do next. Clearly I'm not welcome in the strategy meetings, not that I would have anything of value to offer. Of the clansmen still awake, most seem to know who I am, based on their glaring. I move away from March's tent, feeling rather aimless.

I'm a fucking jumper, for Mary's sake. I don't belong down here. This isn't even my fight. I had nothing to do with the McCulloughs deciding my visit portended Conglomerate interference in local politics. I sigh.

Maybe my basic medical training would make me somewhat useful to Doc, so I head that way. I swing around a crate of disorganized supplies and spot my favorite guardian. To be honest, I register a tiny flicker of relief.

"I've been looking everywhere for you," Jael says, vaulting over the parts. "Tarn's going to fire me if I don't get you out of here."

I can't help but arch my brows. "*That's* your concern? Take a look around, genius. We're in danger of being killed by clansmen, one way or another. If Gunnar-Dahlgren doesn't do it, the McCulloughs will."

"Not on my watch."

A snicker escapes me. "You're the worst bodyguard ever."

"Right, I admit I may not have been as vigilant as I ought. But I had no idea this was a high-risk environment. I didn't do enough research on this fucked-up, Mary-forsaken hellhole."

"You're not enjoying our goodwill tour then?" It ought to be against the law to derive so much amusement from one person.

"Puzzled that out for yourself, did you?"

I realize I haven't asked about the important stuff, so I leave off messing with him. "Is Dina all right? What about the ship?"

He sucks in a sharp breath, as if being reminded hurts him, and shakes his head. "I'm sorry. I don't know whether she'll make it."

My stomach lurches. "Dina? Or the ship."

"The ship's a dead loss," he answers. "I carried our girl in, but she bled out a lot before I tied the wound off. She's lost a leg, for sure, and I don't know if they can replace it."

"You ass!" I can't believe he stood there talking about getting me off planet when Dina might be dying.

I try to push past him, but he snags my shoulders. "Hey, where you going? She's sedated, Jax. You mean to go wake her up with your wailing, inhibit the healing process, and annoy the doc?"

"I just need to see her, that's all."

His icy gaze searches mine for a moment before he gives a short nod. "Right. I'm not letting you out of my sight again, so I'll come along."

I shrug. It doesn't matter if I have a shadow. We weave through the narrow passages leading back to medical. I don't see Doc anywhere, but his friend Rose greets me with a cool glance.

"You're checking on your ship's mechanic?"

My teeth clench. Maybe the vids still show me as a spoiled little nav-star, but I don't use people like that anymore, thinking only of what they can do for me. Dina's my friend. But before I can start a fight—and I'm tempted—Jael says smoothly, "Yeah. Any change?"

Like I'm not even there, she gestures for him to follow her toward the back. As I slink along in their wake, I decide I must be the worst ambassador in the history of diplomacy. Well, except for Karl Fitzwilliam, who started the Axis Wars.

*Now there's a comforting thought.*

The number of wounded has diminished since I dropped Doc here. I hope they recovered, not died, but I don't put much faith in the reality of that outcome. It's going to take a miracle to save us, and maybe the ones who have already gone through that final door are the lucky ones. I'd take a fast death over one that lingers.

*She's so pale.*

At first she doesn't even seem to be breathing. Her fair hair has been brushed back from her brow, and for the first time, I notice she has a heart-shaped face. Her gruff manner disguises the fact somewhat, but in repose, Dina is quite pretty. No wonder Jael can't resist flirting with her, even though he knows it's a lost cause.

"Did you manage to find a prosthetic?"

On some level, I acknowledge it makes sense for him to make the inquiries because he's the one who saved her life. *He's* the one who carried her to safety. A hot, angry sensation boils in my stomach because I wasn't there for someone I care about, as if I could've changed things somehow.

It's not logical. I didn't let Vel down on Emry, and I know I can't be everywhere at once, but damn March anyway. He's infected me with his devastating sense of moral responsibility.

"It's far from ideal," Rose says softly. "But we managed to salvage a limb from . . . elsewhere. So far, no signs of rejection, but we weren't able to do extensive tissue testing. We had to graft or cauterize the nerves. Doc made the call."

*Elsewhere.*

How do you gaze into a pile of dead bodies and decide what leg to harvest? My breath gusts out in a shaky sound, drawing their attention. "Is she stable?"

Rose doesn't meet my gaze. "I'll be honest, Ambassador. We've only been able to save one person, after such a mauling. I'm astonished your friend has lasted this long, between shock, blood loss, and myriad other factors. If you put any stock in any gods at all, now is the time to address yourself to them."

I nod. "Is there anything I can do?"

"Just stay out of the way and let me do my job," she answers.

That's clearly a dismissal, so I turn, sensing Jael fall in step. I know what it was like out there for him amid the rush of wings, carnage at every turn. Yet he came through it, and though he doesn't seem inclined to view himself that way, he's a hero, too. Damn, why am I surrounded by them on all sides?

"You risked your life to save her," I say in neutral tones. "Why?"

He gives me a faint smile. "The fact that you'd even ask proves you don't know anything about me."

# CHAPTER 31

***If you've never tried living underground, I don't recommend it.***

While soldiers conduct a guerilla war in the tunnels, picking off the McCullough scout teams, the rest of us work to build a life in this primitive pit. The raw violence stuns me. I hear distant fighting, day and night, and the screams of dying men. I don't know what they do with the corpses, can't even imagine.

For the first few days, I perform manual labor alongside the clansmen. We make weapons, chemical stoves, and other necessities. At night I bed down with Vel, who handles my presence with inscrutable aplomb.

I don't know whether Tarn knows anything about the mess on Lachion, but even if he does, I can't expect rescue from that angle. This is a fair-sized planet, and locating us where we've gone to ground would be worse than trying to find a needle in a haystack. We'll need to save ourselves, business as usual.

March stays busy with tactical meetings and leads the strike teams himself. This merc, this killer, I hardly know him. Each time he leaves the bunker, I feel sure he's not coming back. I hate how he strides into danger, leaving me behind, but Jael would bodily restrain me if I tried to join the fight.

On the third day, a mission goes bad. I don't know whether we got faulty intel, or what happened out there, but we're drowning in wounded. Lex passes me at a run, barking out, "Doc needs you!" as he goes to work on damage control.

If the McCulloughs find this bunker, we're done.

A chill ripples over me. Surely Doc didn't go out with the grunts himself. That would be madness. But my heart pounds double time as I head for the big gray tent functioning as the clan hospital.

As I push through the parted flaps, I break out into a cold sweat. There are at least twenty bodies in varying stages of dismemberment, and the air feels thick and heavy in my nostrils, sweet with clotting blood. Doc looks up from his work briefly and then goes back to whatever he's doing inside that poor kid.

I say kid because the person Doc's working on can't be much older than Keri, but he's old enough to fight for his clan. Old enough to die, if the operation doesn't go well. I haven't seen March yet today; he could be somewhere among all these bodies. I shudder and try to force that thought away. If he were dead, surely I'd know. I'd feel something. But our connection has thinned, and he doesn't seek me out anymore.

Rose turns then, jerking her head toward the back of the tent. "Change into some scrubs. There's a sealed set in the cupboard. Then stand inside the san-shower on sterile setting for at least sixty seconds."

Maybe the dry heat will do something to calm my nerves. I have a feeling that whatever they intend to ask me to do, I'm not going to like it, particularly if it requires me to dress like a doctor and scrub up like one, too. But I don't protest.

It takes me less than two minutes to get geared up. "What now?"

Doc answers without pausing what he's doing. "There's a device on the table next to Rose. It's dead simple, just point and shoot. I need you to use it to take readings on all our wounded. It will help us calculate triage."

I'm not trained for this. I want to argue, but I don't. If it will help, then I can't say no. I don't even bother asking "why me?" Approaching the wounded men lined up on drab olive blankets, I feel my hands trembling.

Like Doc said, though, it's really basic. From a single point of contact, the gizmo registers temperature, heart rate, and scads of other medical data. All I have to do is enter the patient's number, as present on his clan ID. I feel like I'm tagging corpses, even though some of them move or moan or beg me to make the pain stop.

The third soldier is wide-awake and, Mary help him, coherent. With a wound like the one in his side, I don't know how. He grabs my wrist, fingers grinding against bone. "Did Jerro make it? Where is he? I promised his ma I'd take care of him."

"He's fine," Doc says. "Just try to relax. You're up next."

Whether that's the truth or a platitude, the guy relaxes his grip on me and fades out. I hope he isn't dead. The gadget reassures me he's stable for the time being, and I move on to the next patient.

Soon, we get into a groove. I see why they needed me now, or at least another pair of hands. I choose the next patient, based on need, Doc does patch work, and then Rose finishes up, sealing wounds and incisions. There's also a clansman doing transport, moving patients from the hospital into the recovery area.

By the time we finish, I'm aching from head to toe. People who say being on the med team is easy ought to be shot. Of course that would just make more work for us, so maybe I could let 'em go with a warning.

Before I head back to the tent I share with Vel, I ask, "Why me?"

"You're not clan," Doc says quietly. "Do you really

think I could ask someone who knew these men to help decide who lives and dies?"

I never thought of that. But yeah, the little gadget had determined two of the soldiers wouldn't make it, regardless of treatment, so they got bumped to the bottom of the list. Rose shot them full of painkiller, and they died quietly, which was all we could do for them. I try to imagine someone who knew them, who had lived, worked, fought, and possibly loved those men, being asked to watch them die. My heart seizes up into a Gordian knot.

"I'm glad I could help." My voice sounds rusty. "But I'm busted. I'll be back in the morning if you need me again."

"If you could." He looks so damn tired, too, but he's not leaving.

We find heroes, not on battlefields, but in hospitals that tend the injured. Sometimes I think it's easier to fight than it is to heal. I check the recovery area one last time, making sure nobody needs anything.

Dina has finally come around. Thanks to her rugged constitution, they've developed an antivenom for those who survive Teras attacks. She can't walk yet, but they're hopeful. She doesn't want me around, though. Dina isn't unfair enough to lay all this on me, but she's a bitchy patient, and I seem to rub her the wrong way, no matter my intentions.

I spend the fourth day working in recovery, changing bandages, fetching this or that, and generally entertaining crotchety soldiers who are convinced the war will be lost if they don't get off their cots. March avoids me, and my heart breaks by millimeters. I should confront him. I *will*. When I work up the nerve.

And on the fifth day, Doc takes me aside.

"Things have slowed a bit, so I've had a chance to take a look at your test results, some of the data I couldn't interpret before."

"Oh?"

The bustle of clansmen going about their business muffles

our words somewhat. In the distance I hear the discharge of weapons, echoing oddly through the tunnels. I've never been surrounded by war, not like this. It's a precarious feeling, and I'm itchy with the need to get the hell out of here.

"I've got good news and bad news, Jax."

I brace myself. "Bad first."

"If you want to live, you have to stop jumping."

Of all the things he could've said, this shocks me the most. We all *know* jumping will kill us someday; it's sort of a given. "Yeah, I get that."

Doc shakes his head. "No, I don't think you do. You know how you're receiving daily injections to combat that inexplicable bone condition?" I nod. He's already told me that such diseases are rare in young people. "Let me try to put this in laymen's terms. A normal human brain suffers irrevocable damage after repeated exposures to the stress of grimspace. You're no exception to this. But you differ from other navigators in a DNA . . . mutation that permits you to cannibalize other physical resources to heal the damage you take."

It takes me a few moments to process that. "When I pass out for three days after a bad jump—"

"That's the unique metabolic process at work. But in order to heal, the resources must be taken from elsewhere," he says with a grave look.

"So my body breaks down my bones to fix my brain, so I can keep jumping. And there's no cure?" I can't look at him. My gaze roves the crowd behind him, watching a man assemble shocksticks and taser pistols from spare parts.

"How could there be? I've never heard of a jumper who could do this, and I've studied thousands of medical records."

He doesn't need to spell it out for me. The next time I lapse into a near coma, there's no telling what system might be ransacked in order to regenerate my brain. Vascular or respiratory pillage might kill me on the spot.

"There's no way to regulate it?"

Doc shrugs. "Perhaps. This is uncharted territory, Jax.

I might eventually be able to develop an implant to control what systems are tapped, defaulting to the less vital ones."

The rest goes unspoken. That would require time and facilities, and right now, my welfare simply isn't at the top of his list. He has a whole clan to care for, new wounded coming in daily, and a war raging around us. In the meantime I shouldn't jump, or it will just get worse. I'll die, just not like most jumpers.

*So how the hell are we getting off this rock?* I exhale shakily.

"What's the good news?"

"Over time, we can repair the degeneration to your skeletal system," he tells me. "Maintain the treatments as prescribed, and you won't always be so—"

"Breakable?"

"That is not a word I'd apply to you." He smiles faintly.

Well, he can't see inside me. The man I love risks his life on an hourly basis, and he drifts further away with every heartbeat. Though I can't articulate the impression, I'm losing him. Kill by kill, someone else trickles in to eclipse the light where he used to be.

He needs to walk away from this war. But March cannot excise his sense of obligation to Keri, springing from his inability to repay Mair, Keri's grandmother, for everything she did for him. I remember his words, back on the waterlogged world of Marakeq. I'd asked him why he was always in my head.

*"It means our theta waves are compatible,"* he'd said. *"It's almost always a one-way feed. I get impressions from other people, what kind and how deep depends on how disciplined their minds are and how much I want to know. Used to be uncontrollable, couldn't shut it off."*

*"How did you—"*

*"Mair. She wouldn't teach me the higher forms, but she saw what a mess I was and taught me how to quiet my mind. Shut out the noise through meditation."*

*"I'm sorry. I didn't know."*

*"Before she took me in hand, I wasn't even human, Jax.*

*You have no idea how many people I've ended. Broke minds to set an example, for the hell of it, or just because I needed a quiet kill. I spent years on Nicuan, feeding their endless wars. By the time I stole a ship because they shorted my pay, there was nothing left. Mair rebuilt me, brick by brick."*

Oh, irony, you're such a bitch.

"Thanks," I tell Doc then. I think he reads something in my expression, but he doesn't ask, thank Mary. "I'll let you get back to work. I know you've got people a lot sicker than me to deal with."

"I've prepared sixty days' worth of your treatment, Jax. Just inject yourself once a day, and you should start to see some improvement."

*As long as I don't jump.* Fuck that, it would be kinder to kill me outright. I make myself smile and thank him. Turning, I lose myself in bodies going about their business. The clansmen are tough, stolid as rocks, and they seem to have adapted well to this lifestyle.

Sometime later, Jael finds me as I sit mechanically assembling weapons I'll never use. This isn't my fight; I'm just caught in the middle of it. But if I ever need to, I can get work on low-tech worlds where they make use of cheap human labor.

Part of me acknowledges that's an exaggeration. I still have my post as ambassador, unless Tarn has washed his hands of me. I wouldn't know at this point. They can always hire another jumper to ferry me from place to place, but that option rouses a sick, miserable feeling in the pit of my stomach.

"You look like your best friend died," he says, dropping down beside me.

Given our current situation, that seems particularly tactless. I just shrug. I don't feel like talking, particularly not to him. I can't let myself bond with someone who reminds me so much of Kai.

He misinterprets my gloom. "Look, they seem to think Dina's going to make it. Cheer up, won't you?"

"Is it mandatory?" I'm not ready to share my prognosis

with anyone. It's bad enough that I have to haul a med kit around and shoot up like a chem-head.

"Nope. But this might help. We're getting out of here. Two days, tops."

"How?"

"Your Bug friend has some astonishing resources in that bag of his. We've been monitoring enemy transmissions, and they're discussing a fallback, as the tunnel war isn't going well. When they retreat, we'll sneak out and head for the surface."

"And be left wide open for Teras to pick off? Or any McCullough men that happen to be in the vicinity?" That might be the worst idea I've ever heard.

Jael sighs. "Give us a little credit, will you?"

"What's that supposed to mean?"

I don't have much faith left, I'm afraid. This scheme sounds stupid, dangerous, and highly likely to get me killed, full of adrenaline-inducing moments, and the hot rush of risk. Which means I should be all for it. Haven't I always said I didn't become a jumper to die old and gray? I stop protesting.

"It means we have a plan. I *will* get you out of here, Jax. You have my word."

I manage a smile, but I don't believe much in promises anymore either. "What about Dina? She's not going to be ready to run in two days."

If he suggests leaving her, I'll punch him in the eye. I am not the woman from the vids. People are *not* disposable to me.

"That's going to pose a bit of a problem," he says. "But we'll figure that out, too. I need to get back to Vel. Did you want to be in on the brainstorming?"

My brittle smile softens into something close to real. "Yeah. I would."

He tugs me to my feet. "Well, let's do it. Forget this," he adds, sweeping an arm to indicate the dim, grungy encampment. "Soon it'll seem like a bad dream."

Sure enough, I have plenty of those.

# CHAPTER 32

***We've made our plans.***

In four hours, we're out of here. Vel and Jael have fashioned a back harness, and they'll take turns carrying Dina. Now we just need to say good-bye to Doc, quietly, and collect March, not necessarily in that order. It goes without saying that I'm in charge of the latter.

He's probably in some meeting, so I leave the other two and go looking for him. Chemical stoves emit a burnt polymer smell as I weave my way through the tents. This nomadic encampment has taken on certain clan characteristics by this point. They've allocated a training circle where the rehabilitating men spar to keep from killing each other, and the women occupy themselves across the way devising new uses for old rubbish.

In the distance I hear sounds of combat, cries of pain and rage. Overhead the bombardment has stopped at last, making me think we may have a chance. If Vel's intel is correct, and we time our run to a McCullough retreat, we might get off this rock.

I settle outside the tactical tent and wait. Passing clansmen no longer glare at me, at least. Someone taps me on the shoulder. I glance up and find someone who looks more like a raider queen than a Lachion native.

She's incredibly tall, dusky-skinned, and she wears her hair in a short pouf. Her bare arms reveal whipcord strength. Slim metal rods pierce her nose, lower lip, and left brow. She glimmers with silver at throat, fingers, and wrists, highlighting her exotic allure. In the diffuse light, her eyes gleam tawny gold, like a predatory cat.

"Can I help you?" I don't recognize her, but that doesn't mean much. I haven't met everyone down here.

She folds herself into the lotus position beside me. "Whispers say you're making a break. I want to hitch a ride."

I recognize her accent, match it to a small world in the Outskirts. If I recall correctly, a bunch of artists and poets settled the place. I wonder if she can fight.

"May not be a smooth run. We could die out there."

"We could die down here. I know which *I* prefer."

The woman has a point. I offer my hand. "I'm Jax."

A faint smile creases her mouth. "I know who you are."

But she takes my hand, firm grip. Calluses. Okay, so maybe not a useless arty type after all. "And you?"

"My name is Suraya, but my friends call me Hit."

I have a feeling I'm going to regret asking. "Why's that?"

Her smile widens. "Because I only ever need one to take someone down."

Oh, that type.

"What're you doing on Lachion?"

She shrugs. "Bad idea, this supply run. My whole crew died in the attack. I can pilot, so I won't be deadweight." Hit shows me the shunt in her wrist as if I might doubt her word.

Well, it's never a bad idea to have a backup pilot on board. "I'll need to talk it over with the others. I'm going to assume they don't object, so meet us at the south exit in three and a half hours."

Her eyes gleam. "Done. I won't forget this, Ambassador."

I'm *still* not used to being addressed like that. "Don't thank me yet. We have klicks of enemy territory to cover, and then we still have to find a way off this rock."

"You're the kind of person who makes things happen," she says.

*Am I?*

Just now I feel like I'm the world champion at waiting. Hit climbs to her feet and sets off, presumably to collect her gear. I sit and brood.

An hour later, March comes out of the tent, no surprises there. His expression doesn't warm when he notices me. In fact, he looks mildly annoyed, but that might be projection more than accurate interpretation on my part.

"Jax." He bends to greet me with a light kiss on the mouth. "You caught me just before I take another team out."

"Forget that, let someone else do it. Say your good-byes and pack your stuff. We're getting the hell out of here. Meet us at the south exit in two and a half hours." I clamber to my feet and jerk my head toward the tunnel for emphasis.

His eyes go very dark and still. March studies me for a moment in silence, and then the saddest smile curves his lips. He takes my hands in his and seals a kiss into each palm. I can't *feel* him at all; he hasn't touched my mind in days, and the physical contact seems sharper in contrast.

"Good luck," he says quietly.

*Two words. How can two words make me feel like this?*

For a moment, I can't breathe for the bands tightening around my chest. My eyes sting. I tug my hands away from him and curl them into fists. Against my best efforts to wear a poker face, I feel the tears slipping down my cheeks.

"You don't mean—" I try to say, but my voice comes out strange and strangled.

People passing by give us odd looks, and March tries to take my arm, draw me to a quicter place to talk. *Fuck that.*

I jerk away and glare at him through blurry eyes, jaw clenched.

*Say it here, damn you. Right now.*

He offers an almost imperceptible nod. "I'm staying. I owe it to Mair's memory, *and* the clan, after all they've done for me. They took me in, after I walked away from the merc life. And Mair asked me to look after Keri, when she was just ten years old. You don't need me, Jax. Keri does. This is *my* war—I have the training, the experience, and I'll make the difference between their survival and annihilation here. I have to see this through. But you don't need my help getting to Ithiss-Tor; another pilot can get you there."

So he's cutting me loose. I raise my chin and wipe my face with the backs of my hands. In my heart, I know I've already lost him.

He's going to die down here, and it's killing me. I feel a scream building in my lungs, raw and angry. I don't want him to become a martyr. I want him beside me.

No surprise when he reads me. I'm an open book where he's concerned. His expression softens, and March pulls me into his arms. At first I resist on principle because the bastard is *leaving* me—

"No," he whispers. "I'm not. You'll see me again, I swear. This isn't forever."

Tears course down my cheeks. I squeeze them shut, but it doesn't help. They don't stop falling.

Because I don't believe him. I know a good-bye when I feel one.

His mouth finds mine, blind and hungry. March hasn't kissed me in days, but suddenly it's like the only thing he knows how to do. Lips clinging, he tastes salty and bittersweet from my weeping. Again and again, until we gasp for air and lean our foreheads together.

Grief roars inside me. His breath stirs against my damp cheeks, and I try to memorize everything about this moment. How he feels against me, his scent, and the weight of his arms curled around my back.

I never thought he'd leave me. Whatever he thinks, I *do* need him. Just not in the way he wants. I can't be someone other than I am; I can't love him except the way I know how.

"I know," he whispers, setting his cheek against my downy hair. "It's enough. It is. But I have to pay my debts. If I take everything Mair gave me and walk away from her kin when they're in need, then I've forsaken what little honor she taught me. Can't you understand that? I can't be that guy again."

"Yeah, I get it. But it's killing you," I choke out. "A centimeter at a time. So even if by some miracle you survive, you won't be March, not *this* March. You'll be—" I break off, tipping my head back to search his gaze with mine.

But I don't have the words for the darkness I sense coming for him. What good is honor when compassion is lost? And he knows. I see it in the gravity of his expression.

But he pretends he doesn't, another stone in the wall between us. "I'll come back to you," he promises again.

"Sure." I manage a smile. Soon the pain will crystallize into a diamond in my chest, allowing me to function. "Have you thought about paint?" When he looks puzzled, I add, "To combat the Teras? As things stand, it's all but impossible to fight them without heat-sensitive equipment that you don't have on world. But you could jury-rig a weapon that sprays them, making them easier to target."

The clans left the Teras alone because the danger meant nobody else wanted to settle here. And then the McCulloughs figured out how to harness them, catching the others flat-footed. Maybe March can benefit from this idea.

Mary, I feel raw.

"I'll mention it in strat meetings," he says. "It might make the difference when we start trying to retake surface holdings. Please, Jax, don't look like that."

*Like what? Like my heart is breaking?*

He delves into his pocket and produces a ring that shines, cheap and tawdry even in this light. The red stones shimmer like glass. Without ceremony he shoves it onto my middle finger, where it hangs loose.

"Svet collected trinkets like this. I bought it for her on Gehenna," he says softly. "Last gift I ever got her, and I didn't have a chance to give it to her. It's never left my possession since I heard—" March rubs a thumb over my cheek. "Anyway. I want you to have it . . . for now. I'll repo it someday, Jax. Get you something nicer. That's a promise."

I close my fingers to keep the ring from sliding off. "I'll hold you to that."

He kisses me one last time, and I pretend I believe him, at least until he disappears from sight.

Deep down I'm sure I'll never see him again, and it feels like my heart is dying.

# CHAPTER 33

***I've said my farewells.***

Doc said to check back with him regarding an implant, but I won't do that in person. I'll continue my injections and bounce a message to him when they've restored communications. When things have settled down, I'll see what he can do for me. But that will take time.

We're done here. I'm the first to arrive at the south exit. I doubt anyone else is as eager to get some distance from this place. Each moment I stand here constitutes a bitter reminder that March chose to stay.

Here with Keri.

It stings like hell that he put it that way: *You don't need me. Keri does.* Though I don't want to be jealous, the feeling burns in my veins like an acid cocktail. She's young; she doesn't have all the fucked-up dysfunctions I've collected over the years.

But I can't dwell on petty, baseless jealousy. I have a job to do. As I straighten my shoulders, Jael turns up, with Dina reclining on an air sled like a queen. I smile at that.

"What happened to the harness?"

He shrugs. "Doc said he could spare this. It wasn't even working when I started messing with it. And she isn't bleeding, so it should be safer all around."

"What, like I'm not even here?" Dina mock-glares at me and then reinforces the scowl by whirring over and giving me a whack.

"I'm glad you're mobile," I say. "I was worried about you."

She snorts. "Save the mushy stuff for when we get off this Mary-forsaken rock. Is March almost ready?"

Vel arrives, saving me the trouble of answering. I wonder how they're going to react to the news. A lance of fresh pain stabs through me, but I tamp it down. He made his choice.

"I have confirmed the retreat," he says in lieu of a greeting. "We will not have a cleaner shot at this for months most likely."

"We'll probably still see some fighting," Jael adds. "But I think Vel and I are a match for whatever we find down here."

The bounty hunter nods. "I predict we'll find the enemy wounded and disorganized, separated from the rest of the clan."

"I can do my part," Dina adds. "I'm not helpless."

"Never said you were, darling." Jael ruffles her hair. "I expect you to cover us. You're getting the only disruptor, after all."

We talk a little longer, discussing our game plan. Hit rolls up with a bag strapped to her back, looking elegant and dangerous. "We ready?" she asks.

"Lucky break. I found us a new pilot." I don't pose it as a question.

We *need* her, so it's not open to discussion.

Everyone turns to gape at me, but Dina recovers first. "What about March?"

"He's staying," I answer.

"Give me five minutes with him. Don't go anywhere." The mechanic's mouth firms into an angry white line. With that she whips away.

Maybe she'll convince him where I couldn't. Either way, Jael doesn't seem concerned. Not surprising, he doesn't know March well. But I do notice him inspecting Hit's wrist without any particular subtlety.

"You can take us up?" the merc asks her. "What rigs have you flown?"

She gives him a toothy smile. "You let me worry about that, pretty boy. Find me a ship, and I'll fly the shit out of it."

While they lapse into quiet banter, Vel surprises me with a soft touch on the shoulder. "Are you all right?"

I register his sympathy with a certain amount of irony. The least human among us offers me the most emotional support, it seems. I move my shoulders in an unconvincing shrug.

"I will be."

*Someday.*

Even if I can't imagine that day right now, with the loss so fresh, it'll come. Pain always fades. If I learned nothing else from life, I've certainly mastered that.

More than five minutes pass while we wait for Dina. When she returns, her blue eyes look grim, and she won't meet my gaze.

"Let's go," she says tersely. "We've wasted enough time here."

Taking that as his cue, Vel tinkers with the motion sensors set at the south tunnel. "This will disable them long enough for us to get past without raising an alarm. They'll come back online in sixty seconds, so we need to be quick."

I nod. "Noted. Let's get Dina through first."

She bitches, "What am I, bait?"

But I notice she doesn't hesitate to whip around the barricade and out into the tunnel beyond, faster than me, and I'm hot on her heels. The rest join us in record time. Behind us, I hear the beep that means their motion sensor has come back online, preventing the McCulloughs from sneaking up their backsides. Mentally, I wish them luck with it, but we have our own battle to fight now.

Mary, I hope we're not running in the dark. Vel may have senses that can compensate, but the rest of us are only human. I don't think this group will be as sympathetic to my irrational fear either. They're not like Doc. They won't be patient and understanding about it.

To my vast relief, Jael cracks a torch-tube, and the sickly yellow-green light sizzles into existence, dispelling the hungry shadows to a greater distance. They're not gone entirely, but I can breathe now despite the heavy stone that entombs us.

My palms feel sweaty, but I'll deal. We don't have any Psi with us to reveal how much bravado factors into my façade. I tell myself that's a good thing as I fall in behind Vel.

The merc leads the way, weapons in hand. Jael wields a shockstick in one, a sonicblade in the other, and looks as though he'll be lethal in a fight. I'm overly conscious of our breathing, the scrape of our boots against the rock floor.

I don't know how far we've come. I just watch Vel's back and put one foot in front of the other. The bounty hunter monitors our twists and turns. If anyone can get us out of this, he can. He's my miracle man.

Despite Doc's assurances, I fear that the Teras might have found a way in. Who knows how they burrow? If they turn their claws to it, I bet they could tear through the cave walls and into the warren leading to the bunker.

Maybe that's what drives the McCullough retreat. As soon as they get clear, they'll send the Teras in somehow. I shudder, thinking along those lines. I remember all too well how their wings sounded swarming around me in the night, the screams of the dying, and the grotesque sight of bloodied body parts arcing into the wind, devoured in an invisible monstrous feast.

I'm so busy reliving old nightmares that I don't know we've got company until Dina shouts. The disruptor in her hand flashes with a wild shine, and someone screams in agony. Wherever she hit him will be raw meat, flesh scrambled inside out. Unless she hit him in the heart or the head, shock will kill him, not the injury itself.

As we get nearer, I see five McCullough scouts, red-eyed and rough. Dina has already dropped one, and she stays near the back, waiting for the weapon to cycle back up for another shot. The other three leap into the fray with a ferocity that steals my breath.

I pause, whip out my own shockstick, and assume the position in front of Dina. If anyone gets through our first line, I'm not letting them get to her. I hear her snort at my protective position, but she doesn't protest.

Our new pilot wades in with her bare hands, assuming a fighting crouch that tells me she's had extensive hand-to-hand training. She validates her nickname by dodging a sloppy lunge and lays her first opponent out with an open-hand blow to his brow. He goes down like a stone.

I'm amused when she flashes me a grin. "I wasn't bragging, y'know."

Vel carries hooked blades that he uses as an extension of his hands. Watching him fight, I realize they're intended to substitute for his hidden claws. Beside him, Jael spins like a dervish; he's all offense, all insane fury. He doesn't bother trying to protect himself, but then, I know why.

One of the McCulloughs dodges past, evidently thinking he'll use Dina as a hostage. I know what he figures. I'm small, weak. I'm no threat at all.

Well, the enforced rest has done me good, and after losing March, I feel like a fight. "You should run," I tell him with a feral grin.

*I'm Sirantha Jax, and I have had enough.*

# CHAPTER 34

***The close confines of the tunnel favor the quick. I*** dodge a jab and wind to deliver a stinging blow to his right arm. I know from experience, he'll feel numb from the shoulder down for at least an hour.

These McCulloughs aren't as big as Gunnar lugs, but they're faster by comparison, and desperation lends them strength. They know if they don't kill us, they don't leave here alive. No prisoners, no exceptions.

"I'm gonna break your neck, bitch." His breath reeks from two paces away. They must've been down here a long time. "And then I'll do your crippled friend."

"You'll need two good hands for that." I toss the shock-stick between my hands, distracting him from Dina. The weapon hums with the motion, providing a bass beat for the symphony of grunts and groans.

He lunges at me, probably trying to work a lock. I whirl away, never taking my eyes off him, but he manages to sink a fist into my side. The breath wheezes out of me. I take a moment to be grateful he didn't stress any of my bones, and then he bull-rushes, slams me into the wall. Pain sparks down my spine. I'm slower than I used to be, and he's like a mad beast.

In retaliation, I drive all my weight onto his foot. When he winces, I go for his eyes. There's a soft squish, and he screams like men shouldn't, all upper register and pure anguish. I shudder, but don't hesitate to follow up with a shockstick upside his head. Then he falls, a dull, heavy sound.

Dina holds her fire, too risky now that our bodies are between her and the enemy. I'm glad she doesn't want to rearrange our molecules. Shaking, I wipe my fingers on my pants. I can smell the blood, a sweet, coppery tang.

*If I can, the Teras can.* I try to strangle the thought, but it takes root like a poisonous vine.

"Thanks," Dina mutters. "You know when I get off this thing, I'm gonna repay you for that."

I don't comment, though I hope she'll regain full use of her leg. Doc set her up with an immuno-implant to keep her from rejecting the new limb. He also prescribed a strict regimen of exercises. She's limped a step or two on her own, but the days when she stomps around like she used to are a long way off.

The other three fight with a grace that calls to mind a brutal piece of choreography. I'm afraid I'd just get in the way, so I continue to guard Dina while nursing my sore back. Once all the McCulloughs hit the ground, Jael kneels and cuts their throats with a murderous efficiency that makes me look away. His pale eyes glitter in the torch-tube's citrine glow.

"I don't want them on our backtrail," he says briefly.

"Noted." I maneuver past the bodies.

Stepping over sends a shock all the way down my legs. I wonder if I've dislocated something. It occurs to me that, thus far, my role as ambassador hasn't been as cushy as one might expect.

Dina whirs forward on her sled, and Vel takes point again. He glances back long enough to ask, "Everyone all right?"

"Couldn't be better." Yes, I exaggerate.

"Fine," Hit answers with a smile. "But the smell is nasty. Let's get on."

Nobody else seems to notice that a long slash on Jael's arm has now closed itself up. His blood-soaked clothing offers camouflage as well. With everything happening at once and the uncertain light, it's easy to miss, or to think you were mistaken. I know better.

My bodyguard falls in behind me, serving as rear guard. "Thanks," he murmurs, low. "Most of this crew doesn't know anything about me, and I'd like to keep it that way."

I shrug. "We all have shit we'd rather didn't come to light. In your case, though, Jael, you didn't *do* anything. You didn't ask for any of this."

"That hasn't stopped people trying to kill me just to see how long it'll take for me to die," he returns. "And let's not even get started with the zealots."

"Fair enough."

I push down the raw grief clawing at me, trying to compartmentalize. At this moment I need another Jax, one who's tough and capable, but she won't manifest. I can't banish this loss as I have so many others. March got to me the way nobody ever has, burrowed beneath my skin in a way that I don't think I'll *ever* get over him. And I've lost enough people to know.

Glenna, my best friend from the academy, burned out faster than most. She was twenty-three when she died. I said some empty words at her service, took some mental-health days, and drank myself stupid in some scroungy spaceport bar. And I haven't thought about her in ten turns. Odd that her memory would surface here, now.

I shake off the melancholy, noticing that the tunnels seem to be sloping up. At first I'm not sure because it's subtle, but as we go along, I decide the bounty hunter's leading us in the right direction. The new pilot sticks close to Vel, shadowing him as he guides us around corners. His handheld feeds him data he doesn't bother sharing. We only need to know about bad news coming at us.

So much stone. The ceilings are barely tall enough for Hit to pass without stooping. She's easily as tall as Jael. I draw my fingers along the walls as we move, listening for the telltale sound of wings.

Instead I feel a gust of air, which shouldn't exist down here. A draft can mean only one thing. I pause, spin, and then tilt my head back.

In the darkness I can barely make out a ragged hole above our heads. The broken stone doesn't look as though the Gunnars included this in their original construction either. Dread crawls over me like maggots from an old corpse.

"Shit."

My worst fear, realized.

Everyone glances back at Jael and me. Since he's right beside me, he catches on first. The merc tips his head back, and asks, "How close are we to the surface?"

Vel taps on his handheld. "In a direct vertical line, or as the tunnels run?"

In running a hand through his hair, Jael reveals his impatience with Vel's precision. "As the tunnels run, unless you can take us straight up this shaft."

Even assuming her sled had that much lift, Dina couldn't clear the opening, so I take that for a rhetorical question. I can't imagine how she feels, if she's put the pieces together. These monsters I'm so scared of, they *ate* part of her. I don't know how she isn't one giant ball of terror.

Hit taps a booted foot gently, as if she thinks we're wasting time with all this jawing. Maybe she has a point. The longer we stand around down here, the more chance they'll find us.

"Nearly two kilometers," the bounty hunter answers at last. "But it winds around, so it will take twice as long as a straight hike."

"We have to assume the tunnels ahead are infested," Dina says flatly. "Vel, can you get a message back to camp? They need to know the bunker's not as safe as they thought. With the wounded, the Teras *will* find them sooner or later."

My imagination supplies the details. Death exploding into an unsuspecting camp with claws and fangs. Rending, devouring—I have to shut down the images; they come too quick and violent for me to bear. If they get to Keri, Lex, and . . .

*March.*

Then the McCulloughs win. And I lose everything.

"I can try." Vel punches keys, shifting this way and that.

"Try under here." I step back, making room beneath the hole in the ceiling.

Maybe that will be enough. If he can't, we'll have to go back. Make our last stand with them. The others watch him with varying degrees of tension. I'm not alone in how badly I want off this desolate rock.

"Done," he says, after an interminable moment. "Dr. Solaith should see the warning soon. I hope it gives them time to prepare."

We all heave a collective sigh. Part of me feels it isn't enough. I want to turn and run back down the dark stone passage toward March. It will drive me nuts, not knowing what happens here after we go.

I ache.

Only the fact that he made his choice prevents me from doing just that. Well, that and my secret, shameful fear of the dark. But March made it clear we're on diverging paths, and only time will tell whether that's always going to be the case. I don't have enough faith left in me to believe, but I curl my hand into a fist, fingering the cheap ring he gave me.

Ahead of us lies probable death and dismemberment. Behind us lies an encampment of weary, beleaguered clansmen with a war to fight. Talk about a rock and a hard place.

Two kilometers between us and daylight. I wonder if the dead we left behind will draw them, all hunger and keening sonic rage. Fighting Teras underground sounds like suicide. Fuck that. If I meant to take that route, I'd have chosen an easy death. Made my appointment with a Psych, and then visited a clean, safe Eutha-booth.

I sigh. "So what the hell do we do now?"

Hit's teeth shine in the dark. "We kill the muthafuckers, one and all."

Easier said than done.

# CHAPTER 35

***My heart thuds in my ears.***

I'm conscious of each footfall, each scrape against stone. We try to move as a unit, permitting no space between us, but the soft hum from Dina's sled echoes down the corridors. Can the Teras detect vibrations? Each meter feels like a kilometer since I expect at any moment to hear the terrifying sound of wings.

"The passage will not permit them to swarm us," Vel says.

He's right. We can't even pass two abreast, and from what I recall, the Teras have a two-meter wingspan. So Vel will bear the brunt of a first attack. Perhaps his faux-human skill will shield him somewhat.

That's no guarantee he'll survive, however, if they rend him limb from limb. I wonder how his unique body chemistry will affect the monsters. I can't ask, though.

"Can that thing detect movement?" I nod at his handheld.

"Ordinarily. The rock interferes somewhat with the readings, however."

Dina glances back at me over the rim of her sled. Her eyes glow with an odd radiance, echoes of the torch-tube. When she turns back, the light paints her fair hair with oily green streaks.

"If it comes down to it," she tells me, low. "If it's life and death and I'm slowing you down, you leave me, Jax. They already had a taste of me, so they may as well have the rest."

A chill shivers through me. I remember Loras on his belly, shoving March toward me. I recognize self-sacrifice.

I'll be damned if it happens again.

"No. We're not leaving anyone behind." Not this time. "We'll find a way to fight them."

"Better hurry," Hit says, jerking her head at the red blurs on Vel's data screen. "We got two, just around the corner."

"We *have* a way," Jael says, pushing past me. "Jax, stay back, and keep the other two safe."

The pilot glares at his back. "You think I need your protection? I killed one of those monsters topside with nothing but a knife. I just need a ride."

"Then *you* guard Jax and Dina," comes his response. "You ready, Vel?"

The bounty hunter responds by tossing a weapon to Jael. They take up a position just around the corner, and I shudder, barely registering a keen of pure hunger from the beasts. I remember the way their song nearly killed poor Loras.

A burst of orange lightning zags from their hands, igniting the very air before them. The Teras' camouflage fails under such duress, and for an instant, I watch their silhouettes inside the pocket inferno, watch them writhe. Heat washes over me.

Fearing an explosion, I hit the floor, and Dina guides her sled over me. I appreciate the gesture; even now she's got my back. When I'm greeted by the stench of sizzling meat, I chance a peek. Hit stands her ground, watching the monsters burn. Jael and Vel have designed something that propels an incendiary cloud.

"We will burn a path out." Vel holsters the oddly shaped weapon. "They cannot swarm us in the tunnels, and if we move cautiously, they will not detect us easily. I believe they utilize sonar to locate their prey."

I can't be the only one thinking this. "Will their screams draw others?"

The bounty hunter's answer drifts back to me over the hiss of smoldering flesh. "It is possible."

"Then they can just line up to die," Jael says. "I'm so tired of this planet."

"That makes two of us. Any chance you made a spare?" With a nod, Hit indicates the weapon in his hand.

"Only these. Sorry. We can take turns if you prefer." Trust Vel to be scrupulously fair about who gets to barbecue the horrible things.

Personally, I don't care. I've seen what they can do; so has Dina. I suspect she and I are content to watch the action from a safe distance this time. After checking his handheld, Vel maneuvers past the smoking pile with a precision that once again reveals his inhuman nature, once you know what you're looking for. He waves us on.

The smell damn near makes me sick. There's no climate control down here, no ventilation, and the smell of charred meat flashes me dangerously close to the *Sargasso*. By itself, the dark was bad enough. Add this stench to it, and I struggle to stay in the here and now.

I grit my teeth until pain shoots up my jaw to my temple. I won't lose it. I'm stronger than that. March would've known how bad this is for me. I could've counted on a touch on the shoulder, a reassuring nod. So would Doc, for that matter. But those days are gone.

And I have to deal with what is, not what was. Story of my life.

"Watch your step." Jael guides us around the corpses.

Dina slaps at him, which improves my mood somewhat. I'm not sure she's all right with the battlefield medicine that went into saving her life, but we don't have a Psych on hand. Just as well, most of them are crazy bastards. After all, look what they did to me in the name of mental health. When we get out of here, I'll fix her the Jax way: loads of liquor and some pretty girls.

Vel leads us out of that hallway and into the next turn. It's a maze, and I'm hopelessly lost, just as I was when Doc found our way in. Dirtside, I have no sense of direction, something Kai loved teasing me about. When I got lost at the Gehenna starport market, he never let me live it down.

Oddly, thinking about him takes my mind off March. An older loss doesn't sting as much. The memories offer some comfort and distraction as we creep along, slaves to Vel's handheld.

Listening for the rasp of talons and claws against the rock. A dragging sound or a leathery flap of wings. Sonic shrieks echo in the distance, making the hair on the back of my neck stand on end. My nipples perk from the chills running over me steadily, like I have a fever. But I don't think fear counts as an illness.

They're here with us. Hunting. Coming closer, each turn we make. Mary help us, will I never see the sky again?

In Jael's hand the torch-tube starts to flicker, casting odd shadows along the floor, and then it winks out. At first I'm just blind; it's like that long moment after I jack in, but before we jump. And then the walls kindle with their own light, a pale, ethereal twinkle that reminds me of the stars.

"The stone is full of phosphorus," Vel says in a hushed tone.

Once my eyes adjust, it's better than the tubes, more pervasive. I feel less like we're scuttling along in the oily dark, huddled in our tiny isle of illumination. It also smells fresher now that we've moved away from the funeral pyre.

"Does that mean something?" Hit asks him.

Vel lifts his shoulders. "Probably. But I lack the time for extended study."

"No shit. You remind me of Doc sometimes." Dina sounds more herself, less the sacrificial lamb.

"I will take that as a compliment."

"It wasn't meant as one," she mutters.

Ahead of Dina, Hit smothers a chuckle. "Should we leave you two alone?"

Now I laugh. I sense more than see the puzzled look the pilot casts over her shoulder at me, so I explain, "Dina doesn't like men, and Vel, well . . ."

As a Slider, he can grow human skin to pass among us, concealing his mantis form. But I'm not going to out him since Hit hasn't seen him au naturel. No more than I'll tell her about Jael being Bred. Like I told him before, we all have our secrets.

Vel surprises me by finishing the sentence with a flicker of that dry sense of humor that occasionally rears its head. "Let us say she is not my type."

For the first time, I wonder what that would be. He said he left Ithiss-Tor because sexual relations between his people sometimes became deadly. So that means he's been alone this whole time? Not that it's any of my business.

On some level, I'm aware I'm losing myself in these inane speculations in order to distract myself from the soul-scouring fear engendered by the echoing shrieks. The Teras sound so goddamn close now; they should be on Vel's screen.

Two red signatures blossom on his handheld, dead ahead. Then two more, except they aren't where they're supposed to be.

The ceiling above us shakes, disintegrates like the dry dirt of an insect hive. Crumbles down on us in great clods that shimmer with the eerie light. I can't see them, but I can hear them overhead, claws working. Their terrible keens reverberate inside my skull, making me feel like my brains will bleed out my nose.

"Behind!" Hit yells.

And then they come at us from both sides in a terrible rush.

# CHAPTER 36

***Jael spins and fires, a ruddy orange cone jetting from*** his weapon. Ahead of us, Vel takes the ones coming down the corridor in front. Then we're trapped.

Burning on both sides, like standing in the middle of a charnel house and praying you don't catch, too. I shake all over.

Shrill cries of rage echo through the tunnels. The smell seems to enrage the ones trying to get at us from above, but the opening isn't quite big enough yet. Claws rasping, they make a hole like the one I saw half a kilometer back.

Hit eyes the ones above and then leaps. Her knife shimmers in a silver arc as she stabs at . . . nothing. But somehow she hits. The Tera screams in agony. When she severs the claw, it drops in a spatter of green fluid and lies visible on the softly glowing stone floor, opening and closing as the nerve endings die. Apparently the smell of blood, any blood, maddens them. Because overhead, an ominous thump and another scream says the monsters have turned on each other.

"Move!" Vel shouts.

Agreed. We don't want to be here when the ceiling gives way entirely. Ahead, the two Teras still twist and char, inky black smoke roiling from their putrid flesh.

"Dive and roll," Jael adds. "Apart from Dina of course. You should have enough lift to get past them. If your clothing catches, don't panic."

Easy for him to say. He doesn't have burn scars.

The bounty hunter leaps past with a well-timed spring, hits the stone floor with his hands, and tucks into a neat roll. Hit follows suit with a natural grace that suggests she'd be dangerous on the dance floor, too. Cursing, Dina maneuvers until she can glide by. In its death throes, one of the creatures sends her careening into the tunnel wall.

She skids in a shower of sparks to the end of the corridor, where Hit stops the sled with a boot. "I've seen better flying from a drunk aircab driver."

Occupied with stabilizing the sled, Dina mutters, "Bite me," in lieu of a more creative comeback.

The pilot grins. "I just might."

Dina's head comes up, her face pale. But before I hear what she says, Jael gives me a shove from behind. "Get moving, Jax."

As if to punctuate his words, a huge chunk of rock crashes to the floor just in front of me. The fight going on overhead sounds savage. Terrifying. Five meters above, they're devouring each other alive and shattering stone in the process.

But I can't. There's actual *fire* curling from the sizzling meat. He's lucky I haven't puked all over his boots.

"Jael," I begin shakily.

"Oh, for Mary's sake," he bites out. "It's a good thing you don't weigh much."

"Wha—"

"Vel! Think fast."

And then I'm launched, sailing toward the bounty hunter. Everything blurs as I tumble, crash into him, and go down. Jael lands on top of me in an ungainly pile. I suspect he may have cracked my rib with his knee, but before

I can bitch about that, the tunnel collapses in a great mound of rubble and dust.

There's no going back now. I couldn't get to March even if I wanted to. Mary, I hope the warning came in time.

Three more red shapes appear on Vel's handheld. And lucky us—they're on our side of the block.

Hit nudges Dina farther down the new passage as Jael shoves my head down. Vel fires over the top of us, lighting the closest one. They're not smart, these Teras, because they try to push past, and then shriek as they're burned. We see their flesh where it chars. It's odd, like a tear in consensual reality: seeing a shadow suddenly flare into full view through a tendril of licking flame.

Jael fires twice more in quick succession, engulfing all three of them. In narrow tunnels where we control our movements, these monsters are vulnerable. First they can't spot us easily, and then they're alight.

When we reach the surface, it will be a different hunt for them.

"Halfway there," Vel says as we get our breath. He sets me on my feet. "Anything broken?"

I wince and rub my side. "Not sure. But I'm ambulatory, don't worry."

"You better be," Dina says. "You're not hitching a ride."

Flicking a look at Jael, I ignore her for the time being. "You really believe in tough love," I mutter, sotto voce.

It's a throwaway complaint. I've made thousands of them in my life. In fact, I should be thanking him for saving my ass.

"I don't believe in love at all," he returns, equally quiet. "It's just a name people give the endorphins that spring up after some really hot fucking, and the justification they use to manipulate the shit out of each other afterward. Now move your ass. I want to see starlight sometime soon."

"Is it nightfall?" Hit asks. "I've lost track of time down here."

She's right. I don't even know what time we left the

camp or how many days we were down there. Without a sunrise to help mark its passage or a ship's computer to keep track for me, I have no more sense of time than I do direction.

"There are four hours left until daybreak," Vel advises us, after some tapping on his handheld.

"How long will this last kilometer take?" Dina wants to know.

I'm glad she asked because now I don't have to. My shoulder aches from hauling my pack. I hope 245 is okay in there. After Vel snatched me in Maha City, she asked me to install her in a droid body. She didn't enjoy watching what happened without being able to impact events, which means I was right about her AI chip. Since we've been together, she's evolved from her original function, and I now consider her a friend.

As a bonus, she'll also prove invaluable as an aide. If I upgrade her, she can function as my assistant on Ithiss-Tor, too. She'll coach me on customs and etiquette with a precision no human aide could match. So once we're out of here, I'll see about buying her a body from Pretty Robotics. When I have cred, that is.

Of course I could take Jael's advice and charge it to Chancellor Tarn. He wouldn't quibble over a personal aide, would he? Never mind that I could hire a human one much cheaper than I could requisition a suitable frame for 245.

My internal monologue keeps me sane. I manage to filter out the distant stench of acrid smoke that's burning our oxygen. Block out the tons of stone that make me feel like I've been buried alive. Mary, I have so many hang-ups. If I wasn't scared of *them*, too, I'd see a Psych about it.

People would laugh their asses off if they knew how much of my tough act comes from pure pretense. During our plodding progress, Vel checks and double-checks to make sure there are no deadly surprises lurking around each turn. I keep my eyes on Dina's sled. It has a series of lights along the bottom, giving a faint glow that frosts the metal.

The others watch the tiny screen on Vel's handheld. We're slaves to it. I'm aware that the tiniest mechanical malfunction could cost our lives. And technology has a tendency to break down around me for no apparent reason.

I remember the busted phase drive we suffered on the *Folly*, just after we reached Marakeq. From what Dina said, there was no logical reason for it. And that kind of thing happens to me *all* the time. When our Skimmer exploded, I thought that might've been me, too, until I learned otherwise.

For like the fifth time, Jael asks, "Anything?"

Until even Vel loses patience with him. "Have I failed even once to alert you if there *was*?"

Damn. That's Vel-speak for, *Will you please shut the fuck up already?* I don't think anyone's ever managed to get on the bounty hunter's nerves before. To my knowledge, he's the king of cool. I don't know whether Jael should be praised or pitied for this accomplishment.

"No," the merc says grudgingly. "Sorry. The quiet's just making me nervous."

"It's like the eye of the storm," Hit agrees. "You can sense something's coming, feel it prickling over your skin, but you don't know what until it explodes in your face."

To my surprise Dina laughs. Might be the first time I've heard her do so since the attack that maimed her. "I think I like you."

Hit flicks a look over one shoulder. "You flirting with me?"

"Would you like me to be?" Dina actually tosses back her hair.

"That depends on your intentions." Damn, but the woman put some heat into that. *I* even felt it, and I've never hit on a woman when I wasn't drunk.

"Is it dirty that this turns me on?" Jael asks nobody in particular.

"Yes," Vel answers, without looking away from the device that's saved our lives. I can't fault him for that. I'm also impressed with his coordination; I'd have walked into several walls by now. "Ahead, it looks like the incline to the surface."

As if in answer, a cool, fresh wind blows down over us.

"What are we waiting for?" Hit demands. "Let's get the hell out of here!"

# CHAPTER 37

***There's an actual door at the top of the slope, a solid*** metal one meant to keep stuff out. I hope it's well camouflaged on the other side. We pause here, with freedom on the other side of the door. We'll have to navigate the lock to get out, but one thing at a time. At this point, preparation is key.

"Is anyone bleeding?" Jael asks. "Check carefully. I have some liquid skin if you are. We need to seal you up."

Everyone conducts an inspection, and we find minor scrapes here and there. The merc oversees the application of the liquid skin, making sure we're ready to go out in the wind. Dina's fingers are raw from where she hit the wall.

I find a scratch on my elbow. Hell, I'm lucky it's not worse, the way Jael hurled me like a javelin. I'm not particularly aerodynamic.

"This might sting a little," Jael murmurs.

Why is he smiling? I hiss as he squirts my elbow, and I feel the sealant bond with my existing skin. Best bandage in a bottle that credits can buy.

"Everyone good?" Lofting the liquid skin, Jael checks us all one last time.

"I'm hungry, and I'm sick of your face," Dina bitches beneath her breath. Loud enough for everyone to hear.

Jael really isn't the guy I thought, because he surprises me with a sharp laugh. "I'm sure that goes for everybody else, too. But let's break out the paste. You make a good point. We don't know just how far we'll have to hike to steal a ship."

"What do you mean you don't know?" Hit jabs the merc in the chest with both index fingers. I wince in sympathy, but he doesn't seem to feel it. "I thought you and the professor over here had things planned down to the last millimeter."

"I cannot take topography readings underground," Vel explains in a deceptively mild tone. "But we will make for the nearest public hangar. If it comes to it, we can stay there until the Conglomerate dispatches a ship. There will be rudimentary amenities available."

"Hit." Dina puts a hand on the other woman's arm briefly. "Cool down. Shit, if I'm willing to risk it with a bum leg, you can be sure these guys know what they're doing. 'Cause I don't even like 'em. Especially her."

Now that's the Dina I know and love. Mary, I'm glad to see a spark. I flash her a broad grin. "Right back at you, bitch."

"If you say so." But the pilot does step back, looking perceptibly calmer.

Then we enjoy a meal of nutri-paste. It's been so long since I had real food that my teeth feel like they're getting soft. Maybe you can live forever off this stuff as the manufacturer claims, but I'm starting to think I'd rather die.

I daydream about fresh fruits and vegetables, drizzled with a sweet tangy sauce. Maybe some strong white cheese, just a bit smoky. Oooh, and hot bread, crisp on the outside and tender on the inside, brushed with a hint of butter.

"Close your mouth," Jael whispers. "You're drooling. If you're not careful, people will realize you're thinking about me naked."

"Only if you have a warm baguette and a crock of butter in your hands," I return darkly.

He grins at me. "That can be arranged."

"I hate you." I suck down the rest of my paste, quietly stewing because he destroyed the food fantasy that made this goop tolerable.

Vel clears his throat with a look that manages to be vaguely disapproving. What? I didn't *do* anything.

"Next . . . we need this." The bounty hunter tosses me a tube of Thermud, and I eye it with dislike. Merc grunts swear by this stuff, but surely we don't—oh, *frag*. Of course we do. We're about to emerge from a bunker in the middle of two clans at war. I smear the stuff on without protest.

Hit, on the other hand, looks at Vel like she thinks he's crazy. "I'm already dark enough to blend in, don't you think?"

"Not for high-tech," Jael tells her. "This stuff scrambles your heat signature so it bleeds off into the ground."

"Making thermal goggles useless." She takes the tube from me and covers all her exposed skin.

Dina uses it next, but I can tell by her expression she thinks it's a waste of time. Her sled *is* pretty damn conspicuous. But we can only do so much to stack the deck in our favor—got to leave the rest to chance.

*Too bad Lady Luck's so often a bitch.*

Watching Jael daub himself, I can definitely tell he's used it before. His hands practically blur in the speed of the motions. "We all set?"

"How come he doesn't have to use it?" Hit jerks her head toward Vel.

Who manages an approximation of a smile. He's getting better at pretending to be human. "Because I am special, of course."

He ignores her pissed-off exclamation as he goes to work on the electronic lock. Right now the display shows red. If it requires a ret-scan or a handprint, we are utterly screwed.

Or not.

Vel slips on a clear synthetic glove, pulls the tips tight, and lays his palm on the panel. The AI intones, "Thank you, Dr. Solaith. Clearance granted."

The light flashes green, and the heavy door swings wide. That hint of a breeze we've been feeling for a while turns into a gust. I drink it in without minding the chill racing over me. It's still winter, a lot of darkness and short daylight hours.

"He was kind enough to let me borrow his fingerprints before we left," Vel says as he steps out.

Tentatively, we follow suit, single file, coming up against what seems to be a rockslide. We sidle past the narrow gap, and for a moment, I'm afraid Dina will have to leave the sled. I don't know how the hell we'll carry her.

Without a word, she straps herself in, lowers the back so she's fully horizontal. She tests the strength of her belts and then flips to vertical. Her fingers seem sure on the buttons.

"I'm fine," she says, when Hit tries to help guide the sled. "I got this."

Now and then she scrapes the stone, throwing sparks, but she manages. I admire her so damn much. But her face is taut with tension by the time we step out onto the hillside.

"You okay?" I step closer as she switches the sled back to chair configuration.

"I gotta get out of this thing," she tells me, jaw set. "Or I'll kill somebody."

"You will," I promise. "Get out of it, I mean. I'll help. The killing probably depends on how much they piss you off."

I want to say more, but this isn't the time. We need to move. For just a moment, though, I tip my head back, glorying in the icy stars.

From this higher vantage, I see that the clansmen piled those rocks before the opening to make it look like a natural formation. They did a good job concealing their escape route; I'll give them that. But it's not as impregnable as they thought. It's compromised now, full of dying McCulloughs and hungry monsters.

Mary, I hope March makes it out of there. I touch the ring on my finger out of superstition, faith, or some awkward marriage between the two. In an effort to push back the pain trying to drown me, I suck in several deep, gulping breaths of cold air.

He's *my* pilot, and I have to fly without him soon.

Jumpers aren't made for this.

I expected to emerge amid the wreckage of the Gunnar-Dahlgren compound, but we've surfaced well away from there. No broken machinery, no rubble. No signs of bombardment. There are just barren hills, riddled with signs of the honeycomb caverns that house the Teras.

The open worries me more than the tunnels. Down there we could control the approach, limit how many could get at us. Up here we're free targets, dinner afoot.

"No running," Vel cautions again. "We have no way of knowing how the Teras interpret rapid footfalls or how far sound travels through the caverns."

"Do our best to step lightly," I say. "Check."

The bounty hunter pauses a moment to check the readings, and then adds, "This way. We need to get as far from here as we can before daylight."

"Why?" I ask before Hit gets the chance, and she acknowledges it with a grin. I really like her. She's competent, confident, and doesn't accept things at face value.

If it wasn't for the fact that I'm missing March like a lost limb—glad I didn't say that aloud, or Dina would hurt me—I'd even be glad to have Hit as my new pilot. I'm just not ready to make her part of me.

But when am I ever?

"Because there's a storm coming." Vel flashes his handheld.

The merc sighs. "Looks like a lot of snow. We don't have nearly enough survival gear to handle that. We need to find a ship and fast. All right, people, forced march, double time."

We fall in behind Vel in twos, Dina and Hit, then Jael and me. I hate how he won't leave my side now, as if trying to make up for his prior lack of vigilance. I'm too tired to care at this point or work up any rancor. I just wish he'd leave me alone.

"Damn, it's cold." I don't realize I've spoken aloud until I see his smirk.

"You should really keep a coat in that pack."

"You should really fuck off and die."

"Then who'll save your ass when you panic over a bit of barbecue?"

I give the response my most withering tone. "The next monkey Tarn hires. See, that's my gift. Being the last one standing."

"If everyone you give a shit about is gone, sounds more like a curse."

# CHAPTER 38

***He gets it.***

That startles me. I don't offer confirmation that he's right, though. I don't want to talk.

But yeah, some days it does seem more like a curse, just like that guy from mythology who doesn't die, who's destined to wander and suffer. But I can't sustain that level of mental melodrama.

Pure physical discomfort edges out such self-pity. I can't even find the energy to fret about working with Hit, or how the next jump will affect my condition. I know Doc doesn't want me to jump, but he should've cut off my arm if he wanted to prevent me from jacking in.

Nothing else will keep me from grimspace. Even now, the siren song makes me feel itchy with need. The colors, the feeling that comes howling through me as my mind expands. I need to be there like I need nothing else.

More than March even. I'm sure he knows that. That's what happens when you love a junkie.

As we walk, clouds blot out the shimmer of the stars overhead. The storm Vel predicted appears to be rolling in on schedule, and as the wind kicks up, it goes right through me. You'd think I'd have remembered how cold it is here, though to be fair, I didn't realize I'd never be returning to the ship.

I feel like a prisoner of war.

We can't stop moving, but I can barely put one foot in front of the other. I hate this weakness. Though I feel better than I did on Emry, I'm a long way from full strength. The others seem to be bearing up all right. Up ahead, I hear the low susurration of voices: Dina and Hit, getting to know each other.

As always, Vel leads the way in silence. Though I count him among my closest friends, I don't know much about him. That's not likely to change while we forge a desperate path through these hills.

Up and down we climb, avoiding scout droids, McCullough patrols, and, of course, the Teras, who will swarm and devour us if they catch our scent. But between the liquid skin and Thermud, we've taken as many precautions against that outcome as we can. My thighs and calves burn, taut as drawn wire.

Add that to various aches, including a stabbing pain where Jael landed on me, and I'd give just about anything to lie down. Of course I suspect I'd never get up again. I didn't realize how soft I'd gotten, but a jumper's life *is* well padded.

"You holding up all right?" Jael asks, well after I've lost track of how long we've been walking.

"Does it matter?" I mumble.

I don't see how we'll be in any shape to steal a ship once we finally get there. But we can't pitch camp in the open, and a cavern in these hills would be worse.

"Not really," he answers. "I'm just making small talk."

"I have a better idea. *No* talk. That's been working like a charm for hours."

The bounty hunter glances back at me. In this light, his faux-human skin looks a little mottled. It's probably time for him to slough it off and grow new, but he won't do that while he needs the insulation.

"Sirantha, it will serve no purpose if you become ill." With an annoyed sound, he delves into his pack and fishes out a tissue-thin insulated suit, maybe the same one I wore on the Teresengi Basin.

It's not *that* cold, but I scramble into it. I hope my body heat, thus trapped, will warm me up soon. I wince in anticipation because when the feeling returns, it's going to hurt.

Ahead, Dina asks Vel, "How much farther?"

She isn't asking out of weariness or personal discomfort. Shit, now I know what the lights at the base of her sled mean. They've all dimmed but two. If we don't find a power source before that last light goes out, she'll be stranded.

"Four kilometers due west from here," Vel answers. "We'll find a hangar."

Like the one where we landed the first time instead of going directly to the compound. They're maintained by droids and bots, officially independent of clan allegiance. Merchant ships often put down there when they have to deliver supplies on planet to multiple stops; it forestalls accusations of partisan dealings.

I nearly crack my jaw with a yawn. Four kilometers. Under optimum conditions in the training room, I *ran* that without breaking a sweat.

That was a long time, another lifetime, ago.

Far be it for me to question the leadership that's gotten us this far, but . . . well, someone has to. "What if no ships are docked there?"

They don't tend to stay long between dirtside deliveries anyway. Plus, the recent unrest on Lachion will have made some merchant vessels reluctant to risk it. Things won't return to normal here for a while, though weapons vendors may try their luck. They always do a brisk trade on Nicuan.

"Why borrow trouble?" Jael shakes his head and sighs.

"I never *borrow* it. That implies it wasn't mine to start with."

"It's a good question," Hit puts in quietly. "And I'd like it answered."

Perhaps it's simply the hollow hills, but in the silence that follows, the wind carries in a dolorous howl. I imagine wild animals just beyond my line of sight, less terrible than the Teras, but just as hungry. How do the clans survive such a savage world, so far from city lights and the safety of space?

"I do not know," Vel says at last. By Jael's astonished look, he didn't expect that answer either. We wait, hoping there's more. "If nothing else, we will find a secure place to rest and bounce a message to New Terra. The McCulloughs cannot attack us on neutral territory without breaching seven interstellar accords."

I don't like the thought of waiting for rescue when anything can go wrong and usually does. As if in response, the first delicate snowflakes drift down, stick and shimmer in Hit's dark hair. She brushes them away and spins to see the white curtain coming down. Soon this winter loveliness will sting.

"At least I'll be able to charge this thing." Dina slaps the side of the sled and then tips her head back to study the sky. "But I think we need to pick up the pace."

"Got that right." Beside me, Jael breaks into a jog that looks disgustingly effortless. "Don't fall behind, Jax."

He should be exhausted by now, scruffy and unshaven. Instead he's just bloodstained and dirty like the rest of us. I don't see weariness in his eyes, just a stupidly teasing light, like this is some big adventure.

Well, maybe to him, it is. Maybe Jael has endless reserves, thanks to his Bred heritage. I know he can heal from wounds that would kill anyone else.

As for me, I miss March, and I want a shower. I wouldn't say no to some of the perks that an ambassador is reputed to receive. Thus far, I've gotten nothing but murder attempts out of my time on the job.

With a scowl, I raise my knees and force myself to run. Each jolt over rocky ground sends a shock of pain down my side. No problem. I'll just pretend this is the training room, and I'm in peak form. No injury, no illness.

Shit, if I can do all that, why don't I just *wish* us off this rock?

When Dina accelerates, the second-to-last light flickers and blinks out. Hope that single cell has enough juice to take her four kilometers. Vel doesn't let her pass him, though. He increases his own rate of movement to stay a meter ahead of us.

I don't know how he monitors his handheld and keeps an eye on the horizon at the same time. It must be an Ithtorian gift because I would've tripped over my own feet by now. He keeps one eye on each object, something humans just can't do.

The snow falls heavier with each passing moment. In a way it's good because it'll cover our tracks. Thanks to the Thermud, that also means we're five dark figures streaking over a white hillside and down into the valley.

*Nothing but open plains from here on out.*

Our "camouflage" makes us easier to spot, so I hope no McCulloughs lie between us and the hangar. The snow stings, catching in my lashes and numbing the visible portion of my face. Though I'm not the praying sort, I cycle certain thoughts in a mantra timed to my racing heart.

*Please let there be a ship.*

*Please let us get there safely.*

*Please let Dina's sled hold out.*

Whether I'm entreating Mother Mary or Lady Luck herself, I couldn't say. I just know when the building looms up out of the storm, blocky and ugly as an old Gehenna whore, I've never been so glad to see anything in my life.

Because I don't think I can go another step.

# CHAPTER 39

***Jael winds up carrying me the last two hundred meters.***

I don't even bitch about it, though I know he'll never let me live it down. No, I didn't ask for help, but I guess the part where I stumbled and fell on my face sort of clued him in. He's not an idiot, even if he's beyond annoying.

Because he knows the emergency protocols, Vel keys us into the hangar. The doors hiss open, hinting at the delicious warmth awaiting us within. Since our luck usually works that way, I expect a firing squad to be waiting for us, or maybe a random pack of Morgut. I peer around the place.

*Nothing so far.*

After everything we've gone through in this hellhole, it can't be so easy, can it? But maybe we're due a break. Maybe.

Like desperate pilgrims, we stumble inside. Hard light floods my eyes, a shocking change from the winter landscape. I take quick stock of our surroundings: thick metal walls, high, open ceilings with fans and ducts in plain view. Apart from droids going about routine maintenance, the hangar is quiet.

There's a ship.

A big one, too. Shiny and silver, it dominates the docking area. If there's anyone aboard, they're likely asleep since we've arrived just before dawn. Hopefully, the vessel belongs to some unsuspecting merchant who's out in a land vehicle, innocently delivering spare parts. Maybe stuck in the snowstorm.

And I don't give a shit about stranding him. If things go poorly out there, he might not need his ship back after all. But first we have to figure out how to steal it. I don't expect that'll be instantaneous, because only a fool would outfit a fine cruiser like this and then not lock it up tight as a virgin's legs.

The AI greets us politely as we cross the floor. "Welcome to Hangar 47-A. It is unlawful to participate in aggressive activity in this space. If you use projectile weapons, please activate the safety mechanisms now. Please remove power cells from items such as sonicblades and disruptors. Please stow all other dangerous devices. If you refuse to comply, a Peacemaker unit will be dispatched to your location, you will be neutralized, and we will conduct a thorough inspection of your belongings. All contraband will be confiscated to fund the operation of Hangar 47-A. Thank you for your cooperation."

I laugh softly because all I have is a shockstick. I drop it into my backpack and I'm done. Swaying on my feet, I watch the others scramble to deal with their weapons before we're dubbed dangerous, and the droids react accordingly. Hit removes a ridiculous amount of armament from her person, cursing all the while.

Small circular units hover nearby, monitoring our progress. When we finish, the courteous, inhuman voice says, "Thank you. Please avail yourself of all public facilities until departure."

I'm surprised it didn't ask us to visit the gift shop. We didn't linger long in the hangar, the first time I visited, and I'm starting to see why. Having everything so well orchestrated by machines makes me feel oddly extraneous.

"Is it me, or is there something spooky about being the only living things around here?" Hit asks, glancing around.

She rubs her hands up and down her arms, the first outward sign of nervousness I've seen from her. So the pilot doesn't like droids. Interesting, considering that she'll jack into the ship right next to me.

"Droids are more reliable than people," Dina mutters.

Her sled gives an ominous whine, and I start looking for a place she can recharge. I point. "Over there. You can patch into that power station, I think. Might want to do it soon."

She gives a nod. Hit follows her, as if expecting the mechanic will need a hand. I was going to, but it's probably better if Hit helps. I'm not sure I'm strong enough.

To my vast delight, the climate control works just fine. Heat drifts down from the vents overhead, compensating for the weather. My teeth chatter as I strip out of the insulated suit and return it to Vel with a murmur of thanks. He stashes it in his pack, conduit to all good things.

I've lost count of how many times he's saved my ass now. At this point I should just hand over the deed. Or maybe tattoo it with *Property of Velith Il-Nok*. That clinches it.

I'm so fucking tired I'm losing my mind.

"I need some time with the computer." Vel pitches his voice loud enough to reach the other two, working on the sled. "I can get the boarding codes and access the ship via remote, but I do not know how long that will take. I recommend the rest of you get warmed up and have something to eat. There should be a waiting area over there with basic amenities." He inclines his head. "In case of mechanical difficulties."

I watch Dina's halting steps toward the lounge, one arm slung around the pilot's neck. As they move off, Hit tells Dina, "I'll help you get comfortable, and then scrounge up something to eat. Sound good?"

The mechanic's voice carries back to me. "Mmm, prepacked vending chow. I'll buy. I need to get started on those rehab exercises, though. I've been wearing an EMP band on my thigh, but that can't make up for plain hard work."

I definitely notice a vibe between those two, but then Dina scores more than any man I ever met. More than once, I've seen her take home a girl who never looked twice at her own sex before. She's definitely gifted.

Don't ask me why I'm not right there with them, looking for a place to crash. Or a vending unit that will sell me something to eat that isn't nutri-paste. Anything. I'd kill for some choclaste right about now.

Vel heads toward a terminal, and I trudge after him. The AI warns him that's for official docking personnel only, but it doesn't deter him. After watching him mess with it for a few minutes, I'm surprised that none of his high-tech gear can convince it to let him into their system.

"Maybe I can help."

"How?" Jael asks at my elbow.

I ignore him and dig through my pack looking for 245. She's a closed interface, but she might know of a backdoor in the security or a fail-safe included in the design. Mair provided her with an astonishingly eclectic database. Plus, 245 is the only Lachion native among us. That can't hurt.

I power her up, input my access codes, and she greets me with, "Good morning, Sirantha Jax. It has been eight days since your last entry."

How can the modulated female voice *I* chose from her option files sound so accusatory? I ignore the small surge of guilt over leaving her out of the loop.

But I try to placate her nonetheless. "You wouldn't believe the week I've had. I'll tell you all about it in a bit, but first, we need your help."

She won't be able to resist that appeal, as it would constitute going against her programming. "How can I be of assistance?"

"I need to know everything you do about the Lachion hangar systems."

"Accessing," she responds.

"Good idea." Vel sets aside the code scrambler and waits.

"The system was designed and installed by Jens Donner, a systems specialist formerly employed by Generation Technologies. After ten years with the company, Donner founded his own enterprise, ZapTech. He is credited with revolutionizing the AI matrix that permits droids to maintain a facility without human direction."

"He must've included a fail-safe," I say thoughtfully. "How do techs get into the system to performance maintenance?"

After a moment, 245 responds, "I have found the answer to your inquiry in Mair Dahlgren's partitioned files."

*Partitioned files?* What does that mean?

I frown as if she'll respond to nonverbal cues. "I thought I had access to all data. Why didn't you mention this before?"

"You did not ask." Such a reasonable reply. "Shall I override Mair Dahlgren's directive, Sirantha Jax?"

"Please."

"Mair Dahlgren reports that entering this numerical sequence, interspersed with gaps of precisely 6.4 seconds, will gain you access to a maintenance submenu from which you may attempt to gain access to primary systems."

Jael seems impatient, but if he has any better ideas, he's free to pursue them. The merc shifts on the balls of his feet and casts a longing glance toward the lounge, as if imagining what the two women might be doing in there without him. Or maybe, like me, he's fucking starving.

"*Go,*" Vel says without looking at him. "I will watch over her."

"For Mary's sake. We're in a secure hangar. What exactly do you think is going to happen to me?"

And then the boarding ramp on the ship begins to unfold.

# CHAPTER 40

***Jael flicks me a wry look. "You were saying?"***

I have no fight left in me. No idea what I expect, but I'm braced for the worst when three men come strolling down the ramp. Even though they don't look alike, the conformity of their garb gives the impression of a resemblance. They're tall and slim, well coiffed, and their suits look like they cost a year's pay.

Not government guys then.

One of them strides toward us, and the others fall in behind him. That makes him the boss, I guess. On closer inspection, he's older than his fellows, but he's had good antiaging treatments. I can see the years in his eyes rather than around them. His gaze roves over me like a shark, and I decide I don't want to see his teeth. His men tuck their arms behind their backs and wait, as if for orders.

"Our employer sent us to collect you," the leader says, as if this is a routine aircab pickup. "He requires a face-to-face."

I can't think of anything more eloquent than, "Huh?" so I go with it.

"What employer?" Jael demands. "Do you realize you're attempting to detain the ambassador of New Terra?"

"Of course I do," Boss Man replies.

I glance down at myself. Even my own mother wouldn't recognize me, covered in Thermud. "How?"

"What?" The leader glances away from Jael to regard me with puzzlement.

"*How* do you know who I am?"

He ignores that for the moment. "I believe you've already made Mr. Jewel's acquaintance, Ms. Jax."

That doesn't ring any bells until I notice his intent look, a calm demeanor concealing killer intent. *They're Syndicate, of course.* I remember the jeweled brooch my mother wore, what seems like ages ago now.

*Mr. Jewel. Very clever.*

"What the hell have you done to my mother?"

I should've wondered about that long before now; I'm just not a dutiful daughter, I guess. I take a deep breath, steadying myself as best I can, though fatigue and hunger make it difficult to focus.

"That is, in fact, why we were sent to this backwater burg."

"You've been waiting for me?"

That doesn't track. How could anyone know we'd turn up here? Hell, *I* didn't even know if we'd make it out of those tunnels intact.

The older one inclines his head. "In a manner of speaking. We've been tracking you since you surfaced."

"Tracking?" I hate parroting everything he says, as it makes me sound brain damaged. Then again, it may be better if he underestimates me.

Behind us, Vel continues his attempts to get into the terminal until one of the goons steps up behind him and shakes his head. Vel sighs and puts away his tools slowly, as if wanting them to see his hands at all times. While they're watching him, I slip 245 into my pack. It's just a hunch, but I don't want them taking her away.

Given that we've disarmed ourselves, there isn't a lot

we can do at the moment. Droids will intervene at the first sign of trouble, but it might be too late if these guys are good enough. And they have that air about them.

"Your mother was kind enough to slip an isotope into your drink at your last meeting," the thug explains with a smile. "Perfectly stable and harmless, but it does permit us to monitor your movements."

"Like Fugitive scientists once used to track native populations?" I sputter in pure outrage.

To these assholes, I'm just a blip on a display panel somewhere. *Oh, there's Jax; let's go scoop her up.* If I had a blade in my hand, I'd sink it in his eye right now and fuck the consequences.

"It's perfectly harmless," he repeats, like it's a health risk I'm worried about. I guess he's never had his privacy stolen like this. "I suggest you come aboard, so we can get under way at once. We will convey you safely to your meeting."

"You actually believe I'm going with you? Are you out of your mind, or do you think I'm out of mine?"

One of his thugs takes a step forward as if he doesn't like my tone, but Boss Man waves him off. "No, I think you lack viable alternatives, Ms. Jax. You don't have a vessel. I do. And if you harbored any hope of commandeering it, know this crucial fact. I alone possess the ignition codes, and if they are not entered correctly within three tries, the whole ship goes up."

I glance at Jael and Vel, who looks impassive. They offer no suggestions, though I can feel the merc thrumming with tension at my side. He'd like nothing more than to waste these fools, but that might strand us here indefinitely. I suspect he's no keener than I am to rely on Tarn for our salvation.

But I'm not sure the Syndicate constitutes a wise substitute.

Fuck it. When have I ever been sensible? Even if the decision takes us to Mr. Jewel's private playground, at least we're off Lachion, right?

They must have a jumper on board, which means I can rest. I'll eat choclaste, shoot myself full of the chemical cocktail that's supposed to mend my bones, and try to ignore the junkie in my head. That voice tells me to jack into grimspace and frag the consequences. I have to ignore junkie Jax if I want to live.

I'm not entirely sure I do.

Before, I had March to pull me out of such thinking. I could rely on his warmth, even when I didn't realize I was doing so. Now it's just me, falling into the darkness in my own head. That's a scary place to be.

This hard man wannabe isn't as good as he thinks he is. Neither are his boys. Because while I'm thinking things over, Hit slips up behind the boss man and sets a long, filed nail against his throat.

"Don't move," she whispers against his ear, and her crooning tone raises goose bumps on the back of my neck.

"Suraya," Boss Man says without shifting a millimeter. "The poison pilot. Still doing Madame Kang's dirty work?"

I feel like I should know that name, but my mind's too fuzzy. It slips away like a sleek little fish, back into a jumbled mass of half-formed thoughts and memories.

"Keller," she returns. "Still barking on behalf of bigger dogs?"

He can't shrug, but it's implicit in his tone. "It's a living. I'd say it's good to see you, but . . ." His enforcers make an abortive movement, as if to end the impasse, and Keller apparently catches it in his peripheral vision. "No," he adds, as Hit strokes her nail down his neck. "Don't give her a reason."

Call me thick, but I don't entirely understand why he's so afraid. By the sweat streaking down his now-pasty brow, Keller thinks Hit is the angel of death, standing by his shoulder. Makes me wonder what we don't know about her.

"Hypo-implant," Jael whispers. He sounds admiring. "Black-market ware, costs mad loot. Only the most dedicated killers go for them, ones who prefer quiet jobs, no blood, no mess. The right toxin can even make it look natural, assuming no postmortem lab work."

Ah. No wonder Keller's pissing his pants. Maybe we all should be.

"What do you say?" Hit asks me conversationally. "Should I end him?"

The goon's eyes flicker wildly. I can tell he wants to appeal to my better nature, but at this point, I'm not sure I have one.

*Not so smug now, are you, asshole?*

"Probably not," I say, after a judicious pause. "He's our ride off this rock. I wouldn't mind an apology, though. They've been tracking me like a rogue wildebeest. I think that was pretty damn rude."

Hit smiles, slow and feral. "They never did. Why, I'd call that a violation of basic human rights. How can they possibly make that up to you?"

Somehow I manage to choke back hysterical laughter. Maybe we'll regret this, but I'm having too much fun to stop. "I'm open to suggestions."

To my astonishment, Vel joins the game in dry, scholarly tones. "If given full access to their ship's data, I could search for similar infractions and recommend suitable recompense."

"Fine," Keller says. "I'm sorry, all right? I had nothing to do with that. It was all Jewel. If Suraya will just let me go, we can get under way, all nice and peaceful, and then you can take it up with him in person. That's a rare honor, you know. He seldom participates in face-to-face meets anymore."

"Too many people trying to kill him?" Hit asks, butter smooth. "Now, before I step back," she adds, "I'm going to need your word as a gentleman that there will be no reprisals. I don't want your boys coming in on me while I sleep."

"Yeah, I want a guarantee of safe passage for me and my crew," I add.

"Is your friend sick?" the goon beside Vel asks.

I shake my head quickly. "No. It's just a skin condition." *He really needs to molt.*

"You have my word," Keller growls.

Personally I don't give two shits for his sworn vow, written in blood, but Hit seemed to want to hear it. In a feline motion, she drops back a few meters. Keller blots the sweat from his forehead with his forearm.

One of the goons says, "Can I—"

"No," Keller snaps. "We have a deal, and we need this truce to hold, unless you want to die in your sleep."

Damn, I'm glad Hit's on our side. *If* she is. As it stands, I think we need to find out more about this Madame Kang.

Both his boys mutter, "Yes, boss," as they head back up the ramp.

"Everyone on board before this Mary-sucking storm grounds us," Keller adds.

Well, since he put it that way, we collect Dina and follow as fast as we can.

# CHAPTER 41

***Their pilot is good.***

Despite adverse atmospheric factors, our departure goes smooth as s-silk. I've never been on a ship like this one. Instead of worn fittings, scarred and grimy conduits covered by mismatched panels, and ratty seats, everything looks brand-new. They went the extra mile and outfitted the public areas with a high-quality synth that gleams like mahogany.

With its burgundy s-leather chairs, the hub looks more like a swanky executive lounge than where the crew straps in for a jump. Even the safety harnesses manage to look decorative. At first I'm afraid to touch anything, and then I realize I don't care because I'm not paying for it.

Dina drops down and puts her head back. "I'll wait here for jump."

I'm glad, because watching her struggle breaks my heart. We pause by our assigned rooms and drop off our stuff. Then the rest of us continue learning the lay of the land.

I notice how the light fixtures shine with gilt trim. And droids going about their business have an ultrasleek look, including the cleaning bots. This is a star-class vessel, sold to those with credit ratings I can't even imagine.

It's about time we got a break. I'm not sure this qualifies, but at least it's a nice ride, and we're passengers for a change. That implies a certain loss of control over our circumstances, but tired as I am, I'll take it in trade.

While the pilot gets out of the atmosphere, Keller gives us a quick tour and introduces us to his boys. The blue-eyed one who wants to kill Hit is named Grubbs. His partner's name is Boyle. They aren't in the mood to chat, however, and disappear into the game room, our first stop. Huge wall-screen view panel, four terminals, rigged with virtual sims, and a variety of a comfortable chairs.

Keller's guys mess with the equipment, and then the room reverberates with the distinctive sound of *Real Killer*. I guess that's how enforcers relax. When they aren't cracking heads, they sim it. For a moment I stand in the doorway watching the wall screen mimic the moves they make. That might be fun later.

Keller clears his throat. "Let me show you the rest."

With a nod, I step back, realizing I'm holding up progress. I walk on, only half listening to Keller's running commentary. Vel comments now and then. So does Jael. But it sounds muzzy to me, faraway and indistinct.

As we go along, nobody says much, probably eager to clean up and crash. We can't do that until after jump, though, and we can't power up the phase drive until we're away from the planet's gravitational pull.

I pause on the observation deck, watching Lachion recede. From this height, it's a pale world except for splashes of blue where waters lie. March seems both infinitesimal and ephemeral to me now. Touching the ring on my left hand, like a talisman, doesn't bring him back.

From this height, it's like I imagined him. I ache in body and soul. Forgetting the others behind me, I lean my head against the screen for a moment, distorting the image. This isn't the real Lachion, but an array of light that forms a likeness.

His kiss, his smile, my frozen tears in the Teresengi Basin—a dozen moments run behind my closed eyelids, fragments of how we were together. And aren't anymore. I don't know how I'll bear it.

Vel comes up beside me and puts his hand on my shoulder. Don't ask me how I know it's him, but I've come to expect this kind of quiet, understated comfort from him. He doesn't speak, just tilts his head toward the corridor.

*Come away, Jax. There's a new life waiting for you.*

Maybe he doesn't mean that, or even think it, but I ascribe those words to him as I suck in a deep breath. My eyes sting, but I blink the tears back. Sometimes giving up the old life is fucking hard.

I trail the others as we continue the tour. I don't think I've ever been on a vessel so big. It must cost the annual per capita income of some small colonies to power it. Game room, observation deck, spa: This ship is like a roving resort.

I'm definitely coming back to the spa when I get a chance. I'd love a massage, a facial, and anything else I can think of. The droid attendant bears the Pretty Robotics logo, which means she's top-of-the-line. Even in my navstar days, I never traveled in such luxury. Since the Corp wanted to maximize profit, they squeezed each credit until it squeaked.

Huh. Apparently crime *does* pay.

Just then, the pilot's voice comes over the comm. Deep. Masculine. He has an accent I can't place. "We're ready for jump. Strap in, we go in five."

"How far are we traveling?" I ask.

Jael quirks a brow at me, as if to say, *I thought you'd gone mute. Too bad.* I flick my fingers at him and turn back to Keller.

"One jump and an eighteen-hour haul," he answers.

Pity. That doesn't tell me anything about our destination. We head for the hub, and for the first time in more years than I can count, I don the protective headgear along with everyone else. Envy bubbles in my gut.

Someone else will make this leap. Another jumper gets to blaze through grimspace and find the beacons. Shit, withdrawal might kill me faster than anything else. My palms feel clammy as I try to strap in.

I fumble. Hell, how does this even work? I haven't been a passenger since I was thirteen years old.

"You look funny, Jax." Jael takes the seat next to me. "You all right?"

*No.* I can't do the one thing I love more than anything else in the world, unless I want to die. My reassuring smile comes out stiff and scary, if the way the merc recoils offers any clue about my appearance.

Dina answers for me. "Of course she's not, jackass. She's tired, dirty, and she doesn't know how to put on her harness."

"Here," he says, oddly gentle. "You crisscross this, and then this one buckles to the helmet. This last one goes over the top."

"Thanks," I mutter.

I feel helpless. Old. Used up. I never minded the scars on my body, but this . . . I rub my foot over the plush carpet like a sullen child.

He studies me a moment, his pale eyes eerie in his muddy face. "You've never ridden like this? Not even on vacation?"

"Not in a really long time." Twenty years, to be exact.

He just doesn't get it. Non-jumpers never do, and there's a thrill I can't articulate. But because it might distract me, I try.

"Everyone has something that makes them special." I slant him a pointed look to make sure he takes my meaning. Jael gives me a curt nod. "So imagine if you couldn't do it anymore. Whether your gift is good or bad, losing it cuts out a large core of what made you unique."

Dina cracks, "Your big mouth covers that, Jax."

"I get it," Jael says, after thinking it over. "But you're still you."

No, I'm human detritus, what remains when the best

burns away. I quash that thought on my own since March isn't here to do it for me.

Hit offers the best piece of advice. "Just close your eyes and don't think about it. Pretend you're not missing the jump."

I'll try. Even a ship this size shudders a little when the phase drive comes online. So much energy coursing through the conduits, it couldn't be otherwise.

A minute later, Keller arrives with his goons and they strap in across from me. I'm glad they didn't witness my weakness. I tell myself I'm being a baby, letting the loss hit me so hard. Jumpers retire all the time. They teach. They live otherwise productive lives.

Why am I determined to make such a big deal out of it? Maybe I'm used to being the hero. I expected us to steal a ship, and me to sacrifice more health because my crew counted on me to jump. Take them to safety.

Am I disappointed that I don't get to be a martyr? Shit. I don't like what that says about me. I don't have to be the center of attention. I can sit back and ride like everyone else. I *can*.

I don't remember what that first trip was like back when I was a kid. Too many active jumps have nudged that memory aside. So I don't know what to expect.

Vel sits on my left. He leans over as much as he can within the harness and says, "You will experience some pressure, but it is not unpleasant. Electrical sometimes destabilizes while we pass through grimspace, so the lights may go off or flicker uncontrollably."

He's trying to make it easier. The raw place inside me eases a little. "Anything else I should know?"

"It helps to hang on to something." The bounty hunter offers his hand.

# CHAPTER 42

***Smiling, I curl my fingers through his.***

Vel's hand feels slightly sticky and indefinably wrong. While sight may deceive you, touch rarely does. He's starting to smell moldy, too. After we jump, I don't imagine we'll see him out of quarters until we arrive. I hope that's long enough for him to generate more skin, unless he intends to go as himself. I'm not sure that's a good idea.

Then again, if Syndicate intelligence is worth anything, they already know about him. So perhaps it's a moot point. I remember how Jewel said Bugs couldn't be permitted to mingle freely with humanity. Does he pose a danger to Vel?

Maybe they're using me as a blind when they intended to capture the infamous bounty hunter all along. Though I shake my head at the notion, I can't dismiss it entirely. Good to know my paranoia continues to thrive. It would help if I knew who wanted me dead.

Lightning streams over my skin. I *know* when we enter grimspace. Not because the lights flicker, although they do. No, I can feel it in my blood, in my bones. Like I'm part of the primordial matter boiling all around the ship.

When I shut my eyes like Hit told me to, I can just about see the colors. Oh, they're far away, like looking through the wrong end of a telescope, but I can see them. This can't be a delusion.

I've never heard of anyone who could sense grimspace when they weren't jacked into the ship, but I'm not imagining this. From the pure, vast silence comes the pulse of the beacons. I hear it as an echo of my own heartbeat. Since I don't know where we're going, I can't attempt to find the right ones, but I sense the navigator in the cockpit doing so.

He seems sluggish to me, unsure of our course. This jumper lacks my elation, my passion, my certainty. I never doubt I've targeted the right beacon, never have trouble translating the star charts from straight space. There's something wrong here. I've never watched anyone work before, though instructors sometimes do. If I had a control button, I'd hit the override.

I feel the way we alter course, making for a beacon. But he's overshot the jump. I don't understand how I know, but this isn't the place to phase out. Their jumper's a hack, not an artist; he can barely perceive the beacons at all, and his best guess is our worst nightmare.

The phase drive rumbles, preparing to take us back. I shake my head, struggle against my harness, shouting, "No, no, no!"

It's pandemonium. Everyone speaks at once, either telling me to shut the fuck up or trying to reassure me.

Vel squeezes my hand. "It is nearly over, Sirantha."

"No shit it's almost over, we—"

"Sit tight," the Syndicate pilot barks over the comm. "Do not remove safety gear. This is going to get rough."

Keller depresses a button on the arm of his chair. "What's the problem, Mat?"

"We've emerged in an asteroid field, sir, two days off target. And these little bastards are surrounded by pockets of highly combustible gas."

Oh Mary. I *knew* it. Well, not about the asteroid field,

not exactly, but I knew he'd gotten the jump wrong. I knew it was dangerous.

But how? *How* did I know?

"Why are you chatting with me then?" Keller demands. "Get us out of this mess and then update me."

"Roger that."

"I never realized how good you are." Because of Dina's quiet tone, it takes me a moment to register that as a compliment. "Hell of a backseat driver, but good. You get us there, time after time. Never anything like this."

I shift in my chair. "That's not true. When Vel was chasing us, I jumped us eight days out."

"Not into the middle of an asteroid field," she mutters.

With a nod, I concede the point. Until now, I never wondered how I avoid jumping back under dangerous conditions. I can't explain that knowledge; it works like a sixth sense, and I guess I assumed every other jumper has it, too.

Apparently not.

The ship tilts this way and that, testing the strength of my harness. We sling hard left and then roll. My stomach lurches as we make a full loop.

"Mary," Jael groans. "I hope I don't puke before we die."

"Relax." Keller sounds irritated. "Mat's good. He'll get us out."

A distant boom and a grinding sound belie his words.

"We're hit," the pilot announces. "And we have breach. Droids are sealing off the second deck."

Damn. Good-bye, spa. Maybe I'd better kiss my ass good-bye while I'm at it.

"Not good enough." Hit starts unbuckling her safety gear. "Tell him to give me the chair. I'm not dying today." Another explosion rocks the ship. "Go on, keep waffling, there won't be enough of this thing left to tell what it was."

Keller hesitates only a second before getting on the comm. "Mat, I'm sending someone up. Don't argue, just let her fly."

The pilot sounds oddly, inappropriately chipper. "Your funeral."

We stare at each other, taut-faced, as Hit sprints down the corridor toward the cockpit. I hope she flies as well as she fights.

"She's that good?" Dina asks.

"Better." Coming from someone who hates her as much as Keller seems to, that's high praise. He sighs. "Jewel will have my ass for messing up the new ship."

"Space the guy in the nav chair." I blurt the words before I think better of them. "He screwed up so bad—" I trail off, realizing there's no way I can know that.

Everyone swivels to look at me, the same question burning in their eyes.

"How can you be sure?" Keller asks.

"I'm not. Forget I said anything." Why give people another reason to think I'm a crazy egomaniac?

They don't look particularly convinced, but a shift in the way the ship handles distracts them. We've got Hit in the pilot seat now. The swoops feel faster, more graceful. Smaller explosions trail in our wake, but they don't touch the ship.

Maybe we'll get out of this after all.

Ten minutes later, she comes strolling down the hall from the cockpit, looking pleased with herself. "And that's how it's done. Your boys should be able to take it from here." She smiles at Keller. "And if they can't, I'd have them killed."

The Syndicate boss watches as she helps Dina from her chair, and the two of them head off to quarters. Our girl's moving better already, less drag in her leg, more free movement. Her EMP band must be doing some good.

I think Grubb speaks for all of us when he says, "Damn."

"Madame Kang's best," Boyle agrees with a sigh. "We should recruit her."

Keller shakes his head. "Jewel won't pay what she's worth. If you'll excuse me, I need to talk to those idiots in the cockpit. Deck two is off-limits for obvious reasons, but you're free to freshen up and rest."

*Rest. Finally.*

I realize I'm still holding Vel's hand, though I've damaged his skin some. "Thanks. I'm all right now."

"My pleasure." His vocalizer somehow grants the words a courtly inflection. "I believe I have some research to do now, if you will pardon me."

Warmth floods through me. I need to spend some time with him, find out all about his people, their customs, and how they show affection. If they do. So far, I've been lax, and I only know that Ithtorians don't hug.

"Of course."

Then it's just Jael and me left in the hub. He helps me untangle myself from my harness, and I haul myself to my feet. My bones pop as I arch my back.

Uneasy with the intensity of his regard, I try to smile. "What a day, right?"

"You *did* know, didn't you?"

"Know what?" I begin a slow progress toward my room, which I hope will be as nice as I imagine.

"That the jumper messed things up. Somehow, you went out there with him. You saw . . . something."

"I don't want to talk about this," I tell him tiredly. "I need a shower and then a good eight hours of sleep. Don't you have anything else to do?"

"No. You're not getting out of this so easily, Jax. You may have distracted the others, but I was right beside you. I saw your eyes."

"So what?"

The door to my room recognizes me. As it swishes open, I'm tempted to summon a bot to eject him, but that will only delay the inevitable. He'll never stop once he's got his teeth into something. I don't understand why he wants to know so badly, but he's the stubborn type.

I pause in the doorway, awestruck. This is mine? All of it? Forget the utilitarian quarters I've been used to; this is a suite. As I step onto the thick carpeting, I sink at least a centimeter.

In my inglorious past, I've stayed in hotels that weren't

this nice. I try to take in everything in a single visual sweep, blotting out Jael's droning voice. Full-sized bed with shimmering blue blanket, a bar, a personal assistance unit with gourmet kitchen-mate. The bathroom steals my breath.

"So we're going to talk about it. As your bodyguard, I have to know every last thing about you and try to figure out a way to compensate for every eventuality."

Maybe it's that simple. Maybe he just wants to be sure that whatever happened isn't a threat to my well-being. After all, Tarn is paying him to take care of me, and if grimspace poses a danger, even when I'm not jumping—actually I don't even know the answer. This is all new ground since I'm usually in the nav chair.

I sigh. "Good luck with that. I'll be in the shower."

With that, I start getting naked.

# CHAPTER 43

***It's funny how fast he averts his eyes.***

Not that I blame him. The one good thing you can say about the Thermud caked all over me, it covers my scars. I pad into the bathroom, examining all the different settings. I'm used to a san-shower that just cleans you up. This one promises to unclog your pores, steam off the dead cells, and leave you glowing with health.

"Well, let's see what this thing can do."

Midway through my shower, Jael calls, "You all right in there?"

"Yeah, why wouldn't I be? It's pure bliss."

Sound of throat clearing. "No reason."

Half an hour later, I step out and wrap myself up in an ivory robe. I find Jael sprawled on the sofa, drink in hand. But he appears to be . . . blushing?

"What?" I check the tie to make sure I'm not showing skin.

"Have a good time?" he chokes out. "You were . . . loud."

"Mmm. It was wonderful." Just to tease him, I add, "You did say you'd know the next time—"

"So I did." If anything, his embarrassment intensifies.

I can't believe he really thinks I—well, maybe I can use it to my advantage. "You'd better get used to it since you're determined to be my shadow. Privacy is overrated anyhow."

"You're mad, Jax." But he smiles.

Freshly washed, my hair stands on end like down on a baby bird. I grimace at my reflection and head for the kitchen-mate. Jael tracks me with his eyes.

"You hungry? Don't think I'll make a habit of this, but if you go clean up, I'll make us something to eat. Don't just sit there. You're crumbling all over my couch."

Maybe I can distract him from the discussion he intends to have. It's worth a shot anyway. I can't make him understand what I don't even get myself.

Jael slides to his feet. "Right, you've persuaded me, but don't imagine you're off the hook. We'll talk about it over dinner."

"The hell we will," I mutter.

I half expect him to stride boldly into my bathroom, which offers the interesting dilemma of what he's going to wear when he's done. Instead he lets himself out, pausing to murmur, "I'm just next door."

As if I'm likely to go into panic mode at the prospect of being alone. Well, it *has* been a while. Between sharing quarters with Vel and wandering the crowded Gunnar camp, this is certainly a change.

I look over the options on the kitchen-mate and nearly drool. This thing can make anything I want. Thousands of recipes both common and exotic, right at my fingertips, and now I don't know what I want.

Tapping away, I just decide to conjure us a feast. Steamed fish and rice in spicy ginger sauce, tissue-thin vegetables arrayed in a fan, and four different desserts. I hope he likes choclaste. This gourmet unit even has real wine in stock; forget the nasty synthetic stuff.

By the time I get everything laid out, Jael's back. I make a note to seal my door since it's apparently coded to admit anyone. He looks better, his freshly washed hair gleaming like molten gold.

"What if I'm allergic to fish?" he asks as he joins me at the small table near the kitchen-mate.

I grin. "Good thing this isn't real fish."

He knows as well as I do that this is simulated from base organic, but the beauty of a gourmet unit is that you can hardly taste the difference. These days, only the elite know what it's like to eat fresh fruits and vegetables, and only throwbacks consume real flesh.

"Point."

When there's food like this around instead of paste, you won't find me letting it get cold. I practically inhale mine, down two glasses of wine, and then start eyeing the desserts before Jael cleans his plate. I settle on a rich raspberry-filled truffle and nibble at it while he catches up to me.

By tacit consent, we shift to the sofa for the conversation he refuses to let slide. I close my eyes and tilt my head back, hoping to elicit sympathy, but this is Jael we're talking about. Of course it doesn't work.

"What do you want to know?" I ask with a sigh.

"What happened out there?" He touches my cheek, forcing me to look at him.

"I don't know."

"Make me understand, Jax. If grimspace poses a danger to you, I need to know it. I'm supposed to protect you from all threats, remember?"

I let out a long breath. "I could . . . feel it. Don't ask me how. It's like I'm part of grimspace when I'm not even jacked in. Doc started running tests on me, before . . ." With a weary wave, I gloss over details he already knows. "But he never came to any conclusions about what makes me different. And now he has a lot of other stuff on his plate." Massive understatement.

Both his brows go up, but I don't glimpse the skepticism I dreaded. Jael doesn't know the worst of my unstable tendencies, however, so he isn't likely to dismiss this experience as a "delusions of grandeur" fantasy. I relax a little.

"I've never heard of anything like that," he says at last. "You're a fucking legend, you know. Still jumping at your age. It's inspiring."

Mary, he makes it sound like I'm a geriatric case, beyond the hope of all antiaging treatments. I grit my teeth. Counting to ten doesn't help.

"Well, you do all right for someone who looks like he ought to be in wet naps," I tell him sweetly. "Do you shave yet, princess? I bet you couldn't grow a beard if you wanted one."

He's had enough of the wine not to get riled up, more's the pity. "You've got enough chin hair for both of us."

"Is that why you were staring so hard at my ass when I went to the shower? Because it hasn't got any hair on it?" A flip response, not one I expect to make him choke on his drink. "You *were* looking!"

"Not on purpose," he protests. "Or rather, no more than any man would when confronted with a naked woman. It's practically against the law not to look. They revoke your man membership if you play the gentleman too often. In a way, I was paying you a compliment."

"To be sure. So you haven't been guilty of ogling old ladies before?"

"You're not old in the traditional sense," he says, tilting his head with a judicious look. "Just for a jumper. You know."

Of course I do. In my first five years on the job, I attended the funerals of fifteen classmates from the academy. After that, I stopped offering to speak at their services. I swallowed my sorrows instead. That's how my nav-star legend came to be born. Not the party girl they all supposed, or at least, not for the usual reasons.

Loss seeps out from behind my mental barriers, old wounds, old pain adding to the fresh one, a big jagged hole where March used to be. So many people, gone. What Jael said is true—being the last one standing sometimes *does* feel like a curse. Just like that, my mood dips to low ebb.

I need to be horizontal and buried in blankets. A band

tightens across my chest, burgeoning into an ache that threatens to close my throat. Mary curse it, if I don't get him out of here, I'm going to break down right in front of him.

And I won't have that.

"There's nothing you can do, or need to do about what happened out there, Jael. It doesn't factor into protecting me. Doc figured out why I respond to grimspace damage the way I do, and I know what to do about it. Speaking of which, I'm due for a shot. Unless you just like needles, I suggest you get on your way."

"No," he says quietly. "Do your thing, but this conversation isn't over."

"The hell it's not. This is my room! And I don't want you in it anymore." I get up from the sofa, and my hands shake as I draw the med kit out of my bag.

I'm not sure I can manage the treatment without hurting myself. So I close my eyes. That helps a little, though I'm still millimeters away from losing it. The hypo's preset and automatic, so I just press it against my wrist. A single hiss and it's done. I push my breath out in what's meant as a sigh, but it comes out as a groan.

"Right," he says, low. "You pulled a spike out of my gut and saved my life. That might not mean anything to you, but it's *worth* something to me. I'm doing my best to be a friend to you, and you act like you've never heard of such a thing. A blind man could see you're hurting, Jax, and I know damn well why. It's because of who we left behind."

"Yeah." My head droops. I can't look at him as the tears overflow, trickling down my cheeks. "I'm pretty sure I'm dying of it, and I can't bring myself to care."

He comes to me and touches my cheek, featherlight. "Well, I do."

# CHAPTER 44

***I lean toward him, or fall.***

Jael wraps his arms around me, patting in an awkward way that's meant to be comforting. I can tell he doesn't know much about the job for which he's volunteered. If I wasn't gulping back sobs, I'd laugh at his expression. He leads me toward the sofa while I cry and cry, holding nothing back.

There are so many things tangled up inside me that I don't even know why I'm weeping. March is part of it, of course, but it's more than that: an accumulation of woe that I can't deny anymore. Tears stream freely. My nose starts to run.

"Aren't you a sight?" he whispers. "It's all right. I won't tell anyone what a wet rag you turn into after a couple of drinks. In the vids, they have you up on tables flashing your tits once you down a few rounds, so this is a bit of a shock, innit?"

I mumble into his shirt, "Fuck the vids. They're all posted by assholes."

And then I remember how many members of the gutter

press died on Lachion. That probably qualifies as speaking ill of the dead, but I don't care. I feel his hands on my back, thumping gently. You'd think I was an infant he intended to burp.

I hiccup.

The next thing I know, I'm blinking gummy eyes, and I feel stiff all over. Jael is still curled around me, one hand on my shoulder, but he's out, too. I can't tell how long we've been asleep, but it doesn't matter. We have two days to rest.

On this ship, nobody's trying to kill me, eat me, or otherwise disperse my molecules. That's a welcome change. I'm still tired, so I stagger toward the huge bed and flop down. Then I sink back into the delicious, gauzy darkness.

Much later, I surface again, feeling more coherent this time. I adjust my robe, which has gapped in all the wrong places. Rolling out of bed, I assess the situation.

Poor Jael toppled sidewise on my sofa. He's going to be sore, and it serves him right for being such a stubborn bastard. I *do* feel better, but I would've cried whether he stayed with me or not. It irks me that he shoved his way into my business, but I'm not furious over it. So I wake him by kicking him in the ankle instead of somewhere worse.

He squints up at me and groans. "Maybe you'd keep men around longer if you didn't do *that*."

The joke falls flat, but I pretend it didn't catch me in a raw place. "Yeah, well, I'm not trying to keep you. You have your own room, go to it."

Maybe I should thank him, but mostly I'm embarrassed over the way I melted down. I refuse to hash over my emotional state or give him dewy-eyed looks bursting with boundless gratitude. If he craves that sort of thing, he should hit up a girl named Fawn, who dances at the Hidden Rue on Gehenna.

As he gets up, the door slides open. I turn to see Dina standing there with a wide smile because she's on her own two feet. But the pleasure in her expression dies like light leaving a dead bulb. Her gaze shifts between the rumpled bed, my dishevelment and Jael's sleepy good humor.

"I can't believe I was actually starting to like you," she bites out. "In your mind, he's as good as dead. So why *not* replace him?" She turns so the door closes behind her, leaving her words to accuse me in her stead.

*Shit.*

Even if it stings, part of me understands why she made that mental leap. I didn't grieve years for Kai before falling for March. So maybe Dina thinks that's the way I operate. One man exits; another man enters, and I just love the one I'm with.

But it's not like that. I hope when she cools down I'll be able to explain, although in the strictest sense, it's none of her business who sleeps in my room. I'm conscious of Jael standing beside me, looking shocked. But before I deal with him, I code the door so it's only accessible to me for the duration of the flight.

He arcs a brow at me. "I guess breakfast's out of the question?"

"Out."

"Right, I'm going." And he does.

I dress in black because it suits my mood. At least short hair means I don't have to style it. Looks the same no matter what I do. I pocket 245, who still hasn't forgiven me for cutting her off back in the hangar. Maybe this will cheer her up.

Determined to get some value out of this downtime, I head for Vel's room. He said he had research to do, but I'm supposed to be tapping him as my resource on Ithtorian culture and customs. To date, I haven't been taking my role seriously, and no matter what the Syndicate wants, I can't become another Karl Fitzwilliam. Not even to save my mother's life.

Unlike me, Vel was smart enough to secure his room right away. I tap the panel and say, "It's Jax. Can I come in?"

His disembodied voice responds, "A moment please."

"Thanks."

And then the door allows me access. I slip inside. As I expected, Vel has molted, but he isn't growing any new skin as of yet. I'm not sure whether that's time related, or if he just doesn't want to wear it.

Funny how different people can take the same suite and turn it into something else. Mine has rumpled bedcovers and dirty dishes while Vel has transformed his room into a command center. Scattered devices, wires, and mechanisms make it look as though he's been here for weeks, not hours.

"What can I do for you, Sirantha?"

"I was hoping we could talk about your homeworld. I probably should've asked long before now." I leave it there, choosing not to use the excuses that hover at the tip of my tongue. "But if I came at a bad time . . . ?"

"No, I can resume my research later."

"You're really doing research?"

That surprises me. I thought he said that to explain his need for solitude. People tend to forgive a lot more eccentricity if they believe the person is of a scholarly bent.

"Yes, actually. I will let you know if I find anything."

Does that mean it relates to me somehow? For once, I don't let myself become sidetracked. I just nod.

"May I?"

"Please, have a seat."

I'm more conscious of his vocalizer now because I can see his mandible moving and hear the brief delay before the signals are translated into human speech. I wonder what it's like for him, functioning as a mimic in our world but never truly part of it. Maybe that's where I should begin.

Only the small dining unit isn't covered with various sensors and monitors, so I sit down there. While I'm at it, I order up some breakfast, or whatever meal this is supposed to be. I've completely lost track of time.

I set 245 on the table, power her up, and input my codes. "Okay if I record?"

"Go ahead."

By some miracle, she doesn't chide me for our interrupted session last time, just greets me and gets to work. I wonder if that should worry me. I nibble at a sweetbread while trying to decide how to phrase my opening question.

Finally, I decide on, "Is it hard for you?"

"What?"

Duh. *He* can't read my mind.

"You have to feel really alone sometimes, separated from . . . other Ithtorians." I barely manage not to say "people like you," which would sound prejudicial, even if I don't *feel* that way about him. "How do you cope with that?"

Vel sits down across from me, regarding me with glittering, faceted eyes. If I'm learning to gauge his natural expressions at all, I'd say he looks hesitant. "Let me ask a question of *you*, first."

"Shoot." I cram the last of my breakfast into my mouth and immediately wish I had something to wash it down.

"Do you find it difficult to look at me as I am?" Vel indicates his current form with one claw.

Between the claws, mandible, peculiar side-set eyes, chitin shell, and segmented body, there's no doubt he qualifies as unusual, if not monstrous like the Morgut. While I chew, I consider the question. But if I want honesty from him, I have to give it back. So the answer comes easy.

"At first, yeah. But getting to know you took away the strangeness. And now you're just you."

"I see." He clicks his claws, a habit I've come to identify as pensive. "To your question . . . we are, by nature, a solitary people," he says at last. "We do not form emotional bonds as your species understands them. Our society functions on social obligation, underpinned by self-interest. Temporary alliances may be formed, but not personal attachments. When such an alliance ceases to be profitable or mutually beneficial, the arrangement is terminated."

"When you say alliance, do you mean business or—" But he just said they don't do personal relationships. I have a hard time wrapping my head around that. "Give me an example. Please."

"This could take a while," he cautions me.

I smile faintly. "I don't have anywhere else to be."

"Then let's begin."

# CHAPTER 45

***I spend most of the day with Vel.***

Coming from a xenophobic race that possesses the unique ability to pass among other species and chooses not to, the bounty hunter is a walking contradiction. We spent hours talking, and I still don't have the sense that I know him. Not intimately. I'm not sure whether I can, or if he has the ability to connect as I know it.

By the time I leave his quarters, my head throbs with all the new information. And I don't know how I can remember everything, particularly the seven hundred sure ways to offend an Ithtorian. My favorite is clicking the same claw three times in rapid succession.

They find that gesture especially insulting in casual conversation because it's how partners signify they're finished with one another. Really, it's an impressively rude way to end a conversation. I wonder if snapping my fingers three times would work on people who bore the shit out of me.

I still don't entirely understand the hierarchical system Vel laid out for me. I even have diagrams, but they don't help a lot. Fortunately, 245 promised to go over the entire list with me until I can recite each item by heart.

*Joy.*

"Thanks for your help," I tell her, as we head back down the hall.

"That's why I'm here. Have you given any more thought to our discussion, Sirantha Jax?"

For a moment, I don't know what she's talking about, and then it clicks. Back on New Terra, while we were still sequestered, she asked me a favor. "If we land somewhere I can order the work done, you can pick out a body from Pretty Robotics. Since it's on Chancellor Tarn, price is no object. Have you thought about a name?"

"I am 245," she says, sounding as puzzled as I've ever heard her.

"Yeah, but if you want a humanoid body so you can accompany me to official diplomatic functions, you'll need something else, won't you?" This was her idea as well, but I see the merit in it. Then she'll be my personal assistant in every respect—and she'll be able to signal me if I'm about to make a dangerous breach in etiquette. Her memory will track that better than a human ever could. "But I guess we could call you according to whatever model you pick out. They have Claudia, Julie, Roberta, Paulette, and I forget who else."

That's a Pretty Robotics gimmick since they cater to lonely men who are also fabulously wealthy. If we go this route, 245 will get more attention than the rest of us combined. Maybe that's a good thing.

"This is important?" she asks.

"I just thought you might want to christen yourself. I mean, how many people get to pick out their own names?"

"Then I will consider all the names in my data banks, but I may need your help in a final decision. I don't wish to select one that is anachronistic or inappropriate."

"Sure, narrow down to five or ten favorites, and we'll go from there."

I turn down the hall that leads back to my room, and a

snippet of conversation reaches me from the other end. "Do you think they know?"

It's Keller's goons, Grubb and Boyle, but they haven't seen me yet. I duck around the corner, heart racing.

"Nah," Boyle says. "Keller's the best. They think Jewel really wants to talk."

Grubb laughs at the very idea, and they pass on by, talking about playing another round of *Real Killer*. I stand there a moment, wondering at the implications. Whatever this means, I suspect it isn't good.

*Dammit. We should've waited for a Conglomerate ship.*

Once they've passed, I sprint down the hall and into my room. Having the door between me and the Syndicate thugs helps some, but it's not enough. I need everyone in here now, and we need to figure out a plan of action.

First, I check something for my own peace of mind. I access the terminal, something I should've done right away, admittedly, if only I hadn't been so tired, hungry, and all-around muzzy headed. The workstation powers up readily enough, but when I attempt to access external communications, a big red screen flashes.

"I am sorry," it tells me, although it doesn't sound sorry. Machines never do. "You are not authorized to transmit to bounce-relay satellites."

*Shit.* We're officially prisoners then. No access to the outside world. In retrospect, I realize Keller promised us safe passage. He made no guarantees as to what would happen once we arrive.

I could drive myself crazy wondering whether they've decided I outlived my usefulness, but that's a waste of time. Instead I decide to invite the crew to a "party" in Dina's room. I'd hold the meeting here, but I doubt she'd come, given that she wants my head on a pike at the moment.

I call Vel first. They're probably logging this conversation, but my paranoia is well documented. In this instance it might even work to my advantage.

"Do you have a white-noise generator or something that scrambles any snooping devices that might be present?"

"Well, that certainly qualifies as one of the odder greetings I have received in my life. As it happens, I do."

"Good," I say. "Bring it with you to Dina's room, ten minutes."

Silence.

So I ask, "What's wrong?"

Another hesitation. "This is not a good time, Sirantha."

*Right.* Right after I left, he must've started fashioning the new skin he'll wear for the next three days. "When would be?"

We're both exercising caution now, and I can tell he's copped to the fact that I'm nervous. I wish I could explain, but that would defeat the purpose. And I suspect he wouldn't welcome an in-person visit just now.

"Two hours. If it is urgent, I could—"

"No, that's fine. I'll let the others know."

I spend a few hours pacing and arguing with 245 over why nobody would ever take her seriously as my personal assistant if she takes the name Colette. Her alternatives are worse.

"Dreama? Synara? Those are stripper names."

"Explain." She sounds confused again.

Four choclaste bars later and six terrible names later, I figure it's time. By the time I get there, Dina is on the verge of an eruption because her suite is full of people and she doesn't know why. Her décor looks exactly like mine, but Hit and Jael sit sprawled on her sofa, and Vel is tinkering with some equipment.

The mechanic glowers at me. "You want to tell me what the fuck's going on? Maybe you just wanted witnesses for when I kick your ass."

I can tell she's been putting in hard time with the EMP band and rehab exercises, as she's visibly stronger today. But I have no intention of brawling. Dina might be able to knock me out one-handed, but she has to catch me first.

"Save it," I say with a sigh.

To simplify matters, I produce 245 and replay the brief conversation between Grubb and Boyle. It's handy I still had her in record mode from the long session with Vel. I run it twice to make sure everyone has the gist, and then I take a seat well away from Jael.

"He lied." Hit pushes to her feet, slamming a fist into her palm. "I should've killed that scumsucker when I had him by the throat. I can take them out if Vel helps me disable droid security."

"I could," the bounty hunter says. "But I am not convinced that is the wisest course. If we execute the crew, we are left with a damaged vessel we may not be able to pilot. Keller said only he possesses the ignition codes, so it stands to reason it would require his permission to override the navigational system as well."

"That means we continue on course whether we like it or not." Dina limps over to the kitchen-mate and starts making drinks.

"And when we show up at Jewel's place with a ship full of dead bodies," Jael concludes, "he *really* won't be in the mood to talk."

"Mass murder won't solve our problems this time," I say. "Huh. Who knew?"

"The jumper's already dead." Having dropped that conversational bomb, Hit crosses to the table and helps Dina distribute the cups.

"What do you mean he's dead?" Remembering my impulsive words, I have a sinking feeling in my stomach.

"Last night, I was scouting the place," she answers without inflection. "And saw them spacing the body. I cut out before they made me."

Jael seems to read my expression. "It's not your fault, Jax. You don't get a job like Keller's by being a proper nice guy. He had to show his boss something, prove the failure had been dealt with. Or Jewel might've made an example of *him*. The Syndicate doesn't make any money off valuing human life."

"You know an awful lot about them," Dina says, eyes narrowed. "What do we *know* about you, anyway?"

His pale eyes shine with a cold light, but he masks it

with a smile. "I was a merc in Surge's company, after March's time. After I got out, I did a turn as an enforcer, yeah, for the Syndicate. I didn't much like shaking down old ladies for their pensions, so I stopped."

Hit raises a brow. "Just like that? You said farewell, and they threw you a little party. Let you walk away?"

At first I'm not sure why they're tag teaming him so hard. And then it hits me. Dina wants him to be a bad guy because she thinks I'm sleeping with him. I figure she's already told Hit her side of things. I open my mouth to defend him, but Jael doesn't need any help.

"No," he answers quietly. "I had to kill a few people to get the message across. I've done things I'm not proud of in the name of survival. But I expect that's the case for everyone in this room."

A chill shivers through me at his tone. With the possible exception of Vel, who has more integrity than anyone I've ever known, he's probably right. Silence meets his words, and I think he's even managed to instill some respect in Dina. She won't mistake him for just another pretty face again.

Jael smiles. "Can we get back to business, or do you have further questions?"

# CHAPTER 46

***I let the silence build for another moment. Until just*** now, nobody noticed the steel that braces Jael's pretty exterior.

Then I say, "I think that's a good idea. We don't want them to catch us flat-footed."

"This allows us time to plan," Vel agrees. "Which is to the good."

He's activated the thingie that should jam any snooping devices that might be present. Now he sits beside Jael, hands at his sides. Vel shows a reserve only present in humans who possess some behavioral dysfunction.

"We're still going to see Jewel," Hit points out. "I don't see how we're any better off."

"Can we assume they mean you harm, Jax?" Jael asks.

"It stands to reason. They asked me to fuck up my attempts at diplomacy because they don't want to see interstellar affairs stabilize. Outfits like the Syndicate profit substantially when there's no central authority to question its activities."

I wave away the cup Dina tries to hand me, thinking it

might be poisoned, or at least doctored to give me the shits for a good seventy-two hours. Then I get up and pace, back and forth from the door all the way to the bathroom and back again. Something's niggling at me, but I can't figure out what.

"But Tarn is covering for you," Jael says after a moment. "He's turned our blunders into what looks like heroism on the vids. First we liberate Emry Station, and then we venture into the heart of a war zone, bringing aid? I bet that's how he spun it. If you continue on your goodwill tour as scheduled, the Ithtorians will be properly impressed by the time you arrive."

Dina forgets she's mad at us for a moment. "So they need to detain your ass. If you simply disappear, they can leak whatever story they want."

"You don't think they'll just kill us?" The pilot furrows her brow like that doesn't make sense to her.

I shake my head. "If they wanted me dead, I would be. They caught us off guard in the hangar, and had a clean shot at me before you showed up."

"I agree," Vel puts in. "If they stood to benefit from Sirantha's death, they would have already arranged it. I cannot imagine that they are prone to wasting resources. If your supposition is correct regarding their motivations, they simply need to hold you long enough to ruin your reputation. Once they let you go, you will not be able to adequately account for your failure, and my people will not be disposed toward permitting any further diplomatic overtures."

"Why is that so important?" Dina wants to know.

"Well, for one thing, there's a prejudicial element to it," Jael answers. "They don't want Bugs passing freely among us because it would become impossible to know 'whom to trust.' No offense, Vel."

The bounty hunter lifts a shoulder in an odd half shrug. "None taken."

"That can't be all of it, though." Hit shakes her head, brow furrowed.

I tend to agree. "If it was *just* human supremacy rearing its ugly head again, they'd just kill me. And the next ambassador. And the next, until people got the message and stopped taking the job. Groups like the Pure Populist Front don't operate under the banner of subtlety."

"Point. So what's the missing link?" Jael doesn't seem afraid of what's in the cup, taking a long sip.

I get tired of pacing and resume my seat on Vel's other side. He slides me an oblique look, and then says, "The Morgut."

We all shift, eyeing Vel expectantly.

He goes on without prompting. "I have been researching the increased frequency of Morgut attacks. In the last thirty days, they have targeted twenty remote stations, outposts and/or research facilities. That is a seventy-five percent increase, correlating to one significant event. I posit that Farwan's fall sent the message that humanity is, at this time, weak and disorganized, thus demarcating you as ideal prey. You also possess the side benefit of being delicious."

Was that a joke, albeit a dark and twisted one? I grin in appreciation.

"That's why the Conglomerate is desperate to get the Ithtorians on board. Tarn will do anything to make it happen." Dina slaps her good knee in realization. "My politics are rusty, but this makes perfect sense."

"Enlighten the rest of us," Hit says with a wry smile.

I lean forward as Dina explains, "From what you told me about your encounter with the Morgut on Emry, Vel was the only one they feared. He's Ithtorian, not human, and that makes him a hunter, not prey. He speaks their language, therefore he's considered an equal. If the Ithtorians side with humanity in the burgeoning conflict, that will give the Morgut pause, hopefully preventing an escalation to all-out interstellar war, the like of which we haven't seen since—"

"The Axis Wars," Jael finishes flatly.

*Shit.* For a moment I just sit there, numb, and hellaciously impressed by Dina's insight. She's damn smart beneath her gruff façade. Then again, I keep forgetting that at one time, she used to be royalty, schooled to see nuances like this.

Vel nods. "I concur with that assessment. As before, however, you fail to address the most crucial question."

Thinking isn't my strong suit, so it's a good thing I'm surrounded by geniuses. "What would that be?"

Jael supplies it. "What does the Syndicate stand to gain by promoting a war between humanity and the Morgut?"

"They sell weapons," Hit answers at once. "Increased revenues."

"It was a rhetorical question," the merc grumbles. "I know that. They also hire out as enforcers, which means they could stand to gain a lot in security contracts. Merchant ships in need of protection, special forces hired to guard remote outposts."

Dina nods. "The possibilities are limitless. If they play it right, they could step into the void left by the Corp and edge out the Conglomerate entirely."

"But to achieve that," Vel continues, "they need to discredit Sirantha, not execute her."

"So we've been kidnapped."

My mouth tightens. I have no doubt we'd have figured it out sooner or later, but surely this helps. Instead of taking things at face value, we're going to be looking for a way out from the jump. We'll find a way; we always do.

"I theorize that Jewel intends to keep Sirantha out of trouble until Tarn has no hope of putting a positive spin on her absence," Vel adds.

"In other words, the Syndicate thinks I'll make a fine scapegoat. That sounds familiar. Given my track record, I get to be the worst ambassador ever, possibly rivaling Karl Fitzwilliam."

I decide to risk Dina's hospitality after all, but I program my own drink, just in case. Mmm, hot choclaste makes everything better. Even hearing that you'll be credited with precipitating the worst conflict since the Axis Wars.

"Depends on how badly the war goes with the Morgut,

but yes." Vel finally shifts, steepling his hands together. If he wasn't wearing the faux skin, I have no doubt he would be clicking away as a sign of deep thought.

Jael pushes to his feet. "We'd better disperse before they come to find out why we're meeting in secret. I mean, we can assume they know we know something, and they can try to guess what we know, but nobody really knows what anybody else knows, you know?"

"If you do that again, I will *kill* you." Hit glares at him. "I'm not kidding."

Yep, there's a reason she gets on so well with Dina. Not sure where that relationship is heading, and it's not my business. But it's good to see Her Highness smiling again, whatever the reason.

*Crap.* I just ordered this drink. With a mental shrug, I drain it in one gulp. It's meant to be sipped, not slurped, but I'll be damned if I let it go to waste.

Nobody's surprised when Hit opts to stay, but I let the guys file out first. I pause at the door. "Look, it's not what you think. He's just overzealous, that's all."

To my surprise, Dina flashes me a sheepish smile. "Yeah, Hit talked me out of that. She said she can always tell when somebody's getting down, and you haven't had any since we left Lachion."

My eyebrows feel like they're shooting off the top of my head. "She can do what now? How?"

Hit smiles. "If I told you that, I'd have to kill you."

"Funny," I mutter. "Like I haven't heard that line a thousand times. It was old when your great-grandmamma was young."

In the pilot's case, however, it just might be true. I opt not to stick around long enough to find out. I have work to do.

# CHAPTER 47

***We're on Venice Minor.***

Kai and I vacationed here once, four years ago. There's a unique brilliance in the sunshine, and the quality of the air possesses an indefinable sweetness. It actually soothes the lungs as you draw it in, soft and balmy. Back then, I laughingly called it paradise, but today it's my prison, however prettily they package it.

And let me say, it's a fabulous villa, all shimmering white stone designed in faux-classical style. Spacious grounds with seven open gardens and terraces invite you to take a stroll; tiered balconies overflow with miniature fruit trees. Yes, you can pluck grapes right off the vine and peaches from the bough. Sweetness drizzles from your lips down your chin.

Though Keller and his goons refuse to confirm, I know perfectly well where we are. And the first time I get access to an unsecured terminal, I'll bounce a message so that the whole world knows, too. They're not blaming this on me; I refuse to be held responsible for increased Morgut attacks and diplomatic failure on Ithiss-Tor.

Maybe I took my role lightly at first, but our time on Emry, and later, on Lachion, put me ass deep in human suffering. I won't stand aside. I won't let the Syndicate neutralize me with promises of future meetings and astonishing opulence.

Keller assigned us lavish suites that actually manage to dim the luxury we enjoyed while aboard the ship. I refuse to be distracted by promises of steam baths, pure-earth facials, and deep-tissue massages, however. I pace my gilt-and-ivory cell, feverish with the need to act.

Everything is coded. It practically requires Keller's permission to take a bath. He plays the role of host quite convincingly. If I didn't know better, I'd almost believe him when he says, "Mr. Jewel has been called away unexpectedly, but he wishes you all to avail yourself of his hospitality in the meantime."

*Bullshit.*

I'm starting to wonder if this Mr. Jewel even exists. He might be Keller for all I know. The voice that spoke through my mother's voice was distorted enough that I wouldn't recognize it if I heard it without augmentation.

The first day, I amuse myself playing with the ridiculously sophisticated wardrober that came with my room. The Fashionista 4000 has patterns and styles that I've never seen before. By the time I'm finished, I've come a long way toward replenishing all the clothes I've seen lost or destroyed along the way.

In some of them, I might even look like an ambassador, although Dina refuses to watch me try on outfits and give me her opinion. Too bad, since she's the only one of us with any experience in such matters. But maybe I shouldn't have asked because she wears a queer look when she shakes her head.

"That's all behind me," she says quietly. "I'm a mechanic now."

"Yeah, okay." I turn from the mirror, clad in a filmy scarlet dress that gives me the look of a fetish vid star not afraid to show some skin. "I'm sorry."

"I'm going to go see what Hit's up to." The way she leaves makes me sure I've struck a sore spot.

Damn, I hate when I'm an insensitive asshole. Usually I can see it coming, but this one blindsided me. Now that I'm thinking about it, I can imagine Dina sitting in her sister's rooms, watching them try on clothes, talking about the parties they'll attend. Maybe the coup on Tarnus took place twenty years ago, but she still wears the scars. Hers just go further than skin deep.

With a sigh, I peel off the red gown and don something more sensible: skinny white slacks, white vest, and light woven shoes. While checking to make sure I got the sizing right on the new clothes, I notice that my dark hair's almost three centimeters long now, and it's starting to curl. I'm finally losing the lost-refugee look.

With a shrug, I close the closet door. Most times, when I look at my reflection, I see the scars to the exclusion of all else. They remind me of the people who died for the Corp's greed; I carry their shadows in my skin.

If I'm a walking memorial, my life has to mean something. I never used to think along those lines. Never saw patterns or purpose—I think that's March's influence. I force back the mood shift that threatens at the thought of him. No time for that. I'll yearn or grieve, or whatever the right emotion is, later. For now I'll do some poking around; see what I can find out.

Mary, I can't believe I have to put my faith in a politician like Tarn. Now that I understand his angle—and what he's trying to prevent—it scares the shit out of me. I hope he can come up with an explanation for where I am *this* time. I'm supposed to be on Ielos, inspiring the pioneers that eke out an existence on the winter world.

He must think I'm the biggest fuckup in the world. When we win free, I'm going to take this job seriously. I can do this. I can be more than Jax the jumper. I've already memorized half the list that Vel went over with me. Morning to night, 245 drills me mercilessly, and it's not like I have anything else to do.

Hit would like to slaughter everyone on the estate and steal a ship. But then she tends to solve all problems with a closed fist, which explains why she and Dina get on so well. Fortunately, cooler heads have prevailed so far, and we're doing recon, trying to find out how many men are at this place, what types of ships are docked here, and what security we can expect—Vel's forte.

I hate relying on Vel, but my options are limited. Realizing I'm pacing, I wheel as I come up against the glastique door that bars me from the terrace. I could key it open, as Keller kindly gave me security codes—but it wouldn't help in the grand scheme of things. We're prohibited from wandering off estate grounds—"for your own safety," as Keller put it—and there's a shock field around the perimeter to protect us from marauding native animals, since the undeveloped portions of Venice Minor consist of wild jungle and dense rain forest.

Well, I have to do *something*. In the last two days, the only thing I've achieved is a light tan. While I no longer look so sick or pasty—and daily injections seem to be shoring up my rickety bones—I need to accomplish something substantial. The past months, I've felt like deadweight that just slows people down.

As I'm getting ready to head out, the door bot tells me, "You have a visitor, Sirantha Jax. Allow entry?"

"Who is it?" I've learned something since March walked into my cell on Perlas Station. I always ask the caller's ID now.

After a brief pause, the bot answers, "Vel."

I find that oddly charming. The bounty hunter doesn't use nicknames or terms of endearment, but he's adopted my mode of address for him? From what he's said, his people don't adopt new customs easily, which makes their ability to mimic alternate forms all the more intriguing.

Most Ithtorians would consider the way Vel lives vulgar. There's a certain stigma attached to concealing his true appearance. The ability developed as a trait meant to enhance hunting prowess, not to allow an Ithtorian, who is clearly superior, to pass among the soft skins.

"Let him in."

The door swishes open, and Vel steps inside. He's getting better at smiling in greeting, simulating the type of expression that people wear when they're happy to see someone. I smile back because whenever he's around, I feel steadier.

"They gave you the princess room." He takes in the elevated bed with its elaborate netting, and the furniture that shimmers with gold.

I arch a brow. "I figured everyone's room looked like this, which must make you boys feel less than manly."

He radiates puzzlement, though his face doesn't alter noticeably. "How could a color scheme affect my gender?"

"Never mind." Sometimes I forget that while Vel might be masculine, he is definitely not a *man*. "What's your room like then?"

I figure he'll get around to the reason behind his visit, and it doesn't hurt to be social. I could use the practice since the Ithtorians will be judging my manners.

"It is green," he says.

Well, that doesn't tell me much. Thankfully, it doesn't matter.

"You want something to eat or drink? I have a full gourmet kitchen-mate in here. And there's a peach tree on my balcony." I must admit, playing the hostess doesn't come natural to me. I'm ready to demand what he found out, which doesn't bode well for my aptitude for political maneuvering.

"If it contains citric acid, I will become ill. Thus, I must decline."

At this point, I give up. I can practice the art of patience later. "Have you finished with your recon? What can you tell me?"

He takes a seat on the long, soft white sofa. "I have. I took a look around the compound, examined security measures, and listened to Grubb and Boyle for an extended period of time. When they were otherwise occupied, I managed to access one of their personal communication units and I downloaded all relevant data. After lengthy analysis, I believe I have detected a fault in their security that can be exploited. But it will require complex planning and some sleight of hand."

"Vel," I breathe. I somehow manage to control the urge to hug him around the neck. "I knew you'd come through. Tell me what you need."

"It will take everyone, operating in tandem, to make this work," he says. "But I believe I've located an old terminal in the sublevel of the structure. It has been decommissioned, but if you take Dina with you, you should be able to patch back into the system. I don't believe such a task would surpass her capabilities."

Given that I've seen her repair a ship with glue, copper wire, and pure voodoo, I'm sure he's right. "Okay, what will the rest of you be doing?"

He tells me.

# CHAPTER 48

***"You sure Jael and Hit can pull this off?" Dina mutters.***

She has some reason to worry. We laid out a three-prong plan, and if anything goes wrong, we'll be in the soup for sure. Timing is crucial. It's a good thing we learned to rely on each other in the tunnels; otherwise, we wouldn't have dared risk something on this scale.

We're down in the basement, not somewhere we should be wandering. I doubt we could convince anyone we're sightseeing. This will work, though. It has to.

I cock a brow at her. "Do you think *we're* better qualified to take out targets quickly and quietly?"

Dina responds with a withering look. "Don't be an idiot. You have the schematics?"

After a few uninterrupted days of exercise and EMP stimulation, she's walking so much better that it takes me a minute to understand why she's so touchy. I'd never know she had a transplant such a short time ago. Her limp isn't even debilitating now; it just throws off her gait some. Doc did a good job picking the replacement limb. Wisely, I decide not to mention any of those thoughts.

"Right here." I loft 245, who doesn't say anything. But she's powered up, ready to play her role.

I don't know if this is genius or desperation, but if I had to guess, I'd call it a reckless marriage of the two. The tricky part arises from not being able to check the others' status, because our comms can't connect to the wireless system. Or rather, aren't being permitted to do so. We're welcome to use their terminals for room-to-room calls, of course.

*Yeah, right.*

"If Vel does his part on time, we'll get in and out in less than two minutes."

The alternative goes unspoken. If he doesn't, alarms sound, Keller's goons come running, and—well, I'm not sure what comes next, but I'd guess it's not good. I imagine there's a limit to what they're willing to put up with. They could transfer me to an altogether-less-agreeable prison, or if they lose patience with the babysitting job entirely, they might off me. As Jael pointed out, these guys don't make money off valuing human life.

As we pause outside the door, I scan the hallway, take a deep breath, and then activate 245. "Johann Keller, requesting access."

She can reproduce a voice with a 98.5 percent accuracy. Let's see if that gets us in the door. Vel should've patched into the cameras by now, so if anyone's watching, it looks like we're not here.

"Granted," the bot tells us politely.

We hasten into the room before something can go wrong, and the door slides closed behind us. I draw up short, causing Dina to slam into my back. Her weight makes me *oof*, and I nearly drop 245, who responds with a cautionary, "Be careful, Sirantha Jax. In your current financial state, you cannot afford to replace me."

"I couldn't replace you even if I had a trillion credits," I tell her.

Dina ignores us as she scowls at where we've ended up. Droid parts litter the filthy counters, and a half dozen broken units lean up against the wall—chassis, arms, legs, even heads. Something stands in the far corner, covered by a tarp. No terminals, not even the decommed one Vel's schematics reflected.

*Shit.*

"I don't think we'll find anything useful in here."

The mechanic looks like she wants to slap me. "No shit. They must've made some changes since those plans were uploaded."

"Or they planted the wrong ones on purpose." I wouldn't put it past them.

*Nothing like running us around for entertainment.* It saves them worrying that we might actually accomplish something. Keeps us busy until the elusive Mr. Jewel sees fit to turn up and deal with us.

Well, I'll be damned if I'll wait. There has to be *something* we can use. I start to rummage quickly, not knowing whether there are cameras in here. I can't spot any of the usual tells, but the room is dark and grimy with months of accumulated dust. Whoever used to tinker down here doesn't anymore.

"What're you doing?" Dina wants to know. "This is a complete waste of time."

"Is it?" I yank the cover off the thing in the corner and only just manage not to stagger back in shock.

Her eyes widen, just as mine do. "Well, maybe not."

"What is it?"

She comes over to examine what I've found. At first I thought it was a dead body, but the flesh feels smooth and supple when I poke it. For all intents, we've found a woman down in storage, eyes closed as if in repose. She has brown hair and an aesthetically perfect face that comes from a composite of many beautiful people.

Bracing herself on the wall, Dina bends and lifts its bare foot. "She's a Lila, one of Pretty Robotics's older models. See the logo stamped on her insole? They changed the line about five years ago and shifted away from classical beauty, went more for the lush, showy designs."

"Bigger boobs?" I guess.

"Among other assets."

"Is she broken?" Why else would she have been dumped down here?

"Lemme take a look."

She pops a panel on the droid's forearm, taps a few buttons, but nothing happens. "Looks like her chip is fried. Expensive repair."

"Unless . . ." I look at 245, hold her up beside the Lila. "What do you think? She's been asking for a way to join the action. Could you manage a brain transplant?"

"It's not my forte, but maybe. I have a knack with most machines."

"I can help," 245 volunteers. "Once you begin the process, I can tell you what connections remain to be made and what systems I am able to control."

"Let's try it," Dina decides. "This unit may have security clearances that 245 can exploit. That alone makes it worth tackling. Plus I like a challenge. Jax, find me some tools."

"Right." I barely manage not to salute and call her "Your Highness" just to rag on her. After what happened earlier, I'd rather not test Dina's mood, particularly not when my very helpful, damn-near-indispensable personal assistant depends on her good offices.

"This isn't going to be a quick in and out," she warns me. "In the original plan, Vel only gives us ten minutes to bounce a message out, telling Tarn where we are."

"Then let's hope the third prong works without a hitch. If Jacl and Hit take care of the goons for us, maybe nobody will come looking."

She shrugs. "And maybe this room isn't on camera. We can't worry about it now. The die is cast. Hand me the silver one. No, smaller than that."

I feel like a particularly inept medical assistant, but I pass her the implement as she begins the procedure. Dina actually unscrews the top of the droid's skull, lifting it off, hair and all. Disembodied, the mass of shimmering chestnut hair looks macabre on the dirty table.

I look away in time to find Dina another tool, this one with a curved end. The model's head is empty; they've already scrapped the ruined bits apparently. To my untrained eye, it looks as if she could just set 245 in there. The space inside the droid's skull seems perfectly sized to accommodate my PA.

She confirms that with an astonished murmur. "I had no idea the pleasure models could be adapted for business so easily."

"I believe you will need to remove my external casing," 245 tells us. "If you were not present, Sirantha Jax, and your correct security codes active, such a procedure would destroy me, along with everything in my data banks."

"But it's safe now? Because I'm here, and I've . . . authorized the installation?" I'm not sure what else to call it.

"It should be." But she sounds unsure. "There are risks associated with exposing my inner workings, but they should be minimized if I am swiftly housed in my new casing."

*Heh.* Only 245 would call this slim, perfect body a *casing*. I wonder how she'll deal with men hitting on her. And they certainly will.

"Well, let's get it done before we're interrupted." Dina takes 245 from my hands, and damn if I don't feel like an anxious parent. "How do I get you open? I don't see any seams."

That strikes me weird, too, akin to asking a patient to consult on her own surgery. However, 245 responds with aplomb. "I will raise the temperature of the two spots on either side where you must apply pressure."

Dina closes her eyes, running her fingertips along the sides of the sphere. "Got it. Here and here."

And 245 pops into segments with tiny silver screws showing. "That is correct. Be sure to ground yourself before touching any of my sensitive components."

I feel myself start to sweat. It trickles down my neck to the small of my back. "You sure you know what you're doing?"

The mechanic glares. "Will you shut up? You're making *me* nervous. And I need a steady hand."

"Do not worry," the PA reassures me. "All will be well, Sirantha Jax. But perhaps you should permit us some room to work."

*And stop watching,* I add silently.

"Fine." I take a deep breath. "I'll be over here if you need me. Guarding the door. Or something."

"Thanks." Dina's already lost interest in my angst, getting straight to work.

I turn my back, hoping for the best.

# CHAPTER 49

***The operation is a success.***

For a moment, I just watch 245 taking her first steps. Her movements are jerky and unsure, but she's doing it. The way she moves her head strikes me as unnatural, too, scanning rather than looking, but at least she's ambulatory. I'm so proud.

"This is very interesting," she says in the voice I chose for her.

"Great job, Dina."

She shrugs like it's no big deal, but I can see that she wants to smile. "It wasn't too bad once you left me alone. We should get out of here, though."

"Agreed. Shall we, 245?"

"I have given that a considerable amount of thought," she tells me. "And I believe a numeric designation is no longer appropriate."

"What did you pick?" I fiddle with the controls, but I can't get the door open.

"Constance," she answers. "It means constant or steadfast. I will take the surname Riddle because of my nature."

I like it, actually, not that my approval is paramount. "Good choice. Can you get us out of here, Constance?"

"Let me try." She pauses, head tilted. "This unit possesses basic clearances. Let's see if these codes still work."

They do, and the door slides open. We step out into the dark hallway, so different from the ivory elegance of the upper stories. Keller comes around a corner and heads right for us.

*Too late to run.* My heart races. By his expression, he isn't sure what we're doing down here. Well, that makes two of us. I hope 245, er, Constance keeps quiet. If she speaks, he's going to know she isn't programmed to simulate sexual arousal.

"That unit is broken," he says by way of greeting. "The boys got a little rough with her one night."

*Ew.* It explains why she was in storage, though. "Dina repaired her," I answer, trying to project the old Jax, the party girl people saw on the vids. "It's pretty quiet around here. So we're going to have a little party. You want to come?"

Keller seems undecided. My skin crawls. If he says yes, we'll have to kill him. It won't be as quick and elegant as Hit could manage, but we'll get the job done.

Making matters worse, I'll have to play the femme fatale. Dina doesn't have the hetero skill set, and Constance can't pass as a pleasure droid. I try on what I hope is a flirtatious smile, and run my fingertips down the front of his shirt.

He steps back. "I'm afraid I can't mix business with pleasure. I need to find Grubb and Boyle. But don't let me get in the way of your good time."

Thank Mary, he's going to let us take the bot without questioning the repair. If he knew anything about the damage to this model, he'd realize there was no way to fix her without a new personality chip. We brush past him, heading for the lift, but my pulse doesn't slow until we put a floor between us.

"He's not going to find Grubb and Boyle, is he?" I need a minute to figure out our next move.

We should've gotten a message out by now, and apart from having found a body for 245, which wasn't exactly urgent, we're no better off. I lead the way down the hall, away from this part of the house at least. The other two follow.

"I don't think so. We didn't send a kind, gentle team to take care of them, did we? When Keller finds them—"

"We become Venice Minor's Most Wanted," I finish.

"Would you really have fucked him?" Dina raises a brow at me.

"I was going to distract him so you could hit him in the head."

She grins. "Good thinking."

"His heart raced in an unusual manner," Constance observes. Hearing 245's voice come out of this gorgeous woman gives me a little start. "That signifies excitement, nervousness, or anxiety, does it not?"

"You could tell that?" I realize I have no idea what this Pretty Robotics model is capable of. I always preferred my companions with a pulse.

"I am able to monitor physiological reactions," she confirms. "Pulse, respiration, body temperature. I believe my predecessor may have used it to gauge reactions to her overtures."

"But with some adaptation, you could use it as a lie detector," Dina says. "That could come in handy."

In my role as ambassador, assuming I ever get there, it would prove invaluable. Constance apparently agrees because she answers, "I need more data regarding the normal spectrum for nonhumans, but yes. I could utilize my sensors in that manner."

"My secret weapon," I say.

"Will I be a secret?" the droid asks. "Do you plan to pass me as human?"

I haven't begun to think of that, or the ethical pitfalls involved. "I don't know. Is that legal?"

"I can check my data banks."

Dina shakes her head at both of us. "Stay focused, please. You can worry about the AI precedents later."

As we move, the villa seems ominously silent. But if Vel, Jael, and Hit have done their jobs well, the place might well be devoid of life, except for us. I haven't heard the report of weapons, nothing but the soft rasp of our shoes against the patterned tile floor.

Time runs against us. Every minute I spend here and not on Ielos works against us. Tarn's excuses won't hold forever.

"We need to expedite an escape, do we not?" Constance must've been running the problem over from various angles.

I nod. "That's the idea."

"Perhaps my basic clearances will work on a communication terminal," Constance suggests. "They may not have blocked them because prior to my installation, this unit would never have possessed the impetus to use such a device."

I stare at her for a moment. "That's an astonishingly simple yet brilliant idea. Your room is closest," I add to Dina. "Let's see if this'll work."

The mechanic's room is quite unlike mine, more masculine, done in mahogany and gold. Our quarters share certain amenities, however, such as the spacious floor plan and luxurious appointments. Her bed doesn't have the intricate netting, however, or the fanciful carvings on the headboard.

Constance heads for the terminal and keys in her codes. We share a tense moment, and then she glances at me, as if in search of approval. I step up behind her in time to see the screen flash to a new set of options.

"Security for the whole house uses the same central computer, which accepts the same algorithmic sequences," she explains.

"So what works for the doors also works on the terminals." Being mechanically minded, Dina figures it out much faster. "Don't just sit there, bounce a message."

"I have Chancellor Tarn's node address, but I require content."

With her looking like a vid actress, it's harder to remember how literal she can be. "Tell him we're being held on Venice Minor by the Syndicate, and we need help."

"Can you attach a worm to the message so he can trace the message to its origin?" Dina asks. "That'll help him find us faster. And bury it in the subsystem logs if you can, so it's not immediately noticeable if someone is monitoring communications."

For several tense, nerve-wracking moments, we watch her work the terminal with all the care of a tightrope dancer. She's clumsy with her fingers at first, unused to such an imperfect interface. And then columns of symbols and numbers pour down the display panel, green tinged, yellow tinged.

*So far so good.*

"Yes, yes, and done," Constance tells us at last. "After sending it, I altered the time stamp to conceal it from prying eyes. If there is no secondary screening system, our message should reach the Chancellor within twelve hours."

*Twelve hours.* But we don't know how long it'll take to get somebody out here. Maybe we shouldn't count on him. But maybe he can spin things with the truth. I can see the talking heads now: *The New Terran ambassador has been kidnapped. No ransom demands have been received as yet . . .*

The timing of the door chime makes me jump, and Dina looks edgy as a chem-head in search of her next fix. I look around for a weapon. Find nothing. They confiscated all our hardware before we boarded, and we haven't seen any of it since. Jaw clenched, I take up a heavy bronze statuette on a side table while Dina takes up position on the other side of the door, beside the control panel.

I nod. It's *her* room.

"What?" That's classic Dina right there, down to the irascible tone.

"Everything okay?" Hit asks. "Can I come in?"

"Fine," Dina answers, unlocking the door.

The tension drains out of me as Dina lets the pilot in.

Jael strolls in behind her, but he draws up short when he catches sight of Constance, now sitting on the sofa. Well away from the terminal. Smart.

*This should be fun.*

"Well then. I had no idea you'd made such a charming friend, or I'd have been back long before now. How'd things go by the way?"

"We got the job done," Dina answers briefly. "You?"

Jael smiles. "Us, too."

My gaze fixes on a small splotch of blood on the collar of his pale blue shirt.

Though they don't tell us where they hid the bodies, the Syndicate is down five hired thugs.

# CHAPTER 50

***We're deep in strategy sessions of phase two.***

So far, the best idea is to steal a shuttle that's strong enough to handle straight space, turn on the distress signal, and wait for rescue. I don't like the uncertainty, however. There's no telling who might pick us up.

At least this Jewel has a vested interest in my survival, since he wants to use me. Then again, there's no telling what he might do when he discovers we've been picking off his guys. We need to get out of here, one way or another.

Still, I can't regret leaving Lachion with them. The arrival of another Conglomerate ship might've had disastrous consequences for Gunnar-Dahlgren. Their battle is going to be hard enough.

"I have studied their security in some detail," Vel says. "And the only vessel we can access is the mini scheduled for repair. Using Constance's clearance codes, I assigned some tech droids to begin work immediately. Since it was not scheduled for maintenance until next week, they should not consider it a flight risk."

"How long before it's operational?" Dina asks.

"Eight hours total," the bounty hunter answers. "Seven hours remaining. I could not divert the entire fleet without arousing some suspicion. If this place were not almost entirely automated, questions would have arisen already."

"A point in our favor," Jael notes. "And since the place is so big, they're probably still looking for the guys who went missing."

"How many do you think are on the grounds?" I don't want to think about fighting our way out of here. Syndicate or not, I've seen enough bloodshed to last a lifetime. Plus Dina and I still qualify as the weakest links.

We can't hold our own in a fight yet. I'm stronger than I was—and so is she—but neither of us could take on a trained enforcer. But maybe Vel, Hit, and Jael are strong enough to make up the difference.

"In all?" Hit asks.

I nod.

The pilot looks thoughtful. "For a place of this size, at least ten. Madame Kang would have insisted on twenty, though. But she relied more on manpower than technology. She was old-fashioned in some ways."

"Perhaps the extra guards travel with the one called Mr. Jewel," Constance suggests. "In his absence, there is less to protect, only material goods, which can be replaced more easily than a person of some importance."

Jael squinches up his eyes at the droid, probably in remembered embarrassment. I let him flirt with her for a good five minutes before explaining why Dina and I were snickering.

Vel agrees. "When their leader arrives, we will likely have more men with which to contend."

"All the more reason to get our asses out of here," Dina says flatly. "We should stay together, and in seven hours, we make a run for the shuttle."

"If we have to shoot our way out, so be it." Jael spins a laser pistol he took off one of the guards.

"Don't even think about taking that thing on board," Hit warns him.

The merc glares at her. "You think I'm stupid? I could dismantle that little skiff we're taking up with a sonicblade, let alone one of these. And I don't intend to experience the joy of vacuum firsthand."

*Two alphas, one small ship. This will be fun.*

"Settle down," I say aloud. "Jael won't be taking any laser weapons up. He may look young, but he's not devoid of sense."

To my surprise, he slides me a layered look that ends in a half smile. By his expression, hc read something significant into my defense, but I don't have time to figure out what. Maybe he hasn't been accepted like this before, and he appreciates when I have his back; I *hope* that's all it is. Hit doesn't know he's Bred, though, or she might be reluctant to work with him. I don't know her well enough to gauge her prejudices.

Vel says, "We should pack up our gear and convey it to a central location."

I suspect I won't be able to carry all the clothes I made in the wardrober, let alone fit them all in my pack. That holds three or four outfits at best, so I need to pick my favorites. When I reach Ielos, I want to make a good impression.

I refuse to think about alternative outcomes. We'll do this, and I'll be a *real* ambassador. I'll do anything to make this work with Ithiss-Tor. I'll even stick to Tarn's script if I have to, because I finally understand what's at stake.

I wish the bastard had leveled with me before we left New Terra. Then again, maybe I would have taken his fear as political maneuvering. Maybe I wouldn't have taken the threat seriously without seeing the carnage on Emry Station.

I push to my feet. "Come on, Constance. Let's go make you a new outfit. You can't wear *that* to diplomatic functions."

The droid tips her head, studying her shiny silver halter dress. "It does look more appropriate for one who makes a living selling sexual favors, does it not?"

She startles a laugh out of me although she wasn't joking. The Lila unit does precisely that, so she was stating a fact. Constance watches us, as if trying to puzzle out why Jael, Dina, and Hit are laughing along with me, but she and Vel are not.

"Yep. Let's meet back here in six hours. Get your stuff, take a nap, but one way or another, we're out of here."

"Ideally, Tarn will flag a ship already in the area," Jael puts in. "Send someone to snag us."

"Let's not think about everything that could go wrong." Hit makes herself comfortable on Dina's couch, so I guess she doesn't need to pack. Or maybe her stuff's already here. Not my business, but I admit to a certain amount of curiosity as to how Dina seduces every other woman she meets.

I mean, she's strong rather than svelte, with broad, muscular shoulders and a thick build. She does have gorgeous green eyes, though, and hair that shimmers like gold silk. Maybe it's the contrast between strength and softness.

"Keep staring at me like that, Jax, and I'll think you see something you like." She raises her gaze to give me a smoky half smile.

Okay, even *I* register a small spark when she levels that look on me. I don't even try to play it off. I flirt back a little. "Nice try. But I'm not having you break March's heart by being irresistible."

The mechanic grins. "It's a curse."

"We meet back in six hours," Jael cuts in. At my arched brow, he shrugs. "A guy can only take so much."

"That's right," Hit says. "They always picture themselves in the middle of the action, whether it has anything to do with them or not."

Leaving them to bicker, I head for the door. Constance falls into step beside me; already she moves with more assurance. "Getting the hang of it?" I ask her.

"Of what?"

"The whole having-a-body experience."

She considers that. "I find it difficult to judge distances. I keep walking into walls where I should turn."

"We'll work on it."

The halls remain eerily empty as we make our way back to my suite. First I show Constance how to use the wardrober, and leave her looking at patterns. Then I make myself a snack. She looks so real that I'm tempted to offer her something to eat.

So I ask about that. "Can you eat? As part of your companion function?"

She pauses, tilting her head in a way that tells me she's accessing secondary systems. "This casing has a receptacle for masticated foodstuff, which needs to be emptied within twenty-four hours, or I would become malodorous."

Everything a rich, lonely man needs in order to pretend he has a real woman by his side. "Don't worry, I won't need you to use such social functions."

"I am not worried," she tells me. "I am here to facilitate all matters for you, Sirantha Jax. If that should involve simulating social intercourse, I am happy to oblige, now that I have a casing designed for such work."

I don't quite know what to say to that. Does that mean she'd let me pimp her out? Then again, she's still an AI, no matter how fond I may have become of her. There's a thin gray line between sentient and self-willed. The wardrober hums as it produces a sober black suit. My PA has a strict sense of business attire, I guess.

With no sense of decorum, she immediately begins disrobing. "You may not want to do that with anyone else in the room," I advise.

She peers at me through a white blouse. "It is impolite?"

"Something like that."

I start going through my clothes, picking out the ones that look sophisticated enough to pass on any world, regardless of local fashions. Lots of black, some silvery gray, and a filmy white outfit that does nice things for my newly tanned skin. That will have to do for now. I wonder how March will like the new me.

Where is he now? Lost in the war he shouldn't have

chosen? Does he ever think of me? And will I recognize him if he comes back to me?

I touch the gaudy ring he gave me as a promise, now suspended around my throat on a thin golden chain. That contact doesn't give me any sense of him, not a magical talisman, or a link to what we've lost.

*He might be dead.* For a moment, the need to have March by my side overwhelms me. The longing steals my breath, nearly bends me double.

"Keep an eye on things," I tell Constance. "I'm going to get some sleep."

It's that or weep, and I need to keep it together. I sprawl on the bed.

The next thing I know, my comm beeps red with an incoming message. I have no way of gauging how long I've been out. "Accept," I call to the terminal.

Then a disembodied voice—no accompanying image—says, "Jewel will see you now."

# CHAPTER 51

***As catastrophes go, this one is fairly dire.***

"Warn the others," I mutter to Constance.

I honestly thought we were being held indefinitely. I didn't think there was any such person named Jewel, and if there was, based on what Grubb and Boyle said, he had no intention of meeting with me. We didn't factor this eventuality into the plan. And we're just forty-five minutes from departure, too.

I try to calm down. The others will figure out a way around this. Nobody will interfere with a pleasure droid roaming the halls, so she'll get word to them. I just need to stall for time.

When I come out into the pale, cool corridor, I find Keller waiting for me. "Did you enjoy your party?"

There's definitely an upside to being portrayed as a brainless thrillseeker on the news vids. Generally, my reputation works against me, but here, it serves us well.

"Very much." I offer a sweet smile. "You should have come along."

"Unfortunately, business arose from my employer's imminent arrival. You'll wait in the central salon."

*Right.* That shuts me up as nothing else could have. Instead I listen to our footsteps echoing ahead of us. All too soon, Keller deposits me in a large, overly empty lounge, complete with ornate floral arrangements and a rushing fountain in the center of the room. The chairs grouped here and there look stiff and formal, more for show than comfort.

"Would you like refreshments?" Keller asks, suddenly obsequious. "It shouldn't be long now."

I feel oddly like the prisoner whose last request cannot be denied. So I refuse everything and elect to remain standing. I'd rather be ready to run.

Keller nods, heading for a hallway other than the one we entered through. I wander the room while trying to pretend I'm not conscious of the minutes ticking away. I hope Constance has gotten word to the others by now.

I don't hear any footsteps beneath the rushing fountain, but I sense I have company. Pinning on a smile, I turn—and find my mother standing there. *Shit.* I didn't see that coming.

"They're holding you, too? Are you all right?" I'm not the most dutiful daughter, I admit, but we'll take her with us when we go.

As she glides closer, I see she looks different than she did at the coffeehouse. She carries herself with an indefinable air of confidence down to her perfectly manicured fingertips. Today she's not a trembling bundle of nerves, fearing for her life. Ramona Jax lent me my bone structure, but she fills out a dress better than I do. Rejuvenex treatments have left her smooth-skinned and ageless.

"I'm surprised you haven't put it together," she says with a faint half smile.

"Put . . ." And then it clicks. "You're Jewel. There's no man behind the mirror, or rather . . . *he* is you. How the hell—"

"Did you think your father's pathetic little art gallery funded our lifestyle? Honestly, Sirantha, sometimes I think you're more his child than mine. If I didn't know you'd gotten your need for adrenaline from me, I'd suspect the worst."

She's good, amazingly good, if she fooled March. Maybe she's like me, completely compartmentalized—maybe that's where I got the ability. So she can be the terrified victim one moment and a ruthless Syndicate boss the next.

I don't even know what to ask first. No wonder Jewel didn't want me harmed. Whatever else can be said of my mother, she possesses enough vanity not to want to erase her own genetic legacy.

*Unless she has to.*

Looking at her now, I can honestly say I've never seen her true face before. She's only ever shown me the featherheaded socialite. But in reality, she's pure steel wrapped in shiny paper.

"What do you mean, I got that from you?"

"I always wanted more, too," she answers. "I was always after the next thrill; I just hid it better, that's all. I still can't believe I convinced your father to . . ." Ramona lifts her shoulders in an eloquent shrug. "During a jump. It's no wonder you love grimspace so well."

I actually stagger back a step. "I was . . . conceived in grimspace?"

As if I haven't spoken, she bypasses me in a cloud of expensive perfume, programming a serving droid with a drink order. "Do you still like that dreadful Tokaji Cuvée?"

Fine, I'll pretend this is a reunion. For now. My head reels with the implications. It's a wonder I'm not brain damaged, if that's where I got my start. Mary, Doc would have a field day with this info.

"I haven't had it in years, too dear for my blood these days."

"Come, darling, don't be coy. You've done quite well for yourself, considering the initial course you chose."

Knowing this will irk her, I say deliberately, "I don't have a single credit to my name, Mother. Simon managed to snatch it all, and now my personal assets are tied up in the Farwan financial debacle."

She dismisses that with a wave of the hand. "Nothing a good barrister can't sort out. I meant in terms of prestige, Sirantha. I have use for an ambassador."

"I'm not going to let you use me," I bite out. "Those days are done. They have been for a while."

The bot returns with our drinks, its abdomen opening to reveal a silver tray. I accept mine, but I don't know if I should drink it. Would she stoop to drugging me? I honestly don't know.

I hold the glass to the light, admiring the burnished gold of a good sweet wine. I spoke the truth—haven't had this vintage in years—made from grapes, raisins, peach, apricot, and underlaid with eucalyptus. Everything I drink is either synthetic or some horrendous homebrew that burns like acid going down. Gets you drunk just the same, though, which was my goal back then.

"It's not tainted," she says. "I don't need to resort to such measures. After all, I have you precisely where I want you."

"Do you?"

"Indeed. Or perhaps you think you've accomplished something by sneaking around the villa, lurking here and there like common criminals."

"It's better to be an *uncommon* criminal like you?"

"I'm a businesswoman," she says with unruffled aplomb. "You distressed your father so much, you know, when you left that expensive finishing school. He wanted you to follow in his footsteps and manage the gallery after him. As if he ever earned a single credit without my help."

"You came from a good family." I'm struggling to understand. "How did you fall into . . . this?"

I can't imagine the things she's done for the Syndicate. Don't want to. Her dark eyes have no bottom, and to my fevered imagination, it seems . . . no soul. No moral compass that tells her right from wrong. There's a calculator instead, measuring value versus expenditure.

"I made a few investments with them, quietly, of course, and without your father's knowledge. He never would've approved."

Outrage sharpens my voice. "You think? Maybe that's because he had a conscience, and he wouldn't have wanted to spend credits that came from misery, vice, and murder."

"He didn't mind spending my money on ugly, expensive paintings that nobody ever bought," she snaps. "He had no business or aesthetic sense at all."

Oh, I hit a nerve with that. For a moment, I let myself enjoy the sensation. She doesn't hold all the cards like she thinks she does. Our little group possesses skills she can't imagine.

Nausea sweeps over me when I put it together. "You killed him. Or had him killed. And then put out word that he'd used a Eutha-booth."

She doesn't even try to deny it. "His little hobby was expensive and tiresome. And with the expansion to my territory, I needed the freedom to come and go without awkward questions."

"After so many years together, that's all he was to you? Awkward, expensive, and tiresome?"

I'm gazing into the eyes of a monster. I can't let down my guard—the fact that she's my mother provides no guarantees. I know that now.

"Your father was obsolete," she says in final tones.

*Like machinery.*

I tuck this new hurt away with all the others, to be dealt with later. If I don't get away from her, there will be no later. She'll figure out some way to use me, or she'll dispose of me. For her, there are no other options. She prefers the former, but she won't balk at the latter.

"Well, if you'd kill *him*, of course you wouldn't hesitate to start a war." I sound calm, much calmer than I feel. "You really don't care that thousands of people will die? Do you know what the bodies look like after a Morgut attack?"

"I'm told it's quite painless," she assures me. "The first bite injects a neurotoxin that blocks the nerve endings, resulting in paralysis."

"And there's money to be made. Weapons to sell. Private security contracts." I test our theories to see how close we came to the truth.

"At least you sorted out what, if not who. You're a bright girl, Sirantha."

I wonder if she had anything to do with the assassination attempt on New Terra. "Did you blow up my Skimmer? What happened, you thought better of trying to use me after we had coffee?"

Ramona shakes her head. "That was a simple misunderstanding. I disciplined the person involved in the error."

"How many pieces did he end up in?"

"Twelve." And I don't think she's joking. "I'm sorry my men broke into your quarters. They seemed to think I wanted you terrorized for some reason, as if fear ever governs women like us." She laughs lightly.

I *hate* that she lumps me in with her. If this is how she runs things, I bet she doesn't pay much in pensions. It also explains Keller's handling of the poor bastard who fucked up in the nav chair. Thank Mary, that had nothing to do with me.

"You're one scary bitch," I say, shaking my head. "I had no idea."

"You still don't." She tips back her head and drains her drink. "For instance . . . I'm having your crew killed as we speak."

I turn for the door, draw up short at the sound of laser fire. Unless they changed plans after Constance got to them—*if* she did—they're all gathered together, waiting for me.

*Shit.*

She smiles. "In fact, they might already be dead."

# CHAPTER 52

***I refuse to show fear. "You don't know them as well as*** I do."

For the first time, I'm glad March isn't here. I prefer he never finds out how much crazy runs up and down my family tree.

"You're expecting them to burst in and take me hostage, Sirantha?" Ramona lofts a brow in gentle skepticism. "Keller and his team can handle them. You didn't honestly think Grubb and Boyle were our best, did you? There's a reason I culled you from the herd *now*, darling. I didn't want you caught in the cross fire."

"I don't think you realize you caught one of Madame Kang's best when you cast your net." A shot in the dark, because surely Keller mentioned it.

The name means nothing to me, but it inspired fear in her hired goons. Maybe it'll affect my mother the same way.

Her eyes widen, and something swirls in their empty depths. "Lies. All Kang's girls died when we raided her on Gehenna."

"Not all," Hit calls. "She may be gone, but I remember everything she taught me. You sent ten men for four of us?" Her laugh rings out.

From another direction, echoing oddly, I hear Jael's voice. "You underestimated Jax's crew. Bet you rue that later."

"If we let you," Vel adds.

I can't tell where any of them are. It sounds like they've got the place surrounded, though, and I assume they're all armed. So does Ramona. She makes a great show of holding up her hands.

"You win," she says lightly. But fury seethes in her eyes. "I'm helpless now. Show yourselves so I can surrender."

She's weak as a boa constrictor, but they're not stupid enough to fall for that. Dina and Constance remain unaccounted for, but it makes sense if they went ahead to the ship. Neither of them would be much help in a fight.

Jael steps from behind an ornate decorative screen, spattered in blood and gore. And I've never been so glad to see anyone in my life. I take a step toward him, but he holds up a hand.

"No, I need to deal with her first. It pisses me off when people I don't know try to kill me in my sleep. Well . . . where I would've been sleeping, anyway, if I wasn't such a chary bastard."

Ramona lifts her chin. "Just make it quick."

This is where I'm supposed to intervene, stop him from killing her. Instead I turn my back. I expect to hear the quick whine of a laser pistol, but when I glance over my shoulder, I find Jael tying her up. He gags her before she can say we haven't seen the last of her, or promise to make us sorry.

I'm already sorry she's related to me. Does that count? I watch him wind the thin filament around her wrists. If she struggles too hard, she'll cut herself.

"I thought you don't like leaving anyone alive on your backtrail."

He shrugs. "I can't kill an unarmed woman. Call me old-fashioned. But you can shoot her if you want."

"She's my mother," I point out.

"So that means you can't shoot her?"

For a moment, I consider asking Hit to do it. I certainly can't. Though I suspect I'll regret letting Ramona live, I just don't have that much ice in my veins. I hope she'll walk away, leaving me out of her schemes after this.

"Pretty much." I can't be the reason she's killed. If nothing else, her hungry, junkie spirit made me who—and what—I am today.

"Then let's get the hell out of here before more goons turn up." With that, he signals to the others that we're moving out. "Thankfully she didn't send all her guys after us, or we might've had some trouble."

The way he looks, they did have some, but I don't speak, mainly because our trot steals my breath. I need to do some endurance training one of these days. One hand clamped against my side, I try to keep up with Jael's long, loping strides.

He's apparently been studying the layout because he makes the turns with surety, leading us from the central salon to the corridor that adjoins the docking area. The walls become less decorative, more functional, and tile gives way to plain plaster.

Footsteps echo through the hallway behind us.

"Fuck. She called them faster than I gave her credit for. I should've shot her."

We're nearly to the private docking bay. I don't know how we're getting out, but as laser fire comes hot and hard on our heels, I hope like hell they have a plan. I dive and roll, coming to my feet around the corner.

Jael still has the pistol he was playing with in Dina's room, so he covers me. Orange light flashes all around, searing the ground. I hope Hit and Vel got here before us because it looks like the party's in full swing. I can't tell how many guys Ramona has left, but she should've sent them all at my crew at once. The ragtag remainder fires on us, thinking they can keep us pinned down.

Thing is, lasers can't kill Jael. So he shoves me along

toward the shuttle, taking hit after hit. He groans low in his throat, but he doesn't falter, and Dina pulls us on board. She slams a palm on the comm panel, and barks, "Let's go!"

"Roger that," comes Hit's disembodied voice. "Hang on, it might get rough."

The shuttle engines fire up, drowning out the sound of lasers striking the hull. If we don't get a move on, we might be looking at a breach; and then we're fucked. Damn, I can't get my breath.

"What took you so long?" the mechanic demands.

"Everyone else here?" I bend over, hands on knees.

"Yeah. After she warned us about the change in plan, Constance came in with me, and we prepped the ship. The other three killed a few guys, and saved your ass."

The understatement makes me smile. We lurch as Hit takes us up, and Dina swears beneath her breath when she slams into the wall. I hear more than see her head for the seats. We all need to strap in.

When my vision stops sparkling from oxygen deprivation, I straighten and check on Jael. Propped up against the wall, he looks pale and clammy, eyes clenched tight. He smells of smoke and charred flesh, so a shudder runs through me when I step closer. But he's not dead like the victims on the *Sargasso*.

He needs me.

Steadying myself with a deep breath, I wrap an arm around his waist. "I've got you, come on. They left the last two seats for us."

A muffled explosion rocks the ship, and at first I think we've been hit, but instead of crashing into the roof, we just keep going up. The shock field doesn't have full vertical coverage, so once we get some altitude we're home free.

There's only the cockpit and a small hub on this boxy little skiff, so we don't have far to go. I see Dina sitting beside Vel, so Constance must be up front with the pilot. Jael collapses, and I nearly go down with him before I get my balance.

I know firsthand just how excruciating burns can be. Even through layers of narcotics, I remember lying in medical, feeling each one of my nerve endings curl and char over and over again. There's no pain like it.

"What can I do?"

Eyes still closed, he takes my hand in his. Damn near pulverizes my knuckles. In fact, given my bone condition, fractures might result. Since he took the shots for me, I'll take this. It'll heal. Maybe slower than someone else, but I'm not weak.

I refuse to be.

"This . . . really fucking stings," he gasps, after a moment. "No matter how many times I'm shot, I never get used to it. Just . . . glad they didn't have disruptors. Talk about painful."

"You can heal even that?" I ask without thinking.

Jael raises haunted eyes to mine. "Yeah. Even that."

He'd only know that if he'd healed the damage from it. I want to ask when. Was it in a battle he chose, or part of inhuman lab testing? He doesn't talk about his early life, before the government disbanded the program, and cut the survivors loose.

In a way, I probably understand him better than anyone. I'm pretty damn close to Bred myself, though I'm not ready to talk about it. What kind of freak am I, conceived in grimspace? I wonder if that has anything to do with why technology breaks down around me. Doc would want to run tests, but he's on Lachion, healing the wounded from a war he won't fight.

"You'll be all right." I force a smile and brush back a burnished lock of sweat-damp hair, intending it as a casual, appreciative gesture.

But Jael leans his forehead against my palm. His eyelids drift down as if my touch offers some unfamiliar benediction. Tremors course through him in waves, and I can almost sense the reparation of damaged cells, wracking him. He acts like he needs this small point of contact for reasons I can't begin to delve.

"Looks like we're clear," Hit announces over the comm. "I got stars on the screen and no sign of pursuit."

"Yet. They will find us if we are not collected by another vessel," Vel says.

Drawing back before I yield to the urge to hug Jael, I tap the comm panel on the arm of my seat. "Turn on the distress signal, and let's hope for the best."

# CHAPTER 53

***If you've never tried hauling straight space in a skiff,*** you don't know what you're missing.

I don't mean that in a good way, of course. It feels like I've driven in mudside vehicles that go faster than this. I can still see the jewel-bright hues of Venice Minor behind us, and even though we've been flying for a while, it would only take a real cutter an hour to catch up with us.

Dina sabotaged a couple of their ships, but she didn't have time to be thoroughly destructive. Just cut a few wires, here and there, remove a few parts. They'll get one up and running soon, and then—

The comm crackles, and Hit's voice fills the tiny hub. "Two ships incoming, different trajectories. Both on intercept course."

"Good to know," I mutter.

But it's not like we have weapons or shields or anything to ready us for an attack. A larger ship will just nail us with magnetic tow cables and haul us into its hold. That's how tiny this box is.

"Hope for the best." Dina shifts in her seat to glare over her shoulder at me. "Does that work for you a lot?"

I lift a shoulder. "Never tried it before. We usually have a half-assed plan."

"Life in your vicinity seldom lacks excitement," Vel observes.

Was that a compliment? Or more like the ancient curse: *May you live in interesting times*? Ignoring that, I call the cockpit to respond, "I'd say take evasive action until we find out who it is and what they want, but I don't know how well this thing handles."

"I'll see what I can do," Hit comes back.

"How long before intercept?" I ask.

There's a pause while she presumably checks the data. And then Constance replies, "Approximately twenty minutes."

"Stay strapped in," the pilot adds.

My shoulders feel knotted, a thread of tension wrapping around my spine. I hate that I can't just jump us away from here. We're so close to grimspace—the place where I began—that I can almost sense the beacons, pulsing in echo to my heartbeat. What will my next jump be like? Returning to my place of origin.

No wonder each jump always felt like coming home.

Whether those two ships intend to help or harm us, there's nothing I can do about it. I hate feeling helpless, and I've had that sensation too much lately. Unless they *intend* to destroy us, they won't waste power on weapons, though. This vessel is simply too small and fragile.

Jael sits beside me, silent and distant. I think he regrets that moment where he showed a hint of vulnerability, where he leaned his head against my hand. He won't look at me, but I have other things to worry about. Like those two ships.

We sit in tense silence, wondering about the outcome. Wondering who else is hunting us. Let me just say, that gets old. I'm afraid to hope that Tarn's come through, sent someone to the rescue, but I'll guarantee one of those ships belongs to dear old Mum. She doesn't strike me as a good loser.

"They have arrived," Constance advises us over the comm.

The tiny skiff shakes, and something clunks against the side. Tow cables? I wish I were in the nav chair where I could see what's going on. But this thing doesn't have a nav chair, and Constance is doubtless more help to Hit, analyzing numbers and probabilities with lightning speed.

"Warning shots over our bow," Hit reports. "We've got one set of tow cables on us, but the smaller ship appears to be powering up weapons." Another pause. "Shots fired. They're engaging."

I tap the comm. "Can you make out ship names or numbers?"

After a brief pause, Constance answers, "I recognize the larger vessel from the docking bay on Venice Minor. They are attempting to pull us in."

"Oh no, we're not going back there. Can we break those cables somehow?" I sit forward and look at Vel, my resident answer man.

He replies by calling the cockpit. "A localized electrical surge might short out their magnet. But it might also damage our vessel and leave us dead in space."

My mother intends to kill everyone aboard, maybe even me at this point. "Better dead in space than dead on Venice Minor."

Hit evidently shares the sentiment because she says, "I'll have Constance see what she can do. If anyone can manage the calculations without blowing us all to shit, it's her. Now hang on, I'm going to spiral, see if I can tangle up those tow wires."

*Shit.*

Every time the ship rolls, my stomach does a slow spin as well. I imagine us like fish on a line, struggling with all our strength to break free. I hope we don't get blown up in some dispute we have nothing to do with. Since we're attached to the Syndicate ship, if it goes up, we're likely close enough to take damage as well. And with no shields, no armor plating, we just aren't sturdy enough to soak it.

I say a prayer to the gods of luck.

"Report," I demand, tapping the button again.

At this rate, Hit will cut off communications from the cabin to the cockpit. But she doesn't sound irked. Rather, excitement infuses her voice.

"I've never seen anybody fly like this," she answers. "Whoever's handling the small ship has magic in his hands. He fires, hits, slings sideways, dives underneath the bigger ship, just daring a collision . . . it's beautiful to watch. So far they haven't landed a single shot on him."

*March.* Stupid, I know, but my heart leaps in purely emotional response. Intellectually, I know it can't be him. He's on Lachion, and at this point, I don't know whether he's alive or dead.

"Get that cable off us," Dina barks into the comm. "Or they'll take us with them when they blow."

"Working," Constance responds. "I must be sure of my calculations, or I will damage this vessel beyond repair."

*Bad choice, no choice.* Either way, we wind up dead. Someone's got to make the call, and they seem to think I'm in charge, most days.

"Do it," I tell her. "If the battle's going south out there, we'll wind up as collateral damage. Welcome to my world."

A jolt rocks the skiff as she complies with my order. The lights flicker, giving the cabin a surreal air. Jael shifts and gazes at me in the weird, stuttering light. I glimpse his eyes in staccato flashes, see his lips moving, but I hear no sound.

Red lights come on along the ceiling, lending everything a bloody glow. Then the onboard computer chimes a warning. "Warning. Electrical fault. Please seek safe landing facilities immediately. Life-support failure imminent."

And then we go careening through space. I can tell the difference between a guided roll and the way we're spinning. Hit has limited control, if any, and I don't think the comm's working anymore.

I've always hated tiny vessels, for good reason as it turns out. There's only a thin barrier between merciless vacuum and us. What the hell's going on? I'm tempted to unstrap and fight my way up front to see, but maybe I'm better off not knowing. I'd probably get myself hurt, too, slamming into walls.

Dina swears steadily in front of me, creative curses that I'd be memorizing with great interest at any other time. The bounty hunter remains silent, still, and I can't tell if he's injured or praying to some strange Ithtorian god. We haven't had a chance to go over religion or mythology yet, dammit.

Jael touches my arm. His fingers feel warm and strong, and I consciously check the urge to reach for him. I tell myself it's not personal; at a time like this, it's natural to want to hold on to someone. Nobody wants to die alone.

This time I can make out the words beneath the strident alarm as the ship's computer counts down. "I'm sorry."

I lean over as best I can. "What for?"

He can't possibly blame himself. That's ridiculous. Too many factors converged to land us in this mess, nothing he could've prevented. But his eyes beg for forgiveness just the same.

"Because—"

Before he finishes the thought, I feel another thunk on our side. Tow cable? At this point I can only guess, and try not to toss up.

I hope that means the smaller ship has won and that it's someone we want to see, once we get inside. More to the point, someone with a jumper, and a functional phase drive who will take us far away from here.

We roll, end over end, until something snaps taut. The skiff shudders. My head flies back, my mouth fills with a coppery tang, and I see a red field full of stars that winks to black.

Then I know nothing at all.

# CHAPTER 54

***I awake in the halls of the dead.***

Everything is pale as a fading dream. Then I open my eyes a little wider, take a second look. This seems like any other med bay: white counters, various drawers and compartments. A slim redhead sits at a terminal nearby, examining data on the screen, and there's a droid as well, probably her assistant. This doesn't look like a drug-induced hallucination. I've seen the woman somewhere before.

She murmurs, "Don't worry, we're taking care of everything. According to Chancellor Tarn, Ielos is the next stop on your goodwill tour. We've got guards on board to make sure nothing *else* goes wrong."

But my brain is too rattled to make necessary connections. A dull throb lives behind my eyes, pain made distant by the welcome advent of medication. I'm too tired to ask anything at the moment, so I just drift.

On awakening for the second time, I think:

*Well, holy shit.*

It worked. I can't believe our plan actually worked. I

feel more like an interstellar hitchhiker than a dignitary who commands respect, but what the hell. If this vessel, whomever it belongs to, gets me to Ielos, I'll take it. Now I can start keeping my promises, make up for all the trouble.

I realize I've lost another bag full of new clothes. Mary curse it, I may as well take up nudism. I haven't been able to keep up with my belongings since the *Sargsasso* crash. I sigh.

The sound snags the woman's attention, and when she turns, I place her immediately. Rose looks better than she did on Lachion, more rested, but there's no mistaking her tousled curls, frosted with silver. My heart immediately spikes with excited anticipation.

"You're awake," she says unnecessarily. "Good thing, too. We're nearly there now. How are you feeling?"

I shrug, struggling toward a sitting position. "Been better, been worse. Is Doc on board?" That's not who I want to ask about first. Of course it's not.

*Maybe . . . just maybe . . .*

I'm afraid to let myself hope.

"Yes, he's asleep. It's technically the middle of the night. But someone had to stay. You took quite a knock on the head."

"Sorry for stealing your sleep. But thank you for watching over me." I can't fight a sinking sensation. If March were here, surely he wouldn't have left my side, not until I woke up.

The fact that Rose has carefully avoided mentioning his name says it all. If I were stronger, I'd demand to know what happened, but at the moment, I just can't. I have to pick my battles, and I don't have the fortitude for this one. I refuse to hear it.

I'm not hanging around Med Bay for another second. With unsteady hands I push to my feet and wobble, watching the room swim. After a moment, I manage to let go of the cot and stand, swaying, under my own power. Given another minute or two, I'll be able to walk. *Shit.* I need my bag. I'm sure it's past time for an injection. I'm getting stronger, so I don't want to retard my progress.

"Where's my pack?"

The redhead glances up from the screen at last. "Constance said to tell you she has all of your belongings, including the clothes you left on Venice Minor."

"Thanks." What a PA . . . helpful administrator doesn't begin to cover it. That's the best news I've had in quite a while.

"She's odd," Rose observes. "Very formal."

So they have no idea she's a droid. I guess they've never run across the Lila model. No shock since she was retired in favor of the ones with giant breasts and shiny silver hair.

"Things are better on Lachion?"

She shakes her head as if in disbelief. "Much. The other clans swore fealty to Gunnar-Dahlgren after seeing how it went for Clan McCullough. In fifty turns, that's *never* happened."

*March always said he knew killing.* That seems like a sad epitaph.

I ache. "Where did you find a jumper?"

"There were a number of jumpers stranded on Lachion," she tells me. "They had the bad timing to be delivering supplies when you showed up."

*Fantastic.* I wonder where all the Farwan jumpers wound up.

"Am I cleared to leave?"

"Absolutely," she answers.

After a few steps, I regain my balance, and by the time I reach the door, I've stopped feeling like I might tip over. I need to check on everyone.

Out in the corridor, which is tinted a particularly bilious yellow, I stop the first person I see. "Excuse me, where are we bound?"

The kid looks like he's barely eighteen, running errands for somebody. "We're taking the ambassador to Ielos."

So it's true. Tension I didn't even register flows out of

me, making me aware of various aches and pains. Not debilitating, however—considering what we've been through, I feel strong, stronger than I have in months.

My stride gains speed as I explore the ship. Various crewmen nod at me in passing, like they recognize me as a person in authority. That's a new sensation.

I could go looking for Doc, but as Rose said, it's the middle of the night. I don't want to wake him. I'm also not sure I'm fit company right now.

March must be dead. If the war on Lachion let up sufficiently for Gunnar-Dahlgren to equip a ship in answer to Tarn's plea, enough for Rose and Doc to take off from treating the wounded, then the outcome must be decided, one way or another. I guess they won, but . . . the price was too high.

There's no other reason he wouldn't have come. Unlike most, his promises mean something. No words are sufficient to describe this loss. I thought I knew pain when Kai died, but this—

A hole has opened up inside me.

He won the war for them, and it destroyed him. Though I'd known it would happen when I left him on Lachion, the incontrovertible evidence wrecks me.

Mary, I can't *live* without him. I don't even want to try.

Some mechanistic part of me keeps me walking loops around the ship's deck. It's like I expect to come out somewhere else, but each time it carries me back where I began. The clansmen who make up the crew begin giving me odd looks.

I can't resist the urge to find somewhere quiet to grieve. A primal scream is building inside me, so I duck into the first cabin that isn't keyed to someone else. Must be vacant, or maybe it's mine. I didn't ask Rose about accommodations.

The dark doesn't surprise me, but the weirdly flickering vid screens all over the room certainly give me pause. And then I spy what's on them. Sirantha Jax, asleep in Med Bay, pacing the corridors, and older clips still. Me, as I step off a vessel with Kai. Me, holding both fists in the air as I stagger out of a barroom brawl.

This isn't entertainment so much as a shrine. Someone is mourning *me* as if I were dead. There's only one person who would surround himself with me like this. But it doesn't make sense. I'm *here*. Why isn't he with me?

As my eyes adjust, I see a dark figure sprawled in a chair. I can't make out his features, but all my senses insist it's March. The door whooshes shut behind me.

"I wondered how soon you'd find me," he says quietly.

I mumble something about it being a fair-sized ship. I want to be glad because, whatever else is wrong, at least he's not dead. But what sits in this small, dark room might be worse, if anything could be.

I take a step toward him, but his stillness alarms me. Something prevents me from running to him. He feels . . . wrong somehow.

*If only I could see his eyes . . .*

My voice comes out raw. "Rose was careful not to mention you. I thought—"

"I know. I asked her not to. I'm sorry." He doesn't look at me. I can't make out his features, but I can tell he's still staring at his Jax collection on the screens.

This isn't how I envisioned our reunion, when I dared think about it at all. The silence wears on me, but I don't know what to say to him. Words pile up in my throat, leaving me mute.

March became part of me as nobody else ever had, but this isn't the man who pined for me, who would've killed the world if anything happened to me. Oddly enough, I feel as though I'm standing before a stranger.

"How did it go on Lachion?" I manage to ask.

Pointless small talk. I already got the gist from Rose.

"Slaughtered the McCulloughs to a man," he answers, low. "The tunnels ran with blood, and then the Teras turned on them. After that, we hunted them through all their holdings. I haven't seen killing like that since I left Nicu Tertius."

Where, he told me, he slew thousands.

"I'm glad you made it." That's not what I want to say. It's banal, but the unearthly chill streaming off of him makes me want to turn tail and run.

Intellectually, I understand the need for him to disconnect from his emotions. How could he annihilate his fellow man if he felt anything for them? This, then, is what Mair saved him from before. But the price for such detachment comes steep.

Because I stand on the other side of the wall and I don't know how to reach him. I don't know what Mair did or how to bring him back. He promised I'd see him again, and he's kept that vow. I touch the ring he gave me, hoping for inspiration. Where do we go from here?

Well, for me, there's no direction except toward him. I ignore his body language; his muscles seem coiled and ready to fight. I don't want to believe he'll hurt me, but Mary, I'm afraid. He's like a wounded beast that doesn't recognize a friendly hand.

I reach toward his face with trembling fingertips. He lashes out, a move that would've broken my forearm if he'd connected. I leap back, shaken.

But I don't quit. Maybe I'm not Mair, but I'll figure this out. I won't lose him.

"You know what? I don't care. I *should*, but I don't. You could've put a million McCulloughs in the ground, and I wouldn't care as long as it means you're here with me."

He shudders. "I shouldn't be. I should've cut and run once I saw you were all right. I could hurt you, Jax. Kill you in my sleep. Even though I *remember* how I used to feel about you, I can't—" March makes a slashing gesture with one hand.

I catch on. He can't access it, as if some necessary neurological pathway has been severed. Afraid to touch him, I seal a kiss into my palm and then blow it into the air. It's a romantic gesture, not like me at all, but I intend it to be symbolic of how far I'm willing to go for him.

"I *need* you, March. I was scared as hell to admit it, but I can't do without you, and if that makes me broken . . ." I shrug. "I'll take you any way I can get you. And I don't give a damn what you've done. You will *never* be rid of me."

"You have no idea how much I don't deserve you." He pitches the comment low, almost dispassionate.

His gaze belies his words. March stares at me as if I stand across a chasm he has no hope of crossing. Maybe he can't feel the warmth between us, but it exists. There must be a bridge, so I'll take the first step toward finding it.

"I want you inside me."

After a moment of silent resistance, his icy soul fills mine.

# CHAPTER 55

***It's not a fix, but a reminder of what we lost. By the*** time March pulls out, I'm shivering. I'll never give up on him, but this will take time. We have to figure out how to repair what's been broken, as Mair did.

Instead of walking away, I sit with him quietly in the dark.

Hours later, I locate my crew in the starboard lounge. They all seem to be in good shape, drinks in hand. Vel sits with his handheld, tapping away. The last vestige of fear dissipates, and that's new, too.

I feel responsible for these people, not in the usual way, which involves making sure I get the jump right. In the past, that's all the accountability I acknowledged. What befalls someone when I'm not in the nav chair, well, that's not my fault. Right?

Wrong. For crazy misbegotten reasons, they follow me, so what happens to them, it's on me. They call this leadership, I think, but it's new. I crackle with it.

"Hell of a thing," Dina says with a grin. She pushes from her chair and limps over to me, just about crushing my ribs in a hug.

"I am glad to see you recovered," Constance tells me.

Is she glad? Can she be? For just a moment, I put aside my questions about her nature, or what she can learn, and accept what she says at face value.

"You did a helluva job," I answer. "Without you, everyone would be dead, and I'd be captive to my mother's warmongering."

The PA pauses as if parsing my words. And then she says, delightfully, unintentionally modest: "I am here to help."

We all snicker, and it doesn't matter that Constance regards us with puzzlement. Each of us brings our own gifts to the mix. We stand together, or we fall. I get that now.

Once the chatter dies down, I cross to where Jael sits, slightly apart from the others. I drop down beside him. "What were you trying to tell me? On the skiff?"

He shakes his head with a bittersweet half smile. "It doesn't matter. The moment's passed."

What did he think he needed to apologize for?

Before I can question him, Hit announces, "Planetfall in fifteen minutes, so bundle up in your winter clothes and strap in."

***Four planets in eight days.***

For the first time, I don't envy someone else the nav chair. If I were sitting up there, I'd be dead. I know it. I need to rest and recuperate while taking my daily injections, or I may never see grimspace again. And while the hunger hasn't lessened—I still long to jump like I want nothing else in this world besides March—my ability to tune it out has improved.

I feel drunk with remembered wonder. First glimpse of the sun rising over the glaciers on Ielos, sunset at the Freeport falls, and an afternoon walk along the famed Avenida de Marquez on Axis V, where the bloodshed began so long ago. I tread along the paths where my predecessor Karl Fitzwilliam made his infamous missteps.

So many people waved and cheered when the convoy passed by, as if I deserved those accolades. What have I ever done to *earn* them? I've touched history this last week, seen and smelled it. Perhaps I'm even becoming part of it in ways I can't comprehend. I imagine it like threads of a tapestry woven together with such expertise that I can't see the separate pieces anymore.

Whole worlds fade like that beneath me. The towns become patchwork textures and then blur into misty colors. Finally, I can no longer see the people who believe in me, who seem to think I can step into the breach and persuade the Ithtorians to side with us in the coming war.

Because, make no mistake, I've seen the bodies in the first skirmish. Now more than ever, the Morgut see us as prey. And the only thing that might give them pause is an alliance with Ithiss-Tor.

I'm not ready. I don't know enough. I'm terrified I'll fuck this up, and humanity everywhere will pay the price. Maybe my mother's still banking on that, and that's another thorn in my side.

But I'll step up.

My gut gurgles as if in answer. I'm bloated from heavy food, eaten at too many parties. And my right hand hurts from all the meet-and-greets. I wore the right clothes and smiled for the press, dandled unfortunate children on my knee, and played a politician for the vids. That was the easy part.

Now the last stop on our tour recedes beneath me. Seeing so many worlds rouses an odd sensation; I'd call it wanderlust, but it's more like a fierce need to move on, because I don't *have* anywhere like these folks do.

Whatever its faults, they have somewhere they call their own. One they'd fight for, die for. Home.

I don't put down roots. I live for the next jump, even though the next might be my last. How did somebody like me wind up in charge of something so important?

A disembodied voice tells me, "Five minutes to jump."

Once it would've bothered me to strap in with everyone

else, but today I have far too much on my mind to make room for something so minor. I make my way to the hub and take a seat next to Vel, but this time I strap in without assistance. I'm an expert passenger now.

"Afterward," he says in lieu of greeting, "we have work to do."

Damn right. Constance doesn't ever let up on the customs—I half suspect she recites the list to me in my sleep—but I need to know the rest. By the time we reach Ithiss-Tor, I need to be the foremost human expert in native customs.

I nod. "I'd like to start with religion."

I give my safety gear one last tug. The helmet feels strange, but as the ship trembles, it can't block out my awareness of the beacons entirely. As if through a veil of water, I feel the jumper scanning grimspace. She's better than the Syndicate navigator, more confident, and she takes us right there.

My skin prickles, the hair standing up on the back of my neck. Though I can't see what she sees, the wildfire and the glorious, cascading colors pouring over the hull, I sense it. Grimspace runs through my blood and bones, boiling inside my cells. What that means, I can't begin to guess.

But a tiny part of me withers and dies when we make the jump back. Yearning sears me like a live wire. I wish I could stay there, utterly unfettered.

Beside me, Vel unbuckles and holds out a hand. "Shall we?"

It takes me another moment to get out of the chair, and then I accept his help. If only things come this easy on Ithiss-Tor. But I know better. He's warned me about the reception I'll receive—and given the shame of his profession, they won't be ecstatic to see him either. I just count us lucky to have gained their initial agreement to take the matter under advisement and permit the arrival of our delegation.

Ten minutes later, we settle in my quarters. The room is a little larger than the space I enjoyed when I worked for the Corp, but nothing like Keller offered on the Syndicate yacht. I guess piracy doesn't pay quite as well as being a crime lord.

"I am going to molt," Vel warns me. "If you are to function on my homeworld, you must accustom yourself to the way we look."

"No problem. I'm used to you." I hope that's not an overstatement.

But there are no surprises this time when his faux-human skin drops away. A boxy little cleaning bot activates and whirs into action at his feet, but I don't break eye contact. I'm not uncomfortable gazing into his faceted eyes. He's still Velith, the person who's saved my ass more times than I can count.

Maybe I can do this after all.

"Religion," he says. "We revere something called the Iglogth. Not God as you understand it, but rather vitality that gives life to everything in the universe. My people believe everything is cyclical, and that the spark which makes you unique returns to the Iglogth, only to be reused at a later time."

"Sort of like reincarnation?" Primitive humans put faith in that, before we proved the soul doesn't exist. When I remember everyone I've lost, my father foremost among them, I wish that wasn't true. I wish I believed we might be together again. I left too many words unsaid.

His mandible moves, clicking sounds result, and then his vocalizer translates. It's funny how much I miss beneath that false skin. "In a manner of speaking."

"Is there anything else I should know?"

"Only as relates to death customs," Vel answers. "We burn our dead and scatter the ashes to the four winds in a formal ceremony. It symbolizes the return of the spirit to the great Iglogth."

"No other religious rituals?"

He turns his head from side to side, a learned human gesture for the negative. It sits strangely on his alien face.

"Moving on then."

We work for hours, covering art, architecture, and world history. By the time Constance interrupts us—what a PA, she even reminds me to eat—my head feels like an overripe melon. If there's another human being who knows more about Ithtorian physiology, mating habits, or customs, well—the Conglomerate should've hired him. Because I don't think I can learn another fact before we put down. I eat with one hand and rub my temples with the other.

Vel watches me, his side-set eyes studying me with what I take to be concern. "Are you well, Sirantha?"

"I'm not sure it'll be enough. I can't do more, but what if—" No, I won't give my fears credence by speaking them aloud. I'll bear this by myself. "Can you work with Constance and download everything we've talked about to her database? That way, if I'm about to make a dire mistake, she can nudge me or something."

"Yes, I believe I can."

I need insurance, but that's the best I can do. Shortly thereafter, the bounty hunter and the droid head for his quarters to fulfill my request. I appreciate that, too; I'm sure Vel sensed I need some time alone.

For at least an hour, I wander the ship, trying to calm my ragged nerves. Fear threatens to choke me from the inside out. If I fuck up here, the whole civilized world will suffer. The Conglomerate needs an alliance with Ithiss-Tor—a rebuff at this juncture would be catastrophic. I battle back my doubt, shove it into the dark place where it can't touch my conscious mind. It will return in the form of nightmares, but I can pay the cost later.

If it lets me function, do what I need to do, then that's enough. I wind up in the observation lounge, where the wall has been replaced with a cunning electronic screen that mirrors what's right outside the ship. It mirrors a window, down to the last shimmer of smoky glass.

Even before they make the announcement, I recognize

Ithiss-Tor beneath us. From up here, it's a beautiful world, all pale whorls and dark curls that must be land. My fists clench.

*I can't do this without you, love.* But March is shut away in his quarters, fighting his own demons, so I can't lean. I have to be strong for him now.

He *needs* me.

Thinking of what he's suffered and suffers still, tears fill my eyes, the first I've allowed since I wept in Jael's arms. These can't fall. I will them away, turn them to ice. I squeeze my eyelids shut until the weakness passes. I can't allow it.

When I sense someone behind me, I turn and find March waiting, half in shadow. I should've known he wouldn't let me down, no matter the cost to himself. In this light, I can't see his eyes—best he doesn't see mine.

"Ready?" he asks.

In the frosted pane, I see a slow progression of faces, people I've loved and lost. I carry their shadows in my skin. Then I turn from the window, setting such memories aside for a time when I can afford to indulge in them.

Like my first glimpse of Ithiss-Tor, cloud shrouded and indistinct, the future awaits.